The Twelfth Floor

ALSO BY MICHELLE KIDD

DI JACK MACINTOSH MYSTERIES
Book 1: Seven Days To Die
Book 2: Fifteen Reasons To Kill
Book 3: Sixteen Carved Pieces
Book 4: Twenty Years Buried
Book 5: Three Broken Bodies
Book 6: The Twelfth Floor

DI NICKI HARDCASTLE SERIES
Book 1: Missing Boy
Book 2: The Trophy Killer
Book 3: The Hardwick Heath Killer

THE TWELFTH FLOOR

MICHELLE KIDD

DI Jack MacIntosh Book 6

Joffe Books, London
www.joffebooks.com

First published in Great Britain in 2024

Cover art by Nebojša Zorić

ISBN: 978-1-83526-869-8

PROLOGUE

Time: 6.45 a.m.
Date: Saturday 10 January 2015
Location: Central London

Although he knew he'd already cleaned all the blood from his skin many times over, he reached for the antibacterial soap one more time.

You could never be too careful.

There was a part of him that enjoyed repeating the cleaning ritual — it was a chance to cleanse his soul as well as wash away the blood. But there was another part of him, an ever-increasing part, that detested it. As the water cascaded over his skin, he felt his top lip begin to curl at the thought of their filthy blood on his hands, seeping under his nails and into his clothes.

The initial euphoria that killing brought him didn't last long. Each time he willed the feeling to linger, to hold on to the intense thrill and keep it locked within, but it was like trying to catch smoke; no sooner did he feel it, then it began to evaporate. With twenty-four hours having now passed since he'd killed them, he knew the emptiness would soon

1

be coming — leaving him nothing but a suffocating darkness where once he'd felt elation.

He snatched at the nail brush and began to scrub once more as the hot water continued to cascade from the shower-head above. As he worked, he wondered if anyone had found them yet — *his girls*. He knew it was too early, but the thought made him smile as he scrubbed. He *wanted* them to be discovered; he *needed* them to be discovered. He'd left them out on display this time so it wouldn't take much, not in a place like Acorn House.

No one had ever found the others — which filled him with a curious sense of disappointment. What was the point of any of it if they were never found?

He'd already bagged up his bloodstained clothing back at the flat — ridding himself of the black bin liners on his way out of the estate. With so many rubbish bins and skips littering the grounds, he'd been spoiled for choice in the end.

The flat itself had been perfect, too. He already knew it was empty — and had been for some time. Getting inside had been straightforward enough; no one had batted so much as an eyelid at him as he'd made his way up. Those that did see him had looked straight through him as if he were merely a ghost. He knew the rundown block of flats housed nothing even remotely masquerading as a camera, so his comings and goings would melt into the background. People came and went on the estate, faces dissolving into the night, never really imprinting on anyone's memory for long.

Perfect.

As he rinsed his hair again, his thoughts were dragged back once more to his girls. He imagined the look of horror on the face of whoever stumbled across them. Another chuckle escaped his throat as the scorching water pulsated over his shoulders. His skin was turning pink, but he didn't flinch — not even when the hot water hit the open wounds that were scored across his back. Clenching his jaw, he closed his eyes and welcomed the pain.

Pain was good.

Pain was his release.

Letting the water cleanse him for several more minutes, he reached forward and turned the taps off. Cleansing routine completed for now, his attention turned to the next one.

Because someone would *always* be next.

CHAPTER ONE

Two days later

Time: 11.15 a.m.
Date: Monday 12 January 2015
Location: Riverview Dental Practice, London

"So, do I spit or swallow?" Detective Inspector Jack MacIntosh held the small plastic cup of pale pink liquid in front of his lips.

"It's your choice, but I'd spit this one if I were you."

Nodding, Jack tipped the liquid into his mouth, wincing as he did so. He'd been lucky to get away with just a split lip, the fist connecting with his jaw the way it had. He was convinced he'd be looking at a few loose teeth at the very least, possibly worse.

Adam Sullivan echoed his patient's thoughts. "You were lucky this time, Jack. Your teeth are rock solid, although there are a few nasty abrasions on the inside of the upper lip and left cheek. They might bleed a little today, and you've an impressive split lip. But, structurally, your teeth are sound."

Jack spat the rinsing liquid out into the small ceramic sink next to the dentist's chair. "That's good to hear."

"Just ordinary paracetamol or ibuprofen should help with any discomfort." The dentist gave his patient a mischievous wink. "Although I often find a decent Glenmorangie does the job just as well."

"Thanks. I'll bear that in mind." Jack wiped his nose with a tissue and swung his legs from the chair. "And thanks for coming in on your day off to fit me in. It's appreciated."

Sullivan waved the compliment away. "Not a problem. I'm only upstairs." He lifted his gaze to the ceiling and the small flat above. "And far be it for me to give you advice, Jack, but maybe try and avoid the fist next time? I can't guarantee your teeth will be so lucky second time around."

Jack held up a hand on his way out. "I'll do my best, mate. See you for a pint sometime soon."

Once out in the reception area, Jack glanced down at his wrist. The Fitbit Force had been a birthday present from the team — although Jack had a fairly good idea that DS Cassidy was really the one behind it. He had made the appropriate noises upon opening it and wore a suitably appreciative smile on his face — he may even have uttered the words 'oh, you shouldn't have'. But — *a Fitbit*? Cassidy had then taken great delight in showing him what the device could do.

'*It counts the steps you do each day, and the distance travelled, so you can keep on top of your fitness goals. It even counts the number of calories burned.*'

Up until that point, Jack considered his main goal in life was just making it through the day unscathed — although today's encounter with Neville Henderson made that largely a moot point. He rubbed the side of his face and felt the throbbing intensify. Like his dentist pal had just told him, he needed to learn to duck. But maybe Amanda Cassidy had a point. This birthday had brought him another year closer to the dreaded fifty, and he'd started to notice that climbing the stairs to his mews flat took a little longer than it had before, and he was more out of breath when he reached the top than he probably should be.

'*And it monitors your sleep patterns — tells you whether you've had a good night's sleep or not.*'

Jack had fought hard to keep himself from laughing out loud.

Sleep.

Such an alien concept these days that he wondered if it truly existed.

But at least the Fitbit told him the time — it had some use at least.

Making his way to the reception desk to pay for his emergency check-up, Jack found his thoughts turning back to work. He knew the minute he set foot back in the station that the shit would follow soon after. They had managed to arrest Henderson eventually, but it had taken four uniforms to hold the bugger down. And that was *after* Jack had taken a slug to the jaw for his trouble. Neville Henderson was well known to everyone this side of the water, and Jack knew the man would no doubt claim excessive force the minute anyone chose to listen — it wouldn't be the first time.

But Jack wasn't concerned about Henderson. He'd only been there by chance — it wasn't his collar and he didn't relish being a part of the circus that followed. But at least the uniforms had worn bodycams. With any luck the whole incident was caught on film and the man would soon crawl back under the stone they'd dragged him out from.

After parting with his money, Jack stepped out into the small car park at the rear of the Riverview Dental Practice and headed for the Mondeo. Just as he reached the driver's side, his mobile chirped. A quick glance told him it was DS Cooper.

"Cooper? What's up? I'm just on my way back." Jack pulled open the driver's door and slipped behind the wheel. "If Henderson is kicking off already just tell them to leave him to stew in his cell for a while. And if it's the chief superintendent, tell him you don't know where I am." He shoved the keys into the ignition and fired up the engine.

But the call wasn't about Neville Henderson.

And it wasn't about the chief superintendent, either.

"It's no' that, boss." Cooper's voice crackled in Jack's ear over the sound of the Mondeo. "We've got ourselves a murder."

* * *

Time: 12.30 p.m.
Date: Monday 12 January 2015
Location: Acorn House, Hillside Estate, London

The flats rose up into the slate grey skies above and Jack inwardly groaned.

"Which floor did you say it was, Cooper?"

"Twelfth. Flat 7b."

Of course it is, mused Jack as they left the Mondeo parked in what may have masqueraded as a car park at some point in time but was currently only inhabited by a mound of used tyres, several stained mattresses and an abandoned child's pram missing a wheel. *Of course it is.*

He cast a wary glance over his shoulder. The Mondeo wasn't exactly the height of desirability when it came to vehicle crime, but around this neck of the woods almost anything was nickable for the right price. He silently prayed the car was still there, together with all four wheels, when they returned.

The entrance to Acorn House was via a communal door and Jack soon saw that whatever security locks had once been in place had long since been ripped from their casings. DS Cooper led the way inside, nudging the door open with a booted foot.

As soon as they stepped inside, both detectives' noses wrinkled. The aroma of stale urine, rotting food and something altogether more fetid greeted them.

"Nice place," grimaced Cooper as they made their way towards the lifts. "Oh, and look — no lift."

Jack's heart sank when he saw the *out of order* sign hanging at an angle across the lift's metal doors.

"Just great," he muttered to himself as he scanned the communal hallway for the stairs. "Just bloody great."

By the time they reached the twelfth floor, Jack's legs were throbbing and his eyes were smarting from the foul stench of concentrated urine that only seemed to increase the higher they climbed. He could already see the door to Flat 7b was open, a lone PC standing guard outside. The whole communal walkway had been cordoned off at both ends with blue and white police tape and Jack ducked under the first section that met them at the top of the concrete stairs, heading for the open door.

After being suitably dressed in protective forensic suits, both he and Cooper stepped over the threshold of Flat 7b and into the narrow hallway beyond. Despite the door being wide open behind them, very little light followed them inside. Peering into the gloom, Jack saw several figures up ahead and continued in their direction, keeping to the metal stepping plates that covered the worn carpet under their feet.

The acrid stench from the stairs intensified the further they went and Jack instinctively raised a hand to cover his nose. The narrow hallway led them into an equally narrow kitchen at the rear and, with just three white-suited figures inside, it looked almost full to bursting. Hovering on the threshold, Jack recognised the smaller of the group.

"Elliott," he greeted, nodding towards the figure standing in the centre of the cramped kitchen. "Good to see you."

Elliott Walker, crime scene manager, raised a hand in acknowledgement. "Likewise, Jack. Thanks for coming out so quickly."

Jack was about to say '*no problem*' but then thought about the twelve flights of stairs he had just subjected his leg muscles to, and the precarious place in which he'd left the Mondeo. Instead he responded with, "What have we got?" The details Cooper had relayed to him when he'd got back to the station from the dentist had been fairly sparse.

"Not much so far, Jack. Just what you can see, really."

Jack's gaze swept the tiny kitchen. A battery powered arc light had been set up in the corner to illuminate the scene, its intense beam hitting the back of the crime scene manager's head. Elliott saw Jack's eyes straying towards it, accompanied by a frown.

"No electricity in the whole flat," he explained. "Disconnected some time ago, so I've been told. The place doesn't seem to have been lived in for a while."

Jack nodded. Among the air of stale urine and something more rotten and festering, was the unmistakable sense of abandonment. "And this is all we've got?" He gestured towards the worn and dingy linoleum floor beneath — and the severed limbs at the crime scene manager's feet. Jack was no pathologist but even he could recognise two human legs when he saw them.

"In here, yes." Elliott's wary gaze lifted over Jack's shoulder. "But there's more back there."

As they turned in the doorway they were greeted by another white-suited figure.

"Greetings, Jack." Dr Philip Matthews, the force's forensic pathologist, had a taut look on his lean face. "Another day in paradise no less?"

Jack flashed him a tired smile. "Looks like it. How long have you been here? I didn't see your car outside."

Dr Matthews gave a sly wink. "I've been out this way a few times before, Jack, so I parked the old girl around the back — much safer than that battleground out front, if you catch my drift. Mrs Matthews would be most disheartened if I brought the Volvo home in a state of disrepair."

Jack thought back to where he'd left the Mondeo. *The battleground.* Shit. He ought to have known better. The lack of other vehicles should have given him the heads up. Sighing, he returned his thoughts to the job in hand and gestured back towards the severed legs on the kitchen floor behind them. "What more can you tell me? Male? Female?"

Dr Matthews paused before beckoning both Jack and DS Cooper to follow him along the dim hallway, away from the confines of the cramped kitchen. "Follow me, if you will, gentlemen."

9

They did as instructed and the pathologist took them into what Jack assumed to be a living room — it was too dark to be sure, but there didn't seem to be too much that was living inside it.

"You've obviously seen the body parts in the kitchen, Jack. Two lower limbs. Female, from my limited examination so far."

As Jack's eyes began to adjust to the dimness, he could just about see the outline of a sofa against the far wall, an armchair opposite and a low-rise coffee table in the centre. Otherwise, the room was empty except for several large black bin liners. "And in here we have what?"

"Well, in here I'm afraid we have more." The pathologist pulled out a pocket torch and illuminated the far side of the room. Now bathed in light, Jack could see what was propped up against a set of threadbare cushions.

Arms.

Human arms.

Jack shuddered, watching the torchlight flicker and dance its way along the length of the battered sofa. "I may not have a medical degree like you, doc, but . . ." He paused and glanced up, catching the pathologist's concerned gaze. "But I'm counting three arms there. Not two."

CHAPTER TWO

Time: 12.50 p.m.
Date: Monday 12 January 2015
Location: Acorn House, Hillside Estate, London

"I'm guessing it's too soon to know how many bodies we've got?" Jack stepped out of Flat 7b, strangely appreciative of the fresh waft of concentrated urine that greeted him. It was marginally better than the stench of death at any rate, and feeling his stomach contract he was glad he hadn't had time for much in the way of breakfast that morning — although the taste of the pink mouthwash from earlier still coated his tongue.

With more battery powered arc lights now set up, it soon became apparent that the flat harboured all manner of piles of rubbish, some in plastic bin liners, others in cardboard boxes — no doubt attracting many a four-legged pest if the amount of rat droppings was anything to go by and the putrid smell that went with it. In addition to the obvious human remains, Jack wouldn't be surprised if something else had died in there, too.

The living room, as well a revealing three human arms, also contained a multitude of drug paraphernalia scattered across the coffee table and threadbare carpet beneath. Any number of spoons, pipes, small plastic bags, glass vials, discarded needles and wraps of tin foil could be seen. Jack knew a drug den when he saw one.

Dr Matthews followed him outside. "Too soon," he agreed. "Once I have the body parts back at the mortuary I'll take the usual blood and tissue samples. The legs could very well be from the same body, they look as though they are, but you know as well as I do Jack that you can never count on anything in this line of work. As for the arms . . ." He gave a small shrug of his narrow shoulders. "Obviously, we have more than one victim there — but whether any of them belong with the legs . . . ?" He let the rest of the sentence hang.

Jack took a step towards the metal railings that gave them a bird's eye view of the estate below — and, more importantly, the car park. He felt a not unwelcome flood of relief when he saw the Mondeo still parked where he'd left it — and, by the looks of it, all four wheels were still attached.

"I'll let you know when I'm ready to examine what we have," continued the pathologist, heading towards the stairs. "And you'll have my report soon after."

Jack called after him. "No sign of a torso yet? Or a head?"

Dr Matthews shook his head as he continued along the walkway. "Not as yet. But there's a lot of rubbish in there which I'm sure you saw — plenty of places that could house all manner of delightful surprises." With a flourish of his hand, the pathologist disappeared from view.

Jack felt his stomach shift once more as he thought about what might be inside any number of the bin liners. Elliott and his team had an unenviable job ahead of them. "Come on, Cooper. Let's get ourselves out of here."

"What's the tally so far, boss?" Cooper gestured towards Jack's Fitbit as they started to descend the concrete stairs. "How many steps have you done?"

Jack sighed. *Not you as well, Cooper.* He glanced at his wrist. "Three thousand eight hundred and nine, so it tells me."

"That's a good start."

Start? Jack rubbed his cheek where he still felt a faint throbbing from Henderson's fist, and followed Cooper down the twelve flights of steps to the ground. *You mean I have to do more?*

Pulling open the communal door, the detective sergeant called back over his shoulder. "I fancy a bacon roll, boss — can we stop off somewhere on the way back? Jenny's got me on this health kick at home — I'm living on rabbit food."

Jack swallowed. He couldn't think of anything worse than bacon fat right now — not after what they'd just witnessed inside Flat 7b. The fetid stench had seemed to follow them all the way down to the ground floor. "Is there a time of day where you don't think about your stomach, Cooper?" Jack heard the detective laugh.

"You sound like Jenny. She thinks I'd eat in my sleep if I could."

Out in the car park, Jack spied four hooded youths on BMX bikes starting to circle the Mondeo like hungry vultures, menacing looks on their pinched faces. It seemed like they'd arrived back not a moment too soon.

* * *

Time: 12.55 p.m.
Date: Monday 12 January 2015
Location: Central London

The antiseptic made his skin smart, but he barely felt it these days. Only able to reach some of the open wounds on his back, he knew some would be left untreated.

The discipline rested on a dark velvet throw at the bottom of an ornate, carved wooden chest. He'd made it himself from seven lengths of thick, coarse rope with a tight knot at each end — the discipline was one of his most prized possessions. With the lid of the chest now closed, the temptation to resume his penance was lessened somewhat — but it never went away entirely. The pull towards the pain it could inflict was always there waiting for him.

Wincing, he wiped the antiseptic cloth over the wounds once again. The stinging sensation was a feeling he welcomed, sometimes even as much as the pain from the whipping. He couldn't quite put into words what it was like — the release he felt when the rope seared into his skin. It was a feeling like no other. Pain truly was the greatest cleanser of them all; even the act of killing didn't give the same euphoric state that the discipline could.

But it came close.

Dressing the last of the wounds that he could reach, he wiped the sweat from his brow. He knew the discipline would be used more in the coming days as his hunger for repentance intensified, and the thought gave him a curious thrill. The pain the knotted rope inflicted had now cleared his mind, allowing him to welcome in the crystal-clear clarity of the world around him.

He pulled on a clean T-shirt, careful not to aggravate the raw wounds that were still smarting.

Clarity.

The pain had cleansed his soul but it had also made him hungry — but not for food. He had already selected the hold-alls that he would use — both brand new, they still sat in their plastic wrapping on the floor. Donning a pair of thin latex gloves, he sliced open the packaging and admired his purchase. His smile widened and his eyes gleamed, the pain from the discipline long forgotten.

Perfect.

He had left her back in the lock-up garage after picking her up on Saturday night. But he couldn't bring her here; here there were too many people who would see. But the lock-up was perfect; she would be safe there for a while yet.

And he had already planned where he would take her.

And then where she would be found.

Everything was in the planning.

* * *

14

Jack eased himself into one of the vacant chairs by the side of the cork pin board.

"Judging by the body parts found at the scene earlier today, we have at least two victims. Possibly more. Post-mortem examinations will be carried out later." Pausing, Jack ran a hand over his left cheek, still feeling the force of Neville Henderson's clenched fist. Adam Sullivan might have reassured him that his teeth were intact — *this time* — but Henderson still had a decent sized punch on him. The fresh coffee he'd been handed on entering the incident room sat untouched on the desk next to him, his bottom lip already smarting at the thought of coming into contact with hot liquid. "Cooper — give the rest of the team a quick rundown of what we know at this stage. I appreciate it isn't much."

Jack eyed his team, which was small by most people's standards, but it was equally perfectly formed. Detective Sergeant Chris Cooper was his most experienced officer — a bundle of ginger-haired energy with a deep-seated passion for anything even remotely bacon-flavoured. Jack had lost count of the number of bacon rolls the man could put away in one sitting — he'd already devoured two in the Mondeo on their way back from Acorn House.

Then there was DS Amanda Cassidy. She hadn't been a sergeant as long as Cooper had, but she was one of the smartest officers Jack had ever worked with. Always on a health kick of some description, she was tenacious in her attempts to persuade Jack to make healthier lifestyle choices, which was probably why he'd received the Fitbit for his birthday. She'd tried countless times to wean him off his sugar-laden coffee addiction, but soon acknowledged it was likely to be a hiding to nothing.

And last, there was Trevor. Detective Constable Trevor Daniels had only been part of Jack's team since last September, but it hadn't taken long for him to show himself to be a loyal and hard-working officer. Previously labelled as the station 'nerd', he had a brilliantly quick mind and a love of anything historical or supernatural. He was now an integral part of Jack's close-knit team.

Cooper shook his computer mouse to activate the interactive whiteboard where details from that morning's discovery were starting to populate.

"Like the boss said, there are at least two victims inside Acorn House. The flat is on the twelfth floor, accessed by a communal entrance which is unlocked with no security. Acorn House itself is one of three tower blocks on the Hillside Estate — Beech House and Maple House make up the other two. The lifts in Acorn House have been out of order for some time, so access to the flat is by just the one main staircase. Flat 7b is reported to have been uninhabited in recent weeks, and possibly even months. There was some evidence of drug use in the premises — drug paraphernalia and the like. Possibly being used as a drug den for local gangs. The door wasn't particularly secure, so just about anyone could have got in if they really wanted to. Uniformed officers are conducting door-to-door enquiries as we speak in all three of the tower blocks, so we could get something back from that as the day goes on. But I wouldn't hold your breath — this whole area was caught up in the riots of only a few years ago. Any police presence is likely to be met with a certain degree of hostility." Cooper puffed out his cheeks and leaned back in his chair. "That's pretty much all we have at present."

Jack shifted in his seat. "Cooper's right. I remember the riots well, and I don't think too many of the residents are going to be falling over backwards to help. But we might get lucky. The only positive we do have is that the severed arms still had their hands attached. Fingerprints are being checked against the database which may show up something. In the meantime, we concentrate on the scene as we have it."

Deciding to risk it, Jack reached for the coffee mug, the taste of the mouthwash still clinging to his tongue. The first mouthful stung his lip but he persevered, desperate for the heat and the caffeine. "There's also a distinct lack of cameras around the whole estate. Certainly no CCTV and I seriously doubt any of the residents will have their own private ones. So, it's a blind spot — ideal for our killer."

"Do you think he knew that, guv?" DS Cassidy unwrapped a cereal bar. "Whoever did this knew the area didn't have cameras?"

"Highly likely, I would say, Amanda. Unless it's just one big coincidence." Jack was well known for his intense dislike of the 'c' word and his expression pulled no punches. "Let's get the ball rolling while we wait for the results of the post-mortems and the lab. As the flat has been empty for some time, we need to find out who the last resident was; maybe even the one before that. And anyone else who might have had access to it. Any one of them could be a person of interest."

"I'll get on to the council," offered Daniels, pulling his keyboard across the desk.

"What about Missing Persons?" volunteered Cassidy. "Should we check with them?"

"I'm not sure they're going to be much use to us right now — not until we find some more pieces of these poor souls." Jack placed his coffee mug back down on the desk and let his eyes gravitate towards the cork pinboard where several crime scene photographs had been tacked. It made for sickening viewing. Out of the corner of his eye he saw Cassidy put her cereal bar down and look away.

Over Jack's career, countless sickening images had graced the incident room walls — but these were up there with the worst he'd ever seen. He ran a hand once more over his throbbing cheek, which didn't go unnoticed.

"Henderson's still in the cells, boss. I think someone wants to speak to you before he's interviewed." Cooper emptied the last of his packet of bacon crisps into his mouth. "Walloping a DI probably wasn't his greatest move."

"That's as maybe, Cooper, but he can sit and stew as far as I'm concerned — he's someone else's headache today.

We've got far bigger fish to fry." There was already a message from the chief superintendent waiting for Jack when they'd arrived back from Acorn House, which was another conversation he wasn't especially looking forward to. But he decided Dougie King could also wait a while. News about his run-in with Neville Henderson had most probably migrated upstairs, and although the coffee selection in the chief superintendent's office was far superior to what was currently languishing in the bottom of Jack's mug, he didn't relish being roasted alive just yet.

Just then, the door to the incident room swung open and DS Robert Carmichael's head appeared. "Good, you're back. Got time for a trip upstairs, Jack?"

* * *

Time: 2.10 p.m.
Date: Monday 12 January 2015
Location: Denmark Street, London

Stuart 'Mac' MacIntosh swung his leg over the back of his motorbike and grimaced. Although the air was cold — almost freezing, in fact — he could still feel the sweat gathering beneath his leathers. He had been looking forward to getting back to work, to feeling useful once again, but after just a few hours he found his muscles were aching already.

Not that he would admit that to the boss — or to Isabel, for that matter. Jobs were hard to come by at the best of times, and especially so when you had a history as chequered as his. When your CV documented time spent at Her Majesty's Pleasure, the job offers tended to dry up.

But he needed to work for his own sanity — and the courier job suited him. He knew that the money Isabel had inherited from her parents was more than enough for them both to be financially secure, but he was a proud man – a proud MacIntosh – and he needed to provide. Although he suspected Isabel saw it more as stubbornness than pride at times. Forced to take time off after a fire ripped through the former St Bartholomew's Home for Boys, almost taking him with it, now he was fit again he needed to up his game. He didn't want to rely on Isabel any more than he had already.

As he pulled his visor down, he felt his phone vibrate in his pocket and had a good idea who it would be. Jack had messaged him several times over the weekend to suggest a brotherly catch-up over a few beers. Mac wasn't exactly avoiding it, but he wasn't rushing round with a four-pack, either. Jack meant well, but Mac knew that once he had a few beers inside him talk would turn to Isabel and their trip down to Surrey.

And then Mac would most probably end up mentioning Isabel's fears about being watched, which would then inevitably lead to Jack turning all detective inspector on him, demanding information. His brother's heart was in the right place, but sometimes he just made Mac feel inadequate. The wilder of the MacIntosh brothers, Mac — or Stu as Jack still insisted on calling him, never quite warming to the nickname afforded to him since childhood — had slowly started to accept that life wasn't always going to trip him up and drag him down. He may not have had the greatest start in life, but things were going well for him now. Isabel could take the credit for a lot of that — her calming influence had gone a long way to taming his self-destructive tendencies.

Isabel.

Mac wasn't sure if he truly believed her when she said she thought someone was watching the house in Surrey — but he'd made all the right noises at the time and tried to allay her fears. Eventually they'd decided to come back home, where Isabel quickly relaxed back into the steady routine of running the café. Mac knew she felt disappointed, even saddened in some way, at how disconnected she'd felt back in her childhood home. She'd hoped that crossing the threshold would reawaken some long-hidden emotions, but instead she'd spent much of the time feeling unnerved. The house undoubtedly harboured many memories – some good, others more painful – but it was a step she had needed to take.

Pulling the bike away from the kerb, Mac joined the traffic heading west. Isabel was probably mistaken about the house being watched anyway, and mentioning it to Jack would only stir up a hornet's nest that they could well do without. And Jack would no doubt have enough on his plate without anything else adding to it.

Mac decided the less his brother knew the better.

* * *

Time: 2.15 p.m.
Date: Monday 12 January 2015
Location: Metropolitan Police HQ, London

"What are they cooking up, Jack?" DS Robert Carmichael slid a wary glance sideways as he took his seat. "It makes me nervous — seeing women in a huddle like that."

The canteen was getting busier with the lunchtime crowd but Jack found it easy to follow the detective sergeant's line of sight as he bit into his toasted cheese sandwich. The visit to Acorn House earlier that morning had unsettled his stomach and, coupled with the aroma from Cooper's bacon roll as they made their way back to the station in the Mondeo, had killed his appetite stone dead. But the smells circulating the canteen now reawakened his hunger, his stomach growling. He pushed thoughts of severed limbs as far from his mind as he could and chewed.

Across the other side of the canteen, he saw the three women Carmichael was referring to — Detective Inspector Jane Telford from the Cold Case Unit; the force's criminal profiler and forensic psychologist, Dr Rachel Hunter, and then the newest member of the Met's staff, Detective Inspector Becky Yates.

"You read too much into these things, Rob." Jack wiped his mouth with a serviette and reached for his mug of tea. He had already spied the three as he and Rob had entered the canteen, Jane Telford affording him a brief smile as she caught his eye. He got on well with Jane — and Rachel, too — but he didn't know much about the new DI. Becky Yates had transferred to the Met last August and had had to hit the ground running when she was given a complicated kidnapping case to handle. After a shaky start, she'd acquitted herself well.

Carmichael carried on shaking his head, eyes still fixed on the trio as they made their way towards the hot food counter. "Never underestimate a woman, Jack. Have I not taught you anything? And definitely not three of them together — they're like pack animals out for the kill."

Jack spluttered into his mug. "I seriously doubt they're up to much in the canteen, Rob. You're just being paranoid."

Another shake of the head. "No, I've seen looks like that before, mate. Trust me, they're planning something. And if I'm not very much mistaken I think they're talking about you."

Jack followed Carmichael's gaze once again, noting that all three women were now turned in their direction. Jane Telford sported a curious smile on her face, as did Dr Hunter. Becky Yates merely looked intrigued. This time he locked eyes with Rachel — watching her stifle a giggle and then turn away.

"They could be talking about you," remarked Jack, picking up his sandwich again. "Or it could have nothing to do with either of us. Eat your food — I'm not stumping up for all this only for you to let it go cold." He gestured towards the full English breakfast that the canteen served twenty-four hours a day on Carmichael's plate.

Carmichael stabbed at a sausage. "Believe me, Jack. Your ears should be burning red hot by now. Maybe they're warning the new DI about you — if I remember rightly you've a bit of history with both Jane and the lovely Dr Hunter, am I right?" The detective sergeant gave a good-humoured wink as he stuffed the sausage coated in baked beans into his mouth.

Swallowing a mouthful of his sandwich, Jack fixed his friend with a narrowed gaze. "It's a good job I like you, Rob."

He pushed his plate to the side. "But you can quite quickly go off someone, you know."

Carmichael grinned and turned his full attention to the rest of his breakfast. "You should get back in the saddle though, Jack. The dating game. We both should. Otherwise, we'll end up lonely old men when we get pensioned off."

Jack sighed. He'd lost count of the number of conversations he'd had about his perceived loneliness. As soon as anyone heard about his bachelor existence, assumptions were instantly made. "I'm not lonely, Rob. I might live alone, but that's not the same as being lonely. They're two completely different things. Completely different animals."

Carmichael scraped more beans on to his fork. "That's as maybe — but the company would be nice, don't you think?"

"There's plenty of time ahead for you, Rob — you're still young. But me?" Jack gave a throaty laugh. "I think I'm already on the scrap-heap in that regard. Get to my age and everyone you meet has just a bit too much baggage for my liking. My shoulders aren't that broad."

"You're not past it yet, Jack. Forty-eight, isn't it? That's nothing. And I don't think we can expect no baggage at all — that would be a bit unrealistic in this day and age — but maybe just hand luggage only, eh?"

The two men sat in silence for a few minutes while Jack finished his toasted sandwich and Carmichael made short work of the remaining hash browns and beans on his plate. Jack then watched the trio of Jane, Rachel and Becky exit the canteen armed with their takeaway cartons, not giving either of them even so much as a backwards glance.

"Why do you stick your neck out for me, Rob?" Jack turned towards the detective sergeant who was now mopping up a runny egg yolk with a slice of bread. He was acutely aware that Rob had gone above and beyond for him on more than one occasion in the past, and the man hadn't needed to. Jack didn't have that many people he would class as a friend — Rob was pretty much it.

Carmichael put down his knife and fork and pushed the empty plate away. "You and me — we're cut from the same cloth, don't you think? I feel a connection with you that I don't have with very many other people."

Jack nodded. He had to agree. Despite only meeting Rob relatively recently, the two had clicked almost instantly — well, if you ignored the punch Jack landed squarely on Rob's face, almost breaking the man's nose. Carmichael had been brought up in the care system, much the same as Jack and his brother Stuart had, but with quite a different end result. He'd been fortunate enough to find a foster family who later adopted him as their own — he was one of the lucky ones.

Jack had found a foster family too — but Stuart? The younger MacIntosh brother hadn't fared so well. "I guess," he eventually replied.

"How is your brother anyway? I've not seen him in a while."

"Stu's good, thanks. Getting stronger every day."

"That's good to hear." Carmichael began to play with the serviette by the side of his plate. "Sometimes I find myself envying you. You and your brother — you have that closeness, don't you? Brotherliness, I suppose you could call it — if that's even a word. Don't get me wrong, I'm grateful to my mum and dad for taking me in when they did — but they're not my blood." Carmichael lifted his gaze. "Does that make me sound ungrateful?"

"Not at all mate. I think it's only natural."

"So, it's made me start thinking."

Jack took a swig from his mug of tea. "That could be a dangerous mix, Rob. You and thinking." As he put down his mug, he noted an uncertain look in his friend's eyes. "Something on your mind?"

Carmichael tossed the serviette on to his plate. "Kind of. I want to find someone . . . my sister."

Jack's eyebrows hitched. "Your sister? I never knew you had a sister."

23

A sheepish look crossed Carmichael's face. "I don't really talk about her. To be honest, I don't really remember her that much. I was five when I went into care — Genete was three. I've not seen her since."

Jack was about to say something when DS Cooper appeared from nowhere and slid into the seat next to him. Jack eyed the fresh bacon sandwich oozing with brown sauce on the detective sergeant's plate. "Another one, Cooper? Where do you manage to put it all?" Jack took a sly look down towards his stomach, sucking it in a little, then glanced at his Fitbit for his step count. Over four thousand now. Not bad.

"Jenny calls me a hobbit." Cooper grinned and sank his teeth into the soft white roll. "The way I always need two breakfasts."

"And the rest." Jack drained his mug of tea. "How you're not the size of a house I'll never know."

Cooper swallowed his first mouthful. "I've got good metabolism. Anyhow, I came up here for a reason, not just for another roll. Elliott's been on the phone — wants you to call him back as soon as you can. And while you've been gone, the door-to-door has thrown up a potential witness."

Jack scraped his chair back and stood up. "We'd best get back to it then. Rob?" he turned to Carmichael as he passed. "We'll chat some more, yeah?"

CHAPTER THREE

Time: 3.00 p.m.
Date: Monday 12 January 2015
Location: Acorn House, Hillside Estate, London

"We're going to see a Mrs Annie Palmer." Jack braced him-self for the climb back up to the twelfth floor. "Door-to-door confirm it was her who raised the alarm."

"Can't have been a very pleasant thing to find," com-mented Cooper as they stepped once more through the com-munal entrance of Acorn House. "Something like that."

"Quite."

Several minutes later, out of breath and clutching his stomach from the developing stitch, Jack arrived on the twelfth floor. Cooper was waiting for him.

"When did you get so fit, Cooper?" Jack held on to the metal bannister at the top of the stairs, chest wheezing. "You've had at least three bacon rolls that I know of today."

Cooper grinned. "Jenny has me on a tight rein at home these days, boss. Insists we go on walks on my day off, and she's even got one of those exercise bikes for the spare room." He winked, conspiringly. "But she cannae see what I get up to at work."

Jack glanced down at his Fitbit again. Six and a half thousand steps sounded good to him, but his leg muscles were disagreeing. Stepping out of the stairwell and on to the communal walkway, he noted the familiar aroma of stale urine and rotten takeaways had followed them up through each of the twelve flights.

Mrs Palmer lived at flat number 4a which was only two doors in front of them. As they made their way towards it, Jack cast his gaze ahead towards Flat 7b at the far end, crime scene tape still criss-crossing the entrance and a lone PC on duty outside. Elliott and his team would still be working away inside — and from the hurried conversation he'd had with the crime scene manager before leaving the station, Jack was no closer to finding out just what Elliott had discovered. Jack's thoughts had instantly turned to the piles of rubbish that lined the walls within the flat — and just what might have been found inside one of them.

The thought made him shiver.

The crime scene manager wasn't prepared to enlighten him any further over the phone and Jack said he would drop by once they were finished with Mrs Palmer.

Flat 4a looked well kept, a fresh coat of pale blue paint on the door, a small window to the side sporting a pair of bleached-white net curtains. Just about getting his breath back, Jack gave the door three swift raps. It wasn't long before it was opened.

"Yes?" A small woman, no more than five feet tall in her slippers peered out from the gap between the door and the door jamb. A shiny, metal safety chain held the door firmly in place.

Jack stepped closer, trying his best smile. "Mrs Palmer? My name is Detective Inspector Jack MacIntosh and this here is Detective Sergeant Cooper. We're from the Metropolitan Police and we're investigating that nasty business from just along the passageway there." He gestured towards Flat 7b.

"Yes?" the old woman repeated, safety chain still in place.

"I understand you spoke to one of my colleagues earlier today, but it would really help if we could come in and chat with you some more. They tell me you stumbled across the scene and made the 999 call?" Even though the woman was standing some six or so feet away from him on the other side of the door, Jack could see the wariness in her eyes.

"Yes . . . yes I did," she replied, eventually. "And a fair nasty business it was, too. Almost made my heart go, so it did."

"I'm sure. Well, if you don't mind, maybe we could come in?" Jack held up his warrant card. "We won't stay long."

The old woman seemed to consider the proposition for a few seconds before finally unhooking the safety chain and letting the door swing open. "Of course. Please, come in." As she stepped out of the way, she added. "You can't be too careful these days." She nodded towards the chain. "Especially not around here. Not nowadays."

"I can imagine." Jack stepped into the dimly lit hallway, followed by Cooper. Just as Annie Palmer was about to push the door shut behind them, a white cat with tabby markings darted out from beneath her feet and shot outside.

"Thomas!" Mrs Palmer almost tripped over the cat's tail as it rushed past. Shaking her head, she closed the door. "That cat will be the death of me one day. Come on through." She began leading the way into the flat. "Can I get you lovely young men a cup of tea while you're here?"

Jack opened his mouth, about to decline, but Cooper beat him to it.

"That would be grand, Mrs Palmer. Just the job."

Jack gave the detective a withering look but eventually nodded. "That's very kind of you. So long as it isn't too much trouble."

"No trouble at all, my dears. And call me Annie. You go and pop yourselves through there." She waved a hand towards a door on their left. "I'll be through in just a moment. The kettle has only just boiled."

Jack and Cooper stepped into the old woman's living room, immediately assaulted by an array of photographs, decorative plates and framed cross stitch patterns crammed to the walls. Barely an inch of wall space was left uncovered. A large dark wooden dresser hugged the far wall, again adorned with framed pictures and other ornaments. In front of the dresser was a floral covered two-seater sofa plus a high-backed armchair, both facing a three-bar electric fire which was on full. The room was warm and inviting, with a sweet smell of rose and vanilla.

Despite the multitude of knick-knacks decorating every available surface, the room was immaculate. Not a speck of dust anywhere. Cooper went to sit on the two-seater sofa, while Jack remained standing. It wasn't long before Annie shuffled back in pushing a wheeled trolley before her. Jack saw Cooper's eyes light up like a Christmas tree when the detective sergeant spied the plate of digestive biscuits.

Jack leaned forward to accept the teacup the old woman passed him, watching Cooper deftly swipe up three biscuits at once. "This is very kind of you, Mrs Palmer. *Annie*."

Cooper nodded in agreement as he stuffed the first biscuit into his mouth. "Really kind. I'm starving."

Annie took her own teacup and went to sit in the high-backed armchair by the fire. The chair dwarfed her slight frame, her feet barely touching the carpet.

"We'll try not to impose on you for too long, but could you just run us through what happened earlier this morning? I know it might not be pleasant but it could really help us find out what happened."

The old woman took a sip from her teacup, her hand shaking as she did so. Placing the cup and saucer in her lap, she looked up. "It was the most terrible thing I think I've ever seen — and I've seen a lot around here over the years, I can tell you."

"How did you come to go inside the flat?" Jack sipped at his weak tea. It could do with a few sugars. And less milk. "Did you know who used to live there?"

"It was Thomas."

"Thomas?" Jack frowned. "Your cat?"

Annie nodded. "The little rascal ran outside when I opened the door to shake out my duster this morning. Nearly bowled me off my feet, so he did." She gave a little chuckle. "He's a live wire that one, always scampering about, getting into places he's not meant to." She paused, her face clouding over a little. "I don't like him being outside so much these days. There's too much going on here — too many people up to no good, if you know what I mean. It's not safe for him. So, when he ran out, I went after him."

"What happened next?"

"Well, I couldn't see him anywhere. I called him and called him — but nothing. It was then that I saw the door was open."

"The door? The door to Flat 7b, you mean?"

Annie nodded again. "Yes, wide open it was. I wondered if Tom had gone inside — it wouldn't be the first time he's got into someone else's flat, you know. Always on the hunt for food, that one. So, I went in to look."

Jack took another sip of the tepid tea while Cooper stuffed the second biscuit into his mouth. "And what did you find when you went in?"

The old woman's face paled while she gripped the china teacup in her lap. "I've never seen anything quite like it, detective. And I never want to see it again."

"I'm sure." Jack's stance softened. "Why don't you have some more of your tea before we carry on?"

Annie did as suggested, her pale pink lips quivering as she sipped. The teacup rattled in the saucer when she placed it back down. When she spoke, her voice was so quiet it was little more than a whisper. "I didn't really know what it was to begin with, it was so dark in there. But then there was the smell. It was like rotten meat; like something had gone off." She shuddered. "I called Thomas but there was still no sign of him. Then I thought if he was going to be anywhere, he would be in the kitchen. So I went through and that was . . . that

29

was when I saw them." She broke off and lowered her eyes to the teacup. "That was when I saw what they were. Just lying there. I thought my heart was going to jump right out of my mouth. I was almost sick."

Jack nodded as sympathetically as he could. He placed his half-drunk tea back down on the trolley. "Did you touch anything?"

The question seemed to make the old woman visibly baulk. "*Touch* anything? Good lord no, why would I touch anything?" Jack saw Mrs Palmer shiver beneath her cardigan. "I took one look at what it was, saw that Tom was nowhere to be seen, and ran straight back here to call you."

"And did you happen to see anyone else around at that time? Anyone out on the walkway, or walking past your window earlier in the morning?"

Annie shook her head. "Nobody. I think the weather is keeping everyone inside at the moment."

"What about on previous days? Anything yesterday, for example — or the day before? Anyone you've seen that you're not familiar with?"

Again, the old woman shook her head. "Just the usual people from the flats along here. But having said that, we all keep ourselves to ourselves for the most part. It's very quiet. Just the occasional trip to the shop or the Post Office for our pensions. It's the other levels that have the troublemakers in them — and over at Beech House." She gestured vaguely in the direction of the window.

"Troublemakers? What do you mean by that?"

"Kids. Gangs." Mrs Palmer shuddered again. "They shout and swear at you when you walk past. Follow you along the stairs. I don't go out if I see them hanging around."

"When was the last time you saw anyone in Flat 7b? I'm told it's been empty a while."

The old woman frowned. "I'm not sure, to tell you the truth. The last person to live there was old Bernard Fisher. Lovely man he was, but deaf as a post, mind."

"And when did he leave?"

Another frown. "Must be a good six months now — maybe more. I'm sure it was in the summer anyway. I think he went into a home."

"And no one's been living there since?"

Annie shook her head. "Not that I know of. It's been broken into a few times — kids on the estate you see. They see an empty flat and think it's theirs to do what they want with. I heard they'd trashed the place, taken much of what old Bernard had left behind. I think the inside might have needed a lot of work done to it before it could be rented out again. You'll have to speak to the caretaker — Barry Pierce. He'll know more about that than me."

Jack watched Cooper draw out his notebook and write the caretaker's details down. "Have you noticed the door being left open before? You said it was open, which was why you thought your cat might have got inside?"

Annie considered the question, eventually replying with a shrug. "Sometimes. It's always left unlocked I think — which is how the kids get inside. But I'd never seen it left wide open like that. Part of me thought maybe Barry was in there, getting the place ready for a new tenant. Or maybe Bernard's son — Julian. He sometimes stayed with Bernard, treated the place as his own he did."

Jack watched Cooper write the second name down in his notebook. "Julian Fisher. You know him well?"

The old woman hesitated, her cheeks colouring a little beneath the powder she'd applied that morning. "I wouldn't say well, no. Nice enough chap, though. Always has a smile for you and more than happy to help us oldies out — carry our shopping and the like."

Jack nodded. "OK — thank you for your time, Mrs Palmer. Annie. You've been most helpful. I'm truly sorry you had to witness what you did."

"It's no trouble, detective. I'm tougher than I look, believe me. Have you . . . ?" The old woman broke off, getting to her

31

feet and grabbing the wheeled trolley as she did so. "Have you managed to find out who they were?"

Jack motioned for Cooper that it was time to go, seeing the detective sergeant swipe an extra biscuit as he passed. He gave the woman a sad smile. "Sadly no — not yet."

Annie shuffled past, pulling open the door that led out into the hallway. Just as she did so, Jack's phone began to ring. Elliott Walker.

"Hey, Elliott. We're just finishing up here at Flat 4a — be with you in a moment or two."

* * *

Time: 3.05 p.m.
Date: Monday 12 January 2015
Location: Central London

Julian Fisher knew the most sensible thing to do was to get as far away from Acorn House as he could; to put as much distance between himself and the flat as humanly possible. So why had he come back? He'd been on his way to the lock-up, but this place lured him like nowhere else could. It was as if it were some kind of honey trap; like he was a helpless bluebottle caught in a spider's sticky web.

He ducked behind a lamp-post and watched the scene being played out before him. The car park at the front was usually deserted, but now it was home to any number of police cars and other vehicles. He'd seen a series of portable lights being carried towards the entrance and didn't envy the poor sod who had drawn the short straw to carry them all the way up to the twelfth floor.

For he was sure that was where they were heading.

Flat 7b.

His skin began to prickle beneath his parka jacket. Maybe he hadn't been quite as careful as he should have been, as careful as he *usually* was. He had a key to the flat — good old Dad had given him any number of spare keys for the place which he'd kept long after the old man had moved into the care home, and luckily the place had remained empty ever since, which suited his purposes. But now the place was swarming with police.

Amid the sense of disquiet, a curious smile touched his lips and he willed himself to relax. Eventually they would all leave and things could go back to normal.

He just needed to be patient.

But, in the meantime, he needed to get away from here — back to the safety of the lock-up. There may not be any CCTV around the estate, but there were plenty of pairs of eyes — even if many of them were hidden behind prescription strength spectacles or fogged with cataracts.

People could still see.

* * *

Time: 3.20 p.m.
Date: Monday 12 January 2015
Location: Acorn House, Hillside Estate, London

Jack ducked his head beneath the blue and white police tape that still criss-crossed the entrance to Flat 7b and immediately saw the crime scene manager heading in his direction.

"Put one of these on, Jack." Elliott handed over a white forensic suit plus overshoes. "Then it's just through here."

Once Jack had slipped into the protective suit and covered his shoes, he followed Elliott to the rear of the flat and the small bathroom that lay just off from the only bedroom. Two crime scene investigators stepped out of the narrow confines to make way. Although Jack couldn't see their faces very well behind their masks, he still managed to see the pensive look in their eyes. Experience told him what he was about to witness wouldn't be pleasant.

Jack remembered Elliott telling him that the electricity supply had been disconnected, and with no natural light in the tiny bathroom they'd had to install battery powered lights to see what they were doing.

"We've taken a series of photographs and a video so far." The crime scene manager passed Jack his handset. "I think it's best you see for yourself."

Jack took the device, a frown soon deepening beneath his elasticated cap. It didn't take long for him to see what had caused Elliott to call him so urgently.

"From the first image, you can see that one of the greatest concentrations is in the bath itself."

Jack's eyes widened as he took in the extensive swathes of blue light that the luminol had revealed. A useful tool for any forensic investigation, luminol fluoresces in the dark when it comes into contact with blood — reacting with the iron content and giving off a very distinctive blue hue. But the effects didn't last long so any results needed to be photographed immediately.

"Then there is another even heavier concentration on the floor just in front of the bath panel. We've pulled up the carpet tiles but you can see there's still a huge amount of staining on the floor beneath. Then we have what looks like drag marks leading in from the door."

Jack flicked through the images, seeing the markings Elliott was referring to.

The crime scene manager continued. "It's a plausible theory that your victim was dragged into the bathroom, already bleeding. Then . . ." Elliott paused, his gaze flicking towards the bathtub itself. "Then they were dismembered inside the bath."

"It looks like a bloody massacre," breathed Jack, scrolling through each image once more. The luminol had stained everything blue — the tub, the tiles, the shower curtain; even the taps and showerhead.

Elliott nodded. "Some effort has been made to wash the blood away, but I don't think there's any doubt where your victim, or victims, were butchered — to put it rather bluntly. And that's not all. Just after I called you, we found something else." He took back the handset and skipped forward to another set of photographs. "Inside one of the rubbish bags — two more legs and what looks to me like an upper chest."

Jack squinted at the images, his mouth turning dry. Two human legs were clearly visible protruding from a black bin liner — a second image showed a female chest, sliced from the body just above the belly button. Jack had been to many crime scenes over the years, but he hadn't seen one like this for quite some time. "How long do you think you'll be here?"

The crime scene manager gave a non-committal shrug. "We swabbed everywhere in the bathroom before applying the luminol, and we're in the process of swabbing everywhere else. As this looks like the dismemberment site, we'll take the bath apart, check the drains — the usual. Then we'll go through the rest of the flat, taking up the carpet tiles as we go and see what else we find. We'll stay here for as long as it takes."

Jack noticed another crime scene investigator hovering by the door, brandishing a camera and video recorder. He stepped to the side. "I'll leave you to it, Elliott. I can see you've still got a lot to do." He gestured towards the cameras. "Can you let me have some photos and the video as soon as possible?"

"Sure." Elliott nodded. "I'll email some across right away. And like I say — we'll stay as long as we're needed. I'll let you know if we find anything else once we've pulled the whole place apart. We've already sent the latest finds over to the mortuary as I think Dr Matthews wanted to get started."

Jack didn't need the crime scene manager to elaborate on what they were looking for. With the limbs of at least two victims found so far, and one upper torso, there were plenty of body parts that could still be hidden inside the flat. *Somewhere.*

'Plenty of places that could house all manner of delightful surprises.'

Jack recalled Dr Matthews' soft tone as he backed out into the hallway. As he did so, a familiar figure headed in his direction.

"Boss?" DS Cooper sounded breathless. "I was just heading back down to the car when the mortuary rang." He held up his phone. "They're ready for us."

CHAPTER FOUR

Time: 4.15 p.m.
Date: Monday 12 January 2015
Location: Westminster Mortuary, London

Jack adjusted his elasticated cap as he followed DS Cooper into the examination room. He had an ever-growing list of things he really needed to be getting on with back at the station, and taking time out to attend Westminster Mortuary wasn't really one of them.

Elliott had been true to his word and sent over a selection of images of what had been found so far — none of them particularly pretty. The swathes of blue from the luminol left no one in any doubt as to what had happened in the tiny bathroom of Flat 7b. Calling into the incident room briefly on their way back from Acorn House, Jack noticed DS Cassidy turning a pale shade of green once the crime scene photographs were pinned up on to one of the whiteboards. She had tentatively offered to attend the mortuary, but Jack had waved the notion aside. This one was down to him, as much as the thought turned his stomach. Instead, he'd tasked her and Daniels with trying to track down the caretaker of Acorn House, and also Julian Fisher.

Cooper, on the other hand, was like a dog with a new toy.

Dr Matthews was waiting for them. "Welcome, gentlemen. Good to see you both. Let's get started, shall we?"

Jack nodded — the sooner they started, the sooner they could escape back into the fresh air outside. Although the temperature was possibly a few degrees lower than the post-mortem room, the chill air would be a welcome improvement. His nose was already twitching from the heady mixture currently assaulting it — a curious combination of antiseptics, bleach and decay. He knew he'd be smelling it for the rest of the day, and possibly throughout the night, too.

"Good idea, Doc."

Instead of just the one examination today, there would be two, the second body — such as it was — waiting in the chiller room next door. Dr Matthews took up his position at the side of the central steel examination table and reached above his head to switch on the digital recording device.

"Today is Monday 12 January and the first examination is of a female Caucasian. Age will be difficult to determine until we have more, ideally the skull and pelvic bones. There is a selection of body parts identified as follows. Both arms are present with hands intact. Both legs, upper and lower, are also present, again with the feet intact. For this body there is also a section of the upper chest." The pathologist paused, catching Jack's eye for a second. "There is no head and no abdomen or pelvic area."

"Are you sure these all belong to the same victim?"

Dr Matthews nodded. "Preliminary blood analysis and DNA typing confirms these body parts all belong to the same person."

"Do you think we have a trophy hunter?" Cooper stepped closer to the table, eyes wide. "He or she is taking something from each victim — which is why we don't have a complete body?"

Jack felt his eyes stray across to the door that led to the chiller room, in which lay an almost identical, equally macabre picture. Were they looking at a trophy hunter like Cooper suggested? Jack wasn't sure, but something about what they had discovered at Acorn House made him believe there was more to it than that. "That remains to be seen, Cooper. Anything is possible at this stage." Jack pulled his gaze back to the steel table and motioned for the pathologist to continue.

"Taking the upper limbs first — externally there are visible track marks on both forearms, most apparent on the left. Some evidence of recent drug use." Dr Matthews reached forward and gently turned the arm over. "There is a small tattoo of a rose measuring three centimetres in diameter on the inside of the left wrist." Stepping back slightly, the pathologist made room for the mortuary technician to lean in and take a series of close-up photographs. "Some nicotine staining on the index and middle finger of the right hand, but no other distinguishing marks except for a collection of benign skin lesions on the right upper arm."

The pathologist sidestepped along the table. "Taking the lower limbs next. There is evidence of mild varicosities on both lower legs, but minimal inflammation. Several contusions are evident on both upper thighs, varying ages but some look relatively recent." Once again, Dr Matthews stepped to the side to allow close-up photographs to be taken. "One point of note, Jack, I did perform some pre-procedure X-rays and this poor young woman has had some surgery to her left ankle in the recent past. The medial malleolus has been fixed with a screw, the lateral malleolus with a plate."

"Any idea when?" Jack's eyebrows twitched. If they could locate where the procedures took place it could go a long way to help with identification.

The pathologist shook his head. "Not with any great certainty, I'm afraid. The wounds have healed nicely. I'll let you have copies of the X-rays. The metalwork inside may have identification markers enabling them to trace where and when the surgery took place." Turning to select a shiny scalpel from the instrument tray by his side, he looked up expectantly. "In the meantime, shall we begin?"

* * *

Time: 4.15 p.m.
Date: Monday 12 January 2015
Location: Acorn House, Hillside Estate, London

Elliott Walker snapped on a fresh pair of gloves and ran a finger around the inside of the elasticated cap sitting snugly on his head. Despite the almost freezing temperatures outside, and there being no heating inside Flat 7b, he could feel the sweat collecting beneath his protective suit.

His team of investigators had methodically mapped out the flat and were now embarking on their inch-by-inch detailed examination. All the body parts discovered so far had been sent to the mortuary, but the sombre feeling their discovery had caused still lingered. Small plastic numbered triangles now littered the floor where pieces of potential evidence had been found which warranted further analysis.

Although the flat had been stripped of all major appliances and furniture — even the built-in fridge freezer and oven had been ripped from the walls — there were still plenty of places where further body parts could be hidden. The thought made Elliott shudder beneath his protective suit. No matter how long he'd been doing this particular job, and no matter how many distressing cases he'd dealt with in that time, some crime scenes still had the capacity to shock.

And the contents of Flat 7b shocked him to the core.

Black plastic bin liners were stacked up all around the flat — mostly in the hall and bedroom, a handful in the living room. They would all be carefully opened, the contents examined and photographed. Every investigator inside the flat knew what they were looking for, but Elliott would bet that none of them truly wished to find them. With the discovery of another pair of legs and part of someone's chest inside one of the black bin liners, it was feasible there were more body parts to find. Was this killer so cold and callous that he'd merely thrown his victims out with the rubbish? The thought appalled him, but killers weren't usually known for their compassion.

Bob Snowden, one of the most experienced members of the team, gestured for Elliot to follow him back inside the cramped bathroom. When the luminol had revealed the existence of so much blood, blood that had seeped through the carpet tiles and into the wooden floorboards beneath, both Bob and Elliott had stood there, mouths slack. Jack had been right to call it a massacre — that was *exactly* what it was. The more Elliott thought about it, the more he was convinced that this was the site of at least one of the victims' demise — so they were now preparing to pull the place apart, piece by piece.

Starting with the bath itself.

"You ready?" Elliott gestured towards the bath panel. Bob nodded in reply.

Elliott had recently refurbished his own bathroom at home, and knew that most bath panels came away relatively easily. But he still hesitated. Next to him, he sensed Bob's caution, too. Just what were they going to find?

Bringing a flat head screwdriver out of his pocket, Bob started to prise the panel away from the bath. As expected, it popped out without too much resistance, and Elliott helped to pull the rest of it free and stack it up against the wall. Both men then knelt down, Bob lowering his head to the floor to peer into the dark space beneath.

"Shit," breathed the investigator, his eyes widening. "You see what I see?"

Elliott followed suit and instantly saw what Bob was referring to. He tried to respond but instead he felt paralysed, the words sticking in his throat. All he could do was nod.

Swallowing, even though his mouth was dry, Elliott pushed himself to his feet.

He needed to call Jack.

* * *

Time: 4.30 p.m.
Date: Monday 12 January 2015
Location: Westminster Mortuary, London

"Further examination of both upper limbs shows a rather crude separation at the shoulder level." Dr Matthews teased his scalpel along the top edge of the victim's left upper arm. "See here?"

DS Cooper stepped closer. Jack did not.

"The skin and subcutaneous tissue have somewhat frayed edges, almost jagged in places."

"Meaning what?" Jack felt he already knew the answer and sensed his stomach start to clench even before the pathologist opened his mouth to reply.

"I would say that the instrument used wasn't particularly sharp — it was most certainly a knife but not the sharpest tool in the box, if you pardon the pun. Whoever did this has taken a fair few attempts to disarticulate the joint at the shoulder."

Disarticulation.

Jack fidgeted inside his rubber boots as an involuntary shiver joined the disquiet. Visions of little Maisie Lancaster from eight months before instantly flooded his head, forcing him to clear his throat and refocus. The eight-year-old had been brutally dismembered, ending up in a suitcase beneath London Bridge. It had been a particularly traumatic case, and not one Jack wished to repeat. "So not an expert then? We're not looking for a surgeon or a butcher this time around?"

Dr Matthews gave a wry smile. "Well, I wouldn't be quite so cavalier as that, Jack. Even an experienced professional can have an off day."

The rest of the examination passed by relatively quickly. Dr Matthews confirmed that both legs had been separated from the pelvis in much the same manner as the arms — roughly and inexpertly. The upper chest intrigued Jack — so much so that he took one or two steps closer than he normally would.

"The upper torso has been severed at just below the seventh rib." Dr Matthews angled the remains of the woman's upper chest towards Jack. "The spine itself has been severed at the T11/T12 level in the thoracic region, and also the C6/C7 level in the neck." The mortuary technician stepped forward to take some more close-up shots. "The sternum is intact but ribs eight to twelve are missing."

Photographs complete, the pathologist proceeded to open up the chest cavity. "Heart and lungs *in situ* — no apparent external damage."

Jack and Cooper watched as both organs were removed, inspected and weighed. "Heart looks healthy," commented Dr Matthews as he eventually handed the steel bowl to the mortuary technician. "The lungs, however, show signs of bronchiolar constriction and interstitial oedema. There is also a degree of alveolar haemorrhaging."

"Which means?" Jack watched the pathologist slip both right and left lung into separate steel bowls.

"Without the rest of the body it's hard to be a hundred per cent accurate, Jack, but . . ." Dr Matthews placed his scalpel back on to the examination table. "Even without this young woman's head and neck, I believe the cause of death could very well be strangulation, with the body then dismembered post-mortem."

With the first examination complete, the mortuary technician removed the body parts and secured them in the chiller room next door, then wheeled over the second victim.

After a short break to restock with freshly sterilised equipment, and for Dr Matthews to change into a fresh gown, the second post-mortem began. It proceeded in much the same manner as the first and Jack found himself tuning out much of the pathologist's commentary. Words floated in and out of his head like the ebb and flow of the tide.

Dismembered.

Blunt instrument.

Inexpert disarticulation.

With just both lower limbs and one arm for this victim, the second post- mortem didn't take long. And with such little material to examine, Dr Matthews was unable to give a precise cause of death. Although knowing how someone had died was a useful step in the investigation, Jack always felt it was more important to find out *why* they had died. Because sometimes the *why* would lead them to the *who*: and it was the *who* that they really cared about.

Just *who* was responsible for ending these two women's lives so barbarically? Whoever it was, no one was in any doubt about how quickly they would need to be stopped. Anyone capable of hacking a body apart with a none-too sharp knife needed stopping. And fast. The pathologist hadn't exactly used the word '*hacked*' but Jack knew that was what the man had really meant.

"Come on, Cooper." Jack led the way out of the post-mortem room, leaving Dr Matthews performing his customary bow to those unfortunate enough to end up on the wrong end of his scalpel. "Let's get back."

"Why does he do that?" Cooper let the double doors swing shut behind him as Jack led them back towards the changing rooms. "Bowing to the bodies once he's finished with them."

"I believe it's a mark of respect, Cooper." Jack pulled the elasticated cap from his head and began to step out of his rubber boots. "I recall him telling me about it one time — I think it was the doctor that trained him, a famous pathologist who did the same thing. He told the young Dr Matthews here that anyone who had the misfortune to end up on his mortuary slab had earned a degree of respect — especially if that respect was denied to them in the manner of their death."

Cooper disentangled himself from the rubber apron. "He's a good bloke, I like him. So — what's your initial feeling about our killer, then?"

Jack hesitated for a second, slipping on his shoes and unhooking his jacket from one of the pegs that lined the walls. "Anyone who dismembers a body like that — scattering the pieces, maybe even keeping some of them . . ." He broke off and shrugged. "We need to catch them, Cooper. *That* I do know."

Before they reached the door, Jack's mobile rang with a call from DS Cassidy. Hitting the 'accept' button he ushered Cooper ahead of him. Wrinkling his nose as they headed towards the exit, he noticed how the unique mortuary smell was following them along the corridor.

"I hope it's good news, Amanda. Lord knows we could do with some today."

"Well, you could be in luck, guv."

Jack could hear the excitement in the detective sergeant's tone. "What is it?"

"They've found the heads at Acorn House — both of them. And what also looks like the missing abdomen and pelvic organs of at least one victim."

Jack came to a sudden halt in the corridor. "When?"

"Just in the last hour or so. Elliott rang — said they'd found them hidden behind a bath panel. And . . ." Cassidy's voice crackled on the other end of the line. "We've had a hit on the fingerprint database, too."

CHAPTER FIVE

Time: 5.45 p.m.
Date: Monday 12 January 2015
Location: Acorn House, Hillside Estate, London

Jack groaned as he and Cooper once again ascended the concrete staircase, heading to level twelve. Three times in six or so hours and neither his thighs nor his calves were thanking him. As he hauled himself up the final flight he glanced down at his Fitbit. At least Amanda would be impressed to hear his latest step count.

Cooper led the way towards Flat 7b, still cordoned off with blue and white police tape and a lone PC on guard outside. Once again, both detectives donned their protective suits and then ducked beneath the inner cordon tape.

Jack thought the flat smelled even mustier this time around — but maybe that was because he now knew what lay inside.

Lisa Wood.

Identified through fingerprints flagging up on the system, a subsequent check confirmed she had a tattoo of a rose on her left wrist. Further investigation would be needed, but they were as sure as they could be as to the first victim's identity.

Elliott hadn't pulled any punches when Jack had returned the crime scene manager's call after leaving the mortuary, detecting more than a slight wavering in the experienced investigator's voice.

'We've found both heads, Jack. And more.'

Jack stepped around the numbered plastic markers still littering the floor, and once again made his way towards the compact bathroom at the rear, keeping to the metal stepping plates guiding their way. Cooper dutifully followed on behind.

Thanks to the luminol from earlier, Jack already knew how much blood had been spilled inside the flat's dark walls — most of it seemingly in the bathroom — and he couldn't help but feel his nose twitch, searching for that telltale metallic scent clogging the air as they walked.

More sections of carpet tiles had been lifted and bagged up throughout the flat; time would tell if anything untoward had been discovered beneath.

Elliott's face looked pinched beneath his protective suit and elasticated cap, his eyes dulled. "Apologies for calling you out yet again, Jack, but I thought you might want to see this for yourself." The crime scene manager gestured towards the bath.

Jack had already seen the bath panel resting against a side wall. "No problem." His voice felt thick in his throat. "Let's get it over with, shall we?"

Without further word, Elliott lowered himself to his knees and Jack followed suit. He was glad to hear that it wasn't just his own knees that crunched as they met the floor. It didn't go unnoticed.

"All these years of triathlon training is starting to catch up with me, Jack." Elliot managed a rueful grin. "I don't think there's a part of me that doesn't either creak or ache these days."

"Tell me about it." Jack returned the smile, but knew he didn't have the same excuse as the super fit crime scene manager. Triathlon training didn't feature very high up on Jack's to-do list; or any other kind of training either come to that.

"Just in there." Elliott waved a gloved hand towards the cavernous space below the bath. "You can't miss it."

Placing his hands on two more stepping plates, Jack lowered his head to look. Although he knew what to expect — Elliott had been nothing if not graphic in his description of what they had discovered — the sight of two severed heads still had the power to shock. Jack felt his insides shift once more.

Even in the dimness of the space below the bath, he could see both pairs of eyes staring emptily out towards him. Holding his breath, he leaned in closer and soon saw several mounds of flesh — human flesh would be a good guess at this point — but he didn't want to try and identify exactly what they were. Despite that, he could recognise human intestines when he saw them.

And then there was the smell that clogged his nasal passages.

Deciding he'd seen enough, Jack pushed himself to his feet, placing a steadying hand on the room's door handle. Cooper had remained outside the bathroom, his expression telling Jack that this time he had no desire to step closer.

"We've photographed everything *in situ*, so we'll bag it all up and send it over to the mortuary as soon as we can." Elliott stepped away from the bath. "Doesn't make for very pleasant viewing, does it?"

"It certainly doesn't." Jack and Cooper headed back through the hallway in the direction of the front door and — more importantly — the outside. At this point, even the stench of stale urine and discarded rubbish would be preferable to this. "We've had a potential ID for one of them — fingerprints were a hit on the database. We're still waiting to see if there's a hit for the other."

Elliott nodded. "I've already left a message with the mortuary — if we can get the body parts over tonight, Dr Matthews will examine them as a matter of priority first thing in the morning."

Waving his thanks to the crime scene manager, Jack made his way towards the exit, Cooper following on behind.

"I'm not liking this, Cooper. I'm not liking this one bit."
As they ducked beneath the inner cordon tape, Jack's phone
began to ring. "Daniels? What have you got?" Jack listened
to the detective as he and Cooper headed along the walkway towards the stairs. The conversation was short and sweet.
"OK. We're on our way back."

Jack slipped the phone back in his pocket and turned
towards Cooper. "Looks like we've got ourselves a second ID."

* * *

Time: 6.00 p.m.
Date: Monday 12 January 2015
Location: Ground floor flat, Acorn House, Hillside Estate, London

Barry Pierce placed the bloodied towel into the washing
machine and slammed the door. Stowing the bleach away in
the cupboard below the sink he cursed beneath his breath.

The whole estate was crawling with police and forensics
— he didn't even want to step outside his flat for fear of being
set upon and questioned. Coppers made him nervous at the
best of times, and now they were knocking on doors, asking
their silly questions, traipsing all over the place in their big
size nines.

He might only be the caretaker, but this was *his* domain;
and these were *his* flats. He knew most people looked down
their noses at him, but caretakers like himself were underval-
ued. They were important people; they were *needed*. See how
the residents would like it if he wasn't around anymore. There
would be no one to complain to about the rubbish bins not
being collected often enough; or about the absent or burnt-out
lightbulbs in the stairwells; and then there was the graffiti and
other acts of vandalism in and around the estate that needed
dealing with. Yes, they would need him *then*.

Putting the washing machine on to a hot wash, he
straightened up, grimacing at the bolt of pain that shot across

his lower back. Tossing another couple of painkillers into his mouth, he dry-swallowed and reached for his mobile, placing it on silent. Then he knocked the landline phone from its cradle. He'd done his best to dodge the questions fired at him earlier that afternoon — but the female police officer had been quite dogged and persistent. He thought he'd done all right, said the right things at the right time, expressing his horror at what had happened — but now he thought back he couldn't quite remember what he'd said. Quite how they had obtained his phone number remained to be seen — but it was surprising what information was out there if you knew where to look. Or maybe it had been one of the good-for-nothing residents in one of the flats, thinking they were being helpful. They wanted him to come into the station and make a formal statement — again he'd made the appropriate noises but had no desire or plan to see it through. He wasn't going anywhere near them.

And he didn't want them poking around in his flat either.

Or his lock-up.

The lock-up.

The lock-up was where he kept his things and he couldn't risk anyone snooping around uninvited; especially because of what he had in there at the moment. And what *had* been in there before. The thought made him shiver as he pulled on a thick sweatshirt.

They wouldn't, would they? Just barge in and search it? Surely, they needed some kind of warrant before they could just break open the padlocks and shoulder their way in? He was sure he'd seen it on one of those real-life police programmes that saturated the TV these days. Citizens like him had rights. No, they would need a warrant for sure.

The lock-up, and what was inside it, was safe.

For now.

But he would just go and check — to be sure.

* * *

Time: 8.45 p.m.
Date: Monday 12 January 2015
Location: Kettle's Yard Mews, London

Jack pulled the curtains across the living room window, eager to shut out the night. After arriving back at the station to hear the latest news on the identification of their second body, he had eventually persuaded his team to go home and have a night off.

Tara Coe.

The fingerprint database had given them another hit.

Another name. Another life taken.

Although managing to get both victims identified within the first twelve hours of the investigation was something to applaud, no one had felt much like celebrating. Names now made them human. They were someone's daughter; maybe even someone's mother, sister, wife or girlfriend. A name made them real.

Arriving back at Kettle's Yard Mews, Jack had struggled to put what he'd witnessed back at Flat 7b out of his mind. No matter what he did, the images continued to tumble relentlessly. Shocking didn't even come close. Rubbing his eyes, he winced as his hand caught the side of his lip.

Neville Henderson had been released under investigation, muttering any number of expletives as he went. But Jack wasn't concerned about Henderson. In the grand scheme of things, the man barely registered on his radar. It wasn't his case and he had no interest in what happened to him.

Crossing over to the kitchen, he flicked the switch on the kettle and dragged a jar of instant coffee towards him. Rob Carmichael had bought him a bottle of decent single malt for his birthday, but they'd yet to break open the seal. The bottle stood by the side of the kettle, and Jack found his hand hovered tantalisingly over the cap.

But as much as he might relish the thought of the fiery liquid warming the back of his throat, he knew it wasn't the answer tonight. The pounding in his head would only intensify if he went down that chosen road. Instead, he unscrewed the lid of the coffee jar and tipped a generous amount into his mug.

He gave a small smile. Dr Riches would be pleased with his choices — pleased *and* surprised, most probably. After undergoing a course of hypnotherapy at the end of 2012, trying to find a way to overcome the nightmares that had developed a stranglehold on his life, he found the sessions had worked well. To begin with. But, slowly, the nightmares had started to creep back into the darkest corners of his mind and he was now resigned to their return. He had spoken with Dr Riches a couple of weeks ago, assuring her that all was well. It was a lie, but a necessary one. He'd since avoided her calls.

Jack placed the coffee jar back on the shelf. Amanda had given him a jar of decaffeinated coffee, one of her many attempts to encourage a healthier lifestyle, but it sat unopened on the top shelf above his head. Another smile teased his lips. Amanda and the rest of the team were a good bunch; trustworthy and dependable. But it amused him just how much Amanda seemed to want to mother him — if it wasn't some new exercise class, or a new super food he needed to try, it was trying to get him out socialising.

Socialising.

Even the word jarred.

Kettle boiled, Jack tipped the hot water into his mug — taking another look at his Fitbit as he did so. Eleven thousand four hundred and ten steps today.

Not bad.

Climbing the stairs at Acorn House three times that day had certainly taken it out of his legs, and he could feel the muscles tightening all the while as he made his way over to the sofa. Not quite able to take his own advice and have a night off, he had brought some of the paperwork from the investigation home with him. There wasn't much — just a few crime scene photos and initial statements from the neighbours — but what there was now decorated the coffee table.

Jack collapsed on to the sofa, unable to take his eyes off the crime scene photographs. He couldn't remember such a disturbingly, grisly case.

Disturbing.

It was an apt word. It took a certain type of person to be able to cut up another human being — whether they were dead or alive at the time was largely immaterial. Jack gulped down a mouthful of the strong black coffee. Sleep would be a passing acquaintance tonight, he already knew that, with or without the assistance of the caffeine. So, he swallowed another glug.

Forcing his thoughts away from the investigation, he instead turned them towards his brother. Despite Stu being a grown man — and a married man now, at that — Jack still felt a degree of responsibility towards him. Separated after the death of their mother when they were young, they had negotiated the foster care system with varying results. And when Stu had crashed back into his life a couple of years ago, it wasn't long before the familiar urge to be the overprotective older brother crept back in.

Stu was finally getting back on his feet and was apparently back at work, too. Jack wondered if it wasn't a step too far. He'd been through such a traumatic experience, it wouldn't be that easy to just step back into ordinary life and carry on as if nothing had happened. But in true Stuart MacIntosh style, he'd merely shrugged it off along with his bandages.

Stubbornness, Jack liked to call it. Dogged determination others might say. Whatever it was, it had seen Stu pull through several operations and many hours of intense and painful physiotherapy sessions. Jack had to hand it to him — he hadn't moaned once.

Jack swallowed another mouthful of coffee, making a mental note to catch up with Stu now he and Isabel were back from Surrey. He'd sent a message at the weekend, but it had gone unanswered — which was nothing new when it came to Stu.

Jack found himself reaching for the crime scene photographs once again. With his coffee mug now empty, he felt wide awake — wired even — and knew he was likely to remain that way for much of the night. But it didn't concern him; he often did most of his best thinking while the rest of the city slumbered.

He considered making himself another coffee and going through the investigation papers once again, but instead he got to his feet and pulled his jacket on. If he sat here much longer he would start craving a cigarette. He'd managed to give them up — having his last cigarette some two and a half years ago, slipping up only once,, and he didn't want to cave again.

The two IDs they had managed to get from the fingerprint database had unnerved him. As soon as he read the limited amount of information they had on each of the women, the common connection became clear to see. He hadn't mentioned it to the team, deciding to keep his disquiet to himself for now. But they would work it out for themselves before long. They weren't stupid.

Grabbing his car keys and checking that he had enough cash in his wallet, he headed out.

CHAPTER SIX

Time: 7.30 a.m.
Date: Tuesday 13 January 2015
Location: Metropolitan Police HQ, London

"I thought you'd want to know as soon as possible." Dr Philip Matthews' grave tone filled Jack's ear.

Slipping back behind his desk, Jack saw several more files marked 'urgent' had landed in his in-tray overnight. He sighed and looked away. He'd got back to Kettle's Yard Mews late last night, and hadn't slept much when he'd eventually gone to bed. His head throbbed. As did his jaw. "Thanks, Doc. Anything of note?" Jack noticed the pause on the other end of the line, followed by the rustling of paper. After the further discoveries at Acorn House yesterday, the pathologist had promised he would perform the examination of the body parts found behind the bath panel as a priority — and it looked as though the man was true to his word.

"Both examinations are now complete, Jack." Dr Matthews continued. "The heads were in good condition. Both severed at the base of the neck by a somewhat blunt blade. It did the job, but . . ." The pathologist paused again.

"Neither operation would have been particularly pretty. I've taken the usual samples so you'll soon know if the heads belong to the body parts already discovered. My instinct tells me yes, but you'll need to wait for official confirmation from the lab."

"Of course. And the other organs?" Jack couldn't stop the image of what he'd seen behind the bath panel late yesterday afternoon slipping once more into his already cluttered thoughts. The vision had been with him most of last night, even in his dreams. After eventually falling into a fitful sleep, he'd sat bolt upright in the early hours, sweat pouring from his skin, unable to shift the vision of two decapitated heads surrounded by bloodied internal organs. He cleared his throat. "Anything with those?"

"There were two distinct sets of abdominal and pelvic organs — and again I've sent the usual tests to the lab to ascertain which victim they belong to. Assuming, of course, that they do."

Dr Matthews' words sent a chill through him. If the organs didn't belong to either Lisa Wood or Tara Coe it would mean they were looking for yet more victims. The thought wasn't pleasant and Jack immediately shut it from his mind.

"Both sets of organs had been removed from the abdomen and pelvic cavities in their entirety. I'm sending you the images as we speak."

Jack heard a series of tapping sounds in the background and a few seconds later the email icon on his desktop computer flashed. "Got it, Doc."

"The wonders of modern technology, eh, Jack?"

Jack opened up the email attachment to see a series of colour photographs flood the computer monitor, none of them particularly pretty. He was once again glad that he hadn't chosen to have breakfast before coming to the station. "Jesus."

"Quite. I've labelled each image. As I'm sure you'll understand it can be difficult to identify them, given the degree of mutilation."

Mutilation.

Jack's stomach dropped as he scrolled through each image.

A stomach, sliced into shreds; a liver cleaved almost in two. Coils of intestines showing multiple lacerations that made them almost unrecognisable. Jack was grateful for the identification tags that accompanied each picture. But the greatest amount of mutilation seemed reserved for one organ in particular — the uterus; according to its name tag.

The pathologist seemed to echo Jack's thoughts. "The organ with the most intense mutilations is the uterus — and that is true for both of your victims. Closely followed by the intestines. It may come as small comfort to the families but I found no evidence of sexual assault for either."

Jack felt another shiver ripple as he took in the horrific images. Mutilation — on top of dismemberment. What kind of killer were they seeking here? Jack knew Dr Matthews had seen more than his fair share of horrifying scenes over the years, witnessing first-hand what pain and suffering one depraved human being could inflict upon another — but he distinctly detected a quiver in the pathologist's voice as he spoke.

With the fingerprints identifying both victims, Jack had accessed their police files and managed to obtain headshots of both women from the last time each had come to the attention of the authorities. Copies were currently sitting on Jack's desk, and he compared them to the images attached to Dr Matthews' email. There could be no mistake. He was looking at the severed heads of Lisa Wood and Tara Coe.

"So, Doc — what's your gut reaction? If you pardon the phrase." Jack knew there would be a faint smile on Dr Matthews' thin lips at his vain attempt at gallows humour. "What are we looking at here?"

"Well, it's not good, Jack. That I will say. I haven't seen a case quite like this for many a year." The pathologist's voice cut through Jack's ever darkening thoughts. "My full report will be with you by the end of the day."

"Thanks. Any idea as to a cause of death for either of them? And maybe a time? At the PM yesterday you thought one was asphyxiation. Is that still the case?"

"Time of death is always going to be tricky with cases such as these, Jack. Any estimates given will be just that — estimates. If I was pressed, I'd say both were killed between forty-eight and seventy-two hours before discovery. And as for the cause — like we discussed at the PM, one of your victims showed signs of asphyxiation on the limited material I had to examine. And, on balance, I would say the cause of death is likely to be strangulation, and that they were probably deceased before the dismembering and mutilation occurred. We can hope, anyway." Dr Matthews gave a sigh. "But I don't feel the same can be said for your second victim. They suffered a large basal skull fracture with an associated haemorrhage — certainly enough to be fatal, or at least render her unconscious. But . . . I've been in consultation with your crime scene manager and the amount of blood at the scene concerns me."

"Concerns you how?" Jack almost didn't want to ask. But it wasn't as if this could get any worse, could it?

"Dismembering a body will always be a messy business, Jack, you don't need me to tell you that. But . . ."

Jack was already connecting the dots and he didn't really need the pathologist to spell it out for him.

"That amount of blood suggests that at least one of the victims could have been alive at the time of dismemberment. The heart still pumping, at the very least . . ."

Although he'd been expecting it, the words still came as a shock. "*Alive*? You're sure?"

"Difficult to be sure about any of this, Jack, but it's a distinct possibility. That amount of blood at the scene . . ." Dr Matthews cleared his throat. "From the samples taken, the blood loss in and around the bath matches the blood type of your second victim. The lab will be conducting further analysis, DNA and such like, so you will no doubt hear from them soon. I'll go over things once more before finalising my report."

"OK, thanks, Doc — I think." Jack swallowed, at the same time willing his stomach to settle. "I'll wait for your report and we'll see what the lab has to say."

Dr Matthews sighed on the other end of the line. "If my theories are correct, Jack, then your team are looking for one troubled individual. Troubled *and* dangerous."

The pathologist cut the call as Jack's gaze lingered on his computer screen.

Troubled.

And dangerous.

Just great.

* * *

Time: 7.45 a.m.
Date: Tuesday 13 January 2015
Location: Central London

Julian Fisher clipped the padlock back into place — you couldn't be too careful, especially now. Swinging both bags up on to his shoulder he made his way back towards the road. Barry had called him earlier, warning him that the police were still sniffing about and he might want to give the flats a wide berth for a while longer. They didn't speak often, only when strictly necessary and the man wanted something, so Julian had merely grunted a reply. He didn't like Barry all that much, but he had a feeling it was probably mutual. They tolerated each other — took from the other what they needed; like parasites.

Barry let him use the flat when necessary, and didn't ask too many questions. And Julian kept his mouth shut.

Heading towards the tube, he was glad he'd had the fore-sight to switch his phone off. Not only could Barry no longer bother him, but he knew the police could track your location and movements through it. He watched the TV shows; he wasn't stupid.

Shifting the bags slightly, he felt them rub against his back causing him to wince. Pain shot between his shoulder blades. Glad he was wearing a jacket over his shirt, he was sure he could feel the wounds starting to ooze blood again and the last thing he needed was to attract unwanted attention out on the street — not with what he had in the bags.

* * *

Time: 8.30 a.m.
Date: Tuesday 13 January 2015
Location: Acacia Avenue, Wimbledon

Jonathan Spearing slid the memory stick inside the brown padded envelope and sealed it shut. Katarina had tutted when he'd bought them — another expense she said they didn't need. But they had been cheap enough — shipped in bulk from China at a fraction of the cost of buying them here; not that they were expensive to buy anyway so he didn't quite see the issue.

What are you going to do with yet more memory sticks? Her voice had sounded tired, with more than a little edge of scorn for good measure. But he'd let it pass. He hated upsetting her, and it didn't take much to push her buttons these days, so he usually opted for the path of least resistance. She wanted to move — away from Acacia Avenue, away from the memories the house still held for them both; maybe even away from London entirely. He couldn't really blame her – she'd been kidnapped from within her own home, somewhere she was meant to feel safe and secure. How was anyone supposed to come to terms with that? Consequently, she was keeping a tight rein on their finances.

But more memory sticks? Spearing knew he didn't really need them, but he had a feeling he would find a use for them. Take last night, for example. Something had told Spearing that *he* would be there again — call it a journalist's instinct, or a journalist's nose for a story — and it didn't take long for the reporter to be proved right.

He tapped the padded envelope with a thin finger, a smile creeping on to his lips. What a scoop it would be. He hadn't had that many front-page articles in recent times, not since Katarina's kidnapping, and it was taking him some time to find his feet again at the *Daily Courier*. His editor was being patient — not a quality the man was particularly renowned for — but Spearing knew it wouldn't last. He needed to start earning his Senior Crime Correspondent tag before too long — there were any number of eager, wet-behind-the-ears news-hounds only too willing to take his place and consign Spearing to the journalists' scrap-heap given half a chance.

Another tap of the envelope and his smile broadened. Well, now he'd found it. Something so explosive that he couldn't quite believe his luck. He had kept the original video recording for himself — he'd been doing this job long enough to know he needed insurance — so produced a copy on one of the cheap memory sticks that now sat inside the padded envelope.

He wasn't at all sure how any of it would play out. He fully expected the recipient to try and bury the recording as deeply as they could, to stop it reaching the news portals. Spearing sneered as he drained his coffee mug. They could try and bury it as much as they liked — but he *knew* what he'd seen and, more importantly, *who* he'd seen.

And he wasn't going to let this one get away from him.

Jonathan Spearing was back — and headed for the front page.

* * *

Time: 8.30 a.m.
Date: Tuesday 13 January 2015
Location: Metropolitan Police HQ, London

"The IDs we obtained from the fingerprint database yesterday have been confirmed." Jack dry-swallowed two paracetamol tablets, his head still banging. "Lisa Wood and Tara Coe. Both were sex workers, known to work the streets around Soho."

Three pairs of eyes gravitated towards the cork pinboard where head shots of both victims were now pinned next to the gruesome crime scene photos. "These are the most recent images we have on file. Both were known to us for various low-level offences — mostly soliciting, cautions for possession. Lisa Wood was twenty-nine and lived alone in East London. Tara Coe was thirty-one and lived not far from Lisa, in supported accommodation with her young son."

DS Cassidy's face slackened. "That poor little boy. What's going to happen to him?"

"As far as I know Social Services are stepping in — trying to locate any family members to look after him. Luckily, Tara had left him in the care of a neighbour on Wednesday night so he wasn't left home alone."

"Did this neighbour not raise the alarm," asked Cooper, "when Tara didn't return home on Wednesday?"

"From what I can gather, it wasn't unusual for Tara to disappear for a couple of days so the neighbour wasn't unduly concerned."

"So, neither Tara nor Lisa were missed? Not by anybody? No calls to report them missing?" Cooper's eyebrows arched. "That's a sorry state of affairs if people can just disappear like that and no one notices."

Jack sighed. "Unfortunately, our killer is clever – he's targeting those that won't necessarily be missed, those that easily fall through the cracks."

"That poor little boy will be missing his mother, though." Cassidy gave a sad smile. "I hope they manage to trace the family."

"He's being cared for by one of the key workers from the accommodation block at the moment but I'm guessing that, in the interim at least, emergency foster carers will be found." Jack did his best not to let the words 'foster carers' stick in his throat. His own experience had been positive, his brother's not so — indicative of just how much of a game of Russian roulette the care system could be. "But as cruel as it might sound, our energies and thoughts are not with the son. We need to focus on finding this killer — before two victims turns into three."

Troubled and dangerous.

Dr Matthews' words filtered into Jack's head as he turned away from the cork pinboard. He did his best to shut it out. "The post-mortem report on the body parts found late yesterday afternoon beneath the bath at Flat 7b should be with us later today, but I've had a chat with the doc about it already this morning, which I'll come back to in a minute. We should also start getting something back from the lab sometime today. In the meantime, continue tracing the previous tenants of the flat and reviewing the door-to-door statements as they come in. We only need one piece of information to crack this case apart. And I want to talk to that caretaker."

"Still no joy getting him to come in." Cassidy pulled her notebook towards her. "He was decidedly evasive when I spoke to him yesterday and his phone is now switched off."

"In that case, go to him. And see if we can't pin down this Julian Fisher, too, while we're at it."

Cassidy nodded and put a reminder in her notebook.

"Anything on the cause of death yet, boss?" Cooper unwrapped a large bacon roll as he spoke, the aroma quickly filling the incident room. The detective sergeant had stopped off at the canteen on his way in, treating everyone to a round of breakfast rolls. Jack had waved his away, opting instead for a strong black coffee and painkillers. DC Daniels had eagerly accepted his, but Cassidy had opted for the slightly healthier option of a breakfast muffin.

"Not wanting to put you off your breakfasts . . ." Jack eyed Cooper as the detective wrapped his mouth around the soft white roll, a mixture of red and brown sauce oozing from the side. "When I spoke to Dr Matthews this morning he gave me his opinion on the possible causes of death. What he said doesn't make for pleasant listening. Lisa Wood he believes was killed by asphyxiation — smothered or strangled.

She was then likely dismembered afterwards. But Tara Coe . . ." Jack watched Cooper munching away on his breakfast. "Tara could very well have been alive at the time her body was dismembered. She had a head injury — a fracture with underlying haemorrhage — which could have rendered her unconscious, but the doc feels her heart was beating at the very least."

Jack watched Cassidy's face pale and Daniels' eyes widen. Cooper carried on chewing, but even his expression took on a more sombre tone.

"How . . . ?" Cassidy let her muffin fall to her desk, unable to finish the sentence. She merely shook her head. "I can't even begin to think what that must have been like."

"You and me both." Jack rose from his chair. "Which makes it even more imperative that we find whoever is responsible. And fast. Find out all you can on both our victims now we have positive IDs — and I mean *everything*. No matter how trivial or insignificant it might seem. Something made them a target and we need to find out what that was. Dig into their backgrounds and get their next of kin details."

"You think it's a coincidence that they were both sex workers, boss?" Cooper wiped his mouth with a serviette. "That something else made them a target?"

Jack shook his head as he made his way towards the door. "You know me and coincidences, Cooper. Whoever this is, they targeted these women *because* they were sex workers — I'm sure of it. But we need to know *why* it was Lisa and Tara that he chose. There has to be a reason."

"Random?" Cassidy's eyebrows hitched as one of the desk phones began to trill.

Jack liked random just about as much as he liked coincidences. "Doubtful." Ignoring the ringing phone, he reached the door and pulled it open while shrugging back into his jacket. "Keep digging — and dig deep. And get on to that caretaker again, too. Go out and see him if necessary — but I want him spoken to properly."

Just as Jack stepped out into the corridor, DC Daniels' voice followed in his shadow. "Boss?" Jack ducked his head back around the door frame to see the young detective waving the receiver in the air. "Looks like we might have another witness."

CHAPTER SEVEN

Time: 9.30 a.m.
Date: Tuesday 13 January 2015
Location: Acorn House, Hillside Estate, London

Jack pulled the Mondeo to a stop outside the front of Acorn House. His thighs were still aching from the three times they had climbed up to the twelfth floor yesterday and the thought of doing it all over again that morning didn't exactly fill him with much enthusiasm. His stomach began to growl in protest, too. He'd waved away DS Cooper's offer of a bacon roll that morning, content to watch the detective sergeant devour both of them, while Jack settled for another black coffee. But he could now feel the liquid sloshing uncomfortably inside his stomach.

Sighing, he exited the Mondeo. "Remind me who we're going to see up here, Daniels?"

DC Trevor Daniels slid out of the passenger seat, pulling his notebook from his pocket as they headed for the entrance to the block of flats. "A Mr Howard Watkins. Flat number 3a."

"And put me out of my misery. Which floor is he on?"

A faint smile emerged on to the detective constable's face as they stepped through the communal entrance. "Only level six this time, boss."

"Marvellous." Jack gave Daniels a withering look as he led the way towards the stairs, not even bothering to see if the lift had been repaired. "Just bloody marvellous."

The stairs greeted them with the now all-too-familiar stench of urine and decaying rubbish and, grabbing hold of the metal bannister, Jack began to haul himself up the first flight of steps. Amanda was forever advising that he increase his physical activity and undertake more exercise — apparently it was good for mental well-being as well as for the fat stores. But at least she had given up trying to cajole him into joining the gym or accompany her to some exercise class or other — and thankfully she'd stopped mentioning hot yoga. Furnishing him with the Fitbit seemed to satisfy her motherly tendencies — for the time being.

Puffing, and more than a little red in the face, Jack arrived at level six. Daniels was waiting, patiently, for him, barely out of breath.

"How do you manage to keep so fit, Daniels? I thought you spent most of your spare time playing online chess? Is there something about you I don't know?"

Daniels grinned as they made their way towards Flat 3a. "Amanda got me into a local running club. We train one evening a week and there's a group run every Sunday. I don't always manage to get to it every week — but I go when I can."

"Running?" Jack didn't bother to hide the surprise from his tone. "I never had you down as a Sebastian Coe, Daniels. You're a dark horse, I'll give you that."

"Hardly." Daniels' cheeks coloured a little. "But it suits me — the way that you're out with other people, but you're not really *with* them, if that makes any sense at all? I like the solitary aspect of running — just me and the pavement." Daniels' cheeks coloured some more. "It's fun. You should try it."

Jack thought running and fun had no business being in the same sentence, but he let it pass. "I think I'll just take your word for it, Daniels."

Arriving at Flat 3a they were confronted by a plump man in his mid-fifties who answered the door at the second time of asking. His hair had receded, leaving just a curtain in mousy-brown that began at the centre of his scalp.

Further down, the man's stomach was trying its best to burst out of a hand-knitted maroon cardigan, the buttons straining over a checked shirt beneath. A pair of creased flannel trousers in a shade of olive green completed the look. Jack noticed he wore no socks or shoes, answering the door in his bare feet.

"Mr Watkins?" Jack held up his warrant card. "My name is Detective Inspector Jack MacIntosh from the Metropolitan Police. And this is Detective Constable Daniels. I understand you rang the station earlier with some information for us?" Pausing, he noted the man retained a somewhat blank expression. "We're here to talk about what happened yesterday, up on the twelfth floor?"

The man grunted and turned away, leaving the door wide open as he shuffled back inside the flat.

"I guess that's our invitation in," muttered Jack, leading the way across the threshold.

The flat was set out much the same as Mrs Palmer's from six floors up, but it couldn't have been more different if it tried. There were no floral sofas or dust-free surfaces here; no collection of ornaments or decorative plates on the walls. No embroidery or cross stitch patterns in frames. Instead, Howard Watkins seemed to collect junk.

And a lot of it.

One lonely armchair that had seen better days sat in the centre of what Jack supposed was meant to be the living room. He would hazard a guess at its colour being blue at some point in time — but it was only a guess. Stacked up against all four walls were mounds of newspapers and cardboard boxes — the piles three or four deep in places, leaving just a narrow strip in the centre for the armchair.

On top of the boxes were rusting pieces of machinery that Jack didn't even want to attempt to categorise. Some looked vaguely familiar, as if they should maybe be car engine or motorbike parts, possibly even farm machinery. Others, he hadn't a clue; they could belong in a Victorian torture chamber for all he knew. But everything was covered in a thick layer of grease.

Jack felt his nose wrinkle. He'd been into cluttered homes before, and was familiar with the unique aromas they created. He suspected there must be a pet of some sort roaming around, but he was no closer to naming what it could be.

He just hoped it was alive — but judging by the smell that was largely debatable.

Jack cleared his throat. "Mr Watkins. Thank you for seeing us. We won't take up too much of your time." *I don't want to spend a moment longer in here than I have to*, he wanted to add.

The man had already lowered himself back down into the armchair. He didn't offer Jack or Daniels a seat — but there didn't seem to be any in view, unless the piles of newspapers counted. "Go on, then," he muttered, jowls wobbling from his pale unshaven face as he spoke. "But make it quick. I'm a busy man."

"I don't doubt it." Jack tried a smile to go along with the fake retort. "You mentioned to one of our uniformed officers yesterday that you saw a man climbing the stairs with a suitcase? Can you tell us a little more about that? When exactly did you see him?"

Howard Watkins reached for the tobacco tin balanced on the arm of the chair and began to roll a cigarette in his stumpy, gnarled fingers. "It was last Thursday — quarter past twelve."

Jack's eyebrows hitched. "You're sure about that? Twelve fifteen?"

Watkins nodded. "Thursdays I always go down and look through the bins before they get collected the next morning. You'd be surprised what other folks throw away these days."

Much of which seems to end up in here, mused Jack, casting another look around the cramped room, his nose still twitching. "Tell me what you saw."

"Like I said — I saw him pulling a suitcase up the stairs."

"Care to describe him for me?"

"Describe him? I know him."

Jack's eyebrows arched some more. "You know him?"

"Yeah."

Jack and Daniels exchanged a look. "Care to tell us who he might be?"

"Barry Pierce. He's the caretaker for the estate."

Pierce. The man's name was cropping up again.

"And you said he had a suitcase with him?"

Watkins nodded, flabby jowls wobbling. "Aye. Looked like a new one, too. One of those hard ones — shiny it was. Silver. And it had wheels."

"OK — and he was going *up* the stairs, not down?"

"Definitely up. I could hear the wheels thumping on the steps as he pulled it up after him. I remember saying to myself that he's got something heavy inside there."

"And which floor did you see him on?"

"This one. I'd just reached the top of the stairs along the walkway there. I was on my way back here — the racing was due to start on the telly. That's where I saw him making his way up to the next floor."

"And what did he do then?"

"Carried on up. I asked if he wanted any help. I think he grunted a no, but I can't be sure."

"Do you often see him around the flats with a suitcase?"

The man shrugged. "He's always around doing something or other, poking his nose into other people's business." His face took on a sneer which caught Jack's eye.

"I take it you're not a fan of our Mr Pierce?"

"We're not best friends if that's what you mean. But I don't really know him all that well — other than his taste in women."

"Oh?" Jack flashed another look at Daniels who had his notebook ready. "Care to elaborate?"

The sneer remained. "Likes 'em young, if you know what I mean."

"And you've no idea what might have been in the suitcase?"

A shake of the head now accompanied the sneer. "Nope."

Jack saw very little point in asking the man much more. "Well, thanks for your time, Mr Watkins. It's much appreciated. We'll see ourselves out." He gestured for Daniels to follow him back out into the hallway. "Wipe your feet on the way out, Daniels, if you think you're getting back into my car."

* * *

Time: 9.40 a.m.
Date: Tuesday 13 January 2015
Location: Metropolitan Police HQ, London

Spearing didn't usually go near the police — certainly not if he could avoid it. They enjoyed a wary relationship at best — journalists and the police — although Spearing was sure Jack MacIntosh would have something different to say about that.

Turning up his collar as the biting wind started to cut into his neck, he crossed the street and headed towards the main entrance. He could have posted the envelope — let Royal Mail take the strain and responsibility of delivering this particular time bomb — but Spearing needed to know it had arrived safely. Just handing it over the counter in the Post Office, or slotting through the mouth of a post box, he couldn't be *sure*. Sod's law this would be the one envelope that got lost — and it was one missive that he couldn't afford to go astray.

Although he had placed the memory stick inside the padded envelope without so much as a note, his face was familiar enough around these parts for it not to remain a mystery for too long. *If* they really wanted to know. Spearing somehow doubted they would waste too much time trying to find out the owner of the stick — not when they saw what it contained.

70

He almost yearned to be a fly on the wall when it reached its intended target. Just to see that initial look of surprise, followed quickly by shock, and then no small amount of disbelief. Maybe even embarrassment.

But the nuclear fallout that followed would be worth it.

Jack MacIntosh wouldn't know what had hit him.

* * *

Time: 11.10 a.m.
Date: Tuesday 13 January 2015
Location: Metropolitan Police HQ, London

Jack was not an infrequent visitor to the chief superintendent's office, but always felt like the chastised schoolboy whenever he was summoned so it was a destination he tried to avoid. On arriving back at the station following their chat with Howard Watkins, the request had been delivered personally by Penny, the chief superintendent's PA, and it wasn't one Jack could squeeze his way out of.

But he liked Dougie King — and respected him, too. As the city's first black police officer to rise to chief superintendent status, Jack knew the man had endured his fair share of battles along the way; and still did to some extent. Which made his respect for him grow — a respect that Jack felt went both ways. If he ever felt cornered, or yet another complaint had landed on a senior officer's desk, Jack knew Dougie King would have his back no matter what.

"You're a hard man to track down, Jack." King gestured for him to take a seat.

"Oh, you know how it is." Jack managed a hesitant smile as he slipped into a vacant chair. "Always somewhere to be."

The expression on Dougie King's face told Jack that he wasn't born yesterday. "But — now that I've got you, give me an update on what we have over on the Hillside Estate."

"There's not really much to tell, sir." Jack filled the chief superintendent in on what they had discovered at Acorn

House. And what had later been found beneath the bath. It didn't take long. "As you can see, still very much in the early stages."

"But you have IDs already?"

Jack nodded. It never ceased to amaze him how fast information managed to travel within the walls of the station. "We do indeed. Lisa Wood and Tara Coe. Both sets of fingerprints flagged up on the system. Both known sex workers."

Dougie King's bushy eyebrows hitched a notch. "Sex workers?"

"It's all that links them at the moment — but as I said, we're only just getting started with the investigation."

"Coincidence?"

Jack flinched. He knew the chief superintendent was no more a fan of the dreaded 'c' word than he was. "Not in my opinion, sir, no."

Chief Superintendent King leaned forward, elbows on his desk, a grave look crossing his tired face. "I don't like the sound of this one, Jack. No murder is good news but these . . . ?" He paused. "If the sex worker angle is relevant, then we'll arrange extra patrols in the key areas at night. And we'll need to put out a press release to keep the hacks happy. Just the bare bones, but I doubt that'll satisfy them for long."

At the mention of the word 'press' Jack physically recoiled. Dougie King caught his eye.

"Don't worry, Jack. I'll not schedule a full press conference just now — a simple press release will do just as well for the time being until you have something more for me, that is."

Jack felt his muscles relax. "Sir."

"But we'll need to word it carefully. The last thing I want to do is instil panic on the streets. Just enough to inform and warn of the dangers in certain areas after dark, for all the good it will do. You know the score, Jack. Are you releasing the names yet?"

"No, not yet. We're still tracing next of kin."

Dougie King nodded. "Leave it with me, then. I'll get the PR department on to it. But let's pray there are no more,

Jack. Let's pray there are no more." Jack made to get up, but the chief superintendent's eyes widened. "Not so hasty, there. I'm not quite finished."

Hovering above his chair for a moment, Jack slowly lowered himself back down. "Sir?"

Dougie King rested his chin on steepled fingers, a frown straying across his brow. "You know it's election year this year, don't you? And the Mayor is up for re-election next year?"

"I don't give a monkeys." Jack's tone was clipped. He gave an apologetic smile. "*Sir.*"

A similar smile twitched at the corner of Dougie King's mouth. "I'm sure you don't, Jack, but there are plenty within these walls that do — and outside it, too. I'm quite sure that the current Mayor won't be at all happy that we've another killer on the loose at such a — how can I put it — *delicate time*?"

"I still couldn't care less."

The smile twitched again. "And I echo your sentiments, Jack — I really do. But we have to be seen to be doing the right thing here. Your every decision will be scrutinised, as will mine. We've been here before, I might add. Which is why we need this to be a textbook investigation. Belt and braces, everything by the book. So, I need you to send all you have to the profiler on this one — and the earlier the better."

Jack made to rise from his seat again, but Dougie King wasn't finished.

"No arguments, Jack. I mean it. Everything goes to the profiler — and it goes over *today*."

CHAPTER EIGHT

Time: 11.30 a.m.
Date: Tuesday 13 January 2015
Location: Tanners Road Industrial Estate, London

Leo Hooper took a running kick at the worn-out football, sending it skywards.

"Bloody hell, Hoops!" Jake Callaghan starting charging across the deserted street. "How am I supposed to get that?"

The ball came down behind a wire fence, in an area of dense grasses and weeds on the corner of Tanners Road. The whole area had once been a thriving industrial estate, home to many a bustling business such as vehicle repair centres, masonry yards, garden supplies and even a pet food manufacturer — but now it boasted no more than scores of empty and dilapidated prefab units with broken windows and boarded up doors. Wooden frames had rotted to their core, brickwork crumbled to dust — broken glass littered the empty parking bays.

As the area was a no through road, traffic didn't frequent the industrial estate much anymore. Which made it the perfect location for Leo and Jake to play truant from school. Just over a week into the new school term and they already had itchy feet. It was a place they often came to, passing the hours kicking a football up against any one of the abandoned units, even climbing up on to the roofs when they dared, or pulling shards of jagged glass from the rubble to use as make-believe swords. Even the cold hadn't kept them away this morning.

Leo laughed as he watched his friend haul himself over the wire fence that had, like most things on the estate, seen better days. The fence sagged beneath the boy's weight, then sent him toppling over to the other side, landing in a heap on a pile of crumbling breeze blocks and rusted pipes.

"Jesus!" he shrieked, pulling himself to his feet. "That fucking hurt!"

"Just get the ball and stop bloody whining!" Leo was almost doubled over with laughter as he watched his friend lumber off through the almost waist high grasses to where the ball had landed.

They had both left home that morning on the pretext of walking to school, but once they were around the corner and out of sight of their mothers' beady eyes, they'd legged it in the opposite direction. Leo had managed to hide the football in his PE bag, so it hadn't so much as raised an eyebrow when he'd left the house. Jake had stuffed extra crisps, chocolate and drinks into his school bag before his mum had even come downstairs that morning — so the day was set.

They'd spent the last two hours exploring the abandoned units, much as they had before, then progressed to throwing stones at any panes of glass that were still intact, of which there weren't many. After a while, boredom had started to creep in, as had the cold, turning their hands to ice and their feet numb — so they'd climbed up on to one of the roofs and stuffed their faces with the contents of their lunch boxes, and the extras Jake had managed to lift from the kitchen. They were on their way out of the industrial estate, deciding to head towards the park and the chance of a burger from the van that was usually parked by the pond, when Leo had lobbed the football over the fence.

Jake, still sore from his unceremonious landing, swore under his breath as he kicked the grasses out of the way and headed for the ball. It had come to rest in front of a pile of crumbling brickwork that may have been an outbuilding at some point; it was hard to tell. Collapsed on three sides, the area inside had become a haven to fly-tippers. Bags of rubbish, old mattresses, two bicycles without wheels and a mass of car tyres littered the area. To the side, where the ball had come to rest, was a large rusting fridge, its door swinging wide open.

Kicking the last of the grasses out of the way, Jake bent down to retrieve the ball, glad that he'd had the foresight to keep his gloves on. As he leaned in, he spied two fabric holdalls stuffed inside the cavernous mouth of the empty fridge. One was a navy colour, the other a khaki green. They stood out among all the other detritus because they looked brand new.

Glancing over his shoulder to see Leo kicking at something in the gutter, he advanced on the mysterious bags. Perhaps there was something inside they could sell — maybe even the bags themselves. Gary, at the market, was always on the lookout for gear to sell. He wouldn't give them much for it, but it would be better than the non-existent pocket money Jake currently got.

Ignoring the football, Jake reached for the navy bag first. Grabbing hold of the leather handles, he pulled it towards him, noticing how heavy it was. There was definitely something inside. Excitement started to ripple.

Dragging it out from its hiding place, Jake tugged at the zip and found that it slid open with ease. The grin on his face momentarily widened in anticipation — then it froze on his face.

Stomach shifting, he turned to the side to vomit.

* * *

Time: 12.10 p.m.
Date: Tuesday 13 January 2015
Location: Metropolitan Police HQ, London

"Our Mr Pierce was seen on Thursday last week heading up from level six at Acorn House." Jack slipped off his jacket. "We have a witness, Howard Watkins, who says Pierce was dragging a silver-coloured suitcase behind him."

"Up to Flat 7b?" Cassidy's eyebrows hitched.

"Hard to say. He could have been going anywhere, but it's suspicious enough for me to want to have a chat with him. Anything else of note while Daniels and I have been out?"

DS Cooper scooted his chair across to his computer monitor. "I've requested CCTV from the streets closest to Acorn House. The estate itself might not have any cameras but we might see something in the surrounding area. The killer had to have got to the Hillside Estate somehow."

"Good," nodded Jack. "Let's also pull the phone records of both Lisa and Tara. No phones were found with their remains or elsewhere at Acorn House, but we might be able to see where they've been, and crucially where the phones are now."

"I'll get on to that." Cassidy placed her mug of chai tea down and pulled her keyboard towards her. "We're still working on their next of kin, too."

"Keep digging into their backgrounds and their families' backgrounds. Something might be there that links them. Do we have anything in from the lab yet?"

Cooper made a face. "No' yet, boss. I think they're really backed up, but I'll see if I can get Jenny to speed things up a little."

"You do that, Cooper. In the meantime, I need to send everything we've got over to Rachel Hunter — orders of the chief superintendent." Jack made for the door, scooping up his jacket on the way. "I'll be in my office in you need me."

As Jack stepped out into the corridor, he heard one of the desk phones trill.

* * *

Time: 12.15 p.m.
Date: Tuesday 13 January 2015
Location: Central London

He was as sure as he could be that he hadn't been seen and managed to dump the bags without too much trouble. The location had been textbook. No cameras, no passing traffic, no one to interrupt.

Perfect.

The woman had been surprisingly easy to fit inside the bags — or maybe he was just getting better at it. He'd kept her in the lock-up garage for the last couple of days, but knew she needed to go; she needed to make room for the others — for there was always going to be others. That morning, en route to Tanners Road, he'd even passed a stationary police car at one point, and couldn't help but smile to himself as he drove slowly by. He almost wanted to give them a cheerful wave. They had no idea what he had in the back — *no idea at all.*

The thought still made him smile now, as he closed the door of his flat behind him. But the euphoria he'd felt from his latest killing was already starting to ebb away, replaced by increasing disappointment. At the beginning, the pleasure he derived from the act of taking another human life could last for days, weeks even. Sometimes months. But now it seemed to sate him for an increasingly shorter amount of time — sometimes it was just hours.

His thoughts suddenly darkened. He must be doing something wrong. Why couldn't he feel the thrill for longer? Why couldn't he savour the elation for as long as he wanted? It felt like he was being punished.

The feeling jarred as he threw the lock-up keys on to the sideboard.

He knew all about punishment — both inflicting it *and* receiving it.

* * *

Time: 4.30 p.m.
Date: Monday 21 November 1985
Location: Gravesend, Kent

He pulled the door to the cupboard under the stairs shut behind him. He liked it in here. In here he felt safe. In here he felt protected. In here, *they* couldn't get to him.

He scooted as quickly and silently as he could towards the far corner of the cupboard, to where he kept the shoebox. Tipping up the lid, he felt inside for the comforting touch of the torch. There was a single low wattage bulb hanging overhead, but he daren't use it.

The torch gave off a comforting, muted light as he settled himself down on one of the cushions he'd managed to smuggle in from the back bedroom some weeks before. Mum had wondered where they'd gone, but didn't seem to mind. But it meant he didn't have to sit on the rough wooden floorboards anymore, with the sharp splinters jabbing through his trousers.

The cupboard was empty except for a box of old books that were on their way to the charity shop and a box of Christmas decorations. He didn't know why they kept the Christmas decorations anymore — no one ever put them up.

Not since *he* had come to stay.

Johnny.

He knew that was the man's name because it was the one his mother had screamed when the fists first landed on her cheeks.

Johnny, please don't. Please stop, Johnny!

He felt his stomach tighten at the memory. They had been doing fine, just the two of them — until *Johnny* came. They didn't have much as a family, not compared to others, but even though he was only eleven years old he knew tough times when he saw them. Mum had done her best with what they had, though. The other boys at school teased him about his second-hand uniform — third hand if the truth be told — and his charity shop shoes. But he was always clean and tidy, and there was always enough food on the table to eat.

But then everything changed.

Johnny had made sure of that.

He witnessed his mother's rapid decline playing out before his very eyes. She used to have the most brilliant blue eyes — cornflower blue someone had told him, but he didn't really know what cornflowers looked like. Blue, he supposed. But to him they looked like the summer sky.

But after Johnny moved in, he rarely saw the summer sky reflected in his mother's eyes. Instead, he saw rainclouds, dark and heavy — brooding before the next gathering storm. After the storm had passed they would turn glassy and unfocused, until the whole cycle repeated itself. To begin with it frightened him and he would ask her what was wrong. She wouldn't hear, staring into space as if she were living in her own dream world; her gaze dazed, her words slurred. So, then he would ask again, concern mounting at her lack of response — and eventually she would snap. A hand would lash out, connecting with first his cheek, then his arms, then his legs if he didn't move out of the way quickly enough.

He knew she didn't mean it, not really. He knew because she said so afterwards, pulling him into one of her bear hugs and sobbing quietly into his hair.

But he never forgot that change in her.

The change *Johnny* had brought about.

Eventually, he came to understand that it was the drugs — but *Johnny* had been the one to bring them into the house. So, it was all his fault.

He found a blanket and wrapped it around his shoulders, drawing his knees up towards his chest. He winced. The most recent bruises were turning darker now, and spreading. He never hit him where it would show — Johnny was clever like that.

And then there were the other things Johnny did to him.

Shivering, he pulled the blanket closer. The cupboard was ice cold, but so was the rest of the flat these days. Mum used to put the fire on in the living room when the weather turned — and they would huddle together in front of it, eating buttery toast and spooning hot soup into their mouths. They would laugh as their breath billowed out in front of them, watching the steam rising from their soup bowls.

But there was no fire anymore; no soup or toast, either.

And there was definitely no laughter.

He couldn't remember the last time he'd heard his mother laugh or even seen her smile.

The front door slammed, the sound reverberating around the flat and causing the cupboard door to shudder, followed by the familiar sounding footfall of heavy boots.

Johnny's boots.

Burying his head in his hands, he willed the pain to end.

* * *

Time: 12.20 p.m.
Date: Tuesday 13 January 2015
Location: Central London

He had never forgotten Johnny in all the years that followed — not for a single second. The man had ruined him — and his mother. Not that he particularly cared about either of them anymore. They were as insignificant to him now as they were when he'd choked the last living breaths out of their drug-addled bodies.

His stomach began to rumble, but he knew it wasn't food that he craved. When dark thoughts invaded his head like they were now, all he needed to do was pull open the wooden chest and reach for the salvation that he knew lay inside on the velvet throw. He took the discipline in his hand, feeling its familiar, welcoming weight. With his elation waning by the second, and his self-doubt returning, he knew what he had to do.

* * *

Time: 12.30 p.m.
Date: Tuesday 13 January 2015
Location: Tanners Road Industrial Estate, London

"Shit." Jack pulled the Mondeo to a stop outside the police cordon. Blue and white tape was already stretched across the road, and beyond that was a familiar white tent. "Shit, shit, shit."

He'd had a bad feeling in the pit of his stomach ever since the call had come in — and arriving on the scene had done nothing to stop that same feeling from multiplying.

"I'm not liking the look of this, boss." Cooper echoed Jack's thoughts as they both exited the Mondeo.

"Me neither, Cooper."

The pair made their way towards the outer cordon, and after signing the attendance log and picking up a couple of white protective suits, they headed in the direction of the forensic tent. Jack could already pick out the familiar balding crown of the force's pathologist standing head and shoulders above the rest.

"Jack." Dr Philip Matthews spied the two detectives and was already striding towards them. "Good of you to get here so quickly."

Jack nodded in acknowledgement, his eyes straying over the tall pathologist's right shoulder. "What can you tell me?"

"Not a great deal from my perspective at this stage, I'm afraid. Your friend Mr Walker over there might be of more use." Dr Matthews gestured towards Elliott Walker, crime scene manager, who was in deep conversation with two of his investigators. "I'm just about to head back to the mortuary — I've a full list today but I'll try and squeeze this in once you can get the poor soul delivered to me."

Jack's eyes remained fixed on the forensic tent. "Thanks, Doc. I appreciate it. But can you at least tell me if it's the same — same as the others, I mean? Dismembered?" The word stuck in Jack's rapidly drying throat.

"Yes. There's certainly no doubt about that." The pathologist's voice was grave, his eyes duller than usual. "Two hold-alls. One contains the head, arms and upper torso. The second, contains the legs, pelvis and what appears to be the majority of the abdominal and pelvic organs. I'll know more once I get everything back to the mortuary."

Jack waved his thanks as Dr Matthews left the scene, heading back to where he'd parked the Volvo.

"Another one." Cooper's voice was solemn.

"Another one," breathed Jack, starting to walk towards the tent.

'*Let's pray there are no more, Jack.*' The chief superintendent's words from no more than ninety minutes ago rang in Jack's ears as he walked. '*Let's pray there are no more.*'

Someone had had the foresight to take down part of the wire fence that surrounded the scene, making negotiating it a great deal easier than it could otherwise have been. Jack and Cooper waded through the waist high grasses, noting the abandoned car tyres, bicycles and other rubbish strewn along the way. Ahead of them was a crumbling brick outhouse which housed the forensic tent.

Elliott Walker arrived at Jack's side. "Jack. Chris. Good to see you both again — although not the greatest of circumstances."

"Quite." Jack fixed the crime scene manager with a half-smile. "The doc just filled me in a little on what you've found. But what else can you tell me?"

Elliott gestured for Jack and Cooper to follow him towards the tent. "From what I understand, the call was made around an hour ago. Two young lads playing hooky from school discovered it. Two generously sized holdalls, both hidden inside an abandoned fridge."

Jack looked past the crime scene manager to see the rusty kitchen appliance lying on its side.

Elliott continued. "Curiosity got the better of one of them — unzipping the navy-coloured bag first. Inside was the head, both arms and upper torso. Each arm has been cut in two, at the elbow joint. Luckily, the young man was wearing gloves, so forensically the site is as good as it can be."

Jack grimaced and glanced sideways at Cooper, greeted by the detective's increasingly pale face. He turned back to the crime scene manager. "And the other bag?"

"That one contains the lower half — both legs, again disarticulated at the knees, plus the abdomen and pelvis, including the internal organs from what we can see."

"Mutilated?" Jack couldn't help the images of Lisa Wood and Tara Coe's mutilated organs from flashing unbidden into his mind as he stared towards the forensic tent.

"Difficult to say at this stage. We haven't wanted to disturb what was inside too much. I'm sure it'll be a question for the post-mortem."

Jack nodded and followed Elliott towards the flaps of the white tent. He could already see both holdalls — one navy blue, one khaki green — sitting in the centre of some protective plastic sheeting. Both looked relatively new, somewhat out of place in an abandoned industrial yard. The zips of both holdalls had been pulled fully open, the sides pressed down as far as possible without disturbing what was inside.

But Jack could see enough even from here.

Black wavy hair tumbled around a pale face, glassy eyes open and staring straight ahead. The eyes of the dead.

"Much blood?" Jack didn't know what else to say, taking a step backwards.

Elliott shook his head. "Not from what we can see. And nothing in the immediate area of where the bags were found. We'll obviously process this whole site, but there's nothing obvious."

As both Jack and Cooper took another step back, a crime scene investigator brandishing a top of the range camera proceeded to kneel down by the side of the holdalls and began to take a series of close-up shots. Jack's attention was drawn to the road on the other side of the wire fence, and the industrial estate beyond.

"I don't suppose you can see any cameras in the vicinity, can you, Cooper?"

DS Cooper turned a full three-hundred-and-sixty degrees. "None that I can see, boss. This place doesn't look like it has seen much trade in a long time."

"Agreed." Jack started back towards the hole in the fence. "Let's get back to the station — set the ball rolling on this one. Elliott?" He called back over his shoulder. "Can you get me some photos as soon as?"

The crime scene manager nodded. "Will do."

Heading back to the Mondeo, Jack noticed Cooper hesitate before pulling open the passenger door. "What's on your mind, Cooper?"

Cooper's eyes shot across the wasteland and back towards the forensic tent. "Is this number three then, boss? We're looking for the same killer?"

Jack wrenched the driver's door open. "What does your detective's nose tell you, Cooper?"

"I think we'd be daft not to link it with the others. It might be a completely different dump site but — that doesn't mean it's not our man."

"Indeed it doesn't. And I'm with you." Jack slid behind the steering wheel, waiting for Cooper to settle himself into the passenger seat before starting the engine. "I take it you saw the hands?"

Cooper nodded. "I'll get the fingerprints analysed as soon as possible — see if we get lucky for a third time."

* * *

Time: 12.45 p.m.
Date: Tuesday 13 January 2015
Location: Central London

Placing the discipline back inside the wooden chest, he made his way through to the bathroom. He'd welcomed the pain more than ever this time, casting deep gashes into his skin with each lash from the knotted rope. Salty tears had started to spring from his eyes, but they were tears of joy — pain was his salvation. With every stroke he could feel himself being cleansed.

Thinking about his mother and Johnny had pushed him to the edge, the anger rippling beneath his hot skin. They had both got what they deserved in the end — just like the bitches out on the streets. His mother had been just like them.

Pulling open the bathroom cabinet, he rummaged in among the pill bottles and packets of medication, searching for the antiseptic wipes. Several bottles clattered into the sink before he found what he needed. The blood would soon cease to flow, and the pain would ebb away, but then his desire to find another would resurface; just like it always did.

There was just the one left in the lock-up right now and he fleetingly wondered if she minded being all alone. He knew he should probably move her. But she'd looked so good, lying side by side with Cherry — both of their faces contorted in a mixture of agony and fear. Each had been strangely compliant towards the end — but he supposed there was little you could do when your hands and feet were tied.

He smiled as he began to wipe away the blood.

CHAPTER NINE

Time: 2.30 p.m.
Date: Tuesday 13 January 2015
Location: Metropolitan Police HQ, London

"Fingerprints were a hit almost as soon as they were uploaded, boss." DS Cooper activated the interactive whiteboard to bring up a passport sized photograph. "Cherry Eyres. Last came to our attention in August last year for possession."

Jack studied the picture, comparing it to the two already tacked to the cork pinboard, and then leafed through the brief details Cooper had managed to print off. "I don't think we can argue against the obvious connection between them. All three were sex workers, and all three frequented the area around Soho. We need to find out all we can about each of their backgrounds, and crucially if they knew each other. I take it we don't have next of kin details for Cherry yet?"

"Not yet, boss."

"OK. We will obviously keep the ID to ourselves for the time being. What else is new?"

"Uniforms were out on patrol last night, guv." Cassidy pulled her notebook towards her. "They spoke to a few of the women still out there — no one was that keen to talk, but they managed to find a couple that would. Confirmed that Lisa and Tara did know each other and regularly worked the same area. Although the names hadn't been released to the media, the girls aren't stupid. They already suspected something bad had happened. They told us they hadn't seen either of them since Wednesday last week." Cassidy flicked over a page. "They also spoke to Bryn Morgan who runs the Welfare Truck. He says they're going to organise a few more visits, be as visible as they can to try and make the streets as safe as possible. He and his volunteers know most of the girls by name and they want to help."

Jack sighed but nodded in appreciation. "That's one piece of good news, at least. Follow up with Bryn and get the rest of the volunteers' details." He welcomed the efforts of the street pastors who gave up their time for free to staff the Welfare Truck at night. From all sorts of walks of life, they offered counselling, a shoulder to cry on, someone to vent frustrations to. It wasn't a job that Jack envied one bit. But they also offered practical support — signposting towards drugs and alcohol services, support with benefit issues and even medical advice. The pastors did their best to make the streets as safe as they could, but Jack took little comfort if the truth be told. It was like locking the door after the horse had well and truly bolted. He wasn't convinced that the sight of the Welfare Truck on the streets was going to make this particular killer change his ways. "What else have we got? Anything on the next of kin for Lisa and Tara?"

Daniels cleared his throat. "We've found next of kin for both victims. Lisa has both parents living in Folkestone. They've been contacted by their local force with a view to a family liaison officer paying them a visit. They've already confirmed that Lisa had a rose tattoo on her wrist, and had surgery for a fractured ankle about three years ago. They're talking about wanting to come and see her — make a formal ID."

Jack grimaced. "OK, let me know if that happens. They'll need some additional support as it won't be pretty."

Daniels continued. "For Tara, all we have is a sister in Welwyn Garden City. She's being offered support and has agreed in principle to taking on the little boy, her nephew, to avoid the involvement of Social Services."

Cassidy gave an audible sigh of relief. "Thank goodness for that — poor little mite."

"OK, now we've contacted the next of kin we'll release the names to the media." Jack perched on the edge of one of the desks. "What about the former tenants of Flat 7b? Are we any closer on that?"

Cassidy nodded. "As Annie Palmer mentioned, the last tenant was a Mr Bernard Fisher. He left the property last July to go into a care home and it has remained empty ever since. I managed to get hold of the caretaker, Barry Pierce, again, but he's quite hard to pin down, often has his phone switched off. He lives in a ground floor flat in Acorn House. I mentioned we would need to speak with him in person, but he got quite cagey again about coming in."

"All the more reason for us to go and see him. Let's drop by later. The fact that Howard Watkins saw him dragging a suitcase up the stairs last week makes me nervous."

"I did get some information out of him, though, before he clammed up. He knew Bernard Fisher quite well — said the man lived alone in the flat with the tenancy in his sole name, but he often had his son, Julian, come to stay with him."

"Annie Palmer mentioned him to us yesterday," chipped in Cooper.

Cassidy continued. "Barry Pierce reckons the last time he saw Julian was a few days before the discovery at Flat 7b."

Jack's eyebrows hitched. "Even though his father hadn't been there for some six months?"

"I queried that with him. Apparently, the son had a few friends or acquaintances in the tower blocks, and was quite a regular face to see around."

"Do we have an address for this son?"

"Not yet. Pierce went decidedly cool when I asked."

"Keep digging, knock on a few doors if you need to. If this Julian is a familiar face, then other residents might know of him and crucially know where we might find him. Anything else?"

"Before Bernard Fisher, the last tenant was a Dorothy Edwards — stayed there between 1993 and 1999. Pierce said she died."

"OK — let's concentrate on Julian Fisher. See what you can find out about him, but from what we've gathered so far, that flat was a haven for all sorts of lowlife to frequent — gangs, local kids. There was plenty of evidence of drug use in at least one of the rooms that I saw. And the place looks to have been left unsecured most of the time, so it's anyone's guess how many people have actually had access to it. Forensically, it's going to be a minefield. But we do need to talk to him, even if just to eliminate him."

"And the caretaker?"

"Him too. I don't like it when people actively avoid us, Amanda. We'll go and see him in person — *unannounced*."

"I've been following up on the camera question around the industrial estate, boss." DS Cooper brought his keyboard towards him. "Like we thought, no cameras in the immediate area — the nearest ones are five streets away."

"Pull the footage anyway, as close as you can get. It's more than likely a dead end, but let's take a look. Whoever dumped the holdalls had to get them there somehow. Anything in the boys' statements from this morning?"

Cooper shook his head. "Neither had much to say — I think they were more worried about getting into trouble for playing truant from school than anything else. Neither mention seeing anyone in the area — no cars, no vans. And they were there for some hours before the discovery."

Jack hadn't pinned too much hope on the boys giving them a breakthrough, and he didn't see the point in re-interviewing them. "OK, let's leave them be."

"If it's any consolation, I think they got far more than they bargained for when opening those holdalls," Cooper managed a grin. "I reckon they'll think twice before bunking off school again."

"I'll be sending what we have on this third victim over to the profiler — see what she has to say. In the meantime, keep digging into all three. We need next of kin for Cherry Eyres, too." Jack looked at his watch. After this morning's discovery, news would be travelling through the station like wildfire, and he didn't need enhanced detective skills to know whose ears it would reach soon enough. He reached for his jacket just as the door to the incident room swung open. For a moment his heart stopped, wondering if the chief superintendent had indeed heard the news and was already on the war path. He relaxed a little when he saw it was DS Carmichael, although the expression on the sergeant's face did nothing to reassure him that all was well.

"Heads up, Jack. The chief's in the vicinity."

Jack's heart sank.

"Just saw him upstairs, heading down this way. Pippa from PR was with him — and they had very serious looks on their faces. I think you might have a few minutes' grace, but not much more than that."

Jack knew what would be coming next. The dreaded press conference — with Pippa's involvement it had to be. There looked to be little he could do to derail it, but he could at least try and delay it. But before he could make a move towards the exit, Dougie King's presence filled the door frame.

* * *

Time: 2.45 p.m.
Date: Tuesday 13 January 2015
Location: Central London

Pulling the suitcase out of the lock-up garage, he made his way towards the van. Although the location of the garage was ideal — with no passing traffic, no cameras, no overlooking buildings — it still felt vulnerable. *He* felt vulnerable.

And it wasn't a feeling he enjoyed.

He was used to feeling in control; steady and unflappable. But recently he'd started to notice a change. Even the discipline was struggling to keep his emotions in check. Usually, the searing pain from the knotted rope cutting into his skin would focus his mind and give him a feeling of unshakeable contentment. He would welcome the pain each time it ripped through him, knowing what paradise lay beyond.

And then there would be calm.

And when he was calm he could plan.

Everything was in the planning.

Frowning, he pulled the suitcase away from the row of garages. She couldn't stay here; not any more. But there was no question about taking her back to the flat. *None* of them ever went to his flat — that would be a one-way ticket to earning him a hefty knock at the door from the police. Too many inquisitive eyes and ears surrounded the flat, too many questions he wouldn't be able to answer.

Which only left the house.

He hadn't been there for some time and knew it would largely be in the same state of disrepair as when his father had left it all those years ago. He shuddered at the thought of what he might find in there, but it would have to do — he had nowhere else.

The wheels of the suitcase struggled across the rough paving slabs towards the waiting van. She hadn't been all that heavy — none of them were — but it was surprising how much they weighed after you'd cut them into bits and stuffed them into bags.

Arriving at the rear doors to the van, he stopped and held his breath for a second, listening to the silence.

Silence was good. Silence meant that no one was watching.

Pulling the doors open, he hauled the suitcase up into the rear, the wheels catching on the van's bumper. He swore under his breath — she was much heavier than she'd looked.

The drive over to the house wouldn't take long, but he would take the scenic route. Although it was only late afternoon and his girls might not be out yet, he would drop by just the same. It was dark now, so maybe they would be starting early. Then he could see which ones were begging to be his next victim — for that was what they all did in the end.

Beg.

Admittedly it was begging for their life — but he sometimes wondered if they begged for death to come swiftly, too.

Grinning, he slammed the rear doors shut and headed for the driver's door.

* * *

Time: 5.00 p.m.
Date: Tuesday 13 January 2015
Location: Metropolitan Police HQ, London

Jack took his seat on the raised platform, heart heavy. Press conferences weren't his favourite occupation at the best of times, everyone in the building knew that without having to be reminded. More often than not they would end up with some degree of verbal sparring, heavily laced with hot words and a good sprinkling of acidic retorts. On more than one occasion the firestorm had reached Dougie King's ears upstairs and the chief superintendent had needed to don his firefighting gear to douse the resulting flames. Things had never quite descended into an all-out physical brawl, but there was always a first time.

But even as Jack entered the conference suite, he could sense that today was going to be different. The mood was sombre — even the hardiest of press hacks were unusually subdued. Normally they would be chattering away like a pack of excitable monkeys — but today they sat stock still in near total silence. The news of the last thirty-six hours was beginning to sink in. They hadn't seen a killer like this on the streets of London for a long time. The Yorkshire Ripper sprang to mind, which only served to tighten Jack's already taut insides.

They had three victims now. Three that they knew of, anyway. Would it end there? Dougie King's voice flickered unbidden into his thoughts.

'Let's pray there's no more, Jack.'

It didn't do much to quell his already growing disquiet.

"Ladies and gentlemen, thank you for coming here this afternoon." Pippa Reynolds stood at the front of the raised platform, next to the bank of TV cameras. "Detective Inspector MacIntosh will address you in a moment. Please refrain from asking questions while he is speaking. Questions can be posed at the end, time permitting." She glanced over her shoulder and gave Jack a good-natured wink. Asking the press pack not to blurt out questions was like asking them to stop breathing.

Jack waited for Pippa to leave the platform before beginning. He was flanked by Cooper on one side, Daniels on the other. Cooper was under strict instructions, like always, to jump in if things looked like they were heading for choppy waters. He hadn't quite had to hold Jack back and unleash the life raft before, but at times it had come close.

Clearing his throat one last time, Jack began. "On Monday 12 January the remains of two young women were found at an address on the Hillside Estate. Post-mortem examinations have been completed and we are now confident as to their identities." Jack paused as images of Lisa Wood and Tara Coe appeared on the screen behind him. "Lisa Wood was twenty-nine and lived in East London. She was last seen in the vicinity of The Causeway on the night of Wednesday seventh of January. I'm appealing to anyone who was in the area last Wednesday evening who may have seen her. In particular, any vehicle owners who may have dashcam footage — please contact us as a matter of urgency."

Jack already knew that drivers in a notorious red-light district were unlikely to come forward willingly, but he had to ask all the same. "Tara Coe was the second victim found. She was thirty-one and also lived in East London, not far from our first victim. Again, she was last seen in the vicinity of The Causeway last Wednesday evening. Once again, I'm appealing to anyone who was in that area that night, and any vehicle owners who may have dashcam footage — please come forward, you may have vital evidence for the investigation. Similarly, anyone from the Hillside Estate who saw anything out of the ordinary on Monday morning, or in the week prior, please contact us as a matter of urgency."

Jack's gaze swept the room, seeing multiple pairs of eyes fixed on him, the press hanging on to his every word. "And then we have this morning — where a further set of remains were found at Tanners Road Industrial Estate. We are unable to confirm the victim's identity at this stage. Once more — if anyone was in the vicinity of the industrial estate either this morning or late last night, please come forward."

Jack spent the next few minutes outlining the results of the post-mortem for the first two victims. He didn't elaborate — in some ways the less people knew the better. "The person we are looking for in connection with these horrific murders is a particularly dangerous individual. Please ring the hotline number with any information."

Collapsing back into his seat, Jack surveyed the room. He was quietly satisfied with himself. He had used the word 'please' at least three times that he could count, maybe more — which in Jack MacIntosh's world was almost unheard of. Nobody had yet to jump out of their seats to hurl a question at him. Even Jonathan Spearing of the *Daily Courier* was behaving himself.

Jack had spied the senior crime correspondent taking up his usual position at the back of the conference room, leaning up against the wall. Dressed in his customary band T-shirt — today it looked like it was the turn of The Killers, which was not without a cruel sense of macabre irony — the reporter merely listened in silence while taking down the odd note in his handheld notepad.

Jack and Spearing had crossed swords on many an occasion in the past, and Jack found the new, laid-back version of the often-acerbic crime reporter more than a little disconcerting.

Welcome maybe, but disconcerting all the same. There was something about the wily hack that Jack still didn't trust.

Pippa, sensing that Jack's presentation was over, opened the floor up to questions.

"Are you definitely linking all three murders?" The question came from a *Daily Mail* reporter Jack knew well.

"We are well aware of the similarities of all three murders, but we are keeping an open mind at this stage."

"So, you *are* linking them, then?"

Jack grimaced and held the *Daily Mail* reporter's gaze. "Like I said, we are keeping an open mind at this stage but our view at present is that this is probably one killer."

"Are the streets safe for women to be out at night, Inspector?" Jack tracked the question back to another reporter he was familiar with from the *Telegraph*. It was a question he'd been expecting, but was no closer to knowing exactly how to respond. The streets weren't safe — but he couldn't just come out and say that. Before he could even pretend to cobble an answer together, another quickly rang out to take its place.

"Do you have any specific advice for women out alone at night, Inspector?" This question came from the back of the room; this time a reporter Jack didn't recognise. "Any advice to stop them becoming the killer's next target."

And so it began.

Any false sense of security that Jack had unwittingly allowed himself to be lulled into disappeared in a flash. As did his patience. The curiously solemn feeling that had settled over the room for the last fifteen minutes was instantly swept aside. It was as if someone had flicked a switch.

Handheld recording devices were raised above heads, chairs scraped as people jostled for a better view. Jack felt his jaw tense as numerous pairs of eyes bore into him, waiting for his response. Once more Dougie King's voice filled his head.

'The last thing I want to do is instil panic on the streets.'

Jack echoed the chief superintendent's thoughts — panic was the last thing they needed — but what else could he say? The streets weren't safe, and he'd be crazy to suggest otherwise.

"These are dangerous times for *everyone* in our city. We *all* need to be on our guard."

"What about the area around The Causeway in particular?" pressed Aaron Taylor, a reporter Jack knew worked alongside Spearing at the *Daily Courier* and who was sitting on the front row. "Will the police be providing extra patrols to protect the women still out working the streets at night?"

Jack felt the hairs on the back of his neck prickle. According to Dougie King additional patrols were already underway, some in unmarked vehicles — but he didn't want the killer being forewarned. "I'm not at liberty to discuss operational procedures at this point in time."

"So, what are we doing here?" bit back Taylor, an impatient scowl darkening his features. "If you're not prepared to divulge or discuss your investigation into these murders, then why are we wasting our time sitting here listening to you?"

Jack felt the familiar flames within him begin to ignite. Mouth dry, he fixed the reporter with a stony stare. The man was a mirror image of Spearing — even down to the cocky sneer on his face and the mouth full of chewing gum. Maybe the *Daily Courier* bred them that way. The man was an idiot, that was plain to see, and Jack laced his reply with an extra dose of condescension for good measure. "The reason for this press conference. Aaron, is for the Metropolitan Police, and my team in particular, to ask for the public's help in catching this killer. Is that such an alien concept for you to grasp?"

Jack sensed Cooper stiffen by his side, but he was all fired up now and there was only one way this was heading.

"It's not an alien concept at all, Inspector, I was just voicing the opinion that many of us here feel. I'm sure I'm not alone in thinking that you're holding back on us, not giving us the full picture — and that decision may cost more young women their lives until this killer is caught."

Jack bristled, feeling the heat spreading. "You're free to leave at any time, no one's stopping you." He gestured towards the door at the back of the room.

Aaron Taylor sat up straight, bit now firmly between his teeth, scowl deepening. "All I want is a straight answer, Inspector. What are we doing here if you won't tell us anything? Not anything useful, anyway. What are you hiding? Or is the real truth that you have no idea how to catch this killer and no idea how to protect the residents of this city? Isn't *that* the real story?"

Jack felt his temperature rise another degree, sweat collecting beneath the collar of his shirt. He resisted the temptation to rip away the tie that was starting to constrict his throat. "The last time I looked, the police were here to serve the city and its individual communities. But that goes both ways. Experience tells me the general public ordinarily respond very well to pleas for help — most citizens of this city are more than willing and eager to assist in any way they can. *You*, on the other hand . . ." Jack's hot gaze bore into the young reporter.

Before he could continue, Jack heard Cooper's chair scrape backwards, the detective sergeant no doubt readying himself to spring to his feet and intervene. Jack cast a sideways glance at Pippa Reynolds hovering by the side of the raised platform, a familiar look of trepidation on her face. Jack ignored them both. He was on a roll now and no one was going to stop him. People like Aaron Taylor irritated him and after a tiring day Jack didn't have time for the man.

"*You*, Aaron, seem intent on placing as many barriers in front of us as you possibly can to prevent us catching this offender. Do you actually want me and my team to catch them? Do you?" Jack's thunderous look told the reporter that an answer wasn't required or, in fact, wise. "Because I really don't think you do. You, and all your little bloodsucking weasel friends that masquerade as journalists, are only interested in selling as much garbage as you can in your shitty little newspapers. You don't care about the women on the streets. You don't care about the people living in the capital, you don't care about your neighbours, your friends. You don't give a *toss* about any of them. All you want to do is instil as much fear and panic into as many people as you possibly can and then collect your big, fat pay cheque at the end of the month as a reward for ruining everyone's lives."

Jack paused for breath, noting he could almost hear a pin drop in the conference room. He daren't look up at Pippa, instead he quietened his tone and fixed Taylor with another fierce look.

"*I repeat* — in words of one syllable in case you're still struggling to understand — that I'm here to solve this case, to catch a particularly dangerous killer. And to be able to do that I would appreciate the public's help. I *need* the public's help. Forgive me if I'm repeating myself but you seem to be struggling with the basics here. Now, you can either be a part of this and help, or you can stop wasting everyone's time and get the fuck out of my police station." Stopping just for a moment's pause, Jack lifted his gaze to the rest of the room. "And that goes for the rest of you bastards, too."

CHAPTER TEN

Time: 5.40 p.m.
Date: Tuesday 13 January 2015
Location: Metropolitan Police HQ, London

"What in God's name was that, Jack?"

Jack could see small beads of perspiration breaking out on the chief superintendent's brow. He knew better than to try and provide an answer, instead silently slipping into the vacant chair.

"It won't be surprising to know that I've just got off the phone to those upstairs — and they're not amused."

"Really?" Jack was still smarting from the fallout from the press conference that had ended not ten minutes ago. Pippa had been her usual calm and collected self, quickly disbanding the angry pack of newshounds that were baying for Jack's blood. Cooper had then quietly ushered Jack to a place of safety, DC Daniels bringing up the rear.

"Yes, Jack. *Really.*"

"I wasn't aware my press conferences warranted such special attention."

Dougie King let out a pent-up sigh. "*Everything* you do warrants special attention, Jack — especially from those above us. History has shown that to be a particularly prudent step, has it not?"

Jack gave a shrug. "I'm still not sure what I did wrong."

The chief superintendent leaned forward, elbows on his desk. His shirt sleeves were rolled up, his tie askew; tiredness clouded his eyes. "I get it, Jack. I really do. I get *you* — you know that. But it may surprise you to hear that not everyone approves of or indeed understands your sense of humour."

"I wasn't aware that I'd made a joke."

Dougie King held Jack in his gaze before letting his mouth start to twitch at the corners. Instead of another sigh, a smile followed. "I think telling the esteemed members of our media fraternity to — and I quote — *'get the fuck out of my police station'* — might qualify."

Jack mirrored the chief superintendent's smile. "I wasn't joking. I can promise you that."

"At least we were able to edit that bit out before it went to the news portals." After a moment or two's further silence, Dougie King accepted defeat. "So — this new investigation — what else can you tell me that you didn't want to divulge to our friends in the press? We can't afford to let it run away from us, Jack. Those upstairs are getting nervous enough as it is, and that was before the media circus we've just witnessed."

"I bet they are. We've got three dead women and no clue who we're looking for. That's about the size of it, I'm afraid." Jack's tone was still on the wrong side of calm. "Do you want to tell them the good news or shall I?"

Another smile twitched on the senior officer's face. "You leave them to me, Jack. You just go and catch me a killer. As soon as you can would be good."

"I'll do my best, but idiots like Taylor really push my buttons sometimes."

"Then you can't let them, Jack. Focus on the investigation. Don't rise to the bait quite so much. All you do is play right into their hands." Dougie King paused, another sigh escaping his lips. "Do you need any more resources? And by that I mean ones that my budget will stretch to. I've already sanctioned extra night-time patrols."

Jack shook his head. "No — but we'll definitely be racking up the overtime. The team don't want to stop, let alone sleep."

"Overtime is approved, Jack, within reason. But make friends with the media — that's all I ask, just this once. Or at least refrain from making enemies out of them."

Jack swallowed the acidic taste that had crept into his mouth. *Make friends with the media.* It wasn't the first time he'd been asked to do the unthinkable. Before he could think of a way to steer the conversation in a different and much safer direction, there was a faint knock at the door.

Penny, the chief superintendent's PA poked her head around the door frame. On seeing Jack, she smiled and entered.

"Sorry to intrude, but this arrived downstairs for you a while ago." She hurried over to Dougie King's desk and handed him a small padded envelope. "Hand delivered. Sorry, been down there for some time. I thought it best to bring it up."

While Dougie King took hold of the envelope, Jack took advantage of the brief hiatus and got to his feet. "I'd best be going, sir. Things to do and all that." Before the chief superintendent could utter something in reply, Jack headed for the open door and escaped into the corridor.

He jogged his way down the stairs, heading towards the incident room where he knew the team would still be hard at work. Enough time had passed for Pippa to have herded the reporters out of the building, but he nevertheless kept a wary eye out for any rampaging media types still baying for his blood as he negotiated the corridors. As he jogged, he mulled over the suggestion that he ought to play nicely with the press. The very thought jarred his nerves.

The media could be useful to have on your side, there was no denying it — but most reporters wouldn't think twice about stabbing you in the back if it got them onto the front page. Jonathan Spearing was a case in point. He and Jack had been sparring partners for a considerable time now, and Jack had lost count of the number of newspaper articles where his name had been dragged through the mud. Spearing had been at the press conference but he'd remained mute, which was most unlike him. After Jack had finished trading insults with Aaron Taylor and the conference had been brought to a hasty conclusion, Spearing had hung back a little, briefly catching Jack's eye before Pippa herded him outside. Jack had noted a different look about the reporter — he even appeared to have a smile on his face, instead of the traditional sneer. Jack couldn't quite put his finger on it but something had changed with the man, that was obvious. Maybe coming close to losing your wife did that to you. Jack, eternal bachelor as he was, wouldn't know.

He reached the bottom of the stairs without any unwanted attention and breathed a sigh of relief. The tension that had built up in his shoulders was now starting to wane, but his head and jaw still throbbed. Deciding a detour was in order, he went in search of coffee and painkillers.

* * *

Time: 6.00 p.m.
Date: Tuesday 13 January 2015
Location: Flat 3a Acorn House, Hillside Estate, London

Howard Watkins leaned over the railings and looked down on to the darkened car park below. The whole place was crawling with them; ants they looked like to him. Maybe beetles. Whatever they were, they were nothing better than scavenger's the whole bloody lot of them. *Cockroaches.* Irritation began to bristle beneath his skin.

He was all for helping the police. What had gone on upstairs in Flat 7b wasn't pleasant — even he thought that much. But why did they have to pull apart the bins, having no regard whatsoever for what they touched? They were *his* bins.

He continued to watch as more white-suited ants grabbed another communal waste bin and pulled its contents out on to the floor below.

No respect.

With a final grunt of displeasure, he pushed away from the railings and headed back inside. Slamming the door to his flat behind him, a lopsided grin replaced the irritated sneer that had been there only moments before. As he shuffled along in his slippers towards the kitchen, his growling stomach telling him it was time for dinner, he eyed the freshly stacked pile of black bin bags lining the walls.

The grin widened. It was a good job he'd got down there first and managed to take away all the decent stuff before they got their grubby little mitts on it and squirrelled it away, never to be seen again.

Yes, he'd done well.

It was all in the planning.

With the growling sounds getting louder, he padded across the kitchen and headed for the frying pan.

* * *

Time: 6.10 p.m.
Date: Tuesday 13 January 2015
Location: Metropolitan Police HQ, London

Jack threw his jacket on to his chair and surveyed the chaos on his desk. The in-tray looked just about the same as when he'd last seen it — maybe a few extra files balancing precariously on top, and his morning mug of coffee sat cold and long forgotten.

Slipping behind the desk, he pulled open the top drawer, sure there was a packet of paracetamol lurking in there somewhere.

It was then that he spied it.

A small white envelope — handwritten — sitting squarely in the centre of the desk.

For the attention of Detective Inspector MacIntosh.

For a second or two, Jack merely stared at it, but it didn't take long for the hairs on the back of his neck to prickle. For some reason, he thought he knew exactly what would be inside. Well, maybe not the exact contents, but he was sure he knew who the missive would be from.

Ritchie Greenwood.

Ritchie was now the head of the largest organised crime gang in the city — the capital's Mr Big — and they were a gang that Jack and the rest of the Met were desperate to dismantle. But it wasn't proving that easy — people like Ritchie Greenwood were clever.

Slipping back out from behind his desk, Jack hurried to close the office door. History told him that prying eyes, and ears, were everywhere. Turning back to the envelope, he picked it up between his thumb and forefinger and stared at it once more. It wasn't sealed — which raised the question whether anyone else had already taken a peek inside.

Jack flicked the envelope open and slid out the small piece of card, the contents confirming his suspicions as to its author.

The instructions were simple.

9.30 p.m.

Tonight.

The Hanged Man.

Jack tucked the card back inside the envelope. Ritchie Greenwood and his demands were a complication he could do without right now. As he slipped the envelope into his jacket pocket and pulled a packet of painkillers from the desk drawer, there was a brief knock at the door. DS Cassidy's head appeared around the door frame.

"Guv? You ready?"

CHAPTER ELEVEN

Time: 6.40 p.m.
Date: Tuesday 13 January 2015
Location: Acorn House, Hillside Estate, London

"I don't like people who avoid us, Amanda." It wasn't the first time Jack had uttered those words on the twenty-minute journey to Acorn House. "It makes me suspicious."

"I agree, guv. He was decidedly evasive on the phone — and then there's the suitcase."

"Yes, the suitcase. Tell me what we know about him so far." Jack led the way towards the entrance to the tower block. Thankfully, with the caretaker having a small flat on the ground floor they wouldn't need to climb the stairs this time. Jack could feel the muscles in his thighs thanking him already.

"Barry Pierce — aged forty-five — has been caretaker here for the last fourteen years. As far as we can tell, he's single and lives alone in the flat that comes with the job. Before Acorn House, he worked at Billingsgate Market and before that at Smithfields."

Jack held the door open and let Cassidy step through into the communal hallway.

"There is a county court judgement on file from three years ago — in relation to monies owed to a building company. Came to our attention briefly eighteen months ago after an allegation of malicious phone calls was made by a resident at the neighbouring tower block, Beech House. He received a caution and appears to have hung on to his job." Cassidy led the way past the stairs and to a door that opened out into a narrow corridor. The area was littered with abandoned bicycles, several rusting lawnmowers, a selection of equally rusting garden tools, a mouldy mattress and three battered metal filing cabinets. On the floor were coils of rope and electrical cables.

"Mind where you put your feet, Amanda," warned Jack as they entered. "This place looks like a death trap."

Barry Pierce's flat was at the end of the corridor and it took three rounds of loud knocking before the door was eventually pulled open. The caretaker wasn't at all how Jack had expected. The man stood a good six feet tall, with broad shoulders beneath a grubby pair of dark overalls. His feet were encased in sturdy-looking work boots, a worn baseball cap on his head. In his hand, was a wrench.

Jack took an instinctive step backwards, fixing the man with a cautious eye. "Mr Pierce? I'm Detective Inspector Jack MacIntosh, and this is Detective Sergeant Cassidy whom I believe you've spoken to recently. May we come inside for a moment?"

"Why?" The man's tone was clipped. "I'm busy."

"Well, so am I Mr Pierce." Jack fought to keep the irritation from his voice. "But we're investigating a murder — more than one murder, in fact — and I somehow think that's more important than whatever it is you've been doing with that wrench. Care to put it down and let us in?"

Jack edged in front of DS Cassidy, eyes still fixed on the tool in the caretaker's hand. A moment's hesitation seemed to flicker across the man's features before he gave a curt nod and stepped back. The hallway was just as cramped as the corridor outside, with more junk lining the walls. Jack saw rusting car parts, more garden implements and yet another lawnmower. As they crossed the threshold, Jack gestured for Cassidy to shut the door behind them. He didn't trust Barry Pierce not to make a run for it.

Without a word, Pierce shuffled back into the flat, closing two doors on his right as he passed and leading the two detectives to a narrow galley-style kitchen at the rear. A thick aroma of cooking oil and fried food hung in the air, with a frying pan coated in a layer of burnt offerings resting in the sink. The cooker hob was covered in a thick film of grease, the wall behind it faring no better. Beneath his shoes, Jack felt the linoleum sticking to his feet as he walked.

"How long have you lived here, Mr Pierce?"

"'Bout twelve years now. Been in the job fourteen."

"And you live here alone?"

The caretaker frowned, then gestured around the kitchen with a muscled arm and grubby hand. "Yes, I live alone — I think that's bloody obvious, don't you? What's this all about?"

Jack bit his tongue. "Like I said, we are conducting a murder investigation. You will no doubt be aware of what was discovered up on the twelfth floor yesterday? Flat 7b? I take it you read the papers, Mr Pierce? Listen to the news?" Jack had already spied a folded copy of the *Daily Mirror* on the kitchen worktop, with what looked like the charred remains of the caretaker's fried breakfast on top. The question elicited the smallest of nods. "Then I'm sure, as caretaker of Acorn House, you'll want to assist us as much as possible in finding out what happened." Jack continued to hold the man in a tight gaze, watching the man's jaw muscles clench.

"Of course," Pierce eventually replied, sliding his gaze away from Jack. "But I don't know anything."

"You don't know what I'm going to ask you yet." Jack noted that the greasy wrench was still in the man's hand. "How about you put that down and we go and sit somewhere a little more comfortable?"

"In here's just fine," came the quick reply, the wrench remaining in the caretaker's hand. "Ask your questions."

"What do you know about the previous tenant of Flat 7b? Bernard Fisher."

Pierce shrugged. "Not much. He was an old fella, didn't go out much. Had mobility issues. Christ knows why they shoved him up on the twelfth floor. Never made much sense to me, especially as the bloody lifts never work. And they gave him a bloody garage, too — what was the point in that? The poor bloke couldn't drive."

"Anything else about him?"

Pierce shook his head. "Nope. Never really had much to do with him."

"How about his son, Julian?" Jack detected a slight change in the man's demeanour, his eyes avoiding Jack's once again.

"Didn't know the guy."

"You told one of my colleagues that you'd seen him a few days ago."

"Well, maybe I did — but that doesn't mean that I *know* him. Just see him about."

"And when would the last time be?"

The question earned merely a shrug in response.

"One of the residents told us he was quite a frequent visitor to Acorn House — in particular Flat 7b. In fact, he would often stay when his father lived there."

"I wouldn't know nothin' about that."

"How about anyone else in or around Flat 7b in recent days? Particularly early Monday morning, and the days immediately before? Anyone you weren't familiar with?"

"Plenty of people hang around the flats. I learn to take no notice."

Jack took a breath, keeping a lid on the irritation that was threatening to bubble up at any moment. He was still going over the events of the press conference, annoyed that he'd let Aaron Taylor get under his skin quite so easily. He turned his attention back to the caretaker.

"What about yourself? When was the last time *you* were inside Flat 7b?"

Pierce shrugged again. "Not sure I can remember. Not for a while anyways."

"Nothing inside needed repairing? Repainting? I'm told the place has been in quite a poor state of repair since Bernard moved out — lots of break-ins, that kind of thing. Local youths using it as a drug den."

Another shrug. "I've fixed a few things from time to time, but there's nowt in there to fix these days. And I don't know nothin' about no kids and no drugs."

"Guv?"

Jack cast a sideways glance at Cassidy, following her gaze which was trained on a large pinboard opposite the sink. A selection of tatty business cards and flyers were pinned all over. You didn't need to be a genius to work out the services they offered.

"You make a habit out of visiting sex workers, Mr Pierce?" Jack recalled Howard Watkins inferring how the caretaker had an unusual interest in women — very *young* women.

"It's not a crime."

"Indeed, it's not — and I didn't suggest that it was. I'm just asking — do you make a habit of visiting sex workers? It's a simple enough question."

Pierce shifted his weight from one heavy boot to the other, clasping the wrench in an ever-tightening grip.

Jack sensed the man's disquiet and decided to take a step closer. "Or do I need to rephrase it into simpler language for you?"

"Those cards are old — I haven't used them in a long time."

"You ever go down to The Causeway?"

"I don't pick girls up off the streets."

"No?"

"No."

"Did you ever meet Lisa Wood or Tara Coe — the victims we found inside Flat 7b? We've identified them, by the way. Their names have been released to the press."

"How would I have met them?"

"I'm just asking the question, Mr Pierce. Both were known to be sex workers, operating around The Causeway. It's not beyond the realms of possibility that you might have met them — given your particular habits."

"I thought I told you — I don't pick girls up off the streets."

"So you did — my mistake." Jack gave his most condescending smile. "And it's true that there are no cameras here, nothing across the whole estate? *None* of the tower blocks have CCTV?"

Pierce shook his head. "They tried a few years ago, but no sooner did they go up then they were vandalised. Didn't make much sense to keep replacing them."

"So, you were well aware the estate wasn't covered by any cameras?"

Another flicker of irritation crossed the caretaker's face. "Of course, but that doesn't mean I done nothing. Look, I know how you lot work . . ."

Jack ignored the dig. "Is there anything else you can tell us that might be helpful to our investigation? Anything at all?"

The caretaker quickly shrugged. "Nowt I can think of, no."

"Going back to Julian Fisher. You know where we might find him?"

Irritation started to furrow Pierce's brow. "Nope. Why should I know that?"

"Do you own a suitcase, Mr Pierce? A silver one, maybe?" The sudden change in the direction of questioning caused the caretaker to falter and Jack saw a curious expression cross the man's features — a mixture of confusion and concern. "Again — it's a simple enough question, Mr Pierce. You either do or you don't."

The caretaker let the silence lengthen before shaking his head. "Nope — no need for one," came the eventual response. "I don't go on holiday."

Jack turned and caught Cassidy's eye. "In that case we'll let you get on with your day." He cast another look at the wrench in the man's hand before backing out of the kitchen and heading towards the door. "We'll see ourselves out."

Once back outside into the relative freshness of the cramped corridor, Jack turned to Cassidy. "What did you make of our Mr Pierce?"

"A grubby, slimy man who wasn't at all comfortable in our presence, guv."

Jack nodded as they headed out of the entrance to the tower block and towards the Mondeo. "And he didn't want to part company with that wrench." Visions of the head injury Tara Coe sustained filled his thoughts as they reached the car.

"Plus, he's someone who has a penchant for sex workers."

"You believe him when he says he doesn't go kerb crawling?"

Cassidy pulled open the passenger side door. "I'm not sure I believed much that came out of his mouth, to be fair, guv. He seemed very evasive. Shifty, even."

Jack cast another look back in the direction of the entrance to Acorn House before slipping behind the wheel. "And he certainly didn't want us to see what he had in those two rooms we passed. Did you notice how he was very quick to pull the doors shut before we could see in?"

Cassidy nodded. "And he denied owning a suitcase. Do we believe Howard Watkins when he says he saw him last week?"

Jack shoved the keys in the ignition. "If we do, then the next question is why is Barry Pierce lying about it?" As he gunned the Mondeo's engine, his eyes flickered towards the dashboard clock. And then the envelope still resting inside his pocket.

9.30 p.m.

The Hanged Man.

"Shit," he muttered beneath his breath, as he pulled the car out of the abandoned car park.

* * *

Annie Palmer toyed with the phone cable, winding it around her fingers. She didn't know what to do. Should she ring in? Was it really something they should know about — or was she being silly?

She placed the phone back in its cradle and returned to the kitchen. George had always said she made a mountain out of a molehill.

'Annie — just leave it be. Stop seeing problems where there aren't any.'

Although she always liked watching the news — making a point of tuning in every evening while she ate her dinner — most of it frightened her these days; war and suffering was everywhere you turned; violence on the streets; homes being broken into.

And tonight was no different.

That lovely police detective had been giving a speech at the press conference into the awful goings on at Acorn House; she'd recognised him the moment she switched the TV on. And that young Scottish lad was with him, too — the one that ate most of her biscuits. She chuckled to herself — handsome they were, the pair of them. But the smile soon slipped from her lips.

'Please ring the hotline number with any information.'

Should she?

Reaching for a saucepan, she filled it with water to put on to boil. She didn't fancy much to eat tonight — just something light like a boiled egg — her stomach was in knots.

'Please ring the hotline number with any information.'

She didn't need to leave her name, did she? Maybe she could just say what she needed to say and leave it at that? If it didn't mean anything then they wouldn't take any notice of it, would they? She didn't want to get the man into trouble if it was nothing.

113

But what if it wasn't nothing?

Suddenly the thought of even boiled eggs turned her stomach and she switched the gas off. She didn't want to cause any trouble — and she still needed her tablets. If she told the police about him, what would happen then? Her GP wouldn't prescribe them to her — *he* was her only hope.

The more she thought about it, the more she convinced herself she was being silly — just like George always told her. He couldn't be caught up in all this — he was too nice, too charming. People like *him* didn't do *that*. And the police weren't stupid — they would soon dismiss what she said as being irrelevant.

Letting out a relieved breath, happy that she had come to a decision she could live with, she padded back through to the living room and reached for the phone.

* * *

Time: 6.55 p.m.
Date: Tuesday 13 January 2015
Location: Ground floor flat, Acorn House, Hillside Estate, London

Barry Pierce dragged the silver suitcase out from underneath his bed, cursing once more as another jolt of pain seared across his back; the painkillers from earlier now long forgotten. He needed to get rid of it — and fast — in case they came back. The question had startled him and he wasn't sure how convincing his answer had been. How had they known?

Flicking open the metal clasps, his nose wrinkled. He would need to clean it before getting rid — it was beginning to smell. As he lifted the lid, the pungent aroma hit his nostrils, catching at the back of his throat. Although it made his eyes water, he'd smelled worse. Tipping bleach on to a cloth, he set about cleaning the inside. Blood had a way of finding its way into the smallest of spaces and it would be a difficult, if not impossible, task to get it completely spotless. He noticed

114

one of the internal zips was stained a russet red; tiny bits of flesh trapped in its teeth.

In hindsight it hadn't been the best choice of suitcase for the job, but he hadn't had much time to prepare.

Withdrawing to the kitchen, the caretaker washed the stained cloth underneath the hot water, watching the sink turn rusty red. Just how had they known? Someone on the estate must have blabbed, it was the only answer. The idea rankled him. Returning to the suitcase, he again applied a liberal dose of bleach to the cloth and repeated the cleansing process.

A noise outside the window caused him to momentarily freeze, his hand hovering over the internal zip. He had remembered to double lock the door, hadn't he, after the coppers had left? Not that it would stop them. The fact they'd come to see him so soon still angered him; waltzing in like they owned the place, poking their noses in where they weren't wanted. Seeing things he didn't want them to see. He didn't like surprises — he liked planning; he liked routine.

He liked to be in control.

At least he'd had the foresight to close the other doors before they could see what was beyond them.

Holding his breath for what seemed like an eternity, he heard the insistent yapping of Mrs Robbin's Yorkshire terrier. She was a woman of routine too — taking the little runt out for its evening walk at the same time, day in day out.

Releasing the air from his lungs, a hesitant smile twitched at his lips.

They weren't coming back for him — not yet. He still had time. He would take the suitcase to the lock-up — it would be safe there. *Everything* was safe there.

CHAPTER TWELVE

Time: 9.30 p.m.
Date: Tuesday 13 January 2015
Location: The Hanged Man Public House

What the hell are you doing, Jack?

He left the Mondeo around the back of the Hanged Man — there were already two vehicles parked there, out of sight of the main road.

Just what the hell are you doing?

The pub didn't look like it had changed much since the last time Jack was here — and why would it? The rusting pub sign was still precariously attached to the front of the crumbling red brickwork; the windows fogged with a mixture of condensation and grime. It was like time had stood still.

Jack knew the front entrance would be unlocked — just as it had been before. As he entered, he saw the same rack of rusting coat hooks fixed to the wall, the same solitary umbrella still hanging from one of them. But there was now a cast iron boot scraper sitting below the hooks, with evidence of fresh mud ground into the threadbare carpet at his feet — evidence that someone was in, at least.

As he reached to push open the door marked 'bar', Jack's gaze remained trained to the carpet below. If he'd had misgivings about returning to the Hanged Man before setting out, those misgivings were redoubled now. He had been to enough crime scenes in his career to spot a bloodstain when he saw one — and this one looked fresh.

Once again, he considered turning around and walking straight back out — that would certainly have been the most sensible thing to do.

But when did Jack MacIntosh ever do sensible?

Sighing, and with more than a generous amount of caution now mixed with trepidation, he pushed open the door to the bar and stepped inside.

* * *

Time: 9.35 p.m.
Date: Tuesday 13 January 2015
Location: The Causeway, London

Tanya Maund pulled up the collar of her lightweight denim jacket and crossed the street. Together with the short denim skirt, it did little to ward off the chill that was clinging to her skin. With a light drizzle now starting to fall, she shivered and quickened her step.

The last punter had dropped her off further down the street than she had wanted — but she didn't fancy arguing the toss. He'd had a funny look in his eye and she'd welcomed the relief at pushing open the passenger side door and escaping into the night once their brief encounter was over.

Brief encounter.

That was the man's nickname on the street — due to the fact he never usually lasted very long; which suited the girls just fine.

He wasn't one of Tanya's regulars, but beggars couldn't be choosers these days.

117

Her high heels clattered on the pavement as she walked, the sound echoing along the deserted street ahead. She hated working winter nights — hated working *any* nights if she were brutally honest. It wasn't a way of life she'd willingly chosen — none of them had. Instead, it was something that had chosen them. And once it had you in its clutches, there was precious little you could do to drag yourself back out again.

But drag herself out she would. It wasn't a life she wanted. Some of the others had been stuck in this hellhole for years, and the thought made Tanya shiver. She was better than this. She *deserved* better than this. The girls all told her that life on the streets had changed in recent times — improvements made, if you could call them that. There were outreach programmes now, welfare support networks that hadn't been there before. Had it made the streets safer? Or was it the women themselves who were making it safer for each other? Tanya didn't know and didn't plan to be here long enough to find out.

The Welfare Truck had been out earlier, which always gave her a lift. The volunteers were friendly and understanding, but not in a patronising way; they would never lecture. They seemed to genuinely care and want to help.

And things could be a lot worse, she reminded herself as she hurried through the dimly lit street. She had her regular patch, and knew the other girls that worked it alongside her. She usually stood at the intersection of two roads just past the entrance to the park. It was a good enough spot; there was enough through traffic to make it worthwhile, but not so much that it drew unwanted attention. Most people in the area knew what went on down there — so most stayed away.

Arriving at the entrance to the park, Tanya crossed the road and headed for a tall oak tree on the opposite side — it would at least offer some form of protection from the inclement weather while she waited. She glanced at the cheap watch she'd bought from the market — there was no point wearing anything valuable out on the streets. All that did was make you more of a target than you were already.

The evening was dragging by painfully slowly. Shivering, she decided to give it another two hours and then call it a night. Although it was still early, business was slow — as it had been all week. The New Year slump they called it. Several of the girls had already given up and gone home — and those that remained looked tense.

The only two she could see now were Mandy and Bernice, both standing a little further along the street, puffing away on cigarettes as they jigged from foot to foot to keep themselves warm. The three of them acknowledged each other with a nod. Both somewhat older, Mandy and Bernice had taken Tanya under their wings during her early days on the street, giving her much needed advice.

Trust your instincts.

Money up front and split it up; some in your pockets, some in your purse, some in your boots.

Keep your phone charged.

Never go back to their place.

Stick to the places you know.

It was advice that had stood her in good stead ever since.

But it wasn't just the inclement weather that was keeping the girls off the streets, or sending them scuttling home early. Tension was rife after the news coverage rippled through about the two dismembered bodies found on the Hillside Estate. And, according to the online news portals that evening, there had now been a third.

The girls had told her that stories like these surfaced from time to time, thankfully relatively infrequently, but they surfaced all the same. It made everyone nervous, naturally, but it did little to stop them. They all had bills to pay, children's mouths to feed, crack habits to maintain. And pimps to satisfy. The initial shock at reading about Lisa and Tara might keep some of the girls at home for a night or two, three at best, but then they would return to their street corners as if nothing had happened. What else could they do?

Tanya had only known Lisa and Tara by sight — maybe the odd nod of the head in passing – but had seen the news report that evening. The thought of what had happened to them, how they would have suffered, instantly chilled her; more so than the freezing rain. And then there was the third body found this morning, too. But, despite this, she still found herself getting ready to work the street that night.

Tanya thrust her hands into the tiny pockets of her jacket. She felt safe — well, safe enough anyway. Maybe Tara and Lisa had taken too many risks; not been as careful as they should have been. They all tried to look out for each other — circulating details between them of punters to avoid, vehicles not to get into. It was a way to keep yourself safe. Her punter from earlier had been odd, but hadn't rung any particular alarm bells — and he was well known to them all. He was odd, like many of them were — *odd but safe*.

Hopping from foot to foot, she felt the cold sinking further into her bones beneath the short skirt and skimpy top. Maybe she'd give it an hour instead of two.

Just then, a set of headlights blinked through the drizzle and headed in her direction.

* * *

Time: 9.35 p.m.
Date: Tuesday 13 January 2015
Location: The Hanged Man Public House

"What can I get you, Jack my old friend?" Ritchie Greenwood swept an arm along the length of the small mahogany bar. "I've still got a wide selection here of your favourite malts."

Jack bristled at the man's use of the word *'friend'*.

Ritchie's face broke out into a wide grin. "There's a nip in the air outside, is there not? Maybe something to warm you from the inside, eh? I assume you still partake?"

"I'll pass, thanks. What do you want?"

"Oh, come come, Jack. That's no way to greet a friend, surely? It's been a while since we last saw each other. How was your Christmas and New Year?" Ritchie Greenwood's eyes sparkled even in the dimness of the lighting behind the bar. "Get up to anything nice?"

Jack ignored the man and took a quick glance around the bar area. Although the pub had closed its doors a long time ago, the smell of stale beer and body odour still seemed to be ingrained in its very fabric. Rumour had it that back in the day the Hanged Man would stage illegal bare knuckle fighting right here in the saloon bar. Jack could just imagine the tables being sent flying, blood, sweat and the odd loose tooth raining down on the paying public. Bets would be passed between beer-stained fingers, profanities bouncing off the walls as the fighting intensified.

But, for now, the bar was empty. Stools with worn fabric coverings sat upturned on equally worn looking tables. The open fireplace on the far wall hadn't seen fire or flame for a long time, instead cobwebs and dirt clung to the brickwork.

Jack couldn't resist. "I like what you've done with the place."

The broad smile on Ritchie's face widened as he lifted the flap at the side of the bar and stepped out. "That's what I like about you, Jack. Your sense of humour."

"What do you want?" repeated Jack, the aroma of stale beer starting to churn his stomach. "I'm busy. I've got better things to be doing with my time than wasting it in here with you." Which was true — and if anything it was an understatement. Although heading towards ten o'clock in the evening, with the ongoing investigation Jack would usually still be at the station — and no doubt most of the team would be, too. With three bodies and a killer on the loose, he could do without time wasting exercises such as this one.

"You and me both." Ritchie stood by Jack's side. "You and me both."

"So — what is it? Sixty seconds, then I'm gone."

Ritchie seemed to take the hint, and after a brief pause he turned and walked towards the rear of the pub. "Follow me, my friend."

Sighing, Jack did as he was told, his eyes drawn once more to the worn carpet underfoot. If he wasn't much mistaken there were more bloodstains. Although the Hanged Man would have been no stranger to many a drop of blood being shed in its day, these particular ones definitely looked fresh. Jack decided to watch where he put his feet.

A door at the rear led into a surprisingly spacious room, empty except for a large wooden table in the centre. As Jack stepped across the threshold he recognised the five beefcakes he'd met here last time. Dressed in smart black suits that strained at the buttons, they were eyeing him up in a decidedly unfriendly fashion.

"I see the Backstreet Boys are back in town." Jack gave each of them a condescending smile.

The first of Ritchie's minders took a step closer, hands clenched into fists by his side, his expression distinctly unimpressed.

"Steady now," teased Jack, letting the smile develop. "You might break a nail if you're not careful."

The minder's eyes narrowed, but Ritchie stepped between them. "Not now, Frank. Jack here is one of us. He's here to help."

Jack bristled once more, then he frowned. *Help?* What on earth could he possibly help with in here? It was then that the rest of Ritchie's minders stepped away from the table, allowing Jack to see what, until now, had been hidden from view.

The man was lying face up, dressed in a pair of faded jeans that had seen better days and a checked red and grey lumberjack shirt. His feet were bootless — a pair mud caked boots lying discarded beneath the table.

Jack's eyes slid sideways to meet Ritchie's. "What's this?"

"This, my friend, is Rhys. And, as you can see, he's in a wee bit of a predicament." Ritchie gestured towards the man who was now starting to groan and writhe on top of the wooden table. Incoherent gargling noises came from his throat. Two of Ritchie's minders stepped towards him, pinning him down firmly with muscled arms.

Despite the only light coming from a solitary lightbulb swinging above them, Jack could see the blood. A good deal of it covered the table, the bottom half of the man's shirt already sodden and clinging to his skin. He quickly started to connect the dots — it didn't take a genius to work it out. The bloodstain he'd first seen in the entrance hall, and then the others in the saloon bar, were all leading to here. And the man.

Jack switched his gaze back to Ritchie. "He looks like he needs a hospital to me."

Ritchie shook his head and took Jack by the elbow. "No, Jack. What he really needs is you."

* * *

Time: 9.45 p.m.
Date: Tuesday 13 January 2015
Location: Acacia Avenue, Wimbledon

Jonathan Spearing placed the dishes in the dishwasher and then took his glass of wine through to the small study. Katrina had gone up for a bath, so he knew she would be at least an hour, if not more, and would most likely then just go to bed; so he would have plenty of time to himself to continue with his project.

The study was *his* space — his man cave he liked to call it. The walls were adorned with framed photographs of all his favourite bands — album covers and tour banners, mostly — from the Red Hot Chilli Peppers, through to Razorlight, Stereophonics and Oasis. Then there were the films — movie posters from *Rebel Without a Cause*, *Easy Rider* and *Heat*, were joined by *The Godfather*, *The Matrix* and latterly *The Hunger Games* and *Harry Potter*. It was an eclectic mix and one he defended rigorously.

In between the framed pictures of music and film memorabilia, was his collection of photographs of cars and motorbikes. Spearing loved anything fast, anything angry — anything that made a noise and caught the eye. *Anything dangerous*.

But tonight he wasn't content just to settle back with his wine and gaze at his collection, no matter how much he coveted each and every item — for tonight he had work to do. Slipping behind his mahogany desk, he pulled the laptop towards him. As usual, it was open on a rolling 24-hour news channel — the downside of being a journalist was that you were never *not* a journalist. He suspected it was very much like being a police officer.

The headlines were as expected — full of the discovery of the 'body in the bags' as it had already been dubbed. And the growing panic that was now settling over the city. Not that the Met wanted the media to use the word 'panic' — 'concern' was their preferred term. Spearing thought panic was more justified though.

The press conference had ended on a high as far as Spearing was concerned. MacIntosh rarely failed to disappoint, and when the proceedings descended into an all-out slanging match, he was more than content to sit back and watch from the sidelines. He hadn't gone along to pick up a news story — there were plenty of others at the *Daily Courier* who would want that particular scoop — instead he'd put in an appearance to purely watch Jack MacIntosh squirm.

Grinning, he opened up a fresh word document, intending to continue the research into his latest article, but as he did so he couldn't help but wonder what tomorrow's headlines would be. As much as the nation seemed to be captivated, albeit in a most gruesome way, by the horrific murders in the capital, Spearing thought the headlines that the world could wake up to tomorrow would easily kick these out of the park.

The memory stick should have reached its intended target by now — although he noted there wasn't even so much as a sniff of it online yet. But there would be, he was sure of that. Not even the Met would be able to cover this one up.

Taking another mouthful of the cool, crisp Chablis, he turned his attention away from the carnage that lay in wait for tomorrow and started work.

* * *

Time: 9.50 p.m.
Date: Tuesday 13 January 2015
Location: Central London

The van bounced hard over an uneven section of road — be it pothole, kerb or speedbump, Tanya hadn't a clue; and it didn't much matter. Whatever it was, it sent her hurtling from one side of the van to the other. Her hands were bound fast by cable ties behind her back, her feet tied at the ankles. Thick tape crushed her mouth closed.

Her heart racing, she felt her stomach contract as the van bounced once again. How did she get here? Her mind still felt hazy, as if seeing things through a fine mist. The last thing she clearly remembered was standing by the kerb on The Causeway, her usual spot — and then, nothing.

Trying to control her breathing, she willed her brain to remember something. *Anything*. But no matter how hard she tied, she was met by the same wall of smothering fog. The cable ties were cutting into her wrists, and something else was digging painfully into her back. Rolling to the side, she glanced behind to see a solitary stiletto shoe.

Her heart raced faster as the fear redoubled.

Willing the vomit to remain in her stomach, she felt the van lurch once again, sending her flying back to the other side. Wherever they were going, the driver was taking the corners at speed without a care for Tanya in the back. She almost laughed at her own naivety. Of course he didn't care about her, whoever he was — he'd plucked her from the street and trussed her up like a Christmas turkey without so much as batting an eyelid.

As the van rocked around another corner, she once again willed herself to think back. Had he plucked her from the street — or had she willingly got in the van? She couldn't even picture his face clearly. All she could remember from that night was the punter who had dropped her off . . . had he come back for her?

Tears began to sprout at the corners of her eyes. She was usually so careful — they all were. So, what had gone wrong?

No one wanted to be out on the streets, Tanya especially — she had bigger and better things planned for her future, intending to give up the streets in a couple of months, give up this life. She'd managed to save enough money to move out of London — to get the hell away from this lifestyle and start again somewhere new.

The tears continued to flow, her vision now as blurry as her head. The future she had so carefully mapped out for herself was now hanging by the tiniest of threads.

Rolling to the side, she caught sight of the single stiletto shoe once again, and realisation hit.

She was going to be number four.

* * *

Time: 9.50 p.m.
Date: Tuesday 13 January 2015
Location: The Hanged Man Public House

"No." Jack's voice was firm. "Never in a million years." He made to turn away, but three of Ritchie's minders stepped forward to close the gap between himself and the door. Beneath their shiny new suits, Jack would bet his last pound that they housed more fat than muscle, but their sheer bulk made his options somewhat limited. His jaw still throbbed from where Neville Henderson had clobbered him, and the split lip was only just starting to heal. He flashed an angry look back towards Ritchie, feeling the man's grip still claw-like on his arm. "He needs a hospital. An ambulance at the very least. End of."

"No ambulances, Jack. And no hospitals. You know the score."

And Jack did. Asking how the man had ended up with at least one gunshot wound would be a pointless exercise — wasting precious time that he knew the man didn't have. Jack stepped back towards the table, just as the man started to groan again.

As their eyes connected, Jack saw indescribable pain mixed with a large element of fear. Blood was oozing from a wound just above the waistband of the man's jeans, already soaking through the full thickness of his shirt. The wooden table beneath him was drenched in blood, but at least the stuff wasn't spurting out of his body. Jack took that as a relatively encouraging sign.

One of Ritchie's minders was pressing a hand down on top of the gunshot wound, stemming the flow. Blood continued to seep slowly through his stubby fingers, albeit at a reduced rate.

"No," repeated Jack. "I can't help you. And I can't help him. Whatever this is, it has absolutely nothing to do with me." He tried to turn away once more but Ritchie's grip on his arm tightened.

"Oh I think you'll find it has *everything* to do with you, Jack. And you *will* help me. Remember — you owe me."

Jack kept his voice calm and controlled. "Like I've said countless times before — I don't owe you anything. Now take your hand off me and get these wankers to move out of the way. I'm leaving — and I'm leaving now."

There was enough menace in Jack's tone to cause Ritchie Greenwood a moment or two's hesitation. Eventually he relented, releasing his grip and brushing his long, pale fingers along the sleeve of Jack's jacket, smoothing it out as he did so. "There, there, my friend. No need to get so heated. All I'm asking is for you to help a man in need." Ritchie gestured back towards the table. "This man needs you, Jack. You're a police officer — last time I looked anyway — so surely that's what you do? You help people." He paused, a customary smirk flashing across his pale lips. "You have a choice here, Jack. You can turn your back and walk away — I won't stop you. But you'll have the death of this young man on your conscience if you do."

Jack felt himself bristle again. How many deaths Ritchie Greenwood and his gang had on their hands — and Joseph Geraghty before them — was incomprehensible. Hundreds? Maybe even thousands when you factored in the drugs. He felt his gaze drag back towards the wooden table. The man was still writhing in pain, the blood oozing from his body. He looked young — maybe not even twenty. For some reason Jack thought of his brother.

"You help patch him up, Jack, then that's one less favour that you owe me."

Jack opened his mouth to reply with some quick retort, but Ritchie wasn't finished.

"That brother of yours seems to be doing well for himself, Jack. But he's punching way above his weight with that lovely young wife of his, don't you think?"

Jack stiffened. "Don't bring Stu into this."

"No?" Ritchie's pale eyebrows arched. "I'm just passing on my good wishes, Jack. To him and his lovely lady. They seemed so happy the last time I saw them. Taking a break down in the house at Albury, weren't they?"

Jack's blood chilled. "What do you mean?"

Ritchie merely smirked, and didn't elaborate.

"When were you in Surrey?" Jack's face darkened. "And more importantly, why?"

"We don't have time for idle chit-chat, my friend. Look at him. I know you can help me, Jack. I know you can help *him*." Ritchie gestured back towards the table. "It's just a question of how much it's worth to you, isn't it? I mean, I'd hate for anything to happen to that brother or yours — or his lovely new wife for that matter. Especially after all they've been through, eh?"

Sighing, Jack took another look at the man still writhing in agony on the table and reached for his phone.

CHAPTER THIRTEEN

Time: 10.35 p.m.
Date: Tuesday 13 January 2015
Location: The Hanged Man Public House

"I'm more used to dead people, Jack." Dr Philip Matthews crossed the threshold of the Hanged Man. Jack had advised the pathologist to leave his Volvo parked around the back alongside the Mondeo — away from prying eyes. The less people that knew what they were about to do, the better.

"Sorry, Doc." Jack had apologised half a dozen times, if not more, since Dr Matthews had pulled up outside the abandoned pub. The look on the esteemed pathologist's face told Jack he was already forgiven. "I don't know what happened — and, quite frankly, I don't want to know. The sooner we get in and sort him out, the sooner we get back out again."

"My sentiments exactly, Jack."

Inside the pub, Jack led the pathologist to the room at the rear. Ritchie Greenwood was nowhere to be seen, instead two of his minders filled the doorway. They stepped to the side as Jack and Dr Matthews approached.

Once inside the room, Jack watched the pathologist pushing his way past two more of Ritchie's minders, not giving either of them the time of day.

"Keep that up." Dr Matthews gestured towards one of Ritchie's minders who was still pressing down hard on the man's bleeding wound. "Don't move until I tell you to. Jack — can you go and support this young man's head?"

Jack did as he was told and stood at one end of the table, one hand on either side of the terrified man's head. Placing his bag by his feet, Dr Matthews bent down to rummage inside. As he did so, his clipped tone was directed at the remaining minders loitering by the open door.

"Make yourselves useful by getting me a bowl of boiling water and shutting that door. Let's give this young man some privacy, shall we?"

It wasn't long before one of the minders returned with a steaming bowl of water and a bottle of vodka. The pathologist looked up from where he had been laying out some fresh gauze and a series of syringes. He frowned towards the bottle.

"I think now is hardly the right time for a toast, do you?"

The minder placed the bowl of hot water by Dr Matthews' feet and held the bottle of spirits out. "I thought you might need it. Disinfects wounds, doesn't it?" The man peered out from beneath a pair of piggy, deep-set eyes, his voice gruff. His jowls wobbled as he spoke.

Dr Matthews tutted under his breath and waved the bottle away. "Thankfully, modern medicine has moved on a little since the Dark Ages — I have everything I need with me here." He gestured towards his medical bag while looking sharply over his shoulder towards the door. "And I don't require an audience. If you want me to patch this young man up and potentially save his life, then I'd be grateful if you would make yourselves scarce. You'll know soon enough when we're finished."

The pathologist turned back towards the man on the table. "And I'll take over from here." He motioned for the one remaining minder who still had his hands on the bloody wound to take a step back.

The five minders needed no further instruction to vacate and all had soon disappeared back into the bar, pulling the door shut behind them. Dr Matthews gently teased the man's bloodied lumberjack shirt apart to assess the gunshot wound, while reaching for a section of sterile gauze.

"Far be it for me to pass comment, Jack, but . . ." He pressed the gauze down firmly and caught Jack's gaze. "But just what have you done this time to get yourself mixed up in something like this?"

* * *

Time: 10.40 p.m.
Date: Tuesday 13 January 2015
Location: Central London

The house wasn't much better than the van, but at least she wasn't being thrown around every time it went around a corner. She had no recollection of getting out of the van and into the house, and from the fog that still swirled around inside her head she assumed he must have drugged her.

Again.

Once the fog lifted enough for her eyelids to open, she took in her new surroundings. The room was dark, the only window had a heavy drape pulled across from one side to the other, snuffing out the outside world. There was a lightbulb overhead but it gave no illumination.

Everywhere smelled damp and rotten — in the dim light squeezing in around the sides of the drape she saw piles and piles of rubbish stacked up against the walls. Newspapers, boxes, black plastic bin liners. On the floor were piles of food cartons and supermarket carrier bags.

Tanya was sitting propped up against a pile of cardboard boxes — what was inside them she didn't care to think about.

The smell all around told her that it probably wasn't pleasant. Occasionally she thought she heard a faint scrabbling sound — then the image of rats and mice took over. She shivered and tried to inch herself away from the stinking boxes, but failed. Her hands and feet were still bound by stiff cable ties.

The passage of time was difficult to track, but Tanya thought she had only been in the room a short time when she felt the presence of someone else. She wasn't altogether sure why, just something telling her that she wasn't alone. Peering through the dimness, she squinted over at the corner opposite. Unless her mind was playing tricks on her, she thought she could see someone's head — a pale face catching the muted light. Then a patch of hair. The more she looked, the more she was convinced someone else was there. Now she could see an arm, a hand. Tanya's spirits rose.

"Hello?" Tanya's voice sounded faint, swallowed by the shadows. "Is someone there?"

Emboldened with thoughts of escape, her mind started to race — two heads were better than one, right? Two pairs of hands to wrench open the window; two pairs of legs to kick out with; two voices to yell as loud as they could, although shouting would be difficult with the sticky tape still plastered across her face.

But another person!

It had to be good news.

But that had been before *he* returned. No sooner had Tanya started making plans for her escape, the door had opened and she shrank back against the boxes and closed her eyes. For some reason she felt it best to pretend to still be sedated.

As she sensed him getting close, she opened her eyelids a little, peering through a tiny slit. She could see his feet stepping carefully between the filth that littered the floor heading towards her. She held her breath as best she could and tried to stop herself from shuddering.

But the man shuffled past.

Tanya let her gaze drift after him, watching as he bent over to pick something up from the floor. As he turned back around, she switched her gaze back to her lap and tried to regulate her breathing.

He mustn't see I'm awake.

He mustn't see I'm awake.

Heartbeat quickening, she sensed him retrace his steps and head back in her direction. She heard him clear his throat and spit to the side. As his boots came into view, she let herself raise her gaze slightly.

And then wished she hadn't.

Swinging from the man's right hand was a woman's severed head.

* * *

Time: 11.35 p.m.
Date: Tuesday 13 January 2015
Location: The Hanged Man Public House

Ritchie waited for Jack and the doctor to leave the car park before returning to the room at the rear of the pub. Rhys was still conscious, which he took to be a good sign. Whatever the doctor had given the lad had managed to calm him a little — he wasn't writhing around in agony anymore at least. There was a little more blood on the table and the floor, and the lad looked decidedly pale, but at least he was still alive.

Death didn't usually bother Ritchie Greenwood — on the contrary, it was part and parcel of the business they were in — but he didn't much fancy having the young man's demise on his hands; and even less so in his own pub. The Hanged Man might not be open for business in the usual sense — no paying punters ever crossed its threshold — but plenty of business still went on inside its four walls. He could do without the hassle of getting rid of a dead body, and a bloodied dead body at that.

No, all in all, Jack MacIntosh had acquitted himself well.

Ritchie left Rhys in the hands of Frank and the rest of his crew and headed back behind the bar. He filled a tumbler with several inches of a decent Macallan and threw most of it into his mouth in one go. He winced at the burn as he swallowed.

Jack MacIntosh.

The man was becoming an irritant.

He'd expected the detective inspector to have succumbed by now; to have caved and become Ritchie's inside man. That was what all this was for, after all. It had never before taken quite this long — the police, as a rule, were only human. And humans always had their price.

But not, so it seemed, Jack MacIntosh. As each day passed, Ritchie saw that the man was different. So much so, that he now believed time had run out for the detective inspector.

Ritchie was getting bored.

The detective was no closer to slipping into Ritchie's back pocket than he was when the boss had still been alive — and Ritchie wasn't renowned for his patience. If the man wasn't prepared to play ball, then neither was he.

Ritchie struggled to understand why Joseph had insisted on holding MacIntosh in such high regard. Joseph Geraghty, the capital's hard man right up until the cancer took him, had acted like the father Ritchie had never had, nurturing and preparing him to take over the reins of the organisation when the big man was no longer around.

And part of that nurturing process had involved explaining all about Jack MacIntosh.

Ritchie remembered it well even now — they had been sitting in Geraghty's penthouse apartment in Canary Wharf, looking out over the capital. Even after the explanation, Ritchie struggled to get his head around the concept. But he'd gone along with it — for Joseph's sake.

The man was dying after all.

* * *

"Are we clear?" Joseph Geraghty's pale green eyes simmered behind his spectacles. "Because this is non-negotiable."

Ritchie Greenwood stared at the glass tumbler in his hands. He hadn't been quite sure what to expect when the boss had summoned him to the penthouse. They had spoken on many occasions in the preceding weeks, Joseph becoming concerned about his declining health; wanting Ritchie to be fully briefed as to how to run the organisation when the time came.

But protecting a police officer? *Helping* a police officer?

Ritchie's brow furrowed once again, which did not go unnoticed.

"You're wondering why I want to give our Mr MacIntosh such special treatment, don't you?"

Ritchie was about to deny it, but saw little point. Joseph might be ill, but he wasn't stupid. "A little," he eventually replied.

Joseph placed his glass of water back down on to the marble-topped table and gazed out over the capital. "This is one of my most favourite places in the world, Rich." He nodded across the rooftops of Canary Wharf. "Up here you are completely separated from the rest of the world."

Ritchie returned the nod, but remained mute. He wasn't much struck on the balcony of Joseph's apartment — not a lover of heights, he didn't relish sitting out and watching the world go by quite as much as the boss did. He much preferred his feet to be on terra firma. He took a sip of the whisky from his tumbler and deepened his frown. Where was the boss going with all this? And what did any of it have to do with Jack MacIntosh?

Ritchie didn't have to wait long to find out.

"Families, Ritchie." Joseph turned away from the view from the balcony. "Families. I suspect he might disagree, but our friend Detective Inspector MacIntosh and myself are very similar. He was a foster care kid in much the same way that I was, although I suspect my experience was a little less conventional than his."

The bemused expression on Ritchie's face continued. He knew the pancreatic cancer was eating away at the boss, and had reached several other organs. When he'd entered the apartment, he'd noticed how Joseph seemed smaller, his frame weak and shrunken, and the whites of his eyes were now tinged yellow, his skin having a waxy sheen. But had the cancer reached his brain, too? He decided not to ask.

"Not many people know this, Ritchie, but I was taken away from my mother the moment I was born — I never knew her, and I don't know if she even got to hold me first. I don't even know my real name."

Although Joseph had paused, Ritchie knew he wasn't expected to comment or respond — instead he decided now was a good time for another mouthful of whisky.

"I was taken away and brought up in a convent — then eventually I was given to a family who were desperate for a child of their own. Adopted I guess you could call it — but no paperwork exists to prove it. My mother was unmarried and it wasn't uncommon in those days for babies to be sold illegally to the highest bidder. A commodity, no less." Joseph eyed Ritchie across the marble-topped table, a warm breeze touching their skin. "I know what it's like to grow up without a mother, without a family. And our friendly detective does, too."

"OK." Wariness entered Ritchie's tone as the whisky began to loosen his tongue. "But what does that have to do with anything? What does that have to do with *us*?"

"Justice and revenge, Ritchie. Justice and revenge. They are two of the most powerful words in the English language — but they mean very different things to many different people. Most of the time it's impossible to have both — it's often just one or the other. Justice *or* revenge. Unfortunately, I was denied both — neither justice nor revenge was available to me. But our Mr MacIntosh, however — he could still seek either, or maybe he could be one of the lucky ones and achieve both."

I still don't understand.

Ritchie almost said the words out loud, but instead gulped another mouthful of whisky.

"Which is why I want to help him." Joseph continued to fix his gaze across the table. "Maybe I'm getting soft in my old age, but I feel myself and Mr MacIntosh are cut from the same cloth — and if he can get justice and revenge for losing his mother, then perhaps I can take some of that for myself. Maybe extinguish a few demons at the same time before I go. I believe they call it resting in peace?" Joseph managed a faint chuckle. "I don't know — I've never died before."

Ritchie swallowed and, emboldened by the alcohol, asked, "What do you want me to do?"

"We are going to get justice for Detective Inspector MacIntosh — we are going to help bring down the man who murdered his mother."

Ritchie started to nod. "OK — so that's the justice. What about the revenge?"

Joseph smiled, his pale face crinkling. "I knew you were a bright boy, Ritchie. That's why I chose you. For the revenge — once we have this man where we want him, we are going to kill him."

Ritchie smiled. He may not care much for protecting or helping a police officer, but killing came easily to him. "Justice *and* revenge — got it. And MacIntosh is all right with this?" Ritchie's eyebrows hitched.

Joseph continued to smile. "Well, he doesn't exactly know of my plans, not yet. But he will. And I'm sure he'll come on board once the plan is in action — I don't think he'll be able to stop himself. But I need you to promise me, Ritchie. I need you to promise me that you'll carry out my wishes to the letter. No deviation."

Ritchie found himself nodding. "Of course."

"Say it."

"Say what?"

"That you promise. I need to hear you say it."

"OK." Feeling a little like a chastised schoolboy, Ritchie relented. "I *promise*." He swirled the rest of his whisky around in the bottom of the tumbler, sensing the meeting might be drawing to a close. But the boss wasn't quite finished.

"You are to protect Jack MacIntosh at all costs."

"Protect him?" The frown returned to Ritchie's brow. Justice and revenge for the man he could just about swallow — but protection? "What do you mean?"

"Work with him, create a relationship with him — keep him on side."

"Ah, you want me to turn him?" Ritchie's eyebrows hitched again, starting to see the potential benefit to an otherwise rather unorthodox request. A bent copper would always be useful. And a bent detective inspector was worth its weight in gold. "You want him to be our inside man?"

Joseph laughed and nodded across to the Canary Wharf skyline once again, his chest sounding wheezy. "I'm sure you'll have more chance of bending one of those skyscrapers over there than you do Jack MacIntosh, but by all means try. But what I really mean is keep him sweet. If he needs a favour, then you do it for him. No questions asked." Joseph gave a wink. "And then you never know — he might just do the same for you."

* * *

Time: 11.40 p.m.
Date: Tuesday 13 January 2013
Location: The Hanged Man Public House

Protect Jack MacIntosh?

Ritchie felt the dry laugh bubbling up in his throat and reached for the bottle of Macallan once again. To begin with he had gone along with Joseph's wishes. The two of them had set up James Quinn just as they had planned — and, although it hadn't gone quite the way Joseph had instructed, Quinn still managed to get himself inside a prison cell.

But Ritchie was tiring of Jack MacIntosh and, after Joseph's death, it didn't take long for any loyalty towards his former boss to start to wane. Jack MacIntosh wasn't for bending, just as Joseph had predicted, and it would be a futile exercise to keep trying.

Although tonight's little escapade had proved how useful it could be to have a detective at his beck and call, Ritchie knew it wouldn't last. And he didn't have the patience to keep flogging a dead horse.

Protect him? Ritchie swallowed the laugh with another slug of Macallan. He would no sooner protect Jack MacIntosh than throw himself under a bus. Instead, he planned to cut the man loose. Not being of a religious persuasion, Ritchie didn't believe in the afterlife and wasn't concerned that Joseph would be turning in his grave any time soon.

Placing the bottle of whisky back on to the shelf, Ritchie came to a decision — and it was the easiest decision he had made in a long time.

Detective Inspector Jack MacIntosh's days were numbered.

CHAPTER FOURTEEN

Time: 7.45 a.m.
Date: Wednesday 14 January 2015
Location: Metropolitan Police HQ, London

Jack hadn't got close enough to Rhys last night, but he still spent half an hour in the shower that morning, scrubbing at his fingernails. Blood was like indelible ink — once it was there it was hard to shift. He still felt bad at involving the doc, but the pathologist had taken the whole experience in his usual good-natured stride.

"No need to explain, Jack. But maybe choose your friends more wisely next time."

Friends.

Jack shivered at the thought of Ritchie Greenwood being classed as a friend. But what caused him even more disquiet was the man's veiled threat towards Stu and Isabel.

'I'd hate for anything to happen to that brother of yours. Or his lovely new wife.'

If the man had been watching them down in Surrey, and it certainly sounded like he had been, then what was his game plan? For Jack was sure there had to be one. Ritchie wouldn't get his hands dirty unless there was something advantageous in it for him. But what could he possibly want from Jack's brother? Or Isabel for that matter?

Resolving to finally catch up with Stu later, Jack pushed open the door of the incident room. Despite the early hour, the team were already hard at work, heads down.

"Morning, guv." DS Cassidy stood up from her chair, waving a piece of paper in the air. "We've had some calls in on the hotline number."

"I bet we have," grumbled Jack, reaching for the mug of black coffee Cassidy brandished towards him in her other hand. "Anything useful, dare I ask?"

Cassidy gave a grin. "A fair number of the usual time-wasters, but there was a call from one of the volunteers on the Welfare Truck — one of the street pastors? Said he knew you? Just some background information on Lisa and Tara, but there wasn't really anything we didn't already know."

Jack waved the piece of paper away and took a mouthful of his coffee. "OK, make sure the details are uploaded onto the system and pop the details on my desk. Anything else?"

"I've managed to get an address for Julian Fisher."

"Good work. Arrange to go and see him — take Daniels with you." Jack took a grateful mouthful of coffee before turning towards DS Cooper. "Cooper, what about the CCTV?"

Cooper scooted his chair back from his desk. "I've been reviewing all the CCTV from both scenes, for what it's worth. Cameras closest to Acorn House and the industrial estate. Nothing too useful. I can't find Lisa or Tara anywhere, so they must have been brought in by car or van. There's plenty of vehicles which we could wade through and eliminate if we had the time — but one thing that did catch my attention was on Thursday morning last week." Cooper brought a still image up on to his computer screen and angled it towards Jack. "Our friend Barry Pierce is seen on one of the cameras closest to the Hillside Estate, heading back in the direction of Acorn House, and he's dragging a light-coloured suitcase behind him."

Jack peered over Cooper's shoulder. "The suitcase he tells us he doesn't have. OK, I know it's not the most exciting of jobs but keep trawling the cameras for any other sightings of him or his suitcase. Check out the roads close to where each victim was last seen. In the meantime, let's try and get a search warrant organised. I want to know what he was so keen to hide from us when we were there yesterday, and I want to find that bloody suitcase." Jack drained his mug. "I'm going to head out and see Gina Simmonds. If you remember, she helped us with the investigation into Narelle Williams' murder last year. With her background, she might be able to give us some insight."

Jack wasn't all that hopeful, but they were now approaching the clutching at straws stage. With three bodies, they were still no further forward and the natives were getting restless. He fully expected another request to see the chief superintendent to land on his desk at any moment — so decided a trip out might be best.

"Then I'll swing by Rachel Hunter's office. She's had a chance to look at the investigation papers, so I'll see what she has to say." He began to head for the door. "While I'm gone, give the mortuary a call and see if Dr Matthews has had a chance to examine our third victim yet. I notice her name has been released to the press. And call the lab, too — they should have something for us by now."

* * *

Time: 7.45 a.m.
Date: Wednesday 14 January 2015
Location: Acacia Avenue, Wimbledon

Jonathan Spearing plucked the two slices of toast from the toaster and dropped them on to the plate. He'd persuaded Katarina to stay in bed, although it had taken good deal of coaxing. He knew he was smothering her, but she seemed to take it with enough good humour not to make too much of a point of it. Ever since the events five months ago, he had barely wanted to let her out of his sight for more than a second.

He worked from home as often as he could; he couldn't remember the last time he'd physically been to the *Courier's* offices. With technology such as it was these days, news stories could be penned just about anywhere, so it didn't really matter. On the odd occasion where he did need to go out and physically speak to someone — meetings with his editor or carrying out research in person — he would spend every minute he was away feeling on edge. She told him not to worry; that the chances of being kidnapped for a second time were so remote to be virtually impossible — but he couldn't quite shake it. Couldn't quite get past the feeling of vulnerability. It had happened before, so why couldn't it happen again? And he was sure Katarina was only saying it to make him feel better. He could tell by the look on her face sometimes that she was still terrified. But he'd made the required conciliatory noises and given her space when she asked for it — he just didn't necessarily have to like it.

Pouring Katarina a mug of her favourite coffee, he started to wonder whether the envelope had reached its intended recipient yet. Surely it must have? And if it had, whether the contents had been viewed. There was nothing on any online news portals, so he supposed the shit hadn't quite hit the fan yet. A smile teased his lips. Give it time.

Buttering the toast with the low-fat spread Katarina insisted upon, he balanced the plate in one hand, coffee cup in the other and headed for the hall. As he reached the stairs, his eyes came to rest on the folded copy of the *Daily Express* still lying on the doormat.

And then he froze.

* * *

Time: 9.00 a.m.
Date: Wednesday 14 January 2015
Location: Isabel's Café, Horseferry Road, London

"Thanks for seeing me." Jack eased himself into one of the armchairs at the back of the café.

"No problem." Gina Simmonds seated herself on a stool opposite, placing two mugs on the table between them. "How can I help?"

"Well, I'm not really sure that you can." Jack reached for the mug of freshly brewed coffee, not really wanting another shot of caffeine so soon after the last, and he still felt wired after last night's events at the Hanged Man. "You'll no doubt be aware of what's been in the news for the last couple of days, especially this morning." Jack gestured towards the rack of newspapers and magazines over by the window.

Gina nodded, solemnly, her hands clasped around her coffee mug. "It's awful. Just awful."

"Like I say, I'm not really sure if you can help, but . . ." Jack paused and gave a shrug. "Is there anything in your dealings with the Carson brothers that might be useful to us? I know they're off the scene at the moment, but they'd both been in the prostitution game a long time."

Gina placed her unwanted coffee down, her face taking on a pained expression. "I hate thinking back to those days — I try to avoid it if I can."

Jack gave what he hoped was a sympathetic smile. "I'm sorry — I realise it won't be pleasant. But if you can think of anything we could use, anything that might give us another lead. I'll be honest with you, Gina — we're struggling right now. We've made appeals to the public to come forward and help, but so far we've had nothing. Nothing useful anyway. We're hitting a brick wall whichever way we turn."

Jack knew Gina's past dealings with Lance and Wayne Carson would be buried deep in the back of her mind, and for good reason. Now languishing in prison cells on opposite sides

144

of the capital, neither brother would see the light of day for a while yet, but that didn't make Jack sleep any easier at night. The Carsons were a drop in the ocean and there were bigger and better criminal enterprises out there only too willing to fill the void caused by the Carsons' imprisonment. But Gina had spent time in their clutches — she was as close as Jack would get to first-hand knowledge on how such prostitution rings operated, barring going undercover and infiltrating the ring himself which wasn't an appealing prospect.

"They operate through fear." Gina's voice was steady but quiet. Jack edged forward in his seat. "Every girl I knew was petrified of them. Some put on a brave face, acted like they didn't care, gave the impression none of it was affecting them — but it was all lies. Every girl I met was terrified of what the Carsons might do to them if they didn't comply." Gina gave a shudder. "Even when you did do as you were told, it didn't make any difference. They would still humiliate you. They would still beat you. Any excuse to exert their power over you."

Jack nodded. "It must have been tough."

Gina gave a weak smile. "It wasn't the best time of my life, no." Then she frowned and her gaze gravitated towards the newspaper rack. "You think thugs like the Carsons are involved in this?"

"I'm not sure. All the women were sex workers and were all working in the same area. But that doesn't necessarily mean they all had the same pimp, or indeed if they even had one. But it's a connection we can't ignore."

Gina shrugged. "I guess it would make sense. But do you think the pimp, or whatever prostitution ring controlled them, would kill them? I'm not sure that makes much sense."

"It doesn't," agreed Jack. "Why would they bite off the very hands that feed them? But we're having to consider every avenue, every possible angle — and, to be honest, we have bugger all else."

"I do recall working on a street where other pimps tried to move in and make their mark. The Carsons weren't happy.

145

They were tricky times; I do remember that much. But it never resulted in murder. It's a lonely place out there. Not many people will take it upon themselves to stick up for you. Even fewer would actually stick their neck out and help you." Gina gave another shudder as the memories came flooding back. "But we would always stick together — look out for one another. I'm sure it must be the same now. And when you're as desperate as these women must be, it's all you have."

Jack took a sip of his coffee. "Did you ever get involved with the street pastors?"

Gina shook her head, pulling her gaze away from the newspapers. "Unfortunately, they weren't around then. I've heard good things about them, though. I did another talk with Jason and the Argyle Foundation a couple of weeks ago — over in Greenwich this time. One of the street pastors came along and spoke. It was quite inspiring. They do fascinating work. But the women will be scared, Jack — no matter how many Welfare Trucks are on the streets. But not as scared as they would be if they didn't go out and work."

Jack drained his coffee and got to his feet. "Thanks for the chat. I'd best be off."

"Isabel will be sorry she missed you. She's had to take Livi to the vet for her vaccinations." Gina followed Jack across the café. "I hope you find him — whoever's doing this."

"So do I, Gina. So do I." Just as Jack reached the door, his phone chirped with an incoming message. Fully expecting it to be Dougie King, he felt his stomach lurch in anticipation.

But it wasn't the chief superintendent.

It was worse than that.

Jack, my friend — we need to talk.'

CHAPTER FIFTEEN

Time: 9.45 a.m.
Date: Wednesday 14 January 2015
Location: Lambeth Bridge, London

Jack stared out over the grey waters of the Thames. He'd chosen Lambeth Bridge for the meeting — if you could even call it that. He wanted somewhere public, somewhere neutral; somewhere where he could be seen. But now he was here he wasn't quite so sure. The Hanged Man had its advantages — discretion for one. Out here, anyone would be able to see him — and then wonder what on earth he was up to. But Jack knew the likelihood of the chief superintendent or any of the top brass at the station taking a stroll by this section of the river was highly unlikely — although it still didn't settle his disquiet.

Glancing over his shoulder, he saw the usual swathes of cars, buses and vans streaming across the bridge, paying him and his companion little or no attention. But he still felt vulnerable.

"What do you want from them? I know you've been there. You pretty much admitted it last night." The words were almost whipped from his mouth by the strengthening wind blowing across from the choppy waters below. The weather was on the turn; although the cold snap remained, it was now accompanied by biting winds and the threat of more rain. Possibly even snow if the temperatures didn't pick up.

Ritchie Greenwood remained silent.

"Just leave them alone. They're of no use to you." The exasperation in Jack's tone was evident.

"Oh, everyone has their uses, Jack. Even you." Ritchie turned to face Jack full on, his back to the river. "I've heard from a reliable source that our mutual acquaintance is recovering well from his wounds — all thanks to you and your doctor friend."

Jack bristled. Dr Matthews had been very good-natured about being dragged into Ritchie Greenwood's dirty world — but the man was a friend and Jack didn't like involving his friends in anything to do with Ritchie Greenwood. "That's good to hear," was all he could muster. "But that's the last time you call on me to do anything. I'm going to change my phone number. We're quits."

"We're quits when I say we are, Jack. You know that." Ritchie paused, his gaze steady. "Remember I had Mickey Hatton take the fall for you."

"I didn't ask you to."

"I know you didn't, but that's what friends are for." Ritchie grinned. "Just think of the trouble you could be in if I hadn't stepped in to help out."

Jack sighed, his body having no energy left to go into battle. He gazed out once more over the grey waters of the Thames, then turned away. "This is crazy. I need to get back." He started walking away from the bridge, but soon heard Ritchie Greenwood's laughter following him on the tails of the strengthening wind.

"Not so fast, Jack — you haven't heard what I've got to say yet. I guarantee you'll want to hear it."

Jack didn't break his stride, feeling the first few spots of rain hit his forehead. "I doubt that very much."

Ritchie raised his voice another notch above the sound of the blustering wind. "It's about James Quinn — he's out of prison."

Jack froze mid-step. Suddenly, all the cacophony around him — the car horns, the grumbling bus engines, the revving motorbikes — all was tuned out, and the resulting silence deafened him. Quinn? Out? Despite his better judgement, Jack turned around and walked back to where Ritchie was still leaning up against the side of the bridge, the wind ruffling the collar of his jacket.

"What did you just say?"

"Quinn," smiled Ritchie, his eyes sparkling. "He's out."

Jack smothered a laugh and shook his head. "No he's not. There's no way he'd be considered for release yet. He's still got time left to serve."

"Oh, I didn't say he'd been released, Jack. I just said he was out of prison. Well — he will be before too long." Ritchie made a show of looking at the expensive watch on his wrist. "Right about now, as it goes — the news will hit the media soon enough."

Jack hovered by the side of the road, a double decker splashing through a puddle and sending up a spray of dirty rainwater. He swore beneath his breath, unable to move out of the way in time.

The smile on Ritchie Greenwood's face remained. "I think you know what I mean."

"Why don't you just spell it out for me and quit playing games." Jack brushed rainwater from his jacket and pulled up the collar as he faced the arctic wind. The rainclouds above were darkening by the second and ice- cold sleet began to pelt down. "I'm not in the mood."

"Just keep an eye on the news, Jack. Keep an eye on the news." With that, Ritchie Greenwood spun on his heels and walked briskly away from the bridge. "I'll be in touch."

Jack cursed under his breath as yet another bus splashed through a puddle by his side. What was he doing here other

149

than being led on another merry dance? He didn't have time for Ritchie Greenwood or James Quinn, or whatever games the pair of them were playing. Turning to make his way back to the station, he felt his phone vibrate in his pocket. A message from Penny, Dougie King's PA. Another summons from the chief superintendent.

Jack decided it was time for another detour.

* * *

Time: 10.05 a.m.
Date: Wednesday 14 January 2015
Location: Metropolitan Police HQ, London

Dougie King leaned back in his leather swivel chair and inwardly groaned.

Jesus, Jack — what now?

He was meant to be in a budget meeting with the bigwigs from upstairs, but he'd persuaded Penny to make the necessary excuses on his behalf. Right now, arguing over the pennies wasn't so high on his list of priorities. Fielding whatever shitstorm would now be riding into town in the wake of the package that had landed on his desk yesterday, however, *was*.

He pushed aside the mug of Colombian coffee, freshly made, and sighed once again. Jack was one of his best officers — *the* best if he was forced to be brutally honest — which afforded him some leeway. But sometimes even being the best couldn't save you, and Dougie King was increasingly concerned that they were now fast approaching that point.

They had been here before, of course, on many an occasion in the past. Jack was certainly no stranger to a complaint or three landing on any number of senior officer's desks, but Dougie King had a feeling that this was different, and that maybe this time Jack MacIntosh might not be able to be saved.

He placed the memory stick back inside the padded envelope. He couldn't afford for anyone else to see it — not yet.

Not until Jack had a chance to explain. Quite what that explanation might be didn't fill Dougie King with much reassurance. Jack was heading for a fall this time — the only question was — could the chief superintendent catch him in time?

* * *

Time: 10.20 a.m.
Date: Wednesday 14 January 2015
Location: Metropolitan Police HQ, London

"Lab results are in." DS Cooper angled his computer screen towards Cassidy and Daniels. "The blood on the floor and around the bath at Acorn House definitely belongs to the second victim, Tara Coe."

Cassidy perched on the edge of Cooper's desk, her face slack. "Poor woman. It sounds like Dr Matthews could be right then — that she was alive when she was dismembered, given the amount of blood at the scene." She gave a shudder. "It doesn't bear thinking about, does it? What else do they say?"

"A lot of fingerprints were lifted, but judging by the number of people who could have been in and out of the place I'm not sure that helps us much. But we'll run them anyway."

"How about DNA?" DC Daniels edged closer.

Cooper scrolled through the lab report. "Again, quite a lot of material — quite a few full and partial profiles, mostly from the drug paraphernalia. But whether they're a help or a hindrance only time will tell. It's a busy scene. Nothing matches the victims yet, apart from the blood."

Cassidy sighed and turned to Daniels. "Trevor, you ready to come and see our friend Julian Fisher with me?"

The detective constable grabbed his jacket from his chair. "Ready as ever."

"I'll let the boss know about the lab reports and carry on sifting through the CCTV." Cooper turned back towards his screen.

"Don't have too much fun while we're gone!" smiled Cassidy as she headed for the door, Daniels following closely behind.

"I'll do my best." Cooper reached for the ham and salad sandwich he'd bought from the canteen earlier, and watched the detectives disappear. He'd been tempted by another bacon roll but decided on the slightly healthier option — it had green things inside, so Jenny would be pleased.

Angling the screen back towards him, he closed down the lab report and loaded the camera footage from around The Causeway where both Lisa Wood and Tara Coe were last seen. The grainy images played out as he sank his teeth into the bread. The cameras were focused on a set of traffic lights and only a handful of pedestrians crossed through the camera's viewfinder. What vehicles did pass by, Cooper logged the registrations to check later, but noted that none had stopped, other than at the lights themselves. He managed to identify both Lisa and Tara on several of the images, but then they seemed to just disappear — walking out of shot, never to return.

Cooper was just about to close the recording down and switch to another when one of the vehicles reappeared. Checking the registration against the list he'd made a few minutes before, he noted the van had made its first appearance earlier that evening.

And now it was back — just after the last sighting of Lisa and Tara.

Ham sandwich, now half-eaten and forgotten, he tore the number from his notepad. They needed to find out who this was.

CHAPTER SIXTEEN

Time: 10.45 a.m.
Date: Wednesday 14 January 2015
Location: St James's University, London

Jack settled himself into the chair by the floor-to-ceiling window. He gazed at the same view as he had the last time he'd graced Rachel Hunter's offices at the university — except today's view was grey and cold. The sleet had intensified on his journey across to the university campus and his jacket was now uncomfortably damp.

Outside was deserted and, although the students were now back after the Christmas break, it looked as though they all preferred the warmth of the lecture theatre to the chill outside. Jack didn't blame them.

"Long time no see, Jack. How have you been?" Dr Rachel Hunter slipped behind her uncluttered desk. She was again dressed smartly in a light grey, well-fitting suit, her hair tied back in a loose ponytail. Spectacles sat perched on her nose.

Jack tore his gaze away from the window, feeling the welcome warmth of the central heating beginning to defrost his hands. "Ah, you know. Can't complain." It was Jack's stock answer to the dreaded 'how are you?' question. People habitually said it as a way of greeting, but most really couldn't care less — although, somehow, he suspected Rachel was different. Anyhow, the stock answer was what everyone got. "Can't complain."

Rachel lowered her gaze to her desk, picking up a thin manila folder. "Well, I've read through the information you sent over, including the additional material for your third victim." She glanced up, peering over the top of her glasses, her pale green eyes devoid of their usual sparkle. "It doesn't make for very pleasant reading."

"No, it doesn't," agreed Jack as he leaned forward in his seat. "I'm going to check in with Dr Matthews later — see if he's had a chance to look at our third victim. Do you have any initial thoughts? I appreciate there isn't that much to go on."

"There's more here than you think, Jack." Rachel's eyebrows hitched a little. "Crime scenes can tell me a lot about the perpetrator — the bodies themselves are just additional evidence."

"Go on."

Rachel plucked a single A4 sheet from the folder. "I've made a few rudimentary observations which I'll flesh out later, but I can give you the brief highlights now. First, I'll take the scene at Acorn House and the discovery of the first two victims. I'll start with an overview of the case first, then I'll go into specifics about what I feel will be your perpetrator's likely characteristics."

Jack had never had much time for forensic profiling in the past — far too many 'maybes' and 'possibles' for his liking — but recently he had come around to the idea after using Rachel in a number of his cases. Although he hated to admit it, there was something to be said for psychological input into an investigation.

Nudging her spectacles, Rachel began. "The cutting up of the bodies — and then the mutilation of the internal organs — this process means something to your killer. It isn't just a way to dispose of the victim, and it isn't just a way to try and hide their identification. He leaves the body parts in full view — and those parts that *are* hidden, such as the internal organs and the heads, aren't hidden very well. They are easily found. He doesn't remove the hands — so fingerprint evidence is still possible. Although he removes the head, he doesn't dispose of it. He *wants* you to find them."

"Why?"

"Shock value would be my initial thought. He wants to shock."

"Well, he's succeeded there."

Rachel trained a well-manicured finger down the typed bullet points. "The way he arranges the limbs — he knows someone will find them and he wants that person to feel outrage and disgust when they do. It's a form of exhibitionism. I wouldn't be surprised if your perpetrator had convictions or cautions for indecent exposure at some point in his past."

"You say him? You're sure our killer is a man?"

"Absolutely." Rachel continued. "And then we have the crime scene itself. Your killer knew the flat was empty — it wasn't a random choice. It was planned well in advance. He is a cautious and methodical person. When inside the flat, he has taken his time with his victims. I believe he took both victims to the flat alive and murdered them there. This wasn't just a dump site for him. How he lured them there is up for speculation, but I'll outline some general characteristics shortly. He also appears to have spent some time cleaning up after himself — albeit not very well."

Rachel pulled out the crime scene photographs, including the carnage in the bloodied bathroom with the blue hue from the luminol clearly visible. "He will have cleaned himself enough not to raise suspicion when he left the scene. As far as I can see from the witness statements so far, no one seems to have seen a man covered in blood. And he would have been heavily bloodstained, so I can only assume he took some time to get clean." The psychologist turned over the page.

"He's a risk taker to some degree, maybe even a gambler or someone with an addiction. It was a risky location, with any number of residents in surrounding flats who could have seen him or stumbled across him. Sound travels in buildings like these — I suspect the walls in the flats aren't particularly thick — but still he chose it as his murder location. Which was risky. But as I mentioned a moment ago, he is methodical and a planner — almost to military precision. He will have assessed the risks, and calmly taken steps to minimise them."

"What about the victims?" asked Jack. "Why them? Was it just random? Wrong place, wrong time?"

Rachel gave a quick shake of the head. "There's nothing random about this killer. He's targeting sex workers for a reason. They mean something to him. I strongly believe he will currently be, or at least have been in the past, a user of prostitutes. But at the same time he will feel an almost overwhelming repulsion for them, and also for himself. He will feel angry at himself for using prostitutes — even to the extent of despising himself for it. The act of killing is his way of cleansing his conscience."

"He has a conscience?" Jack didn't hide the derision in his tone. "That I find hard to believe."

"Everyone has a conscience, Jack, even the most violent and depraved in our society. Some people bury it more successfully than others. There's no evidence of sexual assault, so he's not a sexual predator in the usual sense. He isn't getting sexual gratification from the act of killing — it means something else to him entirely. Which makes him all the more complicated to understand."

Jack grimaced. *Great. A complicated killer.* "Anything else?"

Rachel pulled a second sheet of A4 from the folder. "Just a few likely characteristics. I believe him to be in the age range thirty-five to fifty-five. And, like I said, it is definitely a male. I mentioned before that he will have used prostitutes in the past, possibly still currently. He may have convictions or cautions for indecent exposure, stalking, making malicious phone calls, voyeurism, theft of underwear from washing lines — that kind of thing. Or at least he will have undertaken these activities, but he may not have been caught or punished for them. He will be a user of pornography and may have indecent images stored on any number of digital devices. He will have tried animal mutilation in the past."

Jack felt an all-too-familiar feeling creep in. *Animal mutilation*. Memories of the Bishop investigation last year reared its ugly head and filled Jack's thoughts.

Rachel continued. "There is the potential for drug use — current or historical." She raised her gaze and locked eyes with Jack. "I understand drug paraphernalia was found in the flat?"

"It was. But local residents say the flat was sometimes used by local gangs — so we can't be sure who it belongs to."

"He will come across as a quiet individual. He will hold down a steady job and he'll be intelligent, maybe even charming on occasion, or at least persuasive. He may well have a controlling personality. Remember, he gets these women to come with him willingly, without a struggle. He will not want to draw attention to himself, so will distance himself from social gatherings. He won't have many, if any, close friends or work colleagues. He is unlikely to be in a relationship and will live alone." Rachel placed the paper down on her desk. "It will come as no real surprise but he is likely to come from a traumatic upbringing, most probably exposed to sex and other forms of physical abuse from a very early age. He may possibly have been abused himself. He will be a car driver and know the city well." Pausing, she looked across the desk and caught Jack's eye. "That's about it for now."

Jack puffed out his cheeks and gave a sigh. "That's more than enough to be getting on with, cheers. Is there any relevance to the third body's location? And the fact that it was hidden in holdalls rather than out on display? It's very different to victim one and two."

Rachel hesitated as a frown ghosted her brow. "I don't think so. On the face of it, it's another risky location — even though the body itself was hidden. You haven't located the murder site for the third body yet?"

Jack shook his head. "No. Not yet. We're pretty sure Lisa and Tara were killed inside the flat in Acorn House, but we're not sure about Cherry."

"The change in location does bother me a little. It's an escalation of risk — I understand the industrial estate was disused, correct?"

Jack nodded. "Ceased operations about seven years ago."

Rachel pursed her lips. "Even so, there was still the risk of being seen. Your offender is escalating, which is the usual pattern for a serial killer."

"So, he's not going to stop?" Jack knew the answer to that one but asked the question anyway.

Rachel's face slackened. "He's a very disturbed individual, Jack. Killing for him is not for pleasure. He isn't satisfying a desire, sexual or otherwise, from these murders. It's a form of punishment — both for the women themselves but also for himself — that is evident from the violence and degradation he exposes his victims to. But it doesn't appear to satisfy him. He hates himself for what he's done, but all it does is fuel his desire for further murders. Like I mentioned before, killing cleanses his conscience, his soul even, but it doesn't last long. He feels the compulsion to kill again very soon after the effects of the previous one have worn off. And I feel it can only escalate. The time between his offences is likely to shorten." She paused and gave a sad smile. "You've got a prolific killer on your hands, Jack. Unless you can stop him."

It wasn't exactly what Jack wanted to hear but wasn't completely unexpected. "Thanks, Rachel." He gave a humourless smile in return. "I think."

"I don't envy you, if it's any consolation." Rachel rose from her desk and handed Jack the manila folder. "Here. Take my notes for now, I'll email across a full profile later on today. I've got a lecture starting in fifteen minutes but I'll get it to you as soon as I can."

Jack pushed himself up and took the folder. "Cheers. I'm sure there's something in here we can use."

"Sorry there's no magic wand, Jack. But you know by now — I can only narrow the pool of suspects for you. I can't give you their name."

Jack nodded. "Extra patrols are out on the streets at night, but I'm not really sure what else we can do. The media are stressing the dangers, but . . ." He shrugged and headed for the door. "These women still go out there."

"People think it will never happen to them." Rachel followed Jack to the door, scooping up her jacket as she went. "Bad things happen to other people, Jack. Never to us."

* * *

Time: 11.10 a.m.
Date: Wednesday 14 January 2015
Location: Central London

DS Cassidy led the way towards the front door to Julian Fisher's flat.

"You've got a keen eye, Trevor, have a good look around when we get inside. Let me know if you see anything that catches your interest."

Daniels nodded, standing by Cassidy's side as she rapped hard on the door. After the third round of knocking, the door swung open and Julian Fisher stood in the doorway, a wary look on his face.

"Yes? Can I help you?"

"I hope so, Mr Fisher. My name is Detective Sergeant Cassidy, and this is my colleague Detective Constable Daniels. May we come in?" Cassidy noticed the wary look on Fisher's face transform into one of confusion — or was it fear? She inched closer, but not quite enough to get a booted foot across the threshold. She kept a pleasant smile on her face. "We're hoping you might be able to help us. You will no doubt have heard about the discoveries over at Acorn House?" She paused, watching the man's face for any sign of recognition. "In fact, it was the flat your father used to live in."

Cassidy stood her ground, waiting to see if the man made any attempt to close the door or bar their entrance. He did neither. Instead, after another moment or two of hesitation, his expression changed and he took a step back, gesturing behind him.

"Of course, yes, come on through."

Cassidy exchanged a brief look with Daniels before the pair of them entered. It was a flat not all that dissimilar to those at Acorn House — a narrow hallway leading to a kitchen at the rear. Two doors led off from the entrance hall, presumably a living room and maybe a bedroom. Both doors were closed.

Fisher led the way through to the kitchen. "I'm happy to help but I'm not sure what I can tell you. I don't know the estate very well. Haven't been there for a while, in fact, not since Dad moved into his care home."

That's your first lie, thought Cassidy as she and Daniels followed him through into the small kitchen. "I understand you used to stay at your father's flat on occasion. How often was that?"

"Oh, not very often at all. Hardly ever, really."

And there's the second one.

Cassidy's smile remained on her lips. A sly glance to the side alerted her to where Daniels's gaze was centred. An expensive looking laptop was open on the kitchen worktop, the page showing a well-known gambling site.

"Like the odd flutter on the horses, do we, Mr Fisher?"

The question seemed to momentarily fluster Fisher, who then stepped forward to close down the laptop screen, his face tensing. "Not really. But not a crime, is it?" An edge of irritation had entered his tone.

"Not at all, Mr Fisher. I like the odd wager on the Grand National myself from time to time." Cassidy let the lie trip off her tongue. She had no interest in gambling, horse racing or otherwise. She decided to change the direction of the questions. "Do you live here alone?"

Fisher gave a curt nod, his face reddening. "Yes, alone. Again, that's not a crime that I'm aware of. Look, I don't mean to be rude but I don't really know what I can help you with — and I should really get back to work. Like I said, I don't really know the estate that well."

"Yes, you did say that. How about the area around The Causeway? Is that somewhere you know well?"

"If you're asking whether I use *prostitutes*, then the answer is no." More colour flooded Fisher's cheeks and Cassidy noted the man's body language shifting. Up to now he had been leaning up against the worktop, relaxed with his hands in his pockets — now he was standing squarely, arms folded across his chest. In addition to the colour filling his cheeks, there was now a defiance entering his eyes.

Cassidy cleared her throat. "That wasn't specifically my question Mr Fisher but thank you for answering it anyway." Out of the corner of her eye she noted Daniels taking a small step to the side. She followed his gaze. In front of them was a washing machine, the door half open, and spilling out was a light-coloured towel with what appeared to be smears of blood. On the worktop above was a bottle of antiseptic.

"Had a slight accident?" Cassidy nodded towards the bloodied towel.

The response came quickly. "Nosebleed."

"And the antiseptic?"

"Cut myself shaving."

Cassidy noted the clean-shaven chin facing her. "When was the last time you were inside Flat 7b?" She watched Fisher's face tighten, his eyes darting to the side refusing to meet her own. She instinctively knew when someone was about to lie to her.

"Like I said, not for a while. Not since Dad moved out."

"And when did your father leave Flat 7b?" They already had this information from Barry Pierce but Cassidy was interested to see if Fisher would choose to lie again. She didn't need to wait long.

"I'm not sure. Sometime last year. I've not been back there since."

"Not to the flat, or not to Acorn House?"

"Both. I have no reason to be there now Dad's in a home."

"Quite." Cassidy again tried to catch Fisher's eye. "What is it that you do, Mr Fisher? For a living, I mean." She noted that the abrupt change in the direction of questioning seemed to momentarily wrong-foot the man. His eyes flickered towards the closed laptop.

Eventually he replied. "Accounting. Financial services."

"You make a good living from that?"

Fisher shrugged, eyes still avoiding Cassidy's. "I get by."

"And do you have an office that you work from, or do you work from home?"

"I work from home." A faint frown began to ghost the man's brow. "Why is this . . . ?"

"Are you a car driver, Mr Fisher?" Cassidy watched the frown deepen.

"I have a car, yes." Wariness now edged Fisher's tone at the sudden change in direction. "Although I don't tend to drive much anymore — it's always quicker by tube or bus."

Cassidy nodded. "Indeed it is. So, where do you keep your car when you're not driving it?"

Further colour clouded Fisher's cheeks. "I use the garage my dad rented when he lived at Acorn House."

Cassidy's eyebrows hitched. "He still has a garage in his name? I would have thought he needed to relinquish that when he moved out?"

Fisher's face darkened further. "Well, they let me pay the rent on it so I still use it. Again, is that a crime?" The words spat from his mouth, a fire entering his gaze.

"I'm sure it's not. How about Tanner Road Industrial Estate? Do you know the area?" Another abrupt change in the direction of questioning made Fisher frown. Cassidy maintained her smile. "It's not that far from here."

The man eventually shrugged. "I've heard of it — most people have. Not been out that way for ages — there's nothing there anymore."

"I think we've finished here for now, Mr Fisher. Thank you for your time." Cassidy started to make a move, then stopped. "Just one more thing before we go. We've been informed that your dad's flat is often used by local gangs — drug use, and the like. Do you know anything about that?"

Fisher's lips thinned, his reply coming in a controlled, measured tone. "Why would I know about that?"

"No reason." Cassidy held on to Fisher's gaze for a second before glancing towards Daniels. "We good to go?" Daniels nodded and began heading towards the hallway. "Thank you, once again, Mr Fisher. We'll see ourselves out."

Once outside the flat, the door safely closed behind them, Cassidy turned to the detective constable as they made their way over to the pool car. "What did we learn in there, Trev?"

"He was very evasive about his work. And he lied to us about never visiting Acorn House after his dad moved out." Daniels paused as Cassidy unlocked the car. "*And* I have a feeling he's got a gambling problem."

Cassidy grinned as she pulled open the driver's door. "We'll make a detective out of you yet!"

Once inside, Daniels continued. "What did you make of the bloodied towel? And the antiseptic?"

Cassidy frowned as she started the engine. "There wasn't a great deal of blood on it — certainly not enough to suggest it had anything to do with the murders. You saw the crime scene photos for yourself, it was a bloodbath. But . . ." In the end, she shrugged and reversed out of the parking space. "He could have been telling the truth I suppose — about the nosebleed, and cutting himself shaving."

"He has access to a garage. If we're thinking our killer needs somewhere to kill or keep his victims, we could be looking at a garage or lock-up somewhere?"

Cassidy glanced at the dashboard clock. "Let's head back to the station. The guv should be back soon. We'll see what he thinks to us following up on the garage."

* * *

Time: 11.20 a.m.
Date: Wednesday 14 January 2015
Location: Central London

How the police had tracked him down, Julian wasn't quite sure. Someone on the estate had to have blabbed — and his money was on that waste of space caretaker. He may have turned a blind eye to Julian's comings and goings, and helped him keep the garage on after his dad had moved out, but he didn't like the man, even less trust him.

When he was sure the detective had gone, he went to the bedroom and pulled out a holdall from under the bed. He needed somewhere else to store it; here was too risky. But should he take it back to the garage? The police had lured him into the trap of admitting he had access to it — he couldn't believe he'd allowed himself to be tripped up like that, so easily too. Would they find out where it was and pay it a visit?

The thought unnerved him.

It would have to be the house — there was no alternative.

Part of him was glad he hadn't had to sell it to fund his father's care home fees. There was at least some advantage of working in the financial sector; you knew where the loopholes were. The council didn't know about the house — he'd transferred it into a fictitious company name so Dad could get the flat on the Hillside Estate — and now Dad was getting his care fully funded by the taxpayer, while the house sat empty, gathering dust — and grime, knowing his father.

The house.

Although it wasn't far away, still in central London, he didn't go there very often. He couldn't stand it — the mess, the smell, the flies. He could have paid for a house clearance, completely gut the place and fumigate it, but he didn't have that kind of cash lying around. So, instead, he left it to rot. But it had its uses — it was at least good for somewhere to hide things.

Swinging the holdall up on to his shoulder, he grimaced. Back to the house it was, then.

* * *

Time: 11.20 a.m.
Date: Wednesday 14 January 2015
Location: St James's University, London

"You've been avoiding me, Jack."

Jack swung around to see Dr Evelyn Riches heading in his direction, a coy smile on her face.

"I wouldn't go so far as to say that," he responded, eyes darting back to Rachel Hunter's closed office door. Although he had failed to return several of Dr Riches' calls in recent times, he wasn't sure that he was actively avoiding her. Was he? Fleetingly, he wondered if the two women had been in cahoots about the elusive detective inspector's appearance in the building.

The psychologist walked beside him as they continued along the corridor. "My office is just along here if you remember? We could have a catch-up if you have a spare five minutes?"

By now they had reached the stairs that would take them to the ground floor — and the exit. Jack hesitated, but knew he couldn't really keep putting it off. "Of course," he eventually replied, placing a suitably pleasant smile on his face. "Nothing I'd like more."

165

Although it had been some time since he'd set foot inside Dr Riches' consulting rooms at the university, nothing much had changed. The same panoramic view of the university campus stretched out before him from the window. The same heavy grey skies he'd seen from Dr Hunter's window only minutes before were hanging low over the capital that morning, the sleet now slamming against the pane.

Memories twitched as he noticed the walls still housed an assortment of motivational quotes.

> *Difficult roads lead to beautiful destinations.*
> *Don't wait for opportunity. Create it.*
> *Don't try to be perfect. Just try to be better*
> *than you were yesterday.*
> *The pain you feel today is the strength*
> *you will feel tomorrow.*

Dr Riches slid behind her neat and well-ordered desk, moving a thin folder to the side and out of sight. "So, how have you been, Jack? It's been a while since we last spoke."

Jack turned towards the low-rise coffee table and seating area, then lowered himself into one of the familiar chairs by the window. He considered giving his usual response — 'fine' — but was well aware the psychologist was no fool. Instead, he went with, "Oh, you know."

Dr Riches paused momentarily before nodding slowly. "I heard about that incident at your home last year." She gestured towards Jack's shoulder. "How is it now? Healing well, I hope?"

Jack instinctively flexed his arm and gave the shoulder a rub. Six months may have passed since his shoulder took a glancing shot from James Quinn's gun, but it still gave him trouble from time to time — especially in the cold weather. "More or less," he eventually replied. "Only the occasional bit of stiffness now and again. Nothing that bothers me too much." He knew he could lie along with the best of them — he'd had enough practice, after all.

Dr Riches appeared to swallow the lie and returned the smile. "That's good to hear. And your brother? He suffered some nasty burns."

"Stu's doing really well, thank you. All his surgery has been completed now. He's even back at work."

"And I hear he got married, too?"

Jack nodded. "I know — there's hope for us all, eh?"

"Oh, I wouldn't cast yourself out on the scrap-heap just yet, Jack." The coy smile returned. "Never say never."

Jack settled back into the comfort of the cushions behind him, his gaze narrowing. "Why don't you just come out and say it — we both know why I'm here."

Dr Riches' cheeks pinked a little. "Well, I don't know that . . ."

Jack tried to smother the emerging laugh but failed. "It's OK. I don't mind. Yes, in answer to your *real* question. Yes, I'm still having the dreams — nightmares if you want to call them that — but no, they're not as intrusive as they used to be. I'm handling them much better."

"That's good to hear, Jack. I'm glad." Relief flooded the psychologist's tone.

"And in answer to your *next* question — no, I've no desire for you to put me back under hypnosis."

Dr Riches' cheeks pinked even further. "Am I that transparent?"

Jack grinned. "Totally. But I'm at peace with that part of my life now." It wasn't entirely true but he felt the lie was justified. Dr Riches certainly didn't need to be dragged into whatever shit show he might be heading for.

The psychologist's expression told Jack she didn't necessarily believe him, but she gave a slight incline of the head to show acceptance. It was as good as he was likely to get. "Again — that's good to hear," she replied, simply. "You know I'm still more than happy to see you — if you feel you need any further help with the nightmares. We could do some more cognitive therapy, perhaps some more coping mechanisms."

Jack held up his hands. "That's very kind of you but, no — I'm good."

Dr Riches sat back in her chair and studied Jack from across her desk. "So, how do you cope with them? You said they were less intrusive and that you were handling them better. What techniques are you using?"

Jack faltered, his gaze switching across the room to the multitude of posters advertising any variety of self-help therapy techniques. "Oh, you know — the works. Healthy eating. Lots of fresh air and exercise. Meditation. And what was that other one?" Jack made a play at trying to recall. "Ah yes, mindfulness."

Dr Riches' smile broadened, her eyes twinkling. "My my — you have taken everything on board, haven't you?"

Jack stifled a smile. He knew he looked crumpled and more than a little dishevelled. He hadn't shaved for at least three days if not longer; his hair needed a trim, and his skin probably showed he hadn't been exposed to that much fresh air or exercise in the recent past. And as for his diet? He was sure Dr Riches could see past his vain attempts at pulling the wool over her eyes — she was as sharp as they came. So sharp she could probably see the stacks of takeaway cartons piled into his recycling bin at the flat, maybe even smell last night's biryani on his clothes. He tried to give himself a discreet sniff but couldn't quite get past the warm scent of vanilla coming from the air fresheners.

"And the alcohol?" Dr Riches' eyes continued to dance.

"Never touch a drop, doctor." After a second or two, Jack saw the brightness in the psychologist's eyes dim a little, the humour replaced by concern.

"You do know I'm here for you, don't you, Jack? If you need anything — anything at all."

Jack nodded and pushed himself up from the chair. "I know. And it's much appreciated — it really is. But I really need to be getting back to the station. This current investigation is keeping us busy."

Right on cue, Jack's phone trilled. Glancing down at the screen, a frown darkened his brow. He'd been half expecting it to be Penny again, wondering why he hadn't appeared yet, but was surprised to see a different name flash up.

CHAPTER SEVENTEEN

Time: 12.00 p.m.
Date: Wednesday 14 January 2015
Location: Metropolitan Police HQ, London

"It's her. Cherry Eyres." Jonathan Spearing thrust the newspaper towards Jack.

Jack took hold of the copy of the *Daily Express*, scanning the front-page headline.

BODY IN BAGS VICTIM NAMED

He frowned, passing the paper back. "I know it is. We released the name to the media. Look, I'm really busy here — I need to get back." He turned to go, heading for the door to the ground floor interview room where Spearing had been temporarily housed awaiting Jack's return from the university.

"No, I mean I knew her. Well, I'd met her anyway."

Jack's hand hovered above the door handle. "What do you mean you'd met her?" He swivelled around, and after a slight pause he raised his eyebrows. "Oh, you mean you . . . ?"

"No, no, no — nothing like that." Colour flushed Spearing's cheeks. "I mean I spoke to her. Interviewed her, actually. Only a short time ago, as it happens."

Jack's interest was piqued and he edged back towards the newspaper reporter. "Can you be more specific? When was the last time you saw her?"

Spearing thrust a hand into his trouser pocket. "It's all on here." He waved a memory stick in the air. "I recorded the interview — it's all date stamped. I was about to start writing it up today when I . . ." He glanced back down at the newspaper in his hand. "When I saw this."

It took Jack less than five minutes to find a spare laptop. Spearing inserted the memory stick into the USB port and a minute later brought up the interview file.

"I met her on Saturday night. I'd been working on an article about how prostitution has evolved over the years, and how the risks and dangers have changed since the days of the Ripper. And the attitude of the police, too."

"I think the current risks and dangers are pretty bloody obvious," muttered Jack, watching the video file load.

"Quite." Spearing angled the laptop screen towards them. "She agreed to speak with me, so we met in a café on Manchester Road. She was quite candid about life on the streets. She was well aware of the risks — but for her there was no other way. To be honest, from what she told me they seemed to have a good routine going — her and the other girls in that particular area. They all looked out for each other."

"Well, clearly not quite well enough."

Spearing let the video of his interview with Cherry Eyres play in full. As the minutes ticked by, Jack's heart sank further as he listened to the woman describing life working the streets.

'We all look out for each other. If we have a funny feeling about someone, we let each other know. We take down descriptions, car registration numbers. We keep a log of who is safe, and who to avoid.'

The more Jack listened, the more his sense of disquiet grew. Such a waste of a life. Cherry was young, articulate, intelligent. She should have had her whole life ahead of her, not destined to end up cut to pieces and stuffed into a holdall inside a rusting fridge. A life cut short so unnecessarily — and so barbarically.

Somewhere towards the end of the fifteen-minute recording, Jack heard some of the most chilling words he had ever encountered during his career. And they were words that came straight from Jonathan Spearing's mouth.

'Don't you worry about who might be out there? It's well documented — cases of prostitutes being targets for violence, or worse. You only have to think of the Ripper.'

Jack watched Cherry Eyre's response. It was only slight, but he saw a flicker of what might be doubt, or even maybe fear, cross her pale complexion, but it soon vanished.

'I'll be fine,' was her eventual response.

'But you shouldn't be out here,' Spearing had persisted. *'It's not safe. It's not safe for any of you. You can't keep putting yourself in danger like this.'*

'I have to. There's no other way.'

Jack reached forward and froze the screen with Cherry's face in the centre.

I have to.

There's no other way.

By all accounts, she did go out that night, and that decision was to be her last — a decision that cost her her life. From what they knew so far, Cherry could very well have been abducted only hours later. Shocking didn't even come close.

"This is what I find so hard to comprehend. She knew the risks and she was acutely aware of the dangers, but . . ." Spearing just shrugged. "She still did it. I'm not sure what that says about her — or us as a society."

"Can I have a copy of this?" Jack gestured towards the screen.

Spearing nodded. "Of course. You can have this one." He handed Jack the memory stick.

Snapping the laptop shut, Jack tucked it beneath his arm. "I'll show you out." Spearing followed him obediently to the door. "And thanks, for this." He waved the memory stick in the air.

"No problem."

Jack eyed the newspaper reporter as he pulled open the door. There was something strange in the man's eyes, something he couldn't quite read. When they'd first sat down in the interview room, Jack had asked after Katarina — feeling that somehow he should. Spearing had merely said that she was doing well — considering. She'd been offered counselling but had so far refused to take up the offer. After a couple more minutes of strained small talk, they had got down to business. Jack couldn't be sure but he sensed there was something else on the crime correspondent's mind — something that went beyond Katarina and beyond the contents of the memory stick.

But right now he had more important things to worry about.

One of which was avoiding Dougie King.

* * *

Time: 12.15 p.m.
Date: Wednesday 14 January 2015
Location: Central London

He knew Tanya had seen the other woman. She'd tried to pretend to be asleep, or at least unconscious, but he'd known.

He always knew.

Sometimes he wondered if he knew them better than they knew themselves.

On arriving back at the house, he'd pulled the rest of the woman's body through to the kitchen, bit by bit, but Tanya hadn't even flinched. She was a tough one, that Tanya — maybe the toughest he'd had in a while. The thought excited him as he pulled the holdall open and rummaged for the meat cleaver. He hadn't decided how he was going to kill Tanya, which was probably why he hadn't done it yet. She was different to the others and needed more careful thought. There was even a part of him that wondered if he should find her a playmate; they could keep each other company and entertain him while he decided what to do with them. It could be fun.

A cruel smile tugged at the corners of his mouth as he grabbed the cleaver and turned back to the body lying draped on the dirty linoleum floor. The woman's head was already sitting on the draining board, blood congealing around its base, and he now had to deal with the rest of her. But he knew exactly where she was going to go.

As much as he wanted Tanya to witness the process, to see the fear in her eyes as he witnessed her own destiny, there wasn't enough space in the living room. His father had been a hoarder — that was plain for anyone to see — and almost every inch of floor space was covered in some rubbish or other. He was content to let it fester for now, having no intention of turning the place around; he had no plans to live here. Maybe, when he was finished, he would just take a match to it — and then watch it disappearing into a ball of flames, taking his memories of his father with it.

He felt his nostrils flare. He should really stop calling the man his father — he was no father to him, either in name or bloodline.

Wielding the meat cleaver above his head he began to hack at the woman's limbs. The thudding sound the blade made as it came into contact with human flesh settling his nerves. With each stroke he felt his contentment swell. At last, all was right with the world.

And when he was finished, he would wake Tanya up and have some fun.

* * *

Time: 12.20 p.m.
Date: Wednesday 14 January 2015
Location: Westminster Mortuary, London

Dr Philip Matthews reached for the desk phone then changed his mind, hand hovering over the handset. The case was getting to him. Even after several decades' experience under his belt, the case was still getting to him. He'd promised Jack the post-mortem on the body found in the bags would be completed by the end of the day, a promise he had fulfilled — but it gave him no sense of satisfaction. He couldn't recall another case that unnerved him quite like this one had.

There were undoubtedly cases that stayed with him over the years, even haunted him sometimes. But he always managed to put them to one side, leaving his thoughts at the mortuary door before heading home to his wife; it was the only way. But this one — this one was different.

The draft post-mortem report rested on the desk, several areas highlighted in red pen. The pathologist rubbed his chin before his hand strayed towards the phone once more. Jack would want to know the findings as soon as possible, and despite being rushed off his feet he knew the detective inspector would take the call. They hadn't spoken since the trip to the Hanged Man last night, and he knew it wasn't a topic Jack would want to revisit anytime soon. When he'd taken the call, he hadn't asked too many questions — he knew the detective must be cornered and have no one else to call upon for help. Quite *why* he was cornered, Dr Matthews wasn't about to ask. Some things in Jack's world were often best left unsaid.

Do no harm.

It was one of the first things any prospective medical student hears when they embark on their career. If they hadn't stepped in last night, the young lad would have died within the hour — two if he was particularly unlucky. And if by some miracle the blood loss hadn't sent his body into shock and caused his organs to fail, then he would have succumbed to infection not too long afterwards. So there really had been no decision to make in the end.

Do no harm.

Dr Matthews turned his attention back to the report and sighed. The woman had been in perfect health from what he could gather from the remains that had been rather unceremoniously stuffed inside the two holdalls. The internal organs hadn't shown any acute or chronic conditions — apart from the obvious mutilation. The cause of death had been tricky — but the skull fracture and underlying haemorrhage he discovered would have been more than enough to kill her. It bore remarkable similarities to the injuries sustained by the second victim, so the killer was at least trying to be consistent.

And then there was the dismemberment.

Dr Matthews wasn't ordinarily a betting man, but he would put money on this poor woman's limbs being severed after death — and he hoped to God that he was right. There were no obvious signs of strangulation, unlike the first victim he examined, but there were several defence wounds visible on both forearms. Maybe this one had a chance to fight back.

The pathologist couldn't begin to imagine the terror that must have gone through the woman's mind, and contrary to his usual calm exterior, he felt a small shiver ripple. Pulling the report closer, he swept his gaze over the photographs attached to the end. Once more the victim's internal organs had been removed from her body and mutilated. He had managed to reconstruct the body parts on the examination table in a macabre kind of jigsaw puzzle and everything was accounted for — which at least meant the killer hadn't chosen to take away a souvenir of his deed — which was something.

The main concentration of mutilation was once again in the uterus. Long gouges made with a sharp instrument were easily identifiable. The organ itself was almost reduced to shreds. Further examination confirmed that the kidneys, liver and lungs all had similar marks, but the uterus had been subject to the most frenzied attack.

Picking up the desk phone, he punched in Jack's number and hoped the detective inspector hadn't eaten yet.

CHAPTER EIGHTEEN

Time: 12.55 p.m.
Date: Wednesday 14 January 2015
Location: Metropolitan Police HQ, London

Jack rubbed his eyes and leaned back in his chair. He'd managed to slip back into the station undetected, heading straight for the protection of his office. Dougie King was on the warpath and Jack needed to steel himself before he got another dressing down.

The call from Dr Matthews had done nothing to settle the growing sense of disquiet that was languishing in the pit of his stomach. The case was beginning to run away from him, no matter how hard he tried to keep a grip on it. Cherry Eyres had seemed to have met her death in a similar way to Tara Coe, but the knowledge didn't offer Jack much comfort.

As the pathologist took him through the examination, detailing once again the frenzied mutilation of the internal organs, Jack was thankful the update was verbal and no graphic images accompanied it. The vision of both Lisa and Tara's remains still lodged in his head, refusing to budge. He had a feeling they never would. Once seen, things like that could never be unseen.

On his way to the office, Jack had popped his head into the incident room and Cooper had given him an update on the lab reports and the CCTV findings. It came as no real surprise that Tara's blood was that which was located in the bathroom of Acorn House — but seeing Barry Pierce's car in the vicinity of The Causeway only moments before the last sightings of Lisa and Tara put a new spin on things.

There was something about Barry Pierce that Jack didn't trust and he was now firmly at the top of the suspect list. Jack immediately ordered Cooper to add the finding to the search warrant request. Cassidy and Daniels had shown up not long after Jack arrived, and filled him in on their chat with Julian Fisher and he quickly become another person that piqued his interest.

But who was he most concerned about? Barry Pierce or Julian Fisher?

Jack closed his eyes and willed the emerging headache to abate. He was out of painkillers and feeling grumpy. The lab reports hadn't moved things forward by much. The sheer volume of fingerprints and DNA profiles, partial or otherwise, lifted from Acorn House meant it would be an unenviable task to try and wade through the dross and find that golden nugget; if there even was one to find. The world and his wife had been inside that flat.

Dragging his eyes back open, Jack surveyed his desk. It didn't look as bad as he'd expected, only a couple of extra files had materialised during his absence. Moving them to the side, he noticed the phone message Cassidy had taken down earlier was lying beneath his coffee mug. Pulling it out, he tilted it towards himself, noting the name at the top.

Just as he did so, his mobile rang.

Jack hit the accept button. "Sully? That's uncanny. I was just looking at the phone message you left."

Adam Sullivan gave a chuckle on the other end of the line. "Uncanny, indeed. It must be a sign."

"You rang the hotline number — you have some more information on our victims for us?"

"I'm not sure — you probably already know most of it anyway. But myself and my colleagues really want to try and help if we can."

Jack let the note fall back on the desk. "Anything you can tell us would be gratefully received."

"I gave the bare bones to the call handler when I rang in, but if you fancy a more in-depth chat, maybe the pub later?"

Jack eyed the time on his Fitbit. "Sure. I've got a few things to finish up here this afternoon, and then I'm seeing my brother. How about we meet you in the Duke later?"

After exchanging a few more pleasantries, and the dentist enquiring about the state of Jack's busted lip and teeth, Jack hung up. A pint sounded good right now. Maybe more than one.

If his mood had brightened a little after Adam Sullivan's call, the next one shot it down in flames.

* * *

Time: 1.30 p.m.
Date: Wednesday 14 January 2015
Location: The Angel Café, London

Zara McKenna pulled a copy of the *Daily Express* towards her. The café was warm, which was why she had spent the last hour nursing a mug of tea that had now gone cold. She always sat in the same seat; in the corner, out of the way. The café manager, Sally, was kind to her, and would usually let her stay as long as she wanted so long as it wasn't busy. And anywhere was better than Zara's poky bedsit with its ill-fitting windows and leaking radiators.

Sally O'Brian sidled past, a large, almost industrial-sized, chrome tea urn in her hand. Silently, she tipped another cup full of hot liquid into Zara's mug, leaving a couple of plastic UHT milk pots on the table, and then returned to the counter to serve a customer.

Zara liked Sally. Sometimes she even gave her a free toasted sandwich, or a toasted teacake, as well as the top-ups of tea or coffee. Pulling her parka jacket closer around her, Zara placed both hands around the warming mug. The café was full of enticing aromas which made her stomach growl. The Angel Café was famous for its all-day breakfasts and was a popular haunt for taxi drivers and night shift workers. But Zara mostly liked it because she could blend into the background in here — she could be invisible. No one took much notice of her, tucked away in the corner, which was just the way she liked it.

Although ravenous, her stomach rumbling once more as another plate of eggs and bacon found its way to a hungry customer, Zara's appetite had waned once she'd read the newspaper headlines.

BODY IN BAG VICTIM NAMED

Cherry Eyres.
Zara had known Cherry by sight, but was ashamed to admit that she hadn't noticed the woman was missing. The article said she was last seen on Saturday night — had Zara seen her then? She wasn't sure. She hadn't seen her since but she wasn't exactly looking out for her. How bad did that sound? Were people that easy to forget? Would anyone notice if *she* went missing?

Zara shuddered and took a mouthful of her fresh tea, grateful for the warmth, but her eyes strayed back to the newspaper headlines. At twenty-three, Zara knew she was young to be out on the streets, and she felt especially young today. And vulnerable. And scared.

Thinking about Cherry soon made Zara think about Tanya. They were meant to meet here at lunchtime but Tanya hadn't showed. Zara had given it half an hour before she sent her a message — which had gone unanswered. Then she had tried to call her — but the phone went straight to voicemail.

It was most unlike Tanya not to have her phone switched on — it was *never* switched off.

Zara bit the inside of her cheek, mind racing. She knew she was being silly — Tanya may just have forgotten about their arrangement, and the battery on her phone had died.

Maybe.

Zara took another gulp of tea, willing her disquiet to settle. But she just couldn't shake the feeling that something bad had happened.

Just like it had to Cherry.

* * *

Time: 1.30 p.m.
Date: Wednesday 14 January 2015
Location: Metropolitan Police HQ, London

"I can explain." Jack shifted uneasily in his seat and ran a finger along the inside of his shirt collar, feeling the dampness.

As soon as he sat down, he'd got the distinct impression that he was in trouble — and not just the usual trouble that seemed to follow him around like a bad smell. This was different.

And he wasn't wrong.

"I think that would be a very good idea, Jack." Chief Superintendent Dougie King eyed him from across the desk. "And right now, if you would be so kind."

"It's not what it looks like." Jack gestured towards the laptop Dougie King had placed on top of a small pile of folders in front of them. The image frozen in the centre was clear for all to see — despite its poor, grainy quality Jack recognised himself immediately.

"Well, I sure as hell hope it *isn't* what it looks like, Jack, for your sake as much as mine. Because from where I'm sitting it looks as though you are handing money over to a known sex worker." King let an exasperated sigh escape his lips. "Just what the hell have you been up to now?"

Jack took in the image once again. There was no other option; he would have to tell the truth. He could try and dress it up into something it wasn't, try and front it out — but he knew well enough by now that Dougie King wasn't a fool.

"The woman's name is Kim. She works that part of the city on most weekday evenings." Jack paused, feeling yet more sweat accumulate beneath his shirt. The chief superintendent's office felt warmer than usual, despite the freezing temperatures outside, and he could almost visualise the beads of perspiration popping up on his forehead as the silence lengthened. It wasn't a good look; he knew that much.

He looked guilty.

Hell, he *felt* guilty.

Dougie King's eyes flickered back to the laptop and the grainy images that now sprang back into life as he hit the 'enter' button on the keyboard.

"OK — so now you need to explain to me why a senior officer — a detective inspector, no less — is seen blatantly giving her money."

"Which isn't yet a crime." The words escaped Jack's mouth before his brain had a chance to stop them.

A thunderous look exploded across the chief superintendent's face. "I don't need you to instruct me on the law, Jack! This isn't about committing a crime — this is about what the press will do with this footage when they get their hands on it. Because you know they will." Dougie King paused, regaining some sort of composure before continuing. "I need to know what you've been up to, Jack. All of it."

* * *

Time: 10.45 p.m.
Date: Monday 12 January 2015
Location: The Causeway, London

Jack pulled the Mondeo to a stop around the corner from Colville Avenue. It was nearly eleven o'clock and the place was already bathed in darkness, the temperature was dropping fast. But despite the freeze, he knew she would be there.

She was *always* there.

Pulling the collar up on his jacket, he stepped out of the car and began walking towards the corner where The Causeway met Colville Avenue. Instinctively, he glanced around as he walked. The street looked deserted, as it usually was at this time of night — and there were very few properties that overlooked it. But he checked anyway — old habits die hard.

Thrusting his hands into his pockets to combat the chill, he quickened his stride. He didn't want to be out any longer than he needed to be, not in this part of the city. Not out here, anyway. He'd left the investigation papers strewn across the coffee table back at the flat, and he still had several hours work ahead of him before he'd call it a night.

But he needed to do this.

He *always* needed to do this.

It was like a compulsion; something he had no control over.

Turning the corner, he scoured the length of the street ahead and immediately saw two figures hovering close to the kerb.

He headed in their direction.

* * *

Time: 1.35 p.m.
Date: Wednesday 14 January 2015
Location: Metropolitan Police HQ, London

"Who gave it to you?"

"Never mind who gave it to me, Jack. That's rather immaterial, don't you think? This is just one street away from where two of your murder victims were last seen. Did you not stop to *think*, Jack? Even for a second?"

"I didn't know I was being watched." Jack's gaze slid towards the laptop — and the memory stick attached. Instinctively, his hand slid into his pocket and wrapped itself around the same type of memory stick he'd placed in there earlier. It was an unusual brand — not one Jack had seen before. His grip tightened inside his pocket. What were the chances of two turning up at the same time?

He recalled the curious smirk on Jonathan Spearing's face as the reporter handed over the recording of his interview with Cherry Eyres. Any thought that the hostilities between the two of them had been temporarily disabled disappeared in an instant. Once a snake, always a snake.

"Do you really want this to get out into the public domain, Jack?" Dougie King's thundering voice cut into Jack's thoughts. "Because you know it will — it will unless I can shut it down first. And I can only do that if you start being honest with me. What the hell were you doing?"

Jack stared down at his crumpled suit trousers and sighed. "OK, I'll tell you. When I get the chance, which isn't often I might add, I go out to the streets around Soho. Other times it's around King's Cross."

"You have a penchant for red-light districts, Jack?"

Jack heard the iciness in Dougie King's tone. He raised his gaze and gave the senior officer a withering look while shaking his head. "I just talk to them."

"Talk?" The chief superintendent's expression suggested he found that hard to believe. "And talking costs money, does it?" He inclined his head towards the footage still playing on the laptop.

"Yes," repeated Jack, finding an edge to his own voice. "We talk. If they need anything, I try and give it to them. Food sometimes. Medicines. Whatever they need." Jack paused again, the dampness beneath his collar intensifying. "Most of the time I just give them money."

Dougie King's bushy eyebrows continued to rise. "You're admitting giving known sex workers money? *Cash*? And that's supposed to reassure me that this *isn't* what it looks like?"

"But it isn't!" The edge to Jack's tone sharpened. "It *really* isn't. All I want to do is help. And I do it because . . ." He flashed a hot look up across the desk. "If you must know I do it because of my *mother*."

It was then that Jack knew a full explanation had to follow. He was lucky Dougie King hadn't suspended him on the spot the minute he'd seen the footage, and knew the man deserved the truth. And he deserved it now. The man had had his back plenty of times in the past, now it was Jack's turn to return the favour.

"My mother was a sex worker — back when Stuart and I were little. Probably before we were born, too. It was when we lived back at the Old Mill Road flat in Christchurch. I can remember it vividly. She would leave us alone overnight in the flat, while she went out to work. It wasn't great, we all know that now, but back then?" Jack shrugged. "What else could she do? This was the seventies. She was on her own raising two small kids. You know as well as I do, sir, that once a pimp gets his claws into you, there's very little you can do." Jack stabbed a finger towards the laptop screen. "You think they want to be doing this? Night after night? You think they want to be risking their lives just to earn enough money to survive?" Leaning back in his chair, he sighed. His head was throbbing again. So was his shoulder. He really didn't need a grilling on top of everything.

"I just do what I can to help. Shit, I don't even know if it *does* help. I can't offer them a way out — but I can try and make sure that they're OK. That they're safe. As much as I can anyway. I give them money, direct them to other services — things like the Welfare Truck." Another shrug. "I just feel like I have to be doing something."

"That's very philanthropic of you, Jack." Dougie King's tone lowered a notch, but the exasperation remained. "But you can see what it looks like . . ."

"I *know* what it looks like, sir," bristled Jack. "But there was a part of me that also wondered if Kim might know something, something that might help us with the investigation."

"And did she?"

Jack gave a slow shake of the head. "No, she didn't. But I can assure you, everything was above board. Nothing shady went on."

The chief superintendent mirrored Jack's earlier sigh, slumping back in his chair. "I don't doubt it, Jack, really I don't. But I will admit that, just for a second or two, I wondered what it was that I was watching. I understand your reasoning, but it's just not all that wise, is it? Not when you've got three dead women on your hands a stone's throw away from where you're seen to be entertaining sex workers."

Jack ignored the jibe. "Who gave it to you?" He nodded again towards the laptop. "Who gave you the recording?"

Dougie King gave another sigh. "I don't know. It was delivered by hand, anonymously. But that's not really important, Jack. What *is* important is trying to stop it leaking to the press." The look on the senior officer's face told Jack that was unlikely. "I'll do what I can — but I can't promise this will disappear."

Jack nodded.

The chief superintendent reached for his coffee cup, the contents now tepid at best. "Putting this to the side for a moment, fill me in on the investigation. Any updates I need to be aware of?"

Jack welcomed the change in direction of questioning. "We've interviewed the caretaker for the block — there's just something about him that niggles me, and he's lied to us when questioned. He remains on our radar and we're applying for a search warrant to revisit his flat. Daniels and Amanda have followed up another person of interest. He had access to the flat where the first two victims were found, and seemed very cagey when he was questioned. He also has access to a lock-up or garage. Other than that, we're at a bit of a stalemate."

"I see." Dougie King pushed the unwanted coffee to the side and leaned forward on his desk, fixing Jack with a tired look. "I'll try to make this go away, Jack." He gestured towards the laptop. "As best I can, anyway. But you know as well as I do that these things have a habit of surfacing no matter how deep you bury them. I'll do what I can for now, but there are no promises. And as soon as it does, I'll need to pull you from the investigation, is that clear?"

"Sir, I . . ." Jack's response was cut short.

"Is that clear?"

Jack gave a half-hearted nod.

"Have you told the rest of your team?"

"Not yet."

"Then I advise you do just that. Don't keep them in the dark."

Jack got to his feet, dismissed. "I will do, sir."

"And maybe no more late-night excursions for a while, eh? No matter how good your intentions."

CHAPTER NINETEEN

Time: 2.30 p.m.
Date: Wednesday 14 January 2015
Location: Acorn House, Hillside Estate, London

"I'm going to start dreaming about this bloody place, Cooper."
Jack slammed the door of the Mondeo and headed towards
Acorn House. The crime scene investigators had now vacated
the area — leaving behind the odd scrap of police tape as the
only evidence they'd been there. Jack scoured the area for the
gang of BMX youths that had taken a shine to the Mondeo
previously, but the car park was deserted; excitement over for
the time being.

With this being the sixth time he'd visited in the last
three days, Jack's dislike for the rundown tower block was
growing by the second. He was still smarting from his run-in
with Dougie King. Although the chief superintendent hadn't
dragged him over hot coals like he probably should have, Jack
still felt hard done by. All he ever did was try to help.

"You think he'll let us in, boss?" Cooper jogged to catch
up. "He wisnae too happy to see us the last time."

Jack grimaced and tried to put Dougie King and the
video recording out of his mind — at least for now. He'd

been tempted to call Spearing and give the reporter a piece of his mind but knew that was only likely to add more fuel to the, what could end up being, very large fire. He pulled open the communal door, letting Cooper step through ahead of him.

"Well I doubt he'll have the red carpet out for us, but I don't particularly care if he's happy or not. *This* means I can enter with or without his permission." Jack waved the search warrant in the air. He'd been pleased, if not a little surprised, that the warrant had been authorised at the first time of asking. But if Barry Pierce was their man then the stakes were just about as high as they could ever be — this killer wasn't going to stop until he was caught.

Negotiating their way along the passageway that led to Pierce's ground floor flat, Jack noted yet more abandoned and rusting junk had accumulated in the interim. "Watch your step, Cooper," he muttered, narrowly missing tripping over a garden rake. Why there were gardening tools and lawnmowers strewn about when the estate had zero green spaces, Jack couldn't quite fathom. But the landscaping of the Hillside Estate wasn't his concern right now.

Arriving once more at the caretaker's door, he gave it three hard knocks. Like the first time, silence was all they got in return. After two more rounds of knocking, each one louder than the one before, Jack's already evaporating patience grew thinner. "You thinking what I'm thinking?"

Cooper nodded. "Maybe our earlier visit spooked him?"

Jack eyed the door more closely. It didn't look particularly sturdy from the outside, but the twinge from his shoulder reminded him that even a flimsy door could be painful. "You fancy doing the honours, Cooper?" Jack nodded down towards the detective sergeant's boots. "You've got the shoes for it."

Grinning, Cooper took a step back and gave the door a resounding kick.

* * *

190

Time: 2.30 p.m.
Date: Wednesday 14 January 2015
Location: The Angel Café, London

Once the café had quietened down, Sally had slipped Zara a round of hot buttered toast and a bowl of winter vegetable soup. Zara had smiled, gratefully, although her stomach was still too tied up in knots to eat much. She had tried Tanya's mobile again — nothing. She also logged into her social media accounts, but noted Tanya had last been active early on Tuesday evening. Nothing since. That was almost twenty-four hours ago. Twenty-four hours of nothing.

Again, Zara's eyes shifted towards the newspaper headlines. Surely it was too early to call the police? What would she tell them, anyway? She would feel like such a fool if Tanya was just having a duvet day at home and escaping from the world. Zara felt like that sometimes — wanting to escape from the world.

Picking up one of the pieces of toast, Zara dipped it into the thick soup. She flashed another appreciative smile across the café to where Sally was wiping down some of the tables. She felt better once the food hit her stomach, and quickly polished off the rest of the bowl. She hadn't realised how hungry she was.

Getting to her feet, she slipped her phone back in her pocket and folded the newspaper away. She would go and check on Tanya at home. Maybe she was ill and Zara could go and get her some paracetamol or something.

Feeling better for having a plan, Zara made her way outside.

* * *

Time: 2.35 p.m.
Date: Wednesday 14 January 2015
Location: Ground floor flat, Acorn House, Hillside Estate, London

With the door frame splintered, Jack stepped across the threshold. He had very little doubt that Barry Pierce would be long gone by now, but announced their presence anyway. "Mr Pierce. This is the Metropolitan Police. We've a search warrant for these premises. Make yourself known."

Silence.

"Let's start in here, Cooper." Jack gestured towards the first door on their right — one of the two that had been closed on their previous visit. They stepped into a compact room that looked to have been turned into a study. A battered-looking wooden desk sat against one wall, several racks of shelving behind it.

But it wasn't the desk or the shelving that caught both detectives' attention.

It was the walls.

Pierce had tried to explain away the call-girl cards pinned to the board in his kitchen, and if Jack had suspected the man was lying then, he was certain of it now. Tens if not hundreds of similar themed cards were stuck to every wall, so many it was impossible to count. Some were frayed at the edges, others looked brand new. They ranged from escort services, to brothels, massage parlours to telephone chat lines.

So much for *'those cards are old — I haven't used them in a long time'.*

"Let's take a look around before we decide to bring forensics in." Jack moved towards the desk where a selection of carefully cut-out newspaper articles had been pinned to the wall above. In the centre were the salacious headlines from the tabloids reporting on the murders of Lisa Wood, Tara Coe and Cherry Eyres.

'Hunt for sadistic city killer.'
'Crazed killer on the streets of London.'
'Streets unsafe for women.'

Images of all three victims stared out at them, similar to those on the cork pinboard back in the incident room. But what Jack found even more sinister were the yellowing newspaper articles from the 1970s charting the hunt for the Yorkshire Ripper.

Jack fished around in his pocket for some protective gloves, throwing a pair in Cooper's direction.

"Put these on, Cooper — I've a feeling we're going to need them."

Jack hadn't known what to expect from the search of the flat — but he certainly hadn't expected this. As well as the collection of sex worker business cards, adverts for brothels and the newspaper articles on the recent murders pinned to the walls, a search of the desk itself had thrown up an abundance of pornographic material and low-level drug paraphernalia.

No wonder the man had been keen to keep the door shut.

After they were done with the study, they moved on through the rest of the flat. Nothing of note caught their attention in either the bedroom or the living room; in particular, there was no sign of the silver suitcase — which just left the kitchen.

It was Cooper that discovered it — stuffed behind the washing machine, almost out of sight.

Almost — but not quite.

The bedsheet was clearly bloodstained — and wrapped around a knife.

Jack immediately put the call in to Elliott, asking the crime scene manager to get a team down here as fast as he could.

* * *

Time: 3.00 p.m.
Date: Wednesday 14 January 2015
Location: Sampson Terrace, London

Zara knew before she even tried to look through the window that the place was deserted. It had that feel to it — an emptiness. She pressed her nose up against the windowpane, her warm breath misting on the glass. Nothing. The flat was in darkness.

Another resident let her in the communal entrance, and Zara headed for Tanya's ground floor flat. Her knock at the front door went unanswered, as did the call to Tanya's mobile. Several envelopes and flyers were poking halfway through the letterbox, another sight that did little to quell Zara's unease.

Zara didn't know Tanya's neighbours and didn't relish having to explain her worries to them. Instead, she pulled out her phone and called the police hotline.

CHAPTER TWENTY

Time: 4.00 p.m.
Date: Wednesday 14 January 2015
Location: Metropolitan Police HQ, London

"The lab will try and fast track the analysis of the bedsheet and the knife. Elliott and his team are processing the rest of the flat as we speak. There was no sign of our caretaker but he clearly has an unhealthy interest in our investigation." Jack watched DS Cooper tack several images up on to one of the whiteboards. "Elliott has let us have some preliminary photos to be going on with. While we wait for the lab, we'll put out a warrant for Pierce's arrest. Him running off like this makes me think he has something to hide. Amanda, do we have any other address for him? Friends or family in the area?"

Cassidy shook her head while pulling her keyboard towards her. "Not that I've seen, but I'll take another look."

"We need to find him — put a trace on his vehicle registration, see if it pops up anywhere. And his phone."

"Speaking of which . . ." Cooper turned away from the whiteboard. "I ran a plate through the system of a van which was seen a couple of times on The Causeway the night Lisa and Tara were last seen. You'll never guess who it was."

"Pierce," grimaced Jack, hardly needing to see the nod of Cooper's head that followed.

"Aye, boss." Cooper slipped back behind his desk. "I'll check ANPR and see if it pings anywhere else."

"Any more news on the phone records of our victims?" Jack pulled up a chair and sat down.

"None of the phones have been active in recent days." DC Daniels nudged his spectacles up on to the bridge of his nose and peered at his computer monitor. "Lisa Wood was last active on Wednesday lunchtime close to her home address. She sent a text to a friend. The phone last pinged a mast in the area of Acorn House on Monday morning. But nothing since. Very similar story for Tara Coe. She last made a call on Wednesday afternoon, and her phone pinged the same mast as Lisa's on Monday. Again, nothing since."

Jack groaned. It was a long shot but he had hoped for better news. Although Dr Matthews couldn't be sure as to the time of death, it was likely both women were dead by Monday morning, but their phones weren't recovered from the scene at Acorn House. So, where were they? The most logical answer was that the killer had taken them with him. Sighing, he rubbed his eyes. "What about Cherry Eyres?"

"Still waiting for details on that one, but we do now have her next of kin details. Parents live in Eastbourne and have been contacted by the local force."

"OK, I'll check in with them later." Jack added the task to his already growing mental list.

"We did have one other development while you were out, guv." Cassidy opened her notebook. "There was a call to the hotline just before seven last night. For some reason it's taken this long to reach us. I think they're inundated with calls. Remember our Mrs Palmer from Acorn House?"

Jack nodded. "The one with the cat. She made the 999 call early Monday morning."

Cassidy nodded. "She rang in to say that Julian Fisher used to frequent the tower blocks quite regularly — certainly more regularly then he's admitted to us. She didn't want to get him into trouble as, apparently, he's a nice man — her words not mine — but he's known to the rest of the residents as 'the Doctor'."

"The Doctor?" Jack frowned. "Like Doctor Who?"

Cassidy sniggered. "More like a doctor who can get his hands on medication for you. It seems that as well as dabbling in the financial markets, our Mr Fisher is a dab hand at getting hold of all manner of prescription drugs . . . for a price."

Jack's eyebrows hitched. "Drugs? What kind of drugs?"

Cassidy consulted her notebook. "Mrs Palmer only said that Fisher gets her some headache tablets that her GP either can't or won't prescribe. She doesn't elaborate. But she did go on to say that he dishes out other types of pain meds to some of her neighbours."

"So, he's a drug dealer?" quipped Cooper. "If our victims are overcome by this killer, then maybe he's drugging them?"

"Maybe," mused Jack, rubbing his chin, taking care to avoid the healing cut. "Can you check with the lab for any bloodwork from our victims? See if anything shows up?"

Cooper reached for the desk phone. "I'll give Jenny a call."

Jack glanced at his Fitbit. Although it left a particularly nasty taste in his mouth, he knew he couldn't avoid the topic for much longer. The chief superintendent was right. If the video about his late-night expedition was to go viral, then his team deserved to hear it straight from the horse's mouth. "Look, it's been a long day and time is getting on. I've heard that Lisa Wood's parents have arrived at the mortuary, so I'm going to swing by. Once you're done here, get yourselves off home. We can pick this lot up in the morning." Jack paused, knowing he couldn't put it off any longer. "But before you do, there's something I need to tell you."

* * *

Time: 4.15 p.m.
Date: Wednesday 14 January 2015
Location: South London

James Quinn had been scared once or twice in his time, but nothing quite like this. The van he'd been bundled into smelled of animals — quite what animals he wasn't sure. Pigs? Cows? Sheep? It didn't really matter — but it was definitely animals.

Everything had happened so quickly — one minute he had been in the prison laundry, the next he was in the van. He'd been too frightened to put up anything close to a fight — and even that made him uneasy. James Quinn, frightened? The thought would have made him laugh if he didn't still feel so sick. And the smell of manure wasn't helping.

At least they had let him out of that tiny compartment in the floor of the van, and he now sat on a sack of grain in the back. At least he thought it was grain — it could be anything.

The wound on his head had stopped bleeding, but it felt boggy and sticky when he prodded it. He'd been thrown so violently into the van that he'd whacked his head on the side of the compartment on the way in, momentarily seeing stars then blacking out.

The van lurched to the side, sending Quinn tumbling across the floor. He hit his head again and winced.

Ordinarily, being sprung from his jail cell wouldn't have filled him with as much dread as it did now. He was looking at a good stretch on the inside, more if they managed to pin the murder of Stella MacIntosh on him. And then what? Even if he did get out, he'd be an old man — older than he was already. There wouldn't be much left on the outside for him anymore — he would be a has-been — a relic. Younger, fitter and much smarter criminals would eat him for breakfast. Life inside, on the whole, looked preferable.

But, in the end, he hadn't had much choice in the matter. He certainly hadn't been involved in the planning. Someone clearly wanted him on the outside — but who? And why? Any elation he might have experienced was fleeting at best — soon replaced by deep trepidation.

Another bump in the road, another lurch to the side; the van felt like it was off-road somewhere. He'd lost track of time and had no idea how long they'd been travelling. It felt like days but could only have been hours.

The trepidation multiplied with every lurch. Quinn had already 'died' once before by falling off a cross-channel ferry — he didn't much fancy experiencing it all over again.

* * *

Time: 4.30 p.m.
Date: Wednesday 15 January 2015
Location: Metropolitan Police HQ, London

Jack handed the phone across his desk and saw DS Robert Carmichael's brow crease the minute his eyes locked on to the screen.

"Shit."

Jack nodded. "My thoughts exactly." He'd been on his way out of the station, heading for the mortuary, when his phone pinged with the breaking news story. It was every-where. Every online news portal was running it. Brexit had saturated the headlines for months, and Jack wondered if the government were secretly pleased with the distraction.

Prison breakouts were, generally, a rare occurrence — especially from a secure prison like the one Quinn had been held in. Every so often offenders would fail to return from home leave to one of the lower- category and open prisons — but from a category A prison? Jack couldn't remember the last time one had hit the headlines.

The news articles didn't name the prisoner that had absconded — but Jack knew who it would be.

"How do you think he managed it?" Carmichael handed the phone back. "It's some feat."

"Indeed it is." Jack sank into one of the chairs flanking Carmichael's desk. "But he had help, though."

"On the inside as well as the outside?" Carmichael's eyebrows raised.

"Undoubtedly. Quinn isn't renowned for his intelligence. Someone inside must have helped him — and Ritchie Greenwood is up to his eyeballs in it. I know he is. I just don't know why."

"You think he means Quinn harm?" Carmichael voiced the exact same words that were dancing around inside Jack's cluttered mind. "Wants him dead?"

Jack pulled a fresh packet of painkillers from his pocket. "It's a thought, I guess," he conceded, "But it still doesn't sit right with me. Why go to so much trouble for a weasel like Quinn?" As soon as Jack had uttered the words, he knew.

Ritchie Greenwood couldn't care less about James Quinn — didn't care if the man lived or died — but he certainly *did* care about Jack MacIntosh. Dry swallowing the tablets, Jack's fogged brain began to clear. It was obvious really. Quinn was Ritchie's final attempt to reel Jack in and secure him in the back pocket of the biggest crime gang in the capital. There could be no other reason.

Jack switched his phone off, slipping it back in his pocket. "Well, whatever the motives, I'm steering well clear. Something smells off."

"You're not wrong there. Best left well alone." Carmichael eyed Jack from across the desk. "You look even more like shit than normal. What's up?"

Jack managed a rueful laugh, rubbing his eyes as tiredness began to well up. "I'm not really sure where to start."

Jack then spent the next five minutes outlining his recent meeting with Dougie King, and the recording he felt sure Jonathan Spearing was behind.

"Shit, Jack — you don't do things by halves, do you?"

"That I do not," agreed Jack. "And there's more." Jack then updated his friend and colleague on the trip to the

Hanged Man and the not-so-veiled threat Ritchie Greenwood had made towards his brother and Isabel.

Carmichael exhaled, puffing out his cheeks.

"You certainly know how to attract trouble."

Jack nodded, ruefully. "I know, like shit and flies eh?"

"Pub?" Carmichael raised his eyebrows. "You look like you could do with a pint."

"You're not wrong there. Pub sounds like a cracking idea. I've just got to run over to the mortuary, but I shouldn't be there long. I've got Stu coming over for a beer, but I've told Sully we'll meet him over at the Duke a bit later if you fancy it? First round's on me."

"Sounds good. I'll be there."

Jack made to get up when he spied the webpage Carmichael had open on his computer monitor.

'Find Missing Family — British Red Cross'.

"You going ahead with trying to find your sister?"

Carmichael nodded, slowly, following it with a sigh. "I think so. It may come to nothing — I mean, it's been over thirty years since I last saw Genete. Nearly forty, maybe. She could be anywhere."

"But if you don't try, you'll never know."

"There is that, yes."

Jack made it to the door. "I'll see you in the pub, mate."

CHAPTER TWENTY-ONE

Time: 6.30 p.m.
Date: Wednesday 14 January 2015
Location: Kettle's Yard Mews, London

Mac handed Jack a carrier bag. "Thought I should replenish your stocks."

Peering inside, Jack saw two four-packs of Corona and a bottle of Glenmorangie. "Cheers, Stu, but you needn't have."

Mac shrugged out of his biker's jacket. "Call it a belated birthday present."

Jack swung the bag up on to the kitchen worktop but pulled two chilled bottles from the fridge. "Make yourself at home." As he turned and passed one of the beers over, he noticed the new acquisition on his wrist had caught his brother's eye.

"Hey, you got one of those new fitness watches!" A look of humorous delight filled Mac's eyes. "Well I never! Never thought I'd see the day. Christ, you'll be joining the gym next."

"Steady on, Stu." Jack followed his brother into the living room, trying not to smile. "Let's not get carried away. It was a gift — from the team."

Mac continued to grin like a Cheshire cat. "Well, I think it's great. We'll get you back into shape in no time!"

Jack instinctively sucked in his belly. "That's assuming I was ever in shape to begin with."

Mac tossed his motorbike helmet on to one of the armchairs then headed for the sofa. "You're not in bad shape for an almost-fifty-year-old, bro."

"Thanks, I think."

Just as Mac leaned back against the cushions and stretched his leather-clad legs out in front of him, Jack noticed another smile break out on to his brother's face. "Hey, I told you you needed a pet!" Mac pointed his beer bottle towards the window. "And you know I'm always right."

Jack eyed the ginger tabby cat that had made itself comfortable on the windowsill. "Don't get any funny ideas, Stu — he's not staying."

Mac took a pull from his bottle. "What do you mean he's not staying? He looks quite comfy to me. What's his name?"

Jack removed Mac's motorbike helmet from the armchair, placing it on the floor as he sat. "Marmaduke. Old Mrs Constantine from the floor below is in hospital and she asked me to keep an eye on him. Feed him, that kind of thing." Jack took a gulp from his beer. "I'm not really sure what else you're meant to do with cats other than feed them."

Mac raised his eyebrows along with the bottle at his lips. "Looks like he's moved in to me."

Jack made a face. "He's not meant to be staying here, but the bloody thing keeps following me up the stairs."

Mac grinned as Marmaduke leapt down from the windowsill and padded over to the armchair, jumping up and settling into Jack's lap. "Well, he seems to have taken a shine to you, anyway."

Jack made another face. "Don't encourage him." The ginger tabby began to sniff around the neck of the Corona bottle, forcing Jack to raise it above his head.

"Tell me you haven't got the poor thing hooked on to a beer and pizza diet already, though?" Mac gestured towards the two pizza boxes sitting on the coffee table, leaning forward and popping open both lids. The aroma of fresh pizza wafted out.

"Give me some credit, I'm not quite that bad." Jack dislodged the tabby cat and scooped up one of the slices. "But I have discovered he does quite like a bit of Chinese chicken."

Marmaduke, looking rather disgruntled at having been ejected from Jack's lap so soon, hopped up on to the sofa and started nudging Mac's arm instead. Mac gave the cat a tickle behind the ears. "He's cute! You definitely need to keep him!"

They made a decent dent in the two meat feast pizzas and they were on to their third bottle of beer before Jack decided he might as well get it over with. He had been thinking about it all the time he was at the mortuary with Lisa Wood's distraught parents. He couldn't really offer them much by way of information or consolation, but he did his best. The words 'we're doing all we can' escaped his mouth more than once. It was a phrase he hated with a passion, but he really had nothing more to say. It felt cheap and empty and he silently apologised as he spoke.

Turning his attention back to his brother, Jack knew it had to be said — and said now. History told him that waiting for the right moment often backfired with disastrous results. "I need to tell you something." He placed his beer bottle down on the coffee table. "There's no easy way to say it, but . . ."

"I already know." Mac nodded behind the slice of pizza he was shoving into his mouth. "I saw it online. Looks like the tosser's escaped."

News of James Quinn's escape had saturated the evening news — the man in question now being named. "I was told about it earlier today — I wasn't sure how to tell you. How do you feel? It's OK to feel angry."

"I'm not angry, Jack. The law will catch up with him sooner or later." Mac gulped down a third of his bottle. "How many people break out of prison these days and get away with it? His mug shot is all over the news. He won't be able to move without someone spotting him."

"True." Jack knew the odds were stacked against Quinn making it very far. But if Ritchie Greenwood was involved, that put an entirely new spin on things. "As far as I can make out he was about to be transferred — maybe back to Belmarsh or out to Pentonville or maybe Whitemoor."

"I couldn't care less — it's not like I was planning on visiting him any time soon."

Jack felt a change in conversation was needed. "How's work going?"

Mac reached for another slice of pizza, giving Marmaduke another rub behind the ear as he did so. "It's good. I'm just doing a couple of days a week to begin with. I get a bit stiff if I'm out on the bike for too long, but the boss is giving me all the shorter jobs so I don't have to travel too far." He stretched his legs out again. "These bloody leathers make my skin itch, though."

"Don't go undoing all the good you've done with your physio. You ever thought about finding something else? It's not been long since the fire — recovering from something like that takes time." Although his brother looked well — leaner and fitter, and his eyes had regained their sparkle — Jack knew the real damage often went unseen.

Mac merely shrugged and stuffed the pizza into his mouth. "Not much else I can do, not with a history like mine."

"But — and don't take this the wrong way, Stu — you don't really need to work, do you? You could just help out in the café, couldn't you?" Jack saw his brother bristle.

"That's Isabel's money, not mine. I still need to bring a wage in, Jack. I'm not a sponger."

Jack heard the all-too-familiar edge return to his brother's voice and decided to back off. Stu was a proud man and Jack supposed he might feel the same if he was in his shoes. But the likelihood of bachelor Jack marrying a rich bride was getting more unlikely as time went by.

"Well, don't do anything stupid." Jack quashed the laugh that threatened to bubble up in his throat.

Don't do anything stupid. He was a fine one to talk. He was still smarting after his latest trip to see Dougie King — and the recording he felt sure was down to Jonathan Spearing. If the chief superintendent found out about his recent trip to the Hanged Man, then he'd have more than a few uncomfortable questions to answer. Skating on thin ice was a sport Jack was getting very well accustomed to — maybe even to Olympic level — but even ice had its limits; especially the thin variety. As did Dougie King. Jack wasn't sure how much longer he could stretch the man's loyalty.

He decided a change of scenery was required.

"Pub?"

* * *

Time: 7.30 p.m.
Date: Wednesday 14 January 2015
Location: M3 motorway

Ritchie Greenwood pulled the van back out into the traffic and headed for the M3. It was just him and Quinn now — the others would make their way back to London and carry on as if nothing had happened. With fresh registration plates, he let a cruel smile creep in. He had time — he had all the time in the world. The entire country might be hunting for James Quinn, but they would be searching in all the wrong places. They would *never* think to look where they were headed.

The van had been adapted specifically for the job — a compartment in the floor just big enough for one person, even one of Quinn's portly frame. Masquerading as a prison laundry van, it had been textbook stuff. Audacious, most certainly — but textbook all the same.

Ritchie's smile widened into a grin as he exited the round-about and joined the slip road south. It was like something out of *Porridge* the way they had pulled it off. The team had been watching the prison for a while now, monitoring the comings and goings of the laundry vans, noting the lapses in security. It didn't take much in the end. They even opened the gates and waved them inside.

As Ritchie shoved the van into fifth gear, he mentally calculated the time it would take to arrive at their destination. He still had a fair amount of preparation work to do once they got there, if he wanted this part of the operation to go like clockwork, too. But there was no rush. Quinn wasn't going anywhere.

Time they had plenty of — it was Jack MacIntosh whose days were numbered.

Time was running out for him.

* * *

Time: 8.00 p.m.
Date: Wednesday 14 January 2015
Location: The Duke of Wellington Public House

Jack brought the tray of drinks over to their usual table by the dartboard, placing a pint of lager in front of his brother and Carmichael, and a Guinness in front of Adam Sullivan.

"Cheers." Rob Carmichael picked up his pint glass as Jack resumed his seat by the window.

"No problem." Jack took his own pint of lager from the tray and threw a couple of packets of crisps into the centre of the table. "It's been quite a day."

"How are the teeth?" Sullivan gestured towards Jack's face as he took his first sip of Guinness. "Your lip seems to be healing."

Jack grimaced as he swallowed a mouthful of lager. "Yeah, all good." Instinctively, he ran a hand over his cheek. "I live to fight another day."

Sullivan grinned and reached for one of the crisp packets. "Well, maybe not so much of the fighting, eh? There's only so much damage those teeth can take, you know."

"Noted."

Mac took hold of the other packet of crisps, ripping it open. "Yes, Jack — I'm the black sheep of this family set-up. If there's any fighting to be done, it should be me."

Jack spluttered into his pint glass. "I sincerely hope not, Stu. I could do without any more headaches."

"Case getting to you?" Carmichael placed his glass back down on a beer mat. "From what I see it looks quite complex."

Jack nodded. "You're not wrong there." After another sip of lager, he caught the dentist's eye. "You said you might have some more information on our first two victims. Anything you think might be useful?" Jack caught an inquisitive look from his brother. "Sully here is a street pastor. Knows the streets better than we do at times."

"I'm not so sure about that, Jack." Sullivan wiped froth from his lip with the back of his hand. "But we do what we can. I think I told the call handler everything I knew — I don't think it was anything you didn't know already, to be honest. But I did treat both of them — Lisa and Tara. My dental practice offers free consultations as part of the Welfare Truck service — free dental check-ups and the like. It's not much — and to be honest, not many take us up on it. But both women called in from time to time."

"You get to know them at all?" Jack knew he was clutching at straws but anything that could give them an insight into the victims' lifestyles could help. "Anything we might not know about?"

Sullivan pondered the question for a moment, taking a long mouthful of his Guinness. "Difficult to say. I wouldn't say I got to know them that well — probably Lisa slightly better than Tara. But she was just chattier, you know? Tara was more reserved. I think being a dentist is kind of like being a priest in some ways — you'd be surprised what secrets some patients will divulge when they're sat in the chair. They treat it a bit like a confessional. I think it's the nerves that loosen their tongues." Sullivan smiled. "They were both pleasant enough, though, and wanted to get off the streets. But it's difficult for them."

"What's the mood like out there now?"

"It's not good, that I will say. There's a tension in the air — everyone's really on edge." Sullivan offered the packet of cheese and onion crisps around the table. "And that includes us."

"Well, I don't envy you." Jack waved away the crisp packet. "It's not a job I could do, night after night."

"I could say the same about your job." Sullivan nodded once more towards Jack's healing lip. "You need danger money."

"Or boxing lessons," quipped Mac, grinning as he emptied the remains of a packet of salt and vinegar into his mouth. "Anyone fancy some more crisps?"

"Jesus, Stu," remarked Jack. "You had the best part of two pizzas earlier. Where do you put it all? You're like Cooper — a human bloody rubbish bin."

"I'll have you know I'm a growing boy." Mac sunk the last of his pint and made to stand up. "Anyone fancy another?"

Jack eyed his half-drunk pint. He knew he should really call it a night after this one, as he wanted to be back at the station bright and early in the morning. They still had an outstanding warrant for Barry Pierce's arrest to deal with, and they needed to follow up on Julian Fisher, too. But he gave a quick nod. "Go on then, just the one."

Sullivan got to his feet and picked up his and Mac's empty glasses. "I'll come and help."

Once both were out of earshot, Carmichael turned to Jack. "Have you told your brother about the video?"

Jack shook his head. *The video.* After all that had happened with Quinn and the investigation that afternoon, he'd almost forgotten about Jonathan Spearing. *Almost.* "No. I had to tell the team — don't really want them finding out via other means — but I think the fewer people that know about it the better, don't you? It's not my finest hour."

"Maybe it'll all blow over." Carmichael sounded like he was trying to inject more optimism into his tone than he probably felt. "Something and nothing."

"With Spearing involved, which I'm sure he is, then I somehow doubt that very much. He leaked it for a reason and

I don't think he's done with me yet. He won't rest until he's back on the front pages."

"I thought you two had buried the hatchet after the whole kidnapping thing. He owes you."

Jack gave a low chuckle. "I think that particular hatchet is buried even deeper now. The man's barely human."

Mac and Sullivan reappeared with a fresh tray of drinks, and more crisps.

"Any more news on your sister?" Jack finished the remains of his first pint before accepting the fresh one. "You know where to start looking?"

Carmichael considered the question for a moment. "Kind of. I'm going to try the Red Cross first, and I have some good contacts in Social Services. They might be able to point me in the right direction."

"Sister?" Mac pulled a face as he resumed his seat and ripped open a fresh packet of crisps. "I never knew you had a sister."

"It's a long story, mate," breathed Carmichael. "I'll fill you in another time. How was your trip to Surrey?"

"Surrey?" Sullivan raised an eyebrow as he took a mouthful of fresh Guinness. "Lovely part of the world. My grandparents came from down that way."

"Stu's wife has her family home down there," explained Jack. "Albury."

Mac tipped a handful of crisps into his mouth. "Yeah, wasn't bad. We did some work around the house — Isabel wanted to redecorate some of the rooms."

Jack reached for his second pint. Most people would want to give the place a makeover, to try and erase the past. But try as he might, Jack wasn't convinced a fresh lick of paint, some new wallpaper and soft furnishings would eradicate what had happened there. But it was a start.

Mac carried on. "But the break did her good — gave her a chance to unwind away from everything and take stock. She got a bit anxious while we were there, though. Everything is still playing on her mind, but I guess it's understandable."

"Anxious?" Carmichael caught Jack's eyes over the rim of his pint glass. "About anything in particular?"

Mac shrugged. "Something and nothing, I think. She kept thinking someone was there, watching the house. I told her she was imagining it."

Jack felt his stomach tighten and abandoned his new pint. "Did she see anyone?"

Mac shook his head. "I don't think so. It happened a few times, so she says. First time was when she was out in the front garden — she said she felt like someone was there, watching. But when she looked along the road, there was no one. As you know, the house is on a quiet lane, no through traffic to speak of. There's not a lot of places someone could hide. Then she felt it again, like someone was looking in through the windows."

The disquiet Jack had initially felt back at the Hanged Man now resurfaced. He had wanted to ask Stu about it earlier, back at the flat – ask him outright if he saw anyone that could be Ritchie Greenwood hanging around - but there never seemed to be the right moment. "Do you think there really was anyone looking in?"

Mac gave another shrug. "Nah, I mean it's crazy, right? Who would want to watch us? But she just couldn't shake the feeling — she was really worried about it for a while."

"But the house is secure? Locks and everything?"

Mac nodded. "Even has a burglar alarm."

Jack toyed with the pint glass in front of him, his thirst dissipating fast. A burglar alarm — that was something at least. But it didn't totally reassure him. He caught Carmichael's eye again. In the light of Ritchie Greenwood's veiled threat, they both knew that Isabel was probably not imagining it at all.

Sighing, Jack gestured towards his lager, feeling the tiredness washing over him from all sides. He needed to get home. "As nice as this is, I'm going to make a move after this one."

"I'll be off soon, too," agreed Sullivan. "I'm getting too old for this drinking on a school night business."

Jack picked up his pint just as the door to the main bar swung open. He saw DS Cooper hurrying in their direction. "If you're quick, Cooper, Stu's buying a round." He angled his glass towards his brother.

"No time, boss."

Jack saw the tense look on the detective sergeant's face, instantly placing his pint glass back down. "What is it? What's happened?"

CHAPTER TWENTY-TWO

Time: 9.15 p.m.
Date: Wednesday 14 January 2015
Location: The Causeway, London

DS Cooper brought the Golf to a stop by the kerbside. The road ahead was blocked by lots of fluorescent jacketed uniformed officers who were attempting to herd two groups in separate directions, with varying degrees of success. Every so often, one or more would break away from the pack and attempt to cross to the other side, only to find their way blocked by another uniform.

Jack exited the car and caught the eye of a police sergeant he knew well, the sergeant already hastily making his way towards them.

"We had it all under control, but something seems to have kicked them off again."

Jack quickly took in his surroundings. To his left, a group of approximately a dozen, both male and female, were screaming profanities and gesticulating with their hands. The odd word reached his ears above the chaos.

Whores.

Scum.

Filth.

Dirty.

The wall of officers did their best to contain the baying crowd as peacefully as possible, but Jack could see the look of exasperation on many of their faces. It wasn't what anyone wanted to be doing on a cold January night. And if it didn't calm down soon, he could see the whole thing escalating into something grim.

"Thanks, Roger. Any idea what sparked it off?"

Sergeant Roger Davenport shrugged. "We got a call around eight-fifteen to report a disturbance in the street. When we got here, it was just a bit of shouting and bad mouthing, but not much else. But then more turned up and it very quickly turned into this." He gestured back towards the melee. "It's like bloody World War Three."

Jack glanced to the right where a much smaller group was gathered — just three women standing beneath an old oak tree. Jack recognised them instantly. In contrast to the crowd opposite, they stood calmly together, only one deciding to throw back an occasional retort.

Between the two groups was no man's land, and that was exactly where Jack was headed, motioning for Cooper to follow.

At the very utterance of 'World War Three', a bottle flew past Jack's head, missing his ear by centimetres. It crashed to the ground and shattered into multiple shards on impact. Jack whirled round, his face like thunder. The beers from earlier that evening were jostling uncomfortably inside his stomach, and a headache was gathering momentum, so he could do without a riot to contend with as well tonight. With more than his quota of A&E attendances already under his belt in recent months, he wasn't in a hurry to return.

"What the hell do you think you're doing?" Jack strode towards the crowd where the bottle had started its journey. "That nearly took my bloody ear off!"

The line of uniformed officers swayed as several protest-ers began to surge forward. One stood head and shoulders above the others. Jack suspected he was the bottle thrower judging by the second bottle of Budweiser still held in his hand. As their eyes connected, Jack instinctively ran a hand over his bruised and busted lip.

"Henderson? I might have known. What the hell are you playing at?"

Neville Henderson's nostrils flared and he began to shout something in Jack's direction, but the words were lost in among the din. Instead, he attempted to break through the police line but found himself immediately up against several uniforms.

Jack placed a hand on Sergeant Davenport's shoulder. "It's OK, Roger. Let him through."

The sergeant initially looked wary but eventually acqui-esced, letting the man step through the temporary cordon. He flashed a warning look at Jack that said '*on your head be it*'.

As Henderson approached, Jack took a few steps to the side, away from the throng. "You were saying?"

Neville Henderson's eyes were wild, darting from side to side, and he was breathing hard. In his hand he still clutched the second bottle of Budweiser. "They need to get off the streets — it's attracting killers."

"Lose the bottle, Nev, for Christ's sake. And who exactly needs to get off the streets? The police? They're only here because you're creating merry hell." Jack pointed to his lip. "And don't think I haven't forgotten about this, either."

Henderson ignored the request to get rid of the bot-tle, and gestured towards the three women standing on the opposite side of the street. "Them. Doing what they do, it attracts the wrong sort. All it does is attract trouble. And now its attracting killers." The man continued to breathe hard, his face animated. "I've got two young daughters, fifteen and sixteen. I don't want a killer on our doorstep."

Jack sighed. Despite the punch to the mouth, Neville Henderson was generally all mouth and no trousers when it came to confrontations. Violence wasn't usually his thing. "I understand your frustrations, but this doesn't help anybody." He nodded back towards the fracas. "We're doing all we can to find the person responsible."

"Well you're taking too bloody long about it! Every night they're out on the streets is another night that lures that bloody bastard back here. It's not safe for our kids anymore!"

Jack's gaze travelled back towards the three women still clustered together beneath the tree. Apart from the odd remark thrown back across the road, and the occasional hand gesture, they were surprisingly calm.

"We can't ban people from the streets, Nev. You must know that."

"But what they're doing is wrong! It's illegal, surely? You can't sell yourself like that in public."

Jack sighed again. He wasn't about to get into a debate with the likes of Neville Henderson on a freezing cold January night over the legalities of soliciting and prostitution. He suspected the man wouldn't listen to him anyway.

"We're trying to keep everyone safe — and that includes yourself and the rest of the local residents." Jack knew how empty the words sounded as soon as they left his lips. But it was all he had. "But coming down here and throwing your weight around, shouting the odds like this, surely you can see it isn't helping? All it will do is get you locked up for the night. *Again*. You really want that to happen?"

The man seemed to consider Jack's words, his shoulders relaxing somewhat — but the fire in his eyes still smouldered. "They still need to go. Move them on somewhere else. This bloke only kills because they're here. If they go, so does he."

Jack knew Henderson had a point. If the women weren't there, it was likely neither would the killer. But he'd been in the job long enough to know that moving the women on wasn't the answer. All it would achieve would be to move the killer's patch somewhere else and bring death and misery to another part of the city instead. The man wasn't just going to stop — Rachel Hunter had been very clear on that score. Or it could even be worse than that — if they drove him from the streets he might go to ground completely and then they would never find him.

Jack shivered at the thought.

Standing in the cold, listening to the yelling and screaming going on around him, he considered the other side of the coin — a side that made him feel distinctly uncomfortable. As distasteful as it sounded, he knew the team stood their best shot at catching the killer if the women remained on the streets. The fact of the matter was, he *needed* them there. He *needed* them to go about their business as usual, he *needed* them to draw out the killer.

It put them at high risk, but it was still the best chance they had; maybe the *only* chance they had. If the women disappeared from the streets, all the surveillance in the world wouldn't catch this killer.

"We're doing all we can," he repeated, simply, the same empty words leaving the same empty mouth. "But you and your mates need to leave — this really isn't helping. Stay much longer and you're all looking at a night in the cells. Best thing you can do is turn around and walk away. You've said your piece, we've all heard you. But we've all got better things to be doing right now than arguing out here — I know I certainly have. I need to give my attention to catching this prick, but instead I'm freezing my nuts off talking to you and dodging beer bottles. Understand?"

* * *

Time: 9.45 p.m.
Date: Wednesday 14 January 2015
Location: Whiting Street, London

He had sat and watched the carnage for the last fifteen minutes, irritation growing by the second. Even from this distance,

217

parked up on the corner of Whiting Street, he could see the line of uniformed officers still stretched across the road, but at least the yelling had quietened down.

What he needed to happen now was for them all to retreat, for them all to go home — and to leave him with his girls. He could see the three standing beneath the tree, hopping from foot to foot in their high heels. It made him smile.

He turned up the dial on the heater. Once they felt the warmth inside the van, they wouldn't be able to resist getting in. The others hadn't.

But time was marching on and the police didn't look like they would be leaving anytime soon. He felt the irritation hitch a notch. It had to be tonight. The one he had back at the house wasn't going to be enough to satisfy his cravings.

As he shifted in the driver's seat, he felt the wounds on his back smarting beneath his shirt. The discipline would be waiting for him when he got home — but first he needed the girl.

Desire mixed with revulsion coursed through him. He loved the girls — but he hated them too. He could see his dead mother's eyes in every one of them — and when he snuffed the life out of them, he snuffed it out of her, too.

Again.

Pulling away from the kerb, he turned in the street and headed away from the commotion. He had time. He could be patient.

He would return.

* * *

Time: 10.15 p.m.
Date: Wednesday 14 January 2015
Location: The Causeway, London

Jack leaned up against the side of Cooper's Golf and rubbed his eyes. It was now after ten and the uniformed officers had successfully managed to calm down the fractious stand-off and persuade the rest of the crowd to disperse, hinting in no uncertain terms that home was the best place for them unless they fancied seeing the inside of a police cell. Jack could see the relief on the officers' faces as one by one they departed and the crisis was averted.

Cooper had disappeared then returned with two takeaway cups of coffee. Jack had no idea where the detective sergeant had conjured them up from, but was grateful all the same. He took hold of the disposable cardboard cup and breathed in the aroma. It wasn't particularly great — certainly not up to Isabel's standards in the café, or even the chief superintendent's coffee machine — but beggars couldn't be choosers at this time of night.

Zara, Mandy and Bernice were still standing huddled beneath the oak tree and Jack was quietly impressed at how they had handled the confrontation. They hadn't resorted to violence, only the odd expletive hurled back across the police line from time to time when their patience wore thin.

"Got a bit hairy there for a while, boss." Cooper took a mouthful of his drink, making a face as he swallowed. "Sorry about the coffee. It was all I could find."

"No problem, Cooper. It's hot and wet." Jack took a sip and shuddered, feeling the headache still battering his temples. "Thankfully peace has returned to the streets and we can all sleep easy — for now at least." Jack knew as much as anyone that any peace was likely to be short-lived if they didn't come up with an arrest soon. Neville Henderson and his cronies wouldn't be silenced for long.

"You can't really blame them, though" added Cooper. "They've got a point, when you think about it. If the killer preys on sex workers, then the longer they're out here on the streets the longer they'll be a target. It's catch-22."

"They certainly do have a point, Cooper. And it's a valid one at that. Which makes it all the more imperative that we catch the bastard — and soon." Jack downed another mouthful of his foul-tasting coffee, glad of the warmth at least. His gaze travelled along the street to where a vehicle was pulling up at the kerb.

The street pastors had arrived.

Like he had told Adam Sullivan in the pub earlier, he admired the pastors for what they were doing — or at least trying to do. He suspected they didn't get too many thanks for their efforts, but they continued doing it all the same. Which earned them a degree of respect in Jack's book. Squinting across the street, he scanned the vehicle but couldn't see that Sully was on duty tonight.

Jack sometimes wondered if things might have turned out differently if people like the street pastors had been around in his mother's time. If they had, maybe James Quinn would never have come into their lives the way he had. Maybe she would have been able to get herself out of the game and lead a completely different life.

Maybe she wouldn't have died.

Maybe.

One of the pastors was heading in their direction so Jack swallowed the remains of the coffee, grimacing at the bitterness. At least Cooper had attempted to mask the flavour with a generous amount of sugar.

"Bryn." Jack nodded towards the approaching street pastor. Bryn Morgan was someone Jack had met several times before — a tall man, with a neat beard and round-rimmed spectacles. He had a quiet, placid demeanour and Jack sometimes wondered how he fared patrolling the streets at night. But he also had a sense of humour about him which probably kept his sanity in check.

"Evening, Jack." The street pastor gave a nod. "I see the excitement brought you out tonight, too."

"I wouldn't miss it for the world." Jack gestured across to the women still standing some metres away. "Everyone's OK as far as I can tell. Just some hotheads that boiled over."

Bryn followed Jack's line of sight. "We'll stay in the area for a while, make sure it doesn't kick off again. Maybe even persuade the ladies that it might be time to go home for the night. All three are due welfare checks, so we'll have a chat and take it from there."

"Much obliged."

Bryn waved the compliment away. "Not a problem. It's what we're here for." He paused, then added. "Nasty business, though. We come out to do a welfare patrol as often as we can, but we can't be everywhere at once."

Jack nodded. "I hear you."

"But if we can persuade even one to stay home, to take a different path, then we'd consider that a job well done." Bryn gave a faint smile. "I'd best be getting over there. We'll keep our eyes and ears open, let you know if we spot anything."

Jack nodded his thanks and watched the street pastor cross back towards the women gathered underneath the street light. "Come on, Cooper. Let's get out of here before we freeze to death."

He turned back towards the Golf, but noted the detective sergeant was still rooted to the spot, eyes fixed on his phone. Jack felt an unease start to spread which redoubled when Cooper raised his troubled gaze.

"What is it now, Cooper?"

CHAPTER TWENTY-THREE

Time: 1.15 a.m.
Date: Thursday 15 January 2015
Location: Old Mill Road, Christchurch

Ritchie heaved the body of James Quinn up and on to his shoulder, struggling to negotiate the wire fencing that surrounded the abandoned flats. The man could do with losing a few pounds, that was very clear.

He silently congratulated himself on having the foresight to bring a set of wire cutters with him, deftly managing to snip enough of a gap in the fence to push them both through. Sweating despite the cold, he stumbled across the waste ground and eventually reached what would have been the entrance to the Old Mill Road flats.

Dumping Quinn unceremoniously on the ground, not caring that the man's head struck a large crumbling breezeblock on the way down, he grabbed the rusting sheet of metal that was acting as a door and pulled it to the side. Quinn had been heavily sedated and wouldn't feel a thing.

As Ritchie poked his head inside the building, the smell that greeted him was one of damp and mould. He was sure that MacIntosh must look back on his days in the flats through a pair of rose-tinted spectacles, but all Ritchie could see in front of him was neglect. Wrinkling his nose, he decided he wouldn't spend any more time here than was absolutely necessary. But he had a plan.

Taking Quinn beneath the armpits once more, he dragged the slumbering man through the main entrance and deposited him on the concrete floor of what would once have been the communal hall. Illuminating the confined space with his torch, he checked his watch. If he started now, he could be finished by the end of the day.

And then the fun could begin.

* * *

Time: 1.20 a.m.
Date: Thursday 15 January 2015
Location: Whiting Street, London

Returning to the same street corner, he parked by the kerbside and waited. It had taken a while for the streets to empty of both protesters and police, but now the customary silence was back. And the three women from earlier were down to just one.

He liked it when there was just the one.

Keeping the engine running, he turned the heater up to the maximum once again — and then he waited some more.

He knew she would come — they always did.

As he waited, he arranged the usual series of small square tins along the dashboard. The first had individually wrapped pieces of chocolate and other sugary sweets. The second had wraps of rocks of crack cocaine. The third a collection of condoms.

Often, the first two tins were the most popular.

After only a couple of minutes, the passenger door opened and she slipped herself inside. He could see her shivering, the goose bumps on her exposed pale legs visible even in the relative dimness of the van. She pulled her skirt down as far as it would go — which wasn't far. He supposed her knee length black fake-leather boots didn't offer much warmth — but he didn't really care. He pretended he did, but he didn't.

Without speaking, she reached forward for one of the chocolates and hastily unwrapped it. They were always hungry — always looking for that sugar fix, before they sought another kind of high. Maybe it was to sweeten the soul before the horrors of the night unfolded before them. But again he didn't care. Instead, he found it amusing. They were almost like children in some ways. *His* children. *His* girls. Sometimes he brought lollipops with him, too.

"How are you, Zara?" He always asked how they were. Again, he didn't much care and didn't really listen to their responses. He was merely going through the motions, doing what was expected to gain their trust. He'd done it enough times now that it barely registered with him.

He had started to wonder whether the girls would be dissuaded from working, put off by the lurid and shocking headlines appearing in every morning newspaper and on every online news bulletin. Hourly updates on rolling 24-hour news channels suggested the hunt was gathering pace. It was a manhunt not seen on this scale in the capital for a very long time.

It made him smile. They were looking for him. Looking, but not really *seeing*. For he was right here, all the time, right under their very noses.

The warnings in the press were there in black and white for all to see, but still they came. Still they headed out into the cold and the dark. Still they worked.

And still they got into his van.

He smiled as Zara munched her way through a second chocolate, pulling the van away from the kerb. He knew the police patrols would pass by again before too long, so he needed to be gone. He swung down an adjacent street, avoiding the traffic lights and the inevitable cameras at the junction with the main road.

"Same place?" He took a quick glance towards the passenger seat.

Zara looked up, swallowing the last of her second chocolate and wiping her mouth. She nodded. "Yeah. Just off Newhampton Road if you don't mind. It's too bloody cold out there to walk tonight."

He merely nodded and managed another smile, along with a feigned interest in her evening. "How was it tonight? Much business?" Swinging the car down another side street, he noticed the faint flash of concern that crossed Zara's face as she glanced out of the side window. He gave another well-practised smile. "There's a road closed up ahead — some emergency or other. Probably a burst water pipe with this cold snap we've been having."

She seemed to take it well, reaching for another chocolate and then a rock for later. He saw the sheepish, almost apologetic, look in her eyes. Reaching across with his gloved left hand, he patted her exposed thigh. He felt a tingle ripple through his fingers at the touch. "Go ahead — help yourself."

Zara was young. He wasn't quite sure how young, but younger than the others anyway. They often told him how they'd ended up where they had, doing what they did — why it had happened to them. He pretended to be interested but he wasn't. Their lives bored him. Everything about them bored him. And he despised them, too.

He forced another smile on to his face as Zara reached for the bottle of water tucked into the centre console of the van.

It wouldn't be long now.

* * *

Time: 1.35 a.m.
Date: Thursday 15 January 2015
Location: Old Mill Road, Christchurch

Climbing through the rubble that littered the crumbling stairs had taken some degree of effort, and Ritchie was sweating by the time they made it up to Jack MacIntosh's old flat. He flashed a look of contempt mixed with irritation as he dumped James Quinn's body on the ground; the man was beginning to get under his skin, but Ritchie wouldn't have to put up with it much longer.

He had plans for Quinn; and those plans involved Jack MacIntosh.

The last time he contacted the detective inspector, MacIntosh had threatened to change his number. But Ritchie knew they were empty words; merely an idle threat.

He would keep the message succinct — knowing he wouldn't have to go into much detail in order to get his point across; a mere photograph would do the trick. Didn't someone say that a picture could paint a thousand words?

Ritchie gave a throaty chuckle as he hauled Quinn into a sitting position and propped him up against an old oil-fired radiator. The man was still unconscious, but would soon rouse. Binding Quinn's hands behind his back with cable ties, Ritchie then snapped on a metal handcuff connected to a metal chain, and secured it to the radiator. The man wouldn't be going far.

Getting to his feet, he took a few steps back and angled his phone to take in Quinn, the radiator and just enough of the background to show MacIntosh where they were. It would be all that was needed to sow the seed — the detective's imagination would do the rest.

Now sitting up, Quinn started to come round. He was still drowsy, his eyes closed, but Ritchie didn't exactly need him to smile for the camera. MacIntosh would get the message loud and clear.

And then all Ritchie needed to do was wait.

CHAPTER TWENTY-FOUR

Time: 8.30 a.m.
Date: Thursday 15 January 2015
Location: Number 41 bus, London

Violet Spencer grimaced as she pulled herself up to the top
deck of the number forty-one bus. Her legs were heavily band-
aged, the diabetic ulcers throbbing and weeping with every
step. Downstairs had been full and no one had got up to offer
her a seat even though she had hovered in the gangway long
enough to catch someone's eye. Instead, everyone averted
their gaze, heads angled down towards their phones, looking
anywhere but at the little old lady standing by the stairs.

The youth of today she muttered to herself as she hauled
herself to the top deck. Although, to be fair, most of the people seated downstairs weren't exactly spring chickens themselves and didn't have the ignorance of youth as their excuse.

The bus pulled away from the kerb just as Violet reached
the upper deck, sending her lurching to the side. She grabbed
hold of one of the seats to prevent herself from tumbling to
the floor, but her handbag swung from her shoulder and
glanced off a woman's arm seated behind. Violet thought

about apologising, but judging by the haughty expression the woman fired at her she thought better of it.

Instead, she heaved herself towards the back of the top deck where there were some free seats. She needed more space than most, what with her swollen legs and the extra pounds that had collected around her middle in recent years. The doctor kept nagging her to lose weight, for the good of her overall health and her diabetes management — and she had tried, but it was so hard. Made even more so since her Jock had died. Now her days were filled with morning TV . . . then afternoon TV . . . interspersed with trips to the kitchen for snacks. She didn't think she ate all that much, but the bathroom scales strongly disagreed.

As did the doctor.

But she was lonely in the house, all on her own. Jock had always been there, day and night, for the fifty-one years they were married. And now he was gone. And all it left behind was a large hole that she had to fill with something — and for far too long it had been chocolate eclairs, doughnuts and cheese. She smiled to herself as she started to inch herself into one of the seats. Jock had always liked her with curves — he always said as much.

As she turned to sit, the bus chose that moment to turn another corner, sending her lurching once more to the opposite side. This time she grabbed hold of the metal railing in front of her and as she did so, she spied something on the seat ahead.

Two large shopping bags sat side by side.

Any abandoned baggage on public transport these days should start ringing alarm bells, but instead Violet felt intrigue. She hadn't recalled anyone coming down the stairs when she'd got on, anyone who might have left them behind.

The bus began to slow down and came to a halt at the next stop. Violet took full advantage of the relative stability to investigate further. Jock would have advised caution; she knew that much. He was such a worrier, was Jock.

'*You don't know what's inside, Vi. Leave it alone.*'

But curiosity got the better of her and she shut Jock from her thoughts. Both the bags were 'bags for life' that you could now pick up at the supermarkets, getting ready for the charge for plastic bags coming into effect later in the year, and Violet expected both to be full of shopping.

Immediately she began to think about what treats might be inside. She loved looking at what other people had in their shopping baskets when she made her weekly trip to the budget supermarket close to home. Her pension didn't stretch very far these days and she often had to ration her choices. But here was a stroke of luck! Maybe someone had the same sweet tooth that she did. She started to imagine fresh cream cakes, doughnuts oozing with jam, and the rich ginger cake that Jock loved so much.

Knowing she wouldn't have long before the bus started up again, she leaned forward and pulled open one of the bags.

The roar from the engines of the bus almost drowned out the scream that erupted from her mouth.

Almost, but not quite.

* * *

Time: 8.45 a.m.
Date: Thursday 15 January 2015
Location: Metropolitan Police HQ, London

"She wouldn't leave her name." Cassidy flipped over a page of her notebook. "Call came in at around three o'clock yesterday afternoon. I've no idea why it wasn't flagged up and sent to us earlier."

"Did she say anything else?" Jack slid into his chair behind his desk.

"Not a great deal, to be honest. Just that the missing woman's name is Tanya — Tanya Maund. Lives alone on Sampson Terrace. Usually works the same section of The Causeway on weekday nights, but Tanya hasn't been seen since Tuesday evening, and she missed a catch-up with the caller yesterday lunchtime — which isn't like her. Tanya isn't answering her phone and her flat is in darkness. The caller is worried about her."

Jack nodded. "Doesn't sound good, does it? Nothing else?"

Cassidy shook her head. "No. The caller didn't want to leave her name. But she apparently sounded genuine and was really concerned. The caller added that it was completely out of character for Tanya not to be in touch or answer her phone. And with everything that's been happening . . ."

Jack nodded. "I get it. Let's take a trip out to Sampson Terrace later today and see if we can't find her. Did the caller leave any means for getting back in touch with them?"

Another shake of the head. "No, nothing."

"OK — give me fifteen minutes or so then we'll have a briefing. And find some decent coffee if you can."

Jack waited for his office door to close before letting out a pent-up sigh. After getting back from last night's shenanigans on The Causeway, he had sat watching the online news updates as they came in. As the chief superintendent had predicted, Spearing's video had gone viral.

Jack wasn't on any social media platforms and it was at times like these that he was thankful for that rather canny decision. DS Cooper, however, was — and he had swiftly shown Jack how both his Facebook and Twitter feeds were awash with the tale of the London detective inspector seen paying prostitutes when he should be spending his time investigating the horrific murders that had gripped the capital over the preceding three days.

Jack could see their point, as skewed as it was.

He'd scrolled through some of the posts, seeing the comments coming in thick and fast — none of them particularly sympathetic to his actions. After a minute or so he'd handed the phone back to Cooper having seen enough.

As the night progressed, the online news portals started to run the story too. As usual, the reporting was awash with inaccuracies — but it made for a good headline. Jack wasn't ordinarily bothered by what he read about himself in the news — Jonathan Spearing had done the dirty on him more than once. But this time it was different, for this time it was most certainly going to bring the chief superintendent knocking at his door.

After spending ten minutes going through his email inbox and deleting everything that wasn't urgent, he pushed himself up out of his chair and headed for the incident room. He couldn't let something like this cloud his judgement or derail the investigation. With the call about Tanya Maund, he needed to focus.

Upon entering the incident room, Jack noted the team were working in silence — a comfortable silence, but a silence none the less. He knew they would all have seen the news footage by now, and countless social media posts, and if life had taught him anything over the last forty odd years then it was usually that honesty paid off in a situation such as this.

The team seemed to sense he had something to say and all turned in his direction.

"I don't want to make a huge deal out of this — or crucially waste any more time than we really have to . . ." Jack broke off and glanced at the cork pinboard where three faces stared blankly out at him. With the latest call to the hotline, he hoped they weren't about to add a fourth. "But you will all no doubt be aware of what landed online overnight. I don't have anything to add to what I told you all yesterday. I know what it looks like, and it might not be my finest hour as far as my decision-making process is concerned, but I can reassure you all once again that it was all entirely above board. We need to crack on with the investigation and not let idle chit-chat like this affect what we do. Everyone OK with that?"

"Sure thing, boss," replied Cooper, already sinking his teeth into a bacon roll. "Amanda's been to the deli and got us all a frothy coffee."

Cassidy handed Jack a takeaway cup and smiled. "Not so much froth for you, guv."

Jack responded with a grin. "Cheers."

"And Tanya Maund's phone is still off — I've just tried it." Cassidy waved her notebook in the air.

"In that case, we need to make locating her a priority today." Jack took a welcome sip of his coffee, grateful for the extra sugar Cassidy had slipped in. "But before we do, is there any update on Barry Pierce or his vehicle?"

DC Daniels cleared his throat. "Not yet, boss. Neither he nor his vehicle have been seen."

"OK, update me if we hear any more. Has anything else come in overnight?"

Cooper swallowed a mouthful of bacon roll. "Cherry Eyres' phone details are in — they don't really tell us much. The phone is switched off and hasn't been active since last Saturday morning when it pinged a mast close to her home address. I then gave Annie Palmer a call back regarding her message to the hotline yesterday — remember she said Julian Fisher supplied her and some of the other residents with prescription drugs?"

Jack nodded. "I do. Go on."

"Well, she said that the last time she saw him was the morning of the discovery of the first two victims. He'd stopped by to drop off a packet of tablets — this was just before she lost her cat and went into Flat 7b."

"How long before?"

"She didn't really say, but not long."

"Meanwhile, he tells us he hadn't been to the estate in a long time. Not since his father left, if I remember rightly." Jack paused, taking another welcome mouthful of the rich coffee. "It's enough for us to question him again — let's bring him in for a chat."

Glancing at the wall clock, Jack wondered if Dougie King had graced the station with his presence yet. If he had, then Jack fully expected the call to relieve him of his duties to follow soon after. That being the case, he didn't much fancy hanging around to wait for it. Decision made, he drained the coffee cup and pulled his car keys from his jacket pocket.

"Amanda — you're with me. Let's go and see if we can't find Tanya Maund. Cooper and Daniels — go see Julian Fisher and haul his backside back here."

Cassidy crossed the incident room, but before anyone had a chance to do anything else one of the desk phones rang.

* * *

Time: 9.30 a.m.
Date: Thursday 15 January 2015
Location: Central London

Zara's head pounded. As her eyelids fluttered open, she tried to take in her surroundings. Where was she? Was she at home? Almost as soon as she asked herself the question, she knew what the answer was. The smell gave it away; something rotten was close by.

Feeling her stomach contract, she went to rub her eyes, feeling how sticky they were. But she found she couldn't; her hands were tied behind her back, her feet bound by the ankles.

Confusion flooded her thoughts, rapidly morphing into fear as her vision and memory began to clear. Panic welled up inside her but she willed herself to remain calm — freaking out wasn't going to help, she knew that much.

Her mouth and throat felt as dry as sand, as if she hadn't had a drop of water in a week. But her lips were stuck fast, smothered by a thick strip of tape.

The room was dark, but not so dark that she couldn't make out the shape of several pieces of furniture. She saw an old-fashioned armchair and a sofa by the window that was shrouded by a dark, heavy drape. All around were outlines of boxes and bags, piles and piles of them stacked up against every wall. Maybe that was where the smell was coming from.

It was only then that she noticed the rope around her neck.

* * *

He knew she would be awake now; the drugs didn't last long enough in their systems to keep them unconscious for any period of time. But he liked them awake — he liked to see their eyes.

And their fear.

Squinting through the crack in the door from his vantage point in the kitchen, he thought he saw her move a little, her head jerking to the side. He smiled. If she hadn't had her mouth taped shut, he was sure she would be screaming by now.

They all screamed in the end.

He eyed the bag at his feet, noting that his drug supplies were running low. Some girls were greedier than others, but he didn't mind. They all succumbed eventually.

The kitchen smelled like a sewer, but he was used to it now. He didn't eat here; he didn't sleep here. All he did was bring his girls here. He didn't really like using the house, but now he couldn't trust the lock-up anymore, and definitely not the flat. And once you got past the smell, it was OK. At least his father wasn't here anymore.

His eyes strayed once more to his phone. He'd seen the news update a few moments ago; a road closure in the city due to an 'ongoing police incident'. It didn't exactly say as much, but he knew it couldn't be anything else — the bags must have been found. It made his smile even wider.

An *incident*.

He wondered who had found her.

And how long it had taken them to scream.

Pulling his thoughts away from the bags on the bus, he slowly pulled the kitchen door open. He would need to act swiftly before panic well and truly engulfed her; the road may well be deserted the majority of the time, but he didn't want to take any unnecessary risks. Taking a pre-prepared syringe from the bag, he quickly crossed the litter strewn floor and pulled tightly on the rope around her neck; but not so much that it would constrict her breathing. That would come later, when he was ready. He then pumped her full of enough of the drug to silence her once again, giving him time to do what he needed — time to set the scene. Only then would he bring her round properly and watch her come to terms with her new predicament.

He couldn't wait to see her face.

And then there was the other one; Tanya.

It excited him that he now had two under his control, both here with him at the same time. He'd dragged Tanya across the room earlier and propped her up next to Zara; a rope around each of their necks. This one, too, was drugged enough to make her slip from consciousness, dead to the world.

Dead.

It was a good word, *dead.* It was a word that he liked.

Sitting them up side by side, he took hold of the section of rope around Tanya's neck and secured it to Zara. He could barely hide the grin from his face as he worked. Not for the first time, he wondered who would be the first to scream.

He'd got it wrong with his mother and Johnny — he knew that now. But he'd been young and naive back then.

He was better at it now.

* * *

Time: 9.25 p.m.
Date: Thursday 31 March 1988
Location: Gravesend, Kent

Slipping out from the cupboard under the stairs, he paused and listened to the silence. The flat had elicited no noise for the last few hours, but he needed to be sure. There was no room for error if he was really going to do it; not this time.

Creeping along the passageway that led to the living room, he avoided the floorboards that he knew creaked — just in case — and then peered around the door frame and felt his smile grow. Both his mother and Johnny were passed out on the sofa — like they usually were at this time after a binge. He could hear Johnny's snoring from where he stood, and his mother's chest was rising and falling rhythmically.

They were alive — but not for long.

Although he knew he had all night — they rarely had visitors to the flat, and definitely not at this time of night — he wanted to get the job finished. He wanted them gone — out of his life for good.

Entering the living room, he lifted a syringe from the coffee table. It was used, but it didn't really matter. The dirtier it was the better it would look. From his pocket he pulled out the small bag of heroin he'd stolen from Johnny's stash earlier — the man being so far gone he hadn't noticed it was missing.

He'd had the foresight to pull on a pair of gloves. He watched numerous programmes on TV that he wasn't meant to, and knew the police would check for fingerprints. He wasn't stupid, despite what Johnny said.

Picking up a metal spoon from the table, he tipped some of the powder on to it. He hadn't a clue how much he needed, but he wanted it to be enough. After adding some water, he used his mother's lighter to heat the spoon from below. He'd seen the process many times before, but his hand shook with anticipation.

When the powder had dissolved and started to bubble, he took the syringe and drew up as much of the liquid as he could. He spilled some, but it didn't matter.

He chose Johnny first. Standing in front of the sofa, he stared at the man for a moment or two. In some ways he was letting him off easily — he wouldn't suffer this way; he wouldn't know anything about the manner of his death. Part of him wanted to wake the man up and force him to see what damage he had done.

But death was enough.

He didn't really know how to inject anyone — but he'd watched his mother do it so often that he had the general idea.

He was a quick learner, and he hoped a general idea would be enough.

He chose a vein in the crook of Johnny's elbow — and plunged the syringe in.

He then repeated the process — melting a fresh spoonful of heroin and refilling the syringe — for his mother.

Mother.

She hadn't been much of a mother to him for a long time. What kind of parent allowed her child to be abused the way Johnny had abused him? She might be his mother in name, but that was all.

With the deed now done, he placed the syringe down by the side of their bodies and went to retrieve the rope and knife from the cupboard under the stairs. They wouldn't wake now, he was sure of that — he would have plenty of time to set about the remainder of his plans for them.

For death by heroin wasn't quite enough.

* * *

Time: 10.10 a.m.
Date: Thursday 15 January 2015
Location: Central London

Thinking about his mother and Johnny had caused his anger to flare; just as it always did. But he needed to keep calm — when you lost control that would lead to making mistakes.

And he had no intention of making mistakes.

He placed the discipline back inside the wooden chest, breathing hard. The pain gave him focus and allowed him to see things more clearly. Just feeling the weight of it in his hand afforded him an inner peace. He had to bring it with him to the house — the desire to inflict pain was almost over-whelming at times, and he needed a clear head. There were advantages of being here in the house. Back at the flat he would have to make sure he didn't scream, but here he could make as much noise as he wanted; there was no one around to hear. So, he'd whipped himself hard and deep — stroke after gut-wrenching stroke, exerting more force than he had done before; and for longer. The sound of the discipline lashing his skin, along with the pain, had cleansed both his soul and his mind.

And then he'd screamed.

With each lashing, he'd pictured his mother and Johnny with the rope around their necks, their faces contorted in death. He often wondered if maybe he should have woken them up before death consumed them. Made them look him in the eye before ending their lives.

Death was the only thing he had control over. Death and pain; one inextricably linked to the other. And now, as he dressed his wounds, the feelings of relief and contentment flooded his body.

Zara and Tanya would soon experience the pain.

And not long afterwards they would welcome death with open arms; just like the others had.

After dressing the freshly inflicted wounds that he could reach, he slipped on his coat and picked up the plastic bag containing two mobile phones. Although neither had the battery or SIM card inside anymore, he needed to get rid of them; there could be nothing to link himself to the girls, not if he wanted to do this right.

He made his way along the hall to the front door knowing he could leave Zara and Tanya alone. Although he would lock the door behind him, the street was deserted.

No one would be looking for them; not here.

CHAPTER TWENTY-FIVE

Time: 10.45 a.m.
Date: Thursday 15 January 2015
Location: Fairlie Avenue, London

The number forty-one bus was parked by the side of the road, a police patrol car stationed in front and behind. Already crowds were gathering, waving their phones in the air to see if there was anything worthwhile to record and post on social media.

Jack ground his teeth as he brought the Mondeo to a stop a few metres away from the outer cordon. "Bloody vultures." He exited the car and slammed the door. "Just bloody vultures, the lot of them."

Following on behind, Cassidy deftly steered Jack away from the congregation to their left, for which Jack was silently grateful — a public confrontation in the street with so many mobile phones primed to record wasn't a good mix. He was already in enough trouble with Spearing's video without adding more fuel to the fire.

"Why aren't we any closer to catching him, Amanda?" It wasn't a question Jack thought anyone could answer, but felt he needed to air it out loud. *Why* weren't they any closer? They had two credible suspects in Barry Pierce and Julian Fisher, one of whom seemed to have disappeared overnight. But were they right to be focusing all their attention on them? He took a moment to scan the crowds on the opposite side of the street, not putting it past the killer to return and witness the immediate aftermath of his latest crime; to revel in some sort of morbid glory. Glancing to the side, he saw that Cassidy seemed to have had the same idea.

"I can't see either of them here, guv."

Jack grimaced and continued towards the line of police tape that marked the inner cordon. He could already see Elliott Walker suited and booted at the entrance to the number forty-one bus and as soon as he caught the crime scene manager's eye, the investigator waved them forward.

"We're up on the top deck." Elliott waited for Jack and Cassidy to pull on their protective suits before heading back inside the bus.

Taking the lead, Jack noted Cassidy's pensive expression as they climbed the narrow stairs to the top of the bus. He wondered if she was having the same thought as he was — that the dump sites were getting riskier as time went on. This time it was a bus, in broad daylight, on a busy main road. Jack shuddered when he thought what might come next.

They had been intending to go out to Sampson Terrace to call at Tanya's flat and see if she was there, safe and sound, but the call to the incident room had changed their plans. Jack had a heaviness in his heart as they approached the crime scene.

Was it Tanya they would find?

Elliott stepped aside to let Jack and Cassidy through. "Just up ahead. On the seat to your left."

Jack wordlessly made his way towards two white-suited crime scene investigators who were crowded around one of the seats towards the rear. Although he had been appraised of what had been found, the shock still registered when he saw it.

Two shopping bags — and what were clearly body parts stuffed inside.

* * *

Time: 11.25 a.m.
Date: Thursday 15 January 2015
Location: St James's University, London

Rachel Hunter paced alongside the floor-to-ceiling windows of her office. She'd had a restless night and had given up trying to get back to sleep when the clock struck 4 a.m. Instead, she pulled out everything Jack had sent her on the three victims in his current investigation, and analysed it all over again.

The ferocity of the attacks worried her. Whoever it was, they had a deep-seated hatred within them, which was borne out by the frenzied mutilation each of the women suffered at his hands. But there was an even more disturbing element to this killer — and not one that she had voiced to Jack when he'd visited her office yesterday.

But there could really be no other conclusion.

Slipping the phone from her pocket, she dialled Jack's number and predictably it went to voicemail. She considered hanging up and trying again later, but knew that it couldn't really wait. Biting her top lip, she waited for the beep before leaving her message.

"Jack? It's me — Rachel. I've been thinking about your killer. There's something else about him you need to know." She paused and took in a breath. "The age range I gave you, I still stand by. But your killer didn't just start here. He's been doing this for some time — he's just never been caught." Another pause. "He's done it before, Jack. Your killer has done it before."

* * *

Time: 12.00 p.m.
Date: Thursday 15 January 2015
Location: Sampson Terrace, London

The ground floor flat sat at the end of a quiet residential street, nestled next to several large trees. DS Cassidy led the way through the front gate and up the short, neatly kept path. Beneath the porch they saw that the building was divided up into three flats over three levels, all accessed through the one communal door.

They'd left Elliott and his team on the bus, asking to be kept updated as the processing of the scene commenced, but Jack had decided not to return to the station immediately. The chief superintendent would no doubt already be on the warpath about the fourth body being found, and the news that had hit the headlines that morning, catapulting Jack into celebrity status, would only have made an already delicate situation worse. Jack had left several terse messages for Jonathan Spearing to call him, but he didn't expect the crime correspondent to return any of them anytime soon. His loathing for the man increased as each minute passed.

Cooper had then phoned to say that Julian Fisher was nowhere to be found at his flat, which didn't fill Jack with much cheer either. With both Pierce and Fisher going AWOL, they really did need a break with this case soon, otherwise it was going to drag them under.

Jack stepped up and pressed the buzzer for Tanya Maund's ground floor flat. They had no idea if the body on the bus was Tanya or not, but if the woman herself answered, then they could all breathe a sigh of relief.

With the buzzer eliciting no response, Jack pressed it again.

Still nothing.

Cassidy stepped across to peer in through the large bay window at the front. A pair of thick curtains were pulled halfway across, so she shielded her eyes and pressed her face close to the glass.

"Can't see much, guv. It's too dark." Her breath began to mist on the chilled window. "But no movement that I can see."

Jack gave the buzzer one last go before hitting the ones above. It only took a few seconds for one of the other residents to answer. After explaining who they were, the next sound was that of the communal door being released.

Inside, the entrance hall was small and narrow — the floor beneath sporting authentic-looking Victorian blue and white tiles. An ancient radiator hugged one of the walls, but with their breath fogging in front of them as they spoke, it didn't take much to realise that the hallway wasn't being heated.

The door to Tanya's ground floor flat was on the right as they entered, opposite a narrow set of stairs leading to the flats above. Whoever had buzzed them in didn't seem too concerned to come and see who they had just let in, and the stairs remained in darkness. Jack approached Tanya's door and gave it a sharp rap.

"Tanya? Tanya Maund? It's the police. Open up if you're there please."

A familiar silence followed. Cassidy bit her lip. "It doesn't look good, does it?"

Jack rapped on the door again, louder this time. "Tanya? We just want to make sure you're OK in there, nothing else."

More silence.

As Jack raised his hand for a third rap, both he and Cassidy sensed movement behind them followed by faint footsteps. Turning to see a young woman creeping down the darkened steps with a guarded look on her pale face, Jack tried his best smile.

"Do you know the young woman who lives here?" He nodded towards Tanya's front door. "Tanya Maund?"

The woman on the stairs hesitated for a moment before nodding, but she remained silent.

Jack persisted. "Do you know if she's home? She doesn't seem to be answering."

The woman went to shrug, then stopped herself. "I've not seen her for a few days, actually. Is she OK?"

Jack sidestepped the question. "When was the last time you saw her?"

"I'm not sure. Maybe one day last week?"

"Does she normally disappear like this?"

Shaking her head, the woman tentatively descended a few more steps but the wary look in her eyes remained.

"It's nothing to worry about. We're the police." Jack found his warrant card and flashed it in front of him. "We're just checking up on Tanya. Some of her friends are worried that they haven't seen her lately."

The fact that the two people standing in the hallway were police officers didn't seem to fill the young woman with much reassurance. If anything, the guarded look on her face intensified and she took a hesitant step back. Jack turned towards the door and gave it another sharp rap. He didn't really know why — Tanya clearly wasn't at home. Unless she *was* home and just couldn't get to the door for some reason.

The thought filled Jack with fresh unease. He turned to Cassidy standing beside him. "We need to get this door down." Taking a few steps back, he sized up the wooden door. "You see anything we could use to get it open?"

Cassidy scoured the empty hallway and saw nothing; not even the obligatory abandoned bicycle. "Not much here, guv."

Jack took another step back, contemplating how strong the door looked. But it wasn't really the strength of the door that concerned him. It was more the strength of his shoulder. Instinctively, he rubbed it with the opposite hand. Dislocated shoulders hurt and he wasn't keen to repeat the experience.

But before he needed to think of another plan, the young woman descended the rest of the stairs and hovered at the bottom.

"I . . . I have a key . . . if you need one?"

CHAPTER TWENTY-SIX

Time: 12.10 p.m.
Date: Thursday 15 January 2015
Location: Sampson Terrace, London

Relief enveloped them like a tidal wave as Jack and Cassidy stepped across the threshold into Tanya Maund's ground floor flat. There was a welcome absence of the unique metallic aroma of spilled blood, and the flat didn't have that cold, abandoned feeling that only death could bring. But it was clear the flat was empty.

The front room was compact and, judging by the blankets piled on top of the sagging sofa, it also doubled up as a bedroom on occasion. A very narrow galley-style kitchen at the rear led the way to an even smaller bedroom with an en suite. It took seconds for them to search and confirm the place was deserted.

"So, what do you think?" Cassidy stood by the kitchen sink which still had a cereal bowl waiting to be washed up. "Doesn't look like there's anything to suggest something untoward happened here." Next to the kettle was a mug, with a tea bag sitting in the bottom. Next to that was a supermarket meal for one — chilli con carne. Cassidy nudged the carton with a teaspoon. "This looks like it was defrosted some time ago." She wrinkled her nose, but as yet the defrosted dinner hadn't started to smell. "Looks like she just popped out and never came back."

Jack nodded as he swept the room once more. "True. But it doesn't explain why she hasn't at least been in touch with her friends." He paused, eyeing the waiting TV dinner. Something niggled. "I don't like it. Let's take a look around while we're here."

Tanya's bedroom housed a small single bed that didn't look like it had been slept in recently, a bedside table and single door wardrobe. "See if you can find anything to suggest where she might have gone." Jack gestured towards the bed. "Check underneath. I'll have a look in the wardrobe, see if she's taken any clothes."

Jack edged around the tight space, noting there wasn't enough room to swing a mouse let alone a cat. Pulling open the wardrobe door he saw a selection of clothes on the hanging rail, others neatly folded on a series of shelves to the side. Nothing to suggest any hurried packing had taken place. One solitary shoebox sat on the floor.

Realising his powers of search may have reached their limits, Jack hesitated. But something wasn't right, he could feel it. For whatever reason, he felt Tanya was in trouble — so, rules or no rules, he flipped open the lid of the box to reveal just the one item inside.

And it wasn't a pair of shoes.

Diaries were clever things. They afforded a window into another person's life, a window that would ordinarily be shut fast, hidden from view. They could reveal so much about a person's thoughts and feelings — and Jack knew that sometimes during an investigation they threw up a line of enquiry that hadn't materialised elsewhere.

Although he'd never kept one himself, he'd read many a diary in his time — and if they belonged to a victim of crime they could often make for sombre reading. Murder victims were the worst. Sometimes, the very last diary entries were a victim's final words; spoken from beyond the grave.

He flicked through the first few pages, quickly noting that each one had a date at the top. Sometimes days or even weeks went by without Tanya documenting anything at all — and then there would be a flurry of entries all on the same day.

The earlier entries appeared to be a record of Tanya's hopes and dreams — there was mention of moving out of London, getting a house in the country with a dog. Maybe chickens. But as the pages progressed, the content of the diary seemed to change. Gone were her aspirations and hopes for the future — instead the entries were more hurried, the writing less neat.

'Dave'. Short, moustache — smells of body odour. Safe.

Tall, bald, wears earring in left ear. Northern accent. Rough but safe.

Fat, blond hair. London accent. Tattoos on knuckles. Missing front tooth. AVOID! WON'T PAY!

When Jack had spoken to Jonathan Spearing, the reporter told him that the girls would look out for each other, making a note of any suspect punters to keep themselves safe. Was this what he was looking at right now? A list of suspect punters? If so, one of them could be the killer.

Jack flicked over several more pages. As well as physical descriptions, there now appeared to be vehicle registration numbers etched into the pale pink paper.

AM12 BVM — avoid.

BL61 LLT — avoid.

LM58 TNT — safe.

"Amanda?" Jack straightened up, hearing the cartilage in his knees protest as he did so. "You got a bag for this?" He waved the diary in her direction.

Cassidy pulled a plastic evidence bag from her pocket and reached across the bed to take the diary from Jack's outstretched hand. "You think it might be useful?"

Jack gave a shrug as he inched his way back around the bed. "Maybe. Maybe not. Seems to be a list of dodgy punters that might be worth looking into when we get back to the station."

Cassidy shook the plastic bag open, but before slipping the diary inside she leafed through a few of the entries. "I see what you mean." Her brow creased as she flicked over more pages. "Definitely look like descriptions to me. And car registrations. These could be useful."

Jack began to head for the door, desperate to get back to the car and the packet of painkillers he knew were inside. As he passed, he sensed Cassidy's demeanour change, seeing her visibly stiffen and her eyes widen. "Problem?"

Cassidy held the diary out in front of her, open at one of the pages towards the back. "It's just . . . this." She swallowed. "Take a look."

Jack took the diary back, his patience starting to wane. He *really* needed those painkillers now — any examination of the diary could wait until they got back to the station. He sighed and glanced down at the open page.

Then his heart sank.

CHAPTER TWENTY-SEVEN

Time: 2.35 p.m.
Date: Thursday 15 January 2015
Location: Metropolitan Police HQ, London

The journey back to the station had been quiet. Cassidy had sat with the diary on her lap while Jack concentrated on driving, but thoughts had raced through his head like an express train the entire way.

The diary.

Although it gave a unique insight into Tanya's life, it now also placed Jack slap bang in the middle of it. He knew it wasn't something he could bury — but would it end up burying him? Couple that with the voicemail he'd listened to from Dr Hunter, it had made for a very tense journey back.

Jack slid into a chair by the side of the cork pinboard.

"Our fourth body was found at just after eight-thirty this morning on the top deck of the number forty-one bus. Just as the bus pulled in at a stop on Fairlie Avenue, a Mrs Violet Spencer discovered sections of dismembered limbs inside a supermarket bag. A second bag contained the head and internal organs." Jack sighed.

Four.

It wasn't a good number.

"The bus company already sent over the CCTV, boss." DS Cooper tapped his computer monitor. "While you were out, I managed to take a brief look. It makes for interesting viewing."

"Load it up for us and let's see what we've got."

Cooper brought the CCTV recording up on to the interactive whiteboard. "The camera is just above the driver's cab, giving a clear view of the passengers as they board. The bit that I think interests us starts at seven fifty-four." Cooper fast-forwarded the video recording then hit 'play'. "The bus comes to a stop at the top of Cold Acre Road and the person who might be our man is the last person in the queue."

Jack and the rest of the team watched as a series of passengers stepped on to the bus, paying for their tickets or showing a bus pass, then disappeared out of shot. Unlike a lot of CCTV images Jack had had the misfortune to sit through, these were of crystal-clear clarity.

The final passenger stepped on at seven fifty-six and Cooper paused the recording. "Here we have a pretty decent picture of him."

Filling the screen was an image of a man dressed in a dark blue hoodie, pulled up over his head, light blue jeans, and carrying two 'bag for life' shopping bags identical to the ones found on the upper deck.

"He pays for his ticket with a debit card in the name of David Carpenter. Already, initial enquiries show that it belongs to a sixty-one-year-old from Wolverhampton."

"Well, I think we can be sure that the man on the bus isn't our Mr Carpenter." Jack inched his chair closer to get a better view. "No doubt it's a stolen bank card but follow it up with the local force. See if they can pay him an urgent visit. If the card hasn't been reported as stolen yet, get the bank to freeze it and alert us to any unusual activity. Play it on, Cooper."

The recording sprang back into action and the man disappeared from the screen.

"The bus makes three more stops before the suspect leaves." Cooper let the images play on, pausing once more, this time at eleven minutes past eight. "As the bus comes to a halt, we can just see him alighting in the top left of the screen." Cooper ran the images on at a slower pace, showing the man coming into view once more. "We can't see him too well, the only view of him here is from the back, but it clearly shows him getting off the bus via the centre doors. We can't see his face from this angle but the clothing is identical."

"And no shopping bags," added Jack, watching the suspect step off the bus, hands shoved inside the pockets of his jeans.

"I think we can safely assume that this is the fella that left the bags on the upper deck." Cooper restarted the recording at normal speed. "Five stops later, our Mrs Spencer gets on." He paused the recording once more, showing the old woman heaving herself up on to the bus and showing her pass to the driver. "And I think we all know what happens after that."

Jack rubbed his eyes, feeling the grit beneath them prickle. "OK, so we now have our number one suspect and we need to identify him as a matter of priority. We know he's not David Carpenter, he doesn't look much like sixty-one to me, but he has somehow managed to get hold of a debit card in the man's name. And the images from when he boards the bus give us a nice view of his face. Cooper, see if there's any more CCTV in the area to show us where he went. And anything before the stop where he joined the bus — see what direction he came from. Anything to give us a clue as to who he might be."

Cooper nodded and started tapping away at his keyboard.

"In the meantime, we still don't know where Tanya Maund is." Jack proceeded to outline what he and Cassidy had found back at her flat. "The positive is that there doesn't seem to have been any altercation inside, and nothing to suggest anything untoward happened. But . . ." Jack paused, the same question on his lips as the rest of the team.

Where was she?

"You don't think she could be our victim number four, boss?" Cooper continued to stab at his keyboard, biro clamped between his teeth. "From the bus?"

"I have no idea, Cooper." The thought had crossed Jack's mind more than once. They could very well have found Tanya — stuffed inside two bags for life, as ironic as that sounded. "But until we get a positive ID, we treat her as still missing. People are clearly worried about her and her phone is still switched off. See if we can hurry up the fingerprint analysis — I doubt we'll get lucky for a fourth time, but stranger things have happened. And see if we can find a picture of her — a recent one."

"What about the diary, guv?" Cassidy was still sitting nursing the plastic evidence bag on her lap.

Jack momentarily closed his eyes.

The diary.

Pushing himself up from his seat, he sighed. "Take a note of every description, and track every vehicle registration number — our killer could be buried inside those pages. Then let me have it once you're finished with it."

"What does that mean for Barry Pierce and Julian Fisher?" Cassidy pulled a notepad towards her. "Are we still looking for them?"

"Neither one is off the hook yet. They clearly didn't get on the bus with the bags containing our fourth victim, but that doesn't mean they're not involved at all. We still have the blood-stained bedsheet and knife found at Pierce's flat. I don't suppose we've heard anything about that yet?" The blank expressions from around the room gave him the answer he expected as he headed for the door. "So, we keep looking for them."

"Do you think we're looking for more than one killer, boss?" Cooper voiced the words that had already been circulating Jack's head. "That Pierce and Fisher could be in it together? They've both conveniently disappeared."

"Killing partnerships aren't common, Cooper, but . . ." Jack shrugged as he pulled open the incident room door. "Nothing about this case makes much sense to me at the moment. But

Dr Hunter reckons he's done this before — he didn't just start with Lisa Wood and Tara Coe. She left a voicemail earlier saying he's much too confident to be a first offender. He more or less strolled onto the Hillside Estate with two of the victims, not caring if anyone saw him or not. That takes balls. So, search the system and pull any unsolved cases with similar characteristics. Especially dismemberment and mutilation. Maybe drugs, too."

Cooper nodded. "Will do, boss. Oh, and Jenny called earlier — the bloodwork for all three victims indicates no current drugs, or alcohol, in their systems."

Jack made a face. "OK, well our killer overcomes them somehow so it's likely drugs are involved — just not ones that hang around long enough to be detected. Our killer is clever. Let's try and put a name to that man on the bus — and see if our killer just made his first mistake."

CHAPTER TWENTY-EIGHT

Time: 3.45 p.m.
Date: Thursday 15 January 2015
Location: Metropolitan Police HQ, London

"Jesus, Jack. Not again." Chief Superintendent Dougie King closed his eyes and sighed.

Jack could see the man was struggling with what to say next, so he decided to fill the silence. "It's not . . ."

"Don't tell me." Dougie King's eyes snapped open. "*It's not what it looks like.*" He sighed once again and let Tanya Maund's diary fall on to the desk in front of him. "We've been here before, Jack, if I remember rightly."

"Well, it's not." Jack felt his temperature rising. "What it looks like, I mean."

King leaned forward, elbows on the desk, and buried his face in his hands. "I know I'm going to regret this, but why don't you try and explain why your car registration has been noted in a diary belonging to a potential murder victim?"

Jack had been rehearsing what he might say in response to this question during the entire journey back to the station from Tanya's flat. None of the answers he'd practised in his head were all that convincing. What could he possibly say to make any of this look better? Here they had a vital piece of evidence relating to the potential disappearance of a young women — a woman at high risk from a known sexual predator — and slap bang in the middle of it was Jack's car.

"I spoke with Jonathan Spearing."

The chief superintendent raised his head from his hands, flashing a quizzical look across the desk. "Spearing? The reporter that hates your guts?"

"The one and the same," conceded Jack. "It's no secret that we don't see eye to eye, and I'm sure he's behind that memory stick you got in the post, but he spoke to me about our third victim Cherry Eyres. He'd interviewed her the very night we think she went missing."

Dougie King let out an exasperated sigh. "How is that relevant to the diary, Jack?" He tapped the book with his finger.

"I'm getting to that." Jack worked hard to hide the irritation in his tone. "Cherry told Spearing that the girls all looked out for each other. They helped keep each other safe by taking down details and descriptions of any dodgy punters they came across. Blokes to avoid. Car registrations to be wary of."

King's tired eyes widened a little. "I'm not sure that nugget of information is all that helpful, Jack. I fail to see how having your registration number logged in this little black book of potential murder suspects is working in your favour."

"It's a pink book, not black." Jack knew he was skating on thinner ice by the second. The words had escaped his mouth before his brain had a chance to engage. "Sir."

Dougie King's jaw tightened. "I'm well aware of its colour, Jack. But you just said it yourself — the details logged in this diary were more than likely men the women should steer clear of." The chief superintendent paused, his eyes softening a little. "It doesn't look good, Jack. Let's be honest."

"I get that — but my reg number must have been put in there for some other reason. Remember, I told you how I go down there sometimes, trying to help out?"

"Yes, Jack — my memory is just fine. And I'm still trying to work out how to fight *that* particular fire."

"Well, maybe my registration is in there so they know who I am — that I'm one of those they can trust."

Doubt flooded Dougie King's features. "That may be so, but in the light of the video recording that just about everyone has seen by now, I feel I have no option but to take you off the case."

"No, you can't. Not now."

"Yes, I can, Jack. You know I can. I'm being asked some very awkward questions from upstairs. Especially as we have a fourth body. And now this?" King handed the diary back to Jack. "This is *evidence*, Jack. I can't suppress that — as much as I might want to. The video is one thing — this is something else entirely."

Jack knew if he was in the chief superintendent's boots right now he'd do exactly the same. But it didn't make it any easier to swallow. "Give me another couple of days — forty-eight hours. That's all I ask. We've got a potential lead from the bus CCTV from this morning, and we're looking at all the other reg numbers in the diary. It might lead somewhere and I need to see it through."

Dougie King sighed again, rubbing his chin. Eventually he nodded. "Although I might live to regret it, you've got twenty-four hours, Jack. That's the best I can do. Not a minute more. Because once news of this reaches those above us, you'd better think about getting yourself up on to higher ground. Shit has a habit of rolling downhill."

"It's appreciated, sir." Jack made to get up from his seat but the chief superintendent waved him back down. "Not so fast, Jack. There's one more thing. James Quinn."

Jack attempted a shrug, avoiding his senior officer's eyes. "Doesn't really interest me . . ." He hoped he sounded more convincing than he felt. Judging by the sigh that came across the desk, he knew that was unlikely.

"I don't believe that for a second, Jack. Don't take me for a fool. How could you not be interested? I know you believe that man killed your mother . . ."

Jack was about to step in — *I know that man killed my mother* — but Dougie King raised a hand to silence him before the words left his mouth.

"You forget, I know how you work, Jack. I know what makes you tick. It is exactly what makes you the fine officer that you are — even if you are somewhat unorthodox at times. And so I know there is no way that James Quinn somehow managing to break his way out of prison isn't featuring in your thoughts right now. And maybe it's clouding your judgement a little." Dougie King's gaze gravitated back towards the diary.

"They'll catch him, they always do. He's not exactly the brightest spark — he won't survive on the run for long."

"That's as may be," agreed the chief superintendent, "But it must be preying on your mind. The man shot you for God's sake, Jack. He tried to kill you. *And* he knows where you live."

"He won't be coming back for me."

"No?" Dougie King's eyebrows shot up. "You're sure about that?"

Jack nodded. "I'm sure." He wasn't, not really, but he didn't need yet another reason for the chief superintendent to clip his wings.

"I want to put a team outside your flat. Just in case."

"No." The response came out much sharper than Jack had intended. He gave an apologetic smile. "Sorry. I didn't mean to sound so abrupt. But it's really not necessary. Quinn won't be coming back for me; I can assure you of that. He might be daft but he's not completely stupid. He'll be long gone by now — putting as much distance between himself and the city as he can."

Jack avoided Dougie King's steely gaze. He needed the conversation to switch to something other than James Quinn before the whole house of cards Jack was quietly building came crashing down around him — probably taking his career along with it. *If* he still had a career left after the last twenty-four hours, which was debatable.

Dougie King's lips thinned, seemingly unconvinced. "That may be so, but I still want you to take extra precautions. I mean it. No arguments."

Jack gave a convincing nod. "Of course, sir."

The chief superintendent sighed. "Well, just to round off your good news for the day, I've arranged another press conference for five o'clock, which by my calculation means you have an hour to prepare. Against my better judgement, I'd like you to head it up — but keep it brief, Jack. And *polite*. Try not to tell our esteemed members of the press to fuck off this time, if you can?" Dougie King rose from his leather swivel seat, the meeting clearly at an end. "And smarten yourself up before you go in front of the cameras. You still look like you've been involved in a bar room brawl." He nodded at Jack's lip. "It's not a good look. I'm sure DS Cooper must have a spare shirt lying around somewhere, and maybe a tie?"

* * *

Time: 5.00 p.m.
Date: Thursday 15 January 2015
Location: Number 41 bus, London

The irony wasn't lost on him as Michael Dixon boarded the number forty-one bus for the second time that day. He'd managed to lose himself for much of the day in the post-Christmas and New Year crowds, but now the light was fading fast and he needed to head home.

He'd seen the news reports about the road closures around Fairlie Avenue and knew his journey home would take a slightly different route as a result. *The bags had been found*, that was plain for anyone to see.

Nerves started to jitter in the pit of his stomach as he waited in line, clutching David Carpenter's debit card in an increasingly sweaty hand. He didn't really know why he felt nervous. He'd changed his appearance from when he'd boarded the bus that morning — his hoodie was reversible, so he'd simply turned it inside out to give himself a new look. Instead of dark blue, he was now dressed in a pale orange. On his head he sported a white baseball cap with the *Boston Red Sox* logo, generously bought for him by David Carpenter's debit card.

When it was his turn to pay, Dixon flashed the card once more and waited for the machine to spit out the ticket. Instead, the machine emitted a beep, transaction declined. Frowning, Dixon tried again. The same beep sounded, transaction once again declined.

He heard a sigh and tutting sound coming from the passenger directly behind him as he tried for a third time.

"Mate, your card's declined. Either use another card or step to the side — I've a timetable to keep to." The bus driver's monotone voice told Dixon that he wasn't to try it again.

Card declined.

Panic began to well up as all manner of thoughts and consequences began flitting through Dixon's mind. Someone somewhere knew David Carpenter's card had been nicked, or at least cloned. And if they knew that, they might also know he had just tried to use it. And had successfully used it that day in all manner of shops. The trail would go all over London.

Dixon slipped the card back into his pocket and pushed his way back through the rest of the queuing passengers and jumped off the bus. Instinctively he glanced up to see if there were any street cameras nearby, suddenly feeling vulnerable. Although there weren't any CCTV cameras visible, he knew much of London was covered somehow. Pulling the visor of his baseball cap down over his eyes, he ploughed through the rush hour pedestrians and tried to lose himself in the dark.

* * *

Time: 5.05 p.m.
Date: Thursday 15 January 2015
Location: Metropolitan Police HQ, London

The conference room was packed — even more so than usual. The look on Pippa Reynolds' face as they entered spoke volumes. She looked nervous — *everyone* looked nervous. Everyone, that was, except Jack.

"Looks like the world and his wife have come along to see the circus, Cooper." Jack took his seat behind the large wooden table on the raised platform. DS Cooper slipped into the seat next to him. Behind them, a video screen sported the Metropolitan Police logo.

"Aye," grinned Cooper. "They should have sold tickets."

Jack had already noted that all the seats were occupied — late arrivals forced to stand at the back. He'd clocked Aaron Taylor resuming his seat on the front row — just like last time. The man wore a pinched, haughty look on his face which made Jack want to smile all the more widely. Dougie King had asked him to open with an apology — for his behaviour last time and for the unfortunate video that had surfaced late last night. Jack had made all the appropriate noises, even nodding his head to show willing, but the word 'sorry' wasn't going to escape his mouth anytime soon. And certainly not in here. He wasn't sorry for what he said before and didn't intend to pretend otherwise. And as for the video? If sparks started to fly, then he would just sit back and enjoy the show.

Pippa Reynolds took up her customary position at the front and held up a hand to quell the increasing unrest. "If you would all be so kind, ladies and gentlemen, Detective Inspector MacIntosh is about to address you." After a sideways glance towards Jack and Cooper, she gave a curt nod as she retreated, mouthing the words 'all yours' as she did so.

Jack leaned forward, arms resting on the table, and surveyed the crowd. There were many faces he recognised, and many he didn't. But each and every one of them had a look of glee on their faces, in anticipation of what faux pas might next emerge from Jack's mouth, or how many toes he might tread on or people he might insult. Although Jack didn't intend to apologise, he also didn't want to further antagonise the very people who might be able to help him. It was a tightrope he was well used to balancing on. The chief superintendent was right, as much as it pained him to admit — he needed the media on his side. Four bodies were four too many.

Jack slid a sideways look towards Cooper and winked. The detective sergeant had loaned him a fresh shirt and even a tie — and he'd managed to splash his face with cold water and apply a liberal dose of deodorant before heading downstairs into the lion's den. He was ready.

It was showtime.

"Thank you all for coming." Jack returned his gaze to the sea of reporters in front of him. There. He'd opened with a 'thank you'. That had to appease those above, surely? Thank you was a good word — almost as good as *sorry*.

"I'm going to keep this brief as I'm sure we all have better things to be doing with our time than listening to me witter on." Silence held throughout the room as Jack scoured the journalists standing at the rear. Jonathan Spearing would usually be there somewhere, but he couldn't quite make him out this time, which was probably just as well. The anger he felt over the video recording still simmered, and Jack hadn't finished with the *Daily Courier* reporter yet — he hadn't even started. But Spearing could wait, for now.

Out of the corner of his eye Jack glimpsed the video screen behind change its image. Three square headshots flooded the screen.

"As you know, we are currently investigating the murder of three local women — Lisa Wood, Tara Coe and Cherry Eyres — who were all last seen in the vicinity of The Causeway. We are now satisfied that we are looking for one individual in connection with these deaths." He paused to clear his throat. Usually, some clever prick would jump in and start asking questions right about

261

now, just to provoke, stoke the fire and watch the sparks fly. But today there was near total silence. Jack carried on. "Enquiries are continuing, and we would still like to hear from anyone who was in the vicinity of The Causeway or surrounding streets on the evenings of Wednesday 7th and Saturday 10th January. We would also like to hear from anyone who was in those areas during the preceding week. Any car drivers with dashcam footage, please come forward as you may have something vital for the investigation. We have a dedicated hotline number — or alternatively calls can be made to Crimestoppers."

Jack detected a few reporters starting to shift in their seats. He glanced towards Aaron Taylor who was still sporting a face like a smacked arse. He almost willed the man to try and ruffle his feathers again, but so far he remained tight-lipped.

"This morning, body parts belonging to a fourth woman were discovered on a bus in central London. We are not in a position to release the identification of this person at the present time. However, we have obtained CCTV footage from the bus and identified a man who we would like to trace."

Jack paused while an image of the man on the bus joined the other three behind him. "If anyone knows who this person is, please get in touch as a matter of urgency. In addition, anyone who was travelling on the number forty-one bus this morning between Cold Acre Road and Fairlie Avenue, please also ring the hotline number. You may have vital information."

One brave soul had decided enough was enough and it was time to test the waters. "No ID for the latest victim but you're already linking them to the ongoing investigation?"

Jack spied the owner of the voice — Harvey Wallis of *The Times*. "We are," he replied, simply.

"Why is that?" persisted the reporter.

Jack plastered a smile to his face. "The cases are being linked, that is all I can divulge at this time."

"Do you have a cause of death for this latest victim?" This time it was a crime correspondent for the *Daily Mail*, Guy Murphy, who chose to run the gauntlet.

Jack locked eyes with the reporter. "Post-mortem results will be released in due course."

"Is it a police officer? Someone close to the investigation."

Jack felt his heart rate rise a notch. "Why would you say that, Guy?"

Murphy shrugged. "Well, this killer always seems to be one step ahead of your investigation. I don't think it's unreasonable to think it could be someone connected to the case."

One of our own.

Was that where they were going with this? It was something Jack had secretly considered, and the thought still jarred.

One of our own.

But Jack didn't have time to think of a suitable answer, as the questions now came thick and fast from all corners of the room — it was like a dam that had suddenly burst.

"Are you losing control of this investigation, Inspector?"

"Are the streets safe at night?"

"When will the killing stop?"

"Do you have blood on your hands?"

Jack let the heat die down before turning to address the baying crowd. He took a breath and tried counting to five — ten would be optimistic. Cooper's shirt collar was biting into his neck. "This investigation is being handled in a controlled and methodical manner, just like any other. My team are working tirelessly around the clock to catch this individual, and quite frankly comments like these are of no help to anyone." Pressing his fingernails into the palms of his hands, Jack willed himself to keep his cool. The chief superintendent would be watching and he didn't need to give the man any more ammunition to pull him from the case.

It was then that Jack noticed Jonathan Spearing sitting on the end of the front row. He hadn't noticed the reporter before — the *Daily Courier's* crime correspondent not being in his usual position, at the back of the room, leaning up against the wall. All this time, the man had been under his very nose. Their eyes locked for a second, Spearing's face cracking a wide grin.

And then he said what Jack had been dreading all along.

"Do you enjoy frequenting red-light districts, Detective Inspector?"

That did it. Fresh shirt or no fresh shirt, Jack's temper flared. He sprang from his chair, almost knocking the wooden table flying in front of him, and thundered down the platform steps. Spearing's grin faltered for a second, a startled look crossing his face. He inched as far back in his seat as he could, but there was little place for him to go.

Fists already balling at his sides, Jack knew he'd overstepped the mark the minute he'd let Spearing get to him, but he lunged towards the man all the same, sheer momentum carrying him forward. Sweat peppered his brow, and Cooper's tie dug painfully into his neck.

Just as he was about to take a swing at the crime correspondent's scorn riddled face, two hands grabbed his good shoulder and pulled him backwards.

* * *

Time: 6.00 p.m.
Date: Thursday 15 January 2015
Location: Metropolitan Police HQ, London

"Sorry, everyone. I let things get on top of me — again." Jack gave a sheepish smile towards the team. He knew he shouldn't have let the press get to him quite the way they had, but it was as though they did it on purpose — to see how long it would take for him to fully erupt.

This time it hadn't taken long at all.

"And sorry about your shirt, Cooper." Jack gestured towards the large tear on the shirt's right sleeve, so much so it was almost hanging off. "I'll get you another."

"No need, boss." Cooper didn't bother to hide the grin on his face. "It was worth it for the entertainment value alone."

"That may be so, but you'd probably do as well to keep your distance from me for the foreseeable — and that goes for all of you. My name will be like mud around here once word gets out — if it isn't already." Jack pushed himself away from the desk and ran a hand through his hair. He didn't want to think about what he might have done to Spearing if Cooper hadn't got to him first. Whatever it was, it wouldn't have been pretty. "Look it's been a long day — a long few days, in fact. Take the night off, all of you."

"Before we do that, there's something you might want to know about the vehicle registrations we lifted from the diary." DC Daniels pulled out his notebook. "One of them belongs to a van owned by our very own Barry Pierce."

"Pierce?" Despite his tiredness, Jack's eyebrows hitched. "The very man who said he never picked up girls from the street? Good work, Daniels. I take it there's been no further sighting of him or his vehicle?"

Daniels shook his head. "None."

"Well, he remains a suspect in this investigation — even though we now have our guy from the bus CCTV. Anything else before we call it a night?"

"Elliot rang to say that the body parts from the bus were at the mortuary." Cassidy pulled a face. Jack imagined she still hadn't quite been able to shake the vision of what they'd witnessed on the top deck of the number forty-one that morning. "You're to ring Dr Matthews in the morning. And he's sent through some crime scene photos from the bus — I've pinned them to the board." She pointed towards the whiteboard, Jack noticing the shudder as she did so.

"Looks like Wolverhampton have returned my call about our Mr Carpenter." Cooper waved a Post-It Note in the air that had been tacked to his computer monitor. "Says here that the real David Carpenter has been in ITU in New Cross Hospital for the last eight days. Kind of confirms he's not our man."

Jack nodded. "That it does. Anything else?"

"I've started looking into past unsolved cases, boss," replied Daniels. "Ones with similar traits to our current investigation. So far, nothing stands out but I'd like to carry on this evening, if that's OK?"

"Knock yourself out, Daniels. Just don't make it an all-nighter." Jack pulled his phone from his pocket, relieved to see that there were no messages from Dougie King — not yet at any rate.

Give it time, he thought, as he searched through his contacts list. *Give it time*. Stabbing at the phone screen, his call was connected on the second ring.

"Just say yes to the next question I ask you, Rob." Jack snatched up his jacket and headed for the door. "Do you fancy a pint?"

266

CHAPTER TWENTY-NINE

Time: 7.30 p.m.
Date: Thursday 15 January 2015
Location: The Duke of Wellington Public House

DS Carmichael brought the pints over to their usual table, Jack reaching for his almost before the detective sergeant had time to sit down. "Bad day?"

"Could say that, Rob." Jack downed a third of his pint before glancing at his phone again. Still no word from Dougie King. He wasn't sure if the radio silence reassured him or not. "I'm sure you must have heard what happened by now."

Carmichael gave a quick wink before picking up his pint glass. "I may have heard a thing or two on the grapevine." He nodded towards Jack's torn shirt. "I wasn't quite sure I believed the bit about you squaring up to a member of the press, but . . ." He gave a grin. "Maybe I do now."

"Tosser deserved it," grumbled Jack, taking another mouthful of lager. "Just sorry I didn't manage to actually land a punch on him."

"Has the chief super caught up with you yet?"

Jack made a face. "Not yet. I still have that delight to look forward to. I think the only thing that might save my skin is if we manage to come up with a name for this killer."

"But that's not likely?"

"Not in the foreseeable, no. Certainly not soon enough to save me from the gallows, anyway."

The two detectives sat and finished their drinks in companionable silence, neither feeling the need to populate the quiet with small talk. Jack was about to get up from his bar stool and get a fresh round of drinks in when the pint glasses appeared in front of him.

"You been fighting again, Jack?" Adam Sullivan grinned. "I thought I'd told you before about that."

"Take a seat, mate, and I'll tell you all about it." Jack waved at the empty bar stool next to him.

"I would if I could but I can't stop. Flying visit only." He held up a paper bag. "I only popped in to pick up a takeaway."

"Next time, then. Thanks for the beer." Jack raised his glass at the departing dentist.

"A takeaway sounds just the ticket," commented Carmichael, rubbing his stomach. "You fancy it?"

Before Jack had a chance to respond, a familiar figure burst in through the door and headed in their direction.

"Cooper! This is becoming a habit." Jack started to get to his feet again. "Let me buy you a drink to make up for ruining your shirt. It's the least I can do. And Rob, here, has said he'll treat us to a curry."

"No time, boss." Cooper's cheeks were flushed. "Amanda's had an idea."

* * *

Time: 7.45 p.m.
Date: Thursday 15 January 2015
Location: M4 motorway

Barry Pierce pulled the van into the service station car park and headed for the area in front of a bank of trees and woodland at the rear. With one solitary lamp-post emitting a faint, muted light it was the best he could do. A line of three articulated lorries were the closest vehicles to them, their cabs darkened and the occupants presumably asleep.

Pierce killed the engine and turned in his seat. "You need to make it quick. I don't want to hang around here any longer than I have to."

"I don't see why we needed to come at all." Julian Fisher's voice was gruff, his eyes squinting through the dimness of the van. "Running makes us look guilty."

"We *are* guilty." Peirce's voice was equally gruff. "Well, you are anyway."

Julian's eyes narrowed even further. "Don't think you're whiter than white in all this, mate. You're up to your neck in it, just as much as me." Reaching forward, he pulled the plastic bag from the glove compartment.

Pierce bristled, his hands still gripping the steering wheel, his knuckles turning white. "That's rich coming from you. I'm not the one with two dead women's mobile phones in a bag, am I? And I'm not your mate." He nodded towards the bag in Julian's hand. "What the hell possessed you to keep them? Why didn't you just leave them where they were? These fuck-ing things can be tracked, you know?"

Julian grimaced but shook his head. "The phones are switched off, and in any case they don't have batteries or SIM cards in them. They're useless. No one can trace them. You should have just let me chuck them."

Pierce gave a non-committal shrug. It sounded plausi-ble but he didn't trust Julian Fisher as far as he could throw him. And it was his van. He didn't want evidence like that anywhere near him. "Don't shit on your own doorstep. You chuck those things close to home and they'll come back and bite you before you know it. They need to be as far away from us as you can get them."

Julian pursed his lips and stared out of the side window. "And where do you suggest, Einstein?" He gestured towards the woodland in front of them. "Chuck them in a tree?"

Pierce gripped the steering wheel ever tighter. Why he'd picked Fisher up he couldn't quite fathom. He should have just let him dig his own grave. He wasn't sure the service station was far enough away, but right now he couldn't care less. He just wanted the phones, and Fisher, gone. "I don't care what you do with them anymore. Just get them out of my fucking van!"

Pierce watched as Julian flung open the passenger side door and hauled himself out, muttering any number of expletives under his breath as he went. As he followed the man's figure crossing the forecourt towards a bank of recycling bins on the far side of the car park, he felt his hand gravitate towards the ignition. He should never have picked Fisher up like he had. He hadn't asked to get involved, much less wanted to. Temptation gripped him. He could just drive off, leave the bastard here to fend for himself.

Again, his hand gravitated towards the ignition.

* * *

Julian Fisher headed towards the bank of recycling bins, his irritation with Pierce building with every step. The phones couldn't be tracked; he knew that much — but it made sense to dump them as far away as possible. As he passed the line of articulated lorries, he considered depositing them somewhere inside — or maybe he could wedge them underneath somehow. That way, the handsets could be taken to lord knows where, but definitely far away from Acorn House.

Hesitating as he passed, he noticed the cabs were still in darkness, the occupants slumbering behind the closed curtains at the small windows. It would only take a minute. He glanced back over his shoulder at Pierce's van, the man no doubt watching his every move.

But the bins would be better. They probably weren't emptied for days, maybe even longer.

As he approached the bin closest to him, he felt a sharp stab of pain between his shoulder blades. He was sure the wound had stopped bleeding now, but Pierce could well have seen the bloodstains that had seeped through his shirt when he slid into the van earlier. Instinctively, he pulled his coat a little more tightly around him, wincing at the resulting discomfort.

Wrenching the metal lid up, he lobbed the bag and the two phones inside, hearing them clatter to the bottom. The sooner this was done, the sooner he could get back and get some painkillers inside him.

As he let the lid fall back down, he heard the van's engine roar behind him. Whirling round, he caught sight of Pierce through the windscreen, his face set hard and staring fiercely through the glass ahead. Julian expected the van to slow down as it passed by, enabling him to slip back into the passenger seat.

But the van didn't stop.

Instead it shot past him and disappeared into the night.

"Bastard!" fumed Julian, his words lost in the darkness. "You complete and utter bastard!"

What was he meant to do now?

He contemplated knocking on one of the lorry cabs to ask where they were heading, hopefully it was back to London, but decided against it. No one liked to be woken from sleep, especially a tired lorry driver. He suspected he might not get much of a welcome.

Pulling his coat even tighter, he headed for the exit and the slip road that led back on to the motorway. There was nothing for it, he would have to hitch. As he passed the line of recycling bins, he grimaced at the trouble those phones were now causing him.

Why hadn't he just left them behind?

* * *

Time: 7.15 a.m.
Date: Monday 12 January 2015
Location: Flat 7b, Acorn House, Hillside Estate, London

He took a chance that the woman's right hand was the correct one. Both phones were the new iPhone 5s — and both needed a fingerprint to unlock them.

Tutting under his breath, he angled one of the woman's fingers towards the first phone's screen. On the third attempt, the woman's middle finger, the phone gave a reassuring click and the screen sprang into life. He then repeated the process with the second phone, using one of the other hands. This time it took just two attempts.

With both phones now unlocked, he scrolled through the most recent calls and messages, seeing if any tied either of them to flat 7b. And, therefore, to him. After a few tense minutes, he began to relax.

There was nothing.

After a final scroll through, he switched both phones off and removed the batteries and SIM cards. Taking a plastic bag from his pocket, he slipped both handsets inside, then placed the bag inside his rucksack. He would deal with them later but, for now, he needed to leave.

The legs had been neatly arranged on the floor of the kitchen, and he'd been careful not to tread in the blood. The arrangement of the arms in the other room had made him smile, looking a lot like they were hugging the cushions that surrounded them. He felt it was a nice touch, although he was sure it would be wasted on whoever discovered them.

For they *would* be discovered.

Glancing at his watch, he knew he needed to move on. The estate was waking up and he could ill afford to be seen anywhere near the flat. Hoisting the backpack up into his shoulder, he stepped out on to the walkway and headed in the direction of Flat 4a. The old woman had been bleating on about her headaches again, so he'd agreed to up the dosage for her.

For a price.

He chuckled and left Flat 7b behind.

* * *

Time: 8.45 p.m.
Date: Thursday 15 January 2015
Location: Metropolitan Police HQ, London

"I thought I told you all to take the night off and go home. You can't do it, Amanda. I won't let you." The muscles in Jack's jaw tensed. The idea was insane. "It's against all manner of police protocols." Not that that usually bothered him.

"And not to mention it's far too risky." DS Cooper's face was equally taut. "You cannae do it, Amanda."

"But I want to." DS Cassidy sat squarely in her seat. "I *need* to do it. It's the only way. This bloke isn't stopping. He's killed four so far and Tanya is missing. Lord knows who else he's got by now. The only way we'll get to him is if we flush him out in the open."

"I don't necessarily disagree with you, Amanda." Jack rubbed his eyes. The beers from the pub earlier weren't helping his mood. "But this isn't the way to do it. There are established procedures and protocols for something like this . . ."

Cassidy gave a small laugh. "Since when have you cared about protocols or procedures, guv?"

It earned her a small smile.

"She's got a point, boss." Cooper threw a greaseproof paper bag containing Jack's favourite cheese and ham toastie across the desk. "And get that inside you. You look like death."

Jack caught the sandwich bag and began to unwrap it. "You've changed your tune, Cooper. Not two minutes ago you were crowing on about how risky the whole thing would be."

"I know, but . . ." Cooper sank his teeth into the soft white bread of a fresh bacon roll. "I don't see how else we're

273

gonna find him. He's running rings round us right now. Always one step ahead."

"Do you really think it could be a copper, guv?" Cassidy's dark eyes flickered towards the whiteboard where all four faces now stared out at them. "If we think he's one step ahead all the time — knows when the patrols are out and about, and the women seem to go with him voluntarily? The press is already thinking along those lines."

As sickening as it sounded, Jack knew it was a distinct possibility and it had crossed his mind more than once, and that was before Guy Murphy shot his mouth off at the press conference. "I really don't know, Amanda. We can't rule anything out, but for the moment our main suspect is now the man on the bus. We need to find him. And I still have questions for Barry Pierce if we ever track him down again."

Jack paused and took a large bite out of the toasted sandwich, only just realising how hungry he was. Swallowing, he rubbed his eyes again and grimaced. "OK — just so we can rule it out, find me a list of all officers who have been part of the increased patrols in the area. We'll start there."

"I'll start on that now." Cooper scooted his chair towards one of the computer monitors.

Jack turned back to Cassidy. "But you still can't do it, Amanda. It's fraught with danger. If we think we need to go undercover with this, then there are procedures we have to follow."

"Sod the procedures, guv!" Amanda slammed a hand down on her desk, almost knocking over a stack of paperwork. "These women need our help *now*. Not next week!"

Jack gave a deeper sigh, his head throbbing and his shoulder shouting at him for a top-up of painkillers. He turned towards DC Daniels who had been sitting quietly at the back of the incident room, a thoughtful look on his face as he worked on his computer. "What's your take on it all, Daniels? Are we insane for even considering this?"

Daniels continued tapping away at his keyboard for a few seconds before pausing and looking up, his brow creased in concentration. He nudged his spectacles a little further up his nose. "Well, on the face of it, yes. It's blatantly against the rule book, and not to mention fraught with danger."

Jack rummaged in his pocket, bringing out a packet of painkillers. He dry-swallowed the two remaining pills, tossing the empty packet into the bin. "Why do I get the feeling there's a 'but' coming, Daniels?"

Daniels' face flickered into a smile. "*But* — we have to look at the demographics of each victim."

Jack massaged his temples. Demographics? What rabbit hole was the young detective jumping down now? "Although I feel I might live to regret it, Daniels, tell me what you mean. But make it quick, we haven't got all night."

Daniels got to his feet and approached the whiteboard. "Each of our four victims had black hair." He tapped the image of Lisa Wood who in her mugshot was sporting a short, cropped hair cut in ash blonde. "None of the images we have here on the board are recent. In the post-mortem pictures, you'll remember Lisa had jet-black hair." He then moved to the side and tapped the image of Tara Coe. "Tara has red hair in this photograph, but again it isn't recent. She also had jet-black hair at the time of her death. Cherry Eyres was wearing a black wig at the time of her death, and from what we know about this morning's discovery, our fourth victim also had dark hair." Daniels turned to face Jack. "Then we need consider the other demographics. All four victims were between five-seven and five-eight tall and were all medium build. And all were aged between twenty-five and thirty-five." Daniels paused while the information began to sink in.

Jack started to nod. "So, our perpetrator has a type?"

Daniels blinked. "Almost certainly, I would say. I mean, it's not to say his next victim won't be different, but . . . the ones so far have all looked strikingly similar."

Jack stared at the whiteboard images. How had he not spotted this before? Admittedly, the photographs they had were out of date, but why hadn't he checked? He'd read the post-mortem reports — he should have picked up on it sooner.

While Jack was perusing the whiteboard, Cassidy got to her feet and went to stand by Daniels' side, a determined look on her face. "You see, guv? *This* is what I've been saying all along. I'm twenty-eight, five-seven, and I've got jet-black hair." She paused and drew in a breath. "I'm just his type."

CHAPTER THIRTY

Time: 7.15 a.m.
Date: Friday 16 January 2015
Location: Kettle's Yard Mews. London

The beers at the Duke of Wellington had gone some way to helping Jack sleep, but he had still woken up in the early hours, bathed in sweat. Dougie King hadn't yet been in touch but it didn't mean Jack was out of the danger zone — far from it. Didn't someone important say that the quietest moment was before the storm?

After spending longer than usual in the shower, he pulled his last fresh shirt from the wardrobe, deciding yesterday's trousers would be adequate for another day. Amanda's plan to trap their killer had played heavily on his mind all night.

Padding through to the living room, he picked up the mug of coffee he'd started drinking earlier, and placed it into the microwave to reheat. Caffeine would be needed in abundance today; he could feel it. As he made his way back to the sofa to pick up the laptop, Marmaduke came sauntering over, fresh from a nap on the window ledge, and began winding in and around Jack's legs, purring loudly. The window ledge was fast becoming the tabby cat's favourite place to sleep, especially when the heating was on and the warmth from the radiator beneath rose up.

Mrs Constantine had sent a message to say she hoped she would be discharged from hospital on Monday, so Jack would be relieved of his cat-sitting duties. Jack had surprised himself at the not too small amount of disappointment he felt at the news. He'd come to like having the little guy around, enjoying his company, and would be sad to see him go.

Maybe Stu was right — he needed a pet.

Before Jack could ponder whether a trip to Battersea Dogs and Cats Home was in order, his phone pinged with an incoming message. Part of him had wanted to switch it off overnight — less chance of the chief superintendent getting hold of him to inform him of his fate — but he knew he needed to be contactable out of hours, just in case they stumbled across a breakthrough in the case, as implausible as it sounded.

But the message wasn't to do with work.

As soon as he pulled up the image, he instantly recognised it — it couldn't be anywhere else.

And then he recognised the man in the centre of the screen.

James Quinn.

* * *

Time: 8.00 a.m.
Date: Friday 16 January 2015
Location: Flat 3a Acorn House, Hillside Estate, London

Howard Watkins pulled both black bin liners over to his armchair. The cockroaches had vacated the estate now, and things could slowly get back to normal. There hadn't been much left behind when he'd gone down for his customary Thursday trawl through the bins, which had irritated him as he climbed the six flights back to his flat. But there was always next week. And he still had plenty of bags that he hadn't looked through yet — two of which were now sitting at his feet.

He opened the smaller of the two first, ripping a large hole in the side. Several items of clothing fell out, together with a soiled baby's blanket and several broken children's toys. He wrinkled his nose. He didn't like babies, or children for that matter.

Taking a sip from the mug of milky tea he'd made himself earlier, he pulled the second bag towards him. This one was slightly larger, and heavier — it looked promising. Ripping another hole in the side, he plunged a pudgy hand inside.

The contents again seemed to be clothing. Watkins had acquired several useful items from the bins in the past, notably a decent donkey jacket, several trousers and even a pair of boots, so he decided to pull everything out for a closer inspection.

Watkins wasn't a man of the world but he knew blood when he saw it. Even dried blood. And there seemed to be a lot of it. Several towels were drenched in it and, even though dry and hardened by now, there was still the unmistakable metallic scent. Then there was a T-shirt and a pair of trousers.

And then there were the bones.

Watkins dropped the bag and stared hard at them for a moment or two. Although he had his fair share of rubbish in the flat, he wasn't stupid. And he knew what other people thought of him when they saw it. It didn't bother him what other people thought — they weren't important.

But he drew the line at blood.

Blood meant death.

He considered his options for a moment. He could just stuff it all back in the bag and haul it back down to the communal bin, ready for the next collection.

Or — he could ring the police.

* * *

Time: 8.45 a.m.
Date: Friday 16 January 2015
Location: Metropolitan Police HQ, London

"I'll be honest with you." Jack leaned up against the wall by the side of the cork pinboard. "I don't know how long I'll be heading up this team — what with the video recording and now my car reg details showing up in Tanya Maund's diary."

"But you've explained the video recording, guv," volunteered Cassidy, her face fixed. "And your car registration in the diary could mean anything."

"I'm not so sure that's how they'll see it upstairs, Amanda — but thanks for the vote of confidence, it's appreciated. I've managed to avoid the boot so far, so let's just pray my luck holds for a while longer." Jack suspected he'd avoided the boot mostly because he'd avoided Dougie King, but that could change the moment the chief superintendent managed to track him down. He kept a cautious eye on the door. "What we need to do now is prepare for tonight." The words stuck in Jack's throat as he gave Cassidy yet another concerned look. "I still don't like the idea — I don't like it one bit."

"It's the best chance we have, guv," was Cassidy's retort, her voice firm. "I won't do anything stupid — I'll be in contact with you guys the whole time. I won't put myself in any danger."

"You're already putting yourself in danger, Amanda." Jack rubbed his eyes, still feeling the effects of the disturbed night's sleep. The message he'd received earlier that morning from Ritchie Greenwood was gnawing at the back of his skull. He could almost feel the handset burning a hole inside his pocket.

'You know you want to, Jack.'

'It'll be just you and him.'

But he couldn't let Ritchie Greenwood, or James Quinn for that matter, derail the investigation. He needed to focus.

"We'll be checking in with you every few minutes, but any sign of danger, and I mean *any* sign at all, then you leave. Understood?"

Cassidy nodded. "Understood."

"You want me to park up a street or so away, Jack? Keep an eye out on the ground?" DS Carmichael interjected from the back of the incident room. Although it wasn't his case, Jack had been unable to persuade Rob to leave them to it. "My face isn't so well known in connection with this investigation. I could be another pair of eyes?"

Jack shook his head. "Thanks for the offer, Rob, but it's best you steer clear on this one. This is my neck — and my job — on the line, not yours."

Carmichael shrugged. "Point taken. But the offer's there though, just shout."

"What else have we managed to uncover so far? Any more updates?" Jack eyed the four images now pinned to the corkboard. "Anyone heard anything from the mortuary about our fourth victim?"

"They rang earlier, boss." Cooper pulled his notebook across the desk. "Dr Matthews is examining the remains this morning. He'll give you a bell after. Jenny rang, too — with an update from the lab."

Jack's eyebrows hitched. "Anything useful?"

Cooper made a face. "Well, yes and no."

"Hit me with the good news first."

Cooper flicked open one of the pages in his notebook. "At the bottom of one of the bags from the bus was a partially smoked hand-rolled cigarette, and the paper used contained a partial address."

Jack's eyebrows shot up further. "And?"

"I ran a check — it's a property registered to a Shell Harris, aged twenty-eight. I'm checking for next of kin details as we speak."

"OK, good. Tread carefully though, as we don't know who that cigarette butt belonged to. It might just have been inside the bag when the killer used it, alternatively it might be even related to him in some way. Give it high priority — in case it gives us something to work with." Jack felt a little buoyed at the news; it was a potential lead. Then he remembered Cooper wasn't quite finished. "And what's the not so useful result?"

Cooper made another face. "None of the DNA profiles that were lifted from Acorn House have shown up on the database."

"Well, I guess it was a long shot. What about past cases, Daniels? Anything showing up with that yet?"

DC Daniels shifted in his seat and gave Jack an encouraging nod. "As it happens, there have been a few, yes. One is an unsolved case from 2005 — a body found in Hounslow — where the victim suffered sixty-seven separate knife wounds, and a botched attempt was made to remove their heart. A second case is from 1999 — this time the rape and murder of a prostitute from Essex. No attempt to remove internal organs, but the victims head and hands were removed and buried some way away from the rest of her body. Then I found a third — this one goes back to 1988. Two victims were found together in their flat with ropes around their necks, a man and a woman. No more detail than that at the moment, but they were both known drug addicts and had overdosed on heroin. There was also a crude attempt to remove their limbs."

"An attempt? Not successful, then?" Jack wasn't sure he wanted an explanation as to what that might mean.

Daniels shook his head. "Not successful was all it said. I can dig deeper and try and find out more about them — there might be photos somewhere?"

"I don't think that will be necessary just yet, Daniels. We'll come back to it if needed after tonight. I take it there's no further news on Barry Pierce or Julian Fisher?" Jack could see by the expression on everyone's faces that the answer was in the negative. "Or the man on the bus CCTV?" More negative murmurings followed. "Great," he sighed, pushing away from the wall and heading towards the door. "For what it's worth, Daniels, maybe we should get more information on those three unsolved cases. And keep searching for Pierce and Fisher — they can't have just dropped off the face of the earth."

"What's the plan for tonight, boss?" Cooper twirled a biro in his hand. "What time do you want us?"

Tonight.

Jack still had a bad feeling about the whole thing. "The plan, such as it is, is for us to meet back here around eight o'clock. Amanda, you'll be dropped off as close to The Causeway as we can get you without being seen. Cooper and I will manage everything from here, but your comms device is to be switched on at all times." Everyone nodded. "Daniels — I hear you've got one of your running club sessions tonight?"

Daniels nodded. "But it's fine, boss. I'm happy to miss it and help out instead."

"No need, Daniels. You go to your club run — Amanda tells me you've got a marathon or some such torture lined up to train for? We can cope on our own here tonight."

Daniels grinned. "It's a half marathon and I'm not even sure I'm going to enter yet. I really don't mind missing the training run tonight. There's plenty of time before the race if I decide I'm really going to do it."

"Nonsense, Trevor," cut in Cassidy. "You have to do it! I'm coming along to watch!"

Daniels' grin slipped a little. "It's just that I've never done anything like that before. It's a bit daunting."

Jack passed the detective constable on his way to the door. "That's settled then, Daniels. You go to your running club tonight. We're more than capable on keeping an eye on things from here, aren't we Cooper? We'll see you in the morning."

"What about the list of officers connected to the night-time patrols, boss?" Cooper waved a piece of paper in the air. "We managed to find six who were drafted in to be part of the regular drive-bys."

Jack sighed and wrestled with his conscience. Did he really suspect one of their own? He caught Carmichael's eye at the back of the room and the pair exchanged a knowing look. Jack had made a spectacular error of judgement three years ago, thinking Rob was caught up in one of his investigations and he'd never forgotten it. Carmichael had insisted on brushing it all aside, making a joke of it, despite the punch he took to the face. But was Jack about to do the same thing again here?

Jack shook his head. "No, let's park that one, Cooper. We've got more than enough to handle at the moment. The press seems to have latched on to it through — but I'm more than happy for them to bury themselves down that hole for a while. Just keep at it, everyone. Let me know if anything useful comes in, otherwise I'll see you back here at eight. I'm stepping out — I don't think it's wise that my face is seen around here at the moment. I'll be in my office for a bit, then you can catch me at home."

Stepping out into the corridor, Jack was relieved to see it empty — but the twenty-four hours Dougie King had given him was now over. He was living on borrowed time.

* * *

Time: 10.15 a.m.
Date: Friday 16 January 2015
Location: Central London

Julian Fisher felt he had little option but to return to the flat. He needed to check whether the police were on his tail and if they had paid him another visit in his absence. After a brief look around, it was clear that if they had, they left no sign. He then worried about the lock-up, but knew going back there would be too much of a risk.

When Barry Pierce had driven off without him last night, he had spent a good ten minutes shouting all manner of expletives into the night sky. It hadn't solved the problem, but it had made him feel better. The man incensed him.

Once he'd calmed down, he'd headed back toward the slip road to set about making his way back to London. It hadn't taken too long before someone had taken pity on him and stopped to give him a lift. He hadn't been a particularly chatty passenger, he knew that — but the driver soon got the hint and continued the rest of the journey in silence.

But now he was here, he wondered if it was such a good idea. He had kept the lights off, and kept the curtains drawn, but had barely managed a wink of sleep. As far as he knew, no one had seen him arrive under cover of darkness — but he wouldn't be able to stay long, he knew that.

As he sat in the dim light of the kitchen, nursing a coffee he didn't really want, he inevitably thought back to Pierce. The man was on his own as far as Julian was concerned. Any allegiance they'd had in the past was well and truly over. The man had better keep his mouth shut if he knew what was good for him. But although Julian had plenty on Pierce that would interest the police, he had no intention of going anywhere near the cops right now. At least he'd had the foresight to get rid of the phones — one less thing to tie him to Flat 7b.

Pushing the half-drunk coffee to the side, he winced. The wounds on his back were still stinging and he needed to change the dressings he could reach. He just hoped he had enough antiseptic in the flat so he didn't have to go out to search for some.

Deciding he would shower first, he headed for the bathroom. He'd switched his phone off last night and it remained the same way now; he needed to remain off-grid for a while longer while he decided what to do next.

Peeling off his shirt, the bloodstains clearly visible, he snapped on the shower.

* * *

Time: 10.45 a.m.
Date: Friday 16 January 2015
Location: Metropolitan Police HQ, London

Jack put the phone down and sighed. The call from Dr Matthews had gone as expected — it was never going to be great news. The pathologist had confirmed that all the body parts belonged to the same person, which was something at least, and he'd noted the same extensive head injury as two of the previous three victims had sustained.

Then there was the same dismemberment — and the same mutilation.

As they had suspected from the scene on the bus, Dr Matthews confirmed that not all body parts were present in the bag. It didn't come as any great surprise. An adult human was unlikely to fit inside two shopping bags, even if they were cut into manageable pieces — and even if they did the bags would be too heavy to lift. The CCTV images they had seen from the number forty-one bus showed the man who lifted the bags on board wasn't especially large himself.

But all that did was leave Jack with another unanswered question.

Where was the rest of her?

Cooper had followed up on the hand-rolled cigarette butt found in the shopping bag — finding a recent image of Shell Harris from social media. With the images Dr Matthews had just emailed him from the post-mortem, Jack was in no doubt about the identification of victim number four — not that it brought him much joy. All it meant was there would be another loved one answering the door to that fateful knock, their world suddenly being turned upside down from that moment on, never to be the same again.

He slumped back in his seat and downed the remains of the coffee Cassidy had made him. He'd kept the office door closed and so far had successfully avoided Dougie King, but he knew his luck wouldn't last much longer. Deciding he had probably pushed the said luck as far as it would go, Jack began to gather up various pieces of paper and reports. He could continue working back in the safety and sanctuary of his flat, without constantly jumping at the sound of footsteps outside in the corridor or whenever the phone rang.

As he shoved paperwork into a folder, his thoughts strayed back to tonight. The plan was audacious at best; potentially career-ending at worst. Everything about it made him nervous, but what else could they do? They were literally at the end of the line.

Jack had appreciated Rob's offer to help, keep an eye out on the ground, but Jack couldn't do it to the man. It was bad enough that the whole team were involved, he couldn't justify dragging someone else into it, too.

There had been nothing more in the news about Quinn's escape from prison; plenty of theories but nothing that even came close to what Jack suspected had really happened. He knew Ritchie Greenwood was up to his neck in it, the only question was why?

Jack gave his head a quick shake and swore under his breath. He needed to stop thinking about Quinn — and Ritchie, too. There wasn't enough space in his head for anything more than the current investigation — and tonight.

Tonight.

Jack's stomach clenched once more as he headed for the door.

He had a bad feeling about it already.

CHAPTER THIRTY-ONE

Time: 1.15 p.m.
Date: Friday 16 January 2015
Location: Metropolitan Police HQ, London

DS Cooper waved his pen in the air, attracting Cassidy's attention. He put a hand over the mouthpiece.

"We've had a call on the hotline — someone's only gone and identified the bloke on the bus. More than one, in fact. Several have rung in with the same name." He turned his attention back to the phone. "Aye — just let me have the guy's name, we'll do the rest." Pulling a scrap of paper towards him, he began to scribble. "Aye. That's perfect. Cheers." Returning the handset to the cradle, he turned towards Cassidy who had come to perch on one of the desks behind him. "Guy's name is Michael Dixon, lives at an address in Hackney."

"You calling the guv?"

Cooper reached for his mobile. "Aye. Uniforms are already on their way to pick Dixon up, if he's at home. I'll see what the boss wants to do about interviewing him." The detective sergeant scrolled down to Jack's number, and didn't have to wait long for it to be picked up.

"Cooper? What's up?"

"It's good news, boss. We've had a call in on the hot-line, several in fact. The guy on the bus has been named — a Michael Dixon from Hackney. We're getting him lifted as we speak. Just wondered what you want us to do with him when he gets here. You coming in to speak with him?"

Cooper listened to the response. "Aye, OK. I'll give you a bell when he arrives."

* * *

Jack cut the call. He'd had half a mind to switch his mobile off for the rest of the day, less chance that Dougie King would be able to catch up with him, but if he did that then the others wouldn't be able to reach him. And Cooper's call had been most welcome indeed.

Michael Dixon.

The surname was common enough, but it didn't stop Jack thinking about the case that had haunted him for the last quarter of a century — finding the killer of little Carrie Ann Dixon. Although the case had eventually been solved, it had taken its toll on Jack over the years and he would never forget her as long as he lived.

Running a hand over his unshaven chin, he considered his options. He could drop everything and head back to the station, interview Dixon himself. That would probably be the most sensible thing to do, but Jack wasn't known to be all that sensible at the best of times.

And he had the chief superintendent to think about now. Set one foot back inside the station and Dougie King would most likely be on the war path, heading straight for Jack like an Exocet missile. Jack didn't fancy raising his head above the trenches just yet.

Instead, he'd decided to let Cooper handle it. He was more than capable and Jack trusted him implicitly. The min-ute they got anything tangible from Dixon, Cooper would call him. Slowly, he started to feel something akin to relief filter through. Maybe this was the beginning of the end, and with any luck they wouldn't need to go ahead with the foolhardy, if not downright crazy, farce for later that evening.

Jack started to relax and even contemplate some food.

* * *

Time: 1.45 p.m.
Date: Friday 16 January 2015
Location: Hackney, London

The heavy thumping at the front door roused Mike Dixon from his afternoon slumber. He sat up with a start, sending the plate that had been resting on his chest flying. Momentarily dazed by the sudden commotion, he scrambled to his feet just in time to hear the door leave its hinges and crash to the floor.

"Police! Police! Police!"

The door to Dixon's front room was the next to crash open, followed by a swarm of black-clad police officers filing in in its wake. Panic bubbling, Dixon instinctively raised his hands high above his head. "Don't shoot me!" he yelled, eyes widened in fear. "Don't shoot me!"

Dixon couldn't see any guns but that didn't mean there weren't any. He read the news just as often as the next person. Guns were everywhere.

"On your knees, hands on your head!"

Dixon sank to the floor, his knees landing on the litter strewn threadbare carpet while his heart hammered so violently in his chest he thought it would burst. Two police officers appeared like lightning by his side, grabbing hold of his wrists and twisting them behind his back. Within seconds he'd been handcuffed.

"Michael Dixon — I am arresting you on suspicion of murder. You do not have to say anything, but it may harm your defence if you fail to mention when questioned something you later rely on in court. Anything you do say may be given in evidence. Do you understand?"

Dixon's mouth fell open as he was pulled to his feet. Murder?

"Do you understand?" repeated the officer, holding him by the arm.

Dixon nodded. "Yes, I understand, but . . ."

It took less than two minutes for Dixon to be escorted from the premises and herded into a waiting police van parked outside.

CHAPTER THIRTY-TWO

Time: 5.30 p.m.
Date: Friday 16 January 2015
Location: Metropolitan Police HQ, London

DS Cooper sighed and nudged the as-yet uneaten bacon roll to the side of his desk. His initial chat with Michael Dixon hadn't gone well. Their initial exuberance at identifying the man on the bus very quickly evaporated once the man started to speak.

According to the arresting officers, Dixon had verbal diarrhoea the whole way back, despite being told he was under caution and he might want to take legal advice before spilling his guts. The warning went unheeded and Dixon continued to sing. And he'd continued to do so after being booked into the custody suite.

Cooper dialled Jack's number, knowing the boss would pick up the moment it rang. He wasn't disappointed.

"Cooper? What's the latest?"

Trying to keep the deflation out of his tone, Cooper replied "I don't think it's him, boss."

"What do you mean you don't think it's him? It's not the guy from the CCTV images?"

"Oh no, it's the right guy — it's the bloke from the number forty-one bus all right. He admits that's him. That's not the problem." Cooper knew the boss wouldn't want to be kept hanging for long. "He admits taking the bags on the bus but says he was paid to do so. Won't tell us who by."

"Paid?"

Cooper heard the exasperation in the boss's tone. "Aye, paid. Thing is, he won't tell us who by. Clams right up. I get the feeling he's scared witless of spilling the beans. He's not the brightest star in the sky, but he's petrified."

"And you believe him?"

Cooper had been expecting the question. "Aye, I think I do. Or at least I believe he didnae kill the poor wee lass. Whether he was paid to take the bags on the bus is another matter. An initial search of his flat hasn't found much except for a stash of GHB and David Carpenter's bank card."

There was an audible sigh from Jack's end of the phone. "OK, Cooper. Go at him again — I want to know what connection he has to Acorn House, and whether he knows either Barry Pierce or Julian Fisher. Tell him he's looking at conspiracy to murder — see if that loosens his tongue any."

"On it, boss."

* * *

Jack ended the call and closed his eyes. He'd been hoping for better news, almost willing Cooper to utter the magic words that Dixon had confessed and the case was solved. A rueful laugh stalled in his throat. It was never going to happen — he'd been naive to think there was even the smallest of chances. The GHB was an interesting find, though. And if they could establish a link between him and either Pierce or Fisher — or even both — then the case just took an enormous step forward. Whether it was enough to cancel the fool's errand they had planned for later only time would tell.

But it was time they didn't really have.

293

Jack glanced at his Fitbit — his step count was pretty poor today but that wasn't what unnerved him. With less than three hours until Amanda was due to take her position on the streets, the clock was ticking.

* * *

Cooper and Daniels resumed their seats in interview room one.

"Just to remind you, Mr Dixon, you are still under caution." Cooper's eyes lifted towards the red light blinking reassuringly in the corner of the room. "And this interview is being video and tape recorded. The time is now six-fifteen p.m."

Mike Dixon had been provided with a cup of tea and a sandwich during the break, evidence of both on the front of his sweatshirt.

"Mr Dixon, tell me about Acorn House."

Cooper watched Dixon's forehead crease. "Acorn House? Where's that?"

"On the Hillside Estate. When was the last time you were there?"

"I . . . I don't think I've ever been to the Hillside Estate."

"You don't *think* you've ever been — so it's possible that you have?" Cooper knew he was pushing his luck a little, but he'd learned a lot about interview techniques from the boss over the years — not all of them appearing in any of the handbooks or guides on conducting suspect interviews, but they were often effective just the same.

"I . . . I don't know."

"What about Barry Pierce? Do you know him?" Cooper kept his eyes trained on Dixon's face for any hint of recognition. He saw none. "What about Julian Fisher?" The same blank expression. Cooper decided to change tack.

"How did you come to be in possession of a stolen debit card, Mr Dixon?"

"A stolen what?" Dixon's eyes widened.

"Debit card. You used it on the number forty-one bus yesterday morning, and several times again throughout the day. How did you come by it?"

"I . . . I . . ." Dixon reached for the polystyrene cup of lukewarm water and took a sip. "I was given it."

"By who?"

Dixon lowered his gaze to the worn wooden table. "No comment."

"Are you scared of someone, Michael? Or can I call you Mike?" Cooper remembered the boss telling him that using a suspect's first name sometimes encouraged them to open up. "Is anyone threatening you?"

"No comment."

"You do understand that we're investigating the deaths of four women, don't you, Mike? That's four murders."

"I . . . I didn't do it. I didn't do any of them." Panic edged into Dixon's tone. "It wasn't me."

"Then how do you explain depositing the remains of one of those women on the number forty-one bus?"

Dixon swallowed and took another mouthful of water. "I told you — I was paid to do it."

Cooper nodded, exchanging a look with DC Daniels by his side. "Yes, we heard you say that. But if you don't tell us who that person was, we can't corroborate that, can we? Just give us their name."

"I can't."

"Murder is a serious offence, Mike. It carries a maximum of life in prison, you do understand that?"

"I didn't murder anyone. You can't say I did."

"Even if you didn't carry out the murders, Mike — you're involved. You're looking at conspiracy to murder at the very least right now." Cooper noticed Dixon's leg starting to jiggle beneath the table, the man's eyes blinking rapidly. Sighing, he made a decision. "Interview suspended at six-twenty-one p.m."

CHAPTER THIRTY-THREE

Time: 9.30 p.m.
Date: Friday 16 January 2015
Location: Whiting Street, London

Did they really think he was that stupid?

Gripping the steering wheel, he clenched his teeth until they started to hurt.

He'd driven along The Causeway as usual that evening, casually surveying the area. No one acknowledged him as he crawled along. He was safe. He was *always* safe. It made him smile.

The police were chasing their tails at best. It excited him just how far away from the truth they really were. Suspecting one of their own? If the latest news headlines were to be believed, they really were clutching at straws if they were heading down that spectacular rabbit hole. Not that a copper wouldn't be capable of doing what he did — there were plenty of bad apples around in that particular orchard.

But he expected better of Jack MacIntosh. The man was meant to be smart — smarter than most, so he was told — but the best detective the Met had to offer couldn't see what was staring at him right between the eyeballs. This gave him an extra ripple of pleasure for what he was about to do.

Reaching the end of Whiting Street, he turned the corner and parked up just out of sight. He knew a patrol was scheduled soon, but there were still four girls out on the street, all within eye and earshot of each other. Four was too many; experience told him that much. He needed there to be just the one; all on her own, with no one around to see her get into his van.

Despite his desires, he knew he could wait; the discipline taught him that much. The discipline taught him control and patience.

And endurance.

As he shifted in his seat, the wounds on his back reminded him of their presence — but he welcomed the discomfort.

Pain sharpened his senses.

He'd recognised her the moment he saw her, standing a little back from the kerb beneath a broad oak tree as he drove past. *Amanda* — he was sure that was her name. She looked the part, he had to give her that much. They had obviously put some thought into it — but not quite enough to pull it off.

They really *did* think he was that stupid.

He didn't recall Amanda, if that was indeed her name, appearing at any of the press conferences the Met liked to schedule from time to time. Pantomimes he preferred to call them — for that was often what they ended up being. Instead, MacIntosh would usually head them up — aided by that young, ginger-haired detective. Scottish lad, if he recalled correctly.

But it was never Amanda.

He started to relax his grip on the steering wheel.

Amanda.

He liked the name — he'd never had an Amanda before.

His smile widened. He had to hand it to them; they'd done their research. She was *exactly* what he was looking for. She was even dressed how he liked them all to dress — short

297

skirt, but not too short; knee length boots, leaving a section of pale bare skin, exposed to the cold; and then there was the jet-black hair hanging loose over the shoulders — enough for him to grab hold of and pull the head back when the time came.

He liked them *all* that way.

Yes, they had done very well indeed with Amanda.

Lisa, Tara, Cherry and Shell had all ticked his boxes with ease — all a mirror image of the mother he'd once loved and then grown to despise.

So it could be no coincidence that they'd put Amanda on the street to lure him in — the one to finally catch him.

He could imagine the headlines already.

His smile widened some more.

It was clever.

But not quite clever enough.

* * *

Time: 10.45 p.m.
Date: Friday 16 January 2015
Location: Kettle's Yard Mews, London

He could leave the car behind and head back to the station on foot — it wasn't that far — but the weather outside was less than inviting. The temperature might have risen a degree or two but it was still bitterly cold and icy rain was starting to fall.

Jack swirled the dregs of his coffee around in the bottom of the mug — losing count of the number he'd had since arriving home that morning. Part of him wished he'd stayed at the station to wait it out, but with the chief superintendent breathing down his neck he wasn't quite sure how much time he had left, so his continued absence was probably wise. And then, unsurprisingly, bearing in mind the way their luck was going recently, he'd noticed the Mondeo had a puncture just as he was about to set out back to the station. He wished he hadn't bothered now.

The interviews with Michael Dixon had brought the team nothing but more frustration. Cooper was certain that the man was telling the truth, or at least a version of it, but he still wouldn't give up the name of who had coerced him into taking the shopping bags on board the bus. The sensible money was on either Barry Pierce or Julian Fisher — but where were they? People couldn't just drop off the face of the earth these days, not unless they tried really hard.

With Dixon bringing them no further forward, the plan for the evening had gone ahead — against Jack's better judgement. Cooper had dropped Amanda off close to The Causeway earlier that evening and was more than capable of handling things back in the incident room while Jack waited to get the blasted Mondeo's tyre fixed. But he'd left strict instructions for Cooper to keep in contact with her and call in with regular updates.

So far there hadn't been much to report, but it didn't ease Jack's disquiet. He sank the remains of his umpteenth coffee, knowing he probably should have limited his caffeine intake — not wanting his nerves jangling any more than they were already — but it was a bit late for that now.

Everything about tonight's operation was wrong but, try as he might, he just couldn't see what alternative there was. The discovery of the fourth body yesterday morning was like a hammer blow to the investigation — an investigation that was now clearly stalling. The killer was escalating to an unprecedented level and time clearly wasn't on their side. They had thought they'd got a credible new suspect in Michael Dixon, but that idea was disappearing fast.

They had to stop this killer, whoever he was — and Amanda's plan was as good as any they had come up with so far.

Local mechanic Ashley Bell owed Jack a favour or two, and when he said he would be at the flat inside an hour to deal with the tyre, Jack was sure that the man would try his best. But it was the longest hour he could remember and there was still no sign of him. While he waited, Jack turned on the laptop to give himself something else to think about other than what a spectacular mess they were getting themselves into.

When Dougie King had shown him Spearing's video recording, Jack had persuaded the senior officer to give him a copy of the memory stick. Jack had watched the footage a dozen times by now, and knew it didn't offer much by way of an explanation as to his presence on that particular street at that particular time. It was a well-known red-light district and he was a detective inspector.

The two should never meet — and certainly not on film.

But meet they did and Jonathan Spearing, alongside all the other bloodsucking leeches of the media, had rubbed their hands together with glee at the prospect of slamming yet another police officer's reputation into the mud.

It was increasingly becoming a spectator sport.

The recording started several minutes before the snapshot Dougie King had chosen to show him. Jack had never been inside Spearing's car, but instinctively knew the crime correspondent was the one behind the wheel and angling his phone through the vehicle's windscreen.

The footage showed the street ahead to be quiet. Spearing zoomed in and brought two figures into focus, both standing a few feet away from the kerb. Jack didn't need the camera to get any closer — he knew who they were. Just like he knew who was going to appear in the top right-hand corner of the screen any moment now.

He was.

Although Jack knew his presence on Colville Avenue that night was entirely legitimate, or at least he had an explanation of sorts, the camera didn't often lie. And Dougie King was right — all it showed was a high- ranking police officer approaching known sex workers in the street and handing over cash. Whichever way you looked at it, whatever spin you tried to give it, it wasn't good.

Jack let the recording play on, once again watching himself engage in conversation with both women and then pass

300

each of them a handful of cash. After a couple more minutes, he left them alone on the street and headed back to his car. The whole encounter took less than ten minutes, but it was ten minutes that could very well cost Jack his career.

Jack checked the time on his Fitbit again and considered pouring himself another coffee to pass the time. As he did so, he also glanced at his phone. He'd half been expecting to receive another message from Ritchie Greenwood.

The sheer audacity of the man. He had clearly sprung Quinn from prison somehow, and was now gloating in the aftermath — taking great pleasure in taunting Jack as to the man's presence on the outside.

'You know you want to, Jack.'
'It'll be just you and him.'

Jack had spent some considerable time thinking about whether he wanted to come face to face with Quinn again — to finally get the chance to be in the same room as his mother's killer. But what would he say? The thought intrigued him, maybe even to the point of him thinking he would actually do it, but then he shot the idea down in flames. He needed to stop thinking about Quinn — now was not the time.

Just as he was about to pocket his phone and banish all thoughts of Ritchie Greenwood and James Quinn along with it, another message pinged up on the screen.

* * *

Time: 11.20 p.m.
Date: Friday 16 January 2015
Location: The Causeway, London

DS Cassidy hopped from one foot to the other as the chill began to work its way into the soles of her feet. She'd put on two pairs of socks beneath the cheap, fake-leather boots but they did little to prevent the cold from seeping in. Looking at her watch for what seemed like the millionth time that evening, she saw it was only just after eleven. Time seemed to be going backwards rather than forwards. Business along the street had been slow at best, or at least slower than she'd expected.

The other women had been friendly enough when she'd arrived, telling her that Friday was usually one of the busiest nights of the week, with a steady flow of regulars passing through.

But not tonight.

Maybe the message finally was sinking in. Not just for the women themselves, urging them to stay home and off the streets, but for the punters, too. Although the press had stopped short of coming right out and saying it, everyone knew there was a heightened police presence now, with regular patrols throughout the night, it would make even the most confident kerb crawler think twice.

As the evening had progressed, Cassidy watched the other women slipping into passing cars, one by one, disappearing into the night. She kept an eye on the registration numbers, receiving discreet nods from the others confirming that '*this one is safe*'. When the women returned, she gave a small sigh of relief and afforded them a sad smile.

Cassidy admired their camaraderie — how they truly cared for each other's safety. Their hardened faces told her that none of them were here out of choice — if they had their way they would be at home in the warm with their loved ones. The more the minutes slowly ticked by, the more the respect Cassidy had for them swelled. Some might call them foolish, or even reckless — but all Cassidy saw was desperation.

After a while, one of the women Cassidy knew as Frankie decided enough was enough and left for home. That left just the three of them. Cassidy continued to hop from foot to foot. The next patrol wasn't due to drive by for another forty-five minutes or so. She knew Jack wasn't happy about her being out here — but he'd eventually seen the twisted logic behind it. She fleetingly wondered if he was out there somewhere, maybe just around the corner, keeping an eye out for trouble.

Part of her — the part that still retained some degree of fear about the precarious position she had willingly placed herself in — hoped that he was.

But Jack was instantly recognisable. His face had been splashed all over the media for the last five days — and he'd appeared on the front pages numerous times in the past. Their killer wasn't that stupid — Dr Hunter's profile told them that much. If he saw Jack in the vicinity, he would most likely run a mile.

A car's headlights blinked through the gloom and headed towards them, and Cassidy felt her heart rate increase a notch. As the car neared, one of the women opposite, Helena, caught Cassidy's eye and gave a discreet nod as she walked towards the passenger door.

Safe.

Now it was Cassidy and just one other girl, the darkness deepening around them. The rain had started to fall with increasing velocity, and Cassidy's position beneath the oak tree was offering little protection. She could feel her hair clinging to her scalp as the rainwater dripped down her neck. Pulling her short jacket more firmly around her shoulders, she hugged herself to try and keep warm.

"All OK?" DS Cooper crackled in her earpiece which was camouflaged behind a large ornate earring. Cassidy was grateful to hear his voice.

"All good," she confirmed. "Helena has just got into a car. Confirmed to be a safe punter. The others have had a slow night and one's gone home already. There's just me and one other girl left out here. Where's the guv?" Cassidy had been expecting Jack to check in with her.

Cooper's voice crackled once more. "Car trouble. He's on his way in, but I'm afraid you've just got me as backup for the moment."

Cassidy thought she could hear something in the background, something more than just the crackle of the comms device. "Are you eating?" The very thought of food made her stomach growl. She had been too nervous to contemplate eating anything before coming out, but now her stomach was protesting at its emptiness.

Cooper laughed on the other end of the line. "I think you know me well enough by now, Amanda. Rob just brought us down some burgers from the canteen."

Cassidy's mouth began to water as the rain dripped off the end of her nose. She would do almost anything for a greasy burger right now, and that said something. Usually she chastised Cooper for his junk food addiction, trying to tempt him with all manner of healthier options, but at this moment she would happily bite his arm off for a mouthful of cheeseburger.

"I might call it a night soon," she muttered, feeling her thin jacket sticking to her skin. "I'm freezing. And there's not a lot happening here tonight. I think the weather's putting everyone off from coming out."

"I don't blame you. The boss said to bail out any time you wanted. You know he didn't much like you going out there in the first place."

Cassidy let out a relieved sigh. "That's the best news I've had all night, but I don't really want to leave Jade out here alone, though."

Jade was still standing on the opposite side of the road, trying to light a cigarette in the rain. Cassidy watched as the woman gave up trying and thrust the packet of soggy cigarettes back into her jacket pocket, heading across the road in Cassidy's direction. Her hair was plastered to her scalp, long dirty blonde ragged trusses lying limply across her shoulders, and her thick mascara was running down her damp cheeks.

"I'm giving it up for the night — going home." Jade rubbed the raindrops from her nose. "It's way too quiet and I'm soaked through. Plus, I'm starving."

Cassidy heaved a silent sigh of relief. "Good. I'm doing the same." As Jade started to walk away, Cassidy called out after her. "Do you need a lift anywhere? I'm about to get one of my colleagues to come by and pick me up."

Jade shook her head and carried on walking. "Nah, I only live a couple of streets away. I'll be home before you know it."

Cassidy watched Jade disappear into the gloom, just as another set of headlights appeared at the other end of the street. "Did you hear that, Chris?"

"Loud and clear," crackled the reply. "Shall one of us head out and pick you up?"

Cassidy watched the vehicle approach with a small flicker of trepidation. Jade was now out of sight and she suddenly felt very alone; and very vulnerable. The closer the vehicle got, Cassidy's feeling of fear began to be replaced with one of silent relief. The Welfare Truck pulled up by the kerb, the driver's side window already down.

"Horrible evening to be out. Need a lift anywhere?"

CHAPTER THIRTY-FOUR

Time: 11.30 p.m.
Date: Friday 16 January 2015
Location: Metropolitan Police HQ, London

"Sorry I'm so late — what's the latest?" Jack strode across the floor of the incident room, fat droplets of rainwater flying from his hair. The fine rain from earlier had turned into a deluge. The shoulders of his jacket were drenched even from the short distance between the car park and rear entrance to the station. "Have you heard from Amanda?"

"She made contact a short while ago, boss." Cooper scrunched up one of the burger wrappers that still littered his desk. "She's calling it a night and heading back. Very little traffic and the other girls have gone home, too."

"Wise decision," breathed Jack, not bothering to hide the look of relief on his face. "We're going to pick her up I take it?" He half-turned and started heading back towards the door, car keys in hand.

"No need." Cooper stood up and tossed the wrapper into a nearby bin. "One of the street pastors pulled up in the Welfare Truck while I was talking to her. He's bringing her back."

Jack wasn't overly disappointed. He didn't much fancy running the gauntlet back across the car park to the Mondeo. Due to his tardy arrival, he'd had to park on the far side by the gate, and even at a good run he would get soaked again. And it was cold. "Good. We'll hang around here for a while, then — wait for her to get back and tell us anything she might have gleaned from the evening. Then we'll get off home. I'm sure you've got better things to be doing than spending the rest of the night here."

Cooper grinned. "Jenny's got a few of her mates round to the flat for a decorating party tonight. I'm more than happy to give it a miss, boss!"

"Decorating party?" Jack made a face. DIY and any other form of decorating was not his forte. It was one of the many reasons why his flat at Kettle's Yard Mews hadn't seen a lick of paint since he'd moved in. It was neat, it was clean — and it was relatively tidy, unless Stu had been to stay. Jack wasn't one for unnecessary trappings or home furnishings. And he wasn't one for parties, either, decorating or otherwise. "Sounds like my idea of hell, Cooper."

Jack took a seat and slipped his laptop on to the desk. With Amanda now safe and on her way back, his attention turned back to Ritchie Greenwood. The latest text, received when he was back at the flat, made it clear that this was a one-time offer. James Quinn was being handed to him on a plate, but time was ticking on.

I think you know where we are, Jack.

Home sweet home.

But don't leave it too long — twenty-four hours and we'll be gone.

Jack rubbed his eyes. Another twenty-four-hour deadline, but this one he could do without. He turned to Cooper. "You seen anything of the chief superintendent tonight?"

"Not yet, boss — but we've had some good news at last."

"Good news? There's two words I haven't heard in a long time."

Cooper grinned. "Just got word that Barry Pierce was picked up an hour ago filling up his van at a petrol station not far from Acorn House. Looks like he might have been returning home after all. And that's not all. Julian Fisher returned to his flat and was arrested half an hour ago. He's being booked in as we speak."

Pierce and Fisher both in custody? Jack felt the enormous weight of the last few days start to ease. "That's brilliant news, Cooper. What about Dixon?"

"He's tucked up for the night in the cells. Still swears blind he didn't kill anyone, but won't give us the name of who made him take the bags on to the bus."

"OK, well he can sweat overnight. Let's wait for Amanda to get back, then we can all head off home for some kip."

"I also managed to speak to Shell Harris's parents. They haven't seen her for a few weeks, but confirmed she hasn't been answering her mobile. They sent another photo across — and I don't think there's any doubt she's our fourth victim." Cooper nodded towards the cork pinboard where he'd tacked another image of Shell Harris next to the one they'd obtained from social media. "A family liaison officer is being arranged for them."

"OK, good work. We'll follow up on that tomorrow."

Jack allowed himself to sink back in his seat. Tonight's little operation looked to have been a waste of time, but he felt nothing but relief that Amanda hadn't been placed in any unnecessary danger. It was disappointing news about Dixon — but with both Pierce and Fisher now under arrest, the net was closing fast. And with any luck Dougie King would be none the wiser about Jack's latest foray across the border into the danger zone.

Notwithstanding, Jack kept a wary eye on the door and his phone. He turned back towards Cooper. "You got any of those burgers going spare? I'm starving."

* * *

The rain was coming down more persistently now, plastering his hair to his scalp as he ran. But he didn't mind all that much. The night-time training run had gone well — and Trevor Daniels was beginning to think that the half marathon wasn't such a pie-in-the-sky idea after all. Maybe he *could* do it.

They'd ended the run outside the gates to the park on Carlisle Crescent, and the quickest route back home to his flat at Farriers Court would be directly across the open grass, but at this time of night the whole area would be in pitch darkness. The path wound its way through several densely populated areas of trees and shrubbery — not always pleasant during the day let alone the depths of the night. Even a police officer with a degree of self-defence training like Trevor Daniels didn't much fancy the prospect.

So, instead, he skirted the park and opted for the longer route by road.

With another couple of miles to go, he slowed to a jog. The extra distance would be good preparation for the half marathon *if* he decided to take the plunge and enter. Amanda had been bending his ear about it for weeks now, but it wasn't until this evening that he felt enough confidence to take it on.

Amanda.

He hoped she'd got on OK tonight. No one was particularly thrilled at the prospect of her trying to lure a serial killer out of the shadows, least of all Amanda if Trevor knew her as well as he thought he did — but they were so firmly pressed up against a brick wall with this case that there seemed to be no other option. He hadn't wanted to leave them in the lurch by going off to his running club, but Jack had been insistent. They didn't need the three of them monitoring the situation.

As he splashed through an icy puddle, Daniels looked at his watch. Half past eleven. Amanda would most probably still be out there on the street, facing all sorts. He didn't envy her one bit.

Despite the sweat that clung to his skin under his sports clothes, he shuddered. The Causeway wasn't all that far from where he was now. As he jogged, he mentally pulled up a street map into his head, calculating the distance by road. Not far at all — especially if he cut through the back alleys.

But as much as he wanted to check Amanda was OK, he knew his presence could compromise the whole assignment and then Amanda would have been put in danger for no reason at all. With a heavy heart, and not a small degree of misgiving, he headed for home.

* * *

Time: 11.30 p.m.
Date: Friday 16 January 2015
Location: The Causeway, London

"Help yourself." Adam Sullivan gestured towards the plastic box on the dashboard as he pulled the van out of The Causeway. "You look like you could do with a sugar hit."

Cassidy reached forward and grabbed a couple of chocolates, smiling gratefully. "You're not wrong. I'm starving. And freezing."

"Won't be long until we get you back in the warm. I'll turn the heater up." Sullivan flicked the van's heating up to maximum. "There's some water there somewhere, too. Sorry I've nothing hotter." He gestured towards the glove box.

Cassidy's lips felt dry despite the deluge of rain that had fallen on her. She opened the glove box and rummaged around until she located a bottle of Highland Spring. "Thanks."

"Where am I taking you?" Sullivan hesitated at a junction. "Home?"

Cassidy shook her head, unscrewing the lid of the bottle and thirstily draining a third of it in one go. "No. Back to the station if you don't mind? Unless it's out of your way? I can always ring to be collected."

"Not at all. I'll take you anywhere you wish." Sullivan indicated right and took the turn. "It's a slow night tonight. Not that many out on the streets, thankfully. Those that were I've managed to steer in the direction of a hostel to at least keep dry."

"Thanks." Cassidy pulled the comms device from her ear, screwing the lid back on the bottle.

"Was it a useful evening? You get what you wanted?"

Cassidy glanced sideways, catching the man's eye, unsure how much she should divulge. She saw the merriment in his eyes, the corners crinkling as he broke out into a grin.

"It's all right. Jack told me about your little operation tonight. Asked me to keep an eye out if I saw you around." He pulled the van down a side street. "Not a bad idea, trying to flush the guy out like that. You certainly look like the ones he seems to go for. Dark-haired, medium build. Even the short skirt and boots that he has a penchant for. Very clever idea that. But I take it it didn't work?" Sullivan glanced sideways, eyebrows hitched. "You didn't see him?"

Cassidy yawned and shook her head, munching on her second chocolate. "No. I think the weather might have kept him inside."

Sullivan nodded. "Maybe. You going to try it again another night?"

Cassidy reached for another chocolate. "Possibly. Probably." She shrugged and popped the chocolate into her mouth letting the sweetness dissolve on her tongue and the sugar hit her bloodstream. "Not really sure."

If she was being brutally honest, she was glad the under-cover operation hadn't worked. She'd been running on pure adrenalin for the last twelve hours and now felt completely exhausted. Exhausted but safe. But she wasn't sure she could go through it all again. She wrestled with the conflicting emotions now tumbling around inside her head. She was glad she hadn't seen him — the killer — because the thought of coming face to face with the man who had killed and dismembered four women so far scared the living daylights out of her.

But then there was the disappointment, too. Disappointment that her idea hadn't worked; that they hadn't managed to flush him out and trap him like they'd hoped. Cassidy shuddered and swallowed the chocolate, grateful for the velvety sweetness. Sighing, she closed her eyes and rested her head against the side window.

CHAPTER THIRTY-FIVE

Time: 11.50 p.m.
Date: Friday 16 January 2015
Location: Croxley Avenue, London

The car jolted her awake and Cassidy peered out through hooded eyelids to see Adam Sullivan's face grinning at her.

"Sorry — speed bumps."

Cassidy's head had been resting against the passenger side window at an awkward angle, and her neck felt stiff. Groaning, she pulled herself upright and blinked — first once, then twice. Then a few more times. Her eyesight was blurry, her head feeling heavy and dull. Confusion fogged her thoughts.

The van felt stiflingly warm, her damp clothing now almost dry on her skin. She rubbed her eyes, trying to dislodge the blur. "How long was I out for?"

"Oh, don't worry — not long." Sullivan indicated and pulled to the left.

Cassidy frowned through the misted window. "Where are we?"

"It's not far now."

Cassidy's blood chilled.

That wasn't what I asked.

With her mouth drying by the second, Cassidy reached for the water bottle and unscrewed the cap, taking another long swig. Another frown followed. Was she imagining it, or did it taste slightly salty? She glanced down at the bottle, unable to get her eyes to focus on the label. The words swam in front of her eyes.

Confusion now competed for space with the growing sense of disquiet raging inside her head. Had the bottle already been open when she'd drunk from it? Or had she broken the seal? She couldn't remember. More disquiet followed.

"This doesn't look like the way back to the station," she remarked, her voice sounding distant and muffled. "Where are we?" she repeated.

Sullivan seemed to hesitate before pulling the car into another side street. "Not long now."

Cassidy's heart began to pump faster. As well as the water bottle in her lap, there were several scrunched-up chocolate wrappers. Despite the increasing fog inside her brain, she started pulling snippets of information to the forefront, trying to connect the dots.

Where had she seen those wrappers before?

She looked at them again. They weren't a brand she would ordinarily buy for herself — she didn't buy a lot of chocolate, but when she did it definitely wouldn't be these. And she was quite sure she hadn't seen either Chris or Trevor tucking into them at the station, both of whom loved a chocolate hit from time to time. So, where had she seen them before?

Then it dawned on her and her already chilled blood chilled some more.

As the car bumped over yet another series of speed bumps, she self-consciously started to pull the miniskirt down towards her knees. Her skin was covered in tiny goose bumps, but it had nothing to do with the temperature inside the van.

'You certainly look like the ones he seems to go for. Dark-haired, medium build. Even the short skirt and boots that he has a penchant for.'

Cassidy's brain sharpened despite the fog. They hadn't divulged any of that information to the public, keeping it away from all the media briefings. The photographs they had used of Lisa and Tara showed them with ash blonde and red hair respectively. Nothing had been said about them having jet-black hair. And no mention was made of what they had been wearing.

This was information that *only the killer would know*.

Sickness raged inside her, her heart rate rocketing. Even though the van was warm, she felt frozen to the bone.

The killer.

Swallowing the lump that was threatening to suffocate her, Cassidy glanced out of the side window once again. She couldn't see exactly where they were, the raindrops and mistiness of the window distorting her already somewhat blurred vision. But it definitely wasn't on the way back to the station. Where were they going?

Cassidy knew she would have to do something — and do it soon. Tiredness was about to engulf her again. She knew full well what this man was capable of, and she wasn't planning on becoming his next victim. If he managed to get her back to wherever it was they were headed, then it would likely be game over; he'd already managed to overpower four fit and healthy, streetwise women. He would overpower her in seconds.

Instinctively, she fumbled inside the pocket of her skimpy jacket, feeling her heart freeze. Where was her phone? Flashing an increasingly foggy gaze around the inside of the van, she spied the handset resting up on the dashboard.

She could tell from the blank screen that it had been switched off.

Panic fought with exhaustion. If she was going to get out of this alive then she had to act.

And she had to act *now*.

In one swift movement, she released her seatbelt and made a grab for the steering wheel.

* * *

Time: 11.50 p.m.
Date: Friday 16 January 2015
Location: Metropolitan Police HQ, London

"With Barry Pierce in transit, and Julian Fisher already in custody, we may as well use this time to review the evidence against them while we wait for Amanda."

"Once they're swabbed for DNA, surely it won't take too long for a match to be found, to tell us if it's them? Mike Dixon's DNA hasn't been a match." Cooper slugged back the sugar-laden energy drink he'd picked up from the canteen along with two more burgers. "But there were a few full and partial profiles found in Acorn House."

"I'm always nervous about relying solely on DNA, Cooper." Jack swallowed a mouthful of burger. "Science is a wonderful thing but we need good old-fashioned evidence to back it up. Let's take another look at the crime scene photos and other evidence for both Acorn House and the Tanners Road Industrial Estate. Neither will be interviewed until the morning, but it'll be good to get ahead of ourselves."

Cooper scooted his chair back to his desk and started to bring various images up on to the interactive whiteboard. "These are the first set of crime scene photos taken at Acorn House, boss." The screen was instantly populated with pictures depicting the horrific scene in the one-bedroomed flat — including those from the bathroom.

"What about the evidence log?" Jack pulled his chair closer to the whiteboard, stuffing the rest of his burger into his mouth. "What was taken away to the lab? We might see something we can track back to either of our suspects. Both, if I recall, seemed insistent that they hadn't been inside or even near Flat 7b for some time. We need to see if we can find something to disprove that."

Cooper tapped the keyboard and soon brought up the evidence log. "Here you go, boss." He began to read from the itemised list. "Drug paraphernalia including a set of brass scales, lighters, metal spoons, tin foil and also three hundred and fifty pounds in cash. Then we have an old duvet, a sleeping bag, two pint glasses, three ceramic mugs, two pairs of jeans and a woollen coat. Lastly, there was a selection of confectionary — chewing gum wrappers, empty packets of biscuits and also some chocolate wrappers. Looks like whoever had been there had an attack of the munchies."

Cooper found the corresponding photographs to go with the evidence log, populating the screen with a selection of images showing the crumpled biscuit and chewing gum packets, and piles of chocolate and other sweet wrappers.

Jack frowned towards the screen, inching his chair forward a little. "Can you enlarge that a bit, Cooper? The picture in the bottom right?"

Cooper did as instructed, making one large image fill the entire whiteboard.

Jack's brow creased further. "These look familiar to you, Cooper? The chocolate wrappers?"

Cooper gave a shrug and a brief shake of the head. "Not sure they do, boss. Jenny isn't one for having sweets in the house. And I'm more of a boiled sweet kind of guy than chocolate."

"Hmmm." Jack kept his eyes on the screen, feeling that somewhere in the depths of his memory he'd seen that particular brand of chocolate before. It was an unusual brand, which was why it had registered with him. But where had he seen it?

"What time did you speak to Amanda, Cooper?" Jack looked at the time displayed on his Fitbit. "It shouldn't take this long to get back to the station, should it?"

Cooper glanced up at the wall clock. "She called only a couple of minutes before you showed up, boss. So I'd say she should be here any minute. Maybe there was traffic."

Mind starting to race, Jack pulled his laptop towards him. "I'm going to see if I can find something out about these chocolates while we wait. For some reason, they remind me of something." Laptop open, he went to click on the Google icon but saw that the video recording taken from Spearing's car was still frozen on the screen. About to close it down, Jack's finger hovered over the mouse.

The recording had played on in full, reaching the very end before it froze in time.

Jack's stomach lurched, and he felt the hastily-eaten burger threaten to make a reappearance.

Shit.

* * *

Time: 12.05 a.m.
Date: Saturday 17 January 2015
Location: Grantham Corner, London

When asked about it later that night, Daniels couldn't be sure whether he saw the vehicle crash first or heard it. The van had careered across the road in front of him, its headlights momentarily dazzling him as he jogged in the direction of home. Jumping out of the way just in time, he watched the vehicle speed past, mounting the pavement, still accelerating all the while. The force sent it flying through a row of thick bushes that surrounded the park, and it quickly vanished.

Instinct kicking in, Daniels turned on his heels and sprinted in the direction of the bushes. Where the vegetation had been flattened, he could see the van had come to a stop several metres inside the park, colliding with a low wall. Its headlights were still on and an indicator was flashing.

Pulling his mobile free from the pocket in his Lycra running top, Daniels saw movement up ahead. Movement was good. Movement meant that whoever was inside was still alive. He hit triple nine as he cleared the pavement and ran into the bushes. Just as the call connected, he saw movement once again.

The driver's door was hanging open and whoever had been in the driving seat was pulling themselves out of the stricken vehicle and making a dash across the deserted park. Daniels ran towards the van, squinting in through the rear window to see another figure still inside. As he approached the passenger side door, he began to relay details to the operator on the other end of the phone.

Then he stopped in his tracks.

Amanda.

It was a difficult decision, but Daniels chose to leave her and race after the driver, having ensured that the emergency services were on their way.

Adrenaline kicked in fast. Despite the numerous miles he'd already covered that night with the running club, Daniels found a fresh source of energy from somewhere, but the rain was now falling in sheets, making the ground underfoot slippery.

The driver of the van had disappeared into the night, heading deeper into the park. Daniels had been through the area several times before and knew there was a small pond some way up ahead, together with a bandstand. After that there was more open space until they reached the road on the other side. If the man reached the road before he did, then Daniels would have no chance of finding him. All he would need to do was disappear down any one of the side streets and be swallowed up by the night.

Daniels pressed on with renewed vigour, his thigh muscles screaming at him to stop — but he powered on through the pain. As far as he could tell, Amanda was OK — she was breathing at least, but extremely groggy. It looked as though her head had hit the windscreen on the car's impact, blood trickling from a wound to her forehead. As Daniels thundered on, he saw the man up ahead stumble and fall to the ground, regaining his stride quickly afterwards. But it was enough for the detective to close the gap. Now much closer, Daniels could see the man was limping, dragging his right leg behind him.

The pond and bandstand came into view and Daniels again lengthened his stride, pushing through the pain. His

319

discomfort would be nothing compared to Amanda's. The sound of sirens started to filter through the rain, and Daniels felt a renewed energy grip him. The road would be upon them soon and the van driver would have any number of escape routes open to him.

Clenching his fists, Daniels skirted the bandstand, closing on his quarry all the while. He willed his leg muscles to carry him that bit further, that bit quicker — he couldn't let the man get away; not after everything Amanda had been through.

Just when Daniels thought he'd reached his limit, his legs starting to cramp, the figure up ahead gave a muffled cry and fell to the ground.

Daniels was on him in seconds.

CHAPTER THIRTY-SIX

Time: 3.25 a.m.
Date: Saturday 17 January 2015
Location: London City Hospital

"I blame myself." Jack waved away the polystyrene cup of murky brown liquid. "I should never have sanctioned it."

Cooper placed the unwanted coffee on to the side of the reception desk. "It was a tough call, boss — but it's worked out in our favour. In the end, anyway. We got him."

Jack grimaced. They may well have caught who they believed to be the killer, but at what price? And the fact that it had been Adam Sullivan only served to make it worse. Jack still couldn't quite believe it. *Sullivan?*

On arrival at the hospital, Amanda had been taken for an urgent head CT, her responsiveness suddenly deteriorating during the journey from the scene. One minute she was conversing with the ambulance crew, making all the appropriate responses, but then she seemed to go very quiet.

"That's as maybe, Cooper — but I should never have put her in harm's way like that. What was I thinking?" Jack moved out of the way of a hospital trolley as it passed them by, scouring the busy Accident and Emergency department for the doctor that had initially examined Amanda when they arrived. But the doctor was nowhere to be seen. Jack had already pestered the rest of the A&E staff for an update on her condition, but wasn't getting anywhere.

She'd been gone a while now — it didn't bode well.

What was I thinking? Jack knew full well that the main problem was he *wasn't* thinking; not as straight or as much as he should have been anyway. Once again he was getting distracted by things that had no business interfering with his professional life. It was a weakness he knew he had — a weakness that began and ended with James Quinn.

The double doors at the end of the department swung open and DC Daniels, still clothed in his running gear, headed in their direction. Jack tried to read the expression on his face as the detective neared.

"Daniels? Any news?"

"She's on her way back now. I had a chat with the radiologist and the doctor on the way back. CT was all clear. Just an external head wound and probable concussion. They'll stitch the wound and then admit her for observations overnight."

Jack's eyebrows raised a notch. "How did you manage to find that information out so quickly? No one would tell me anything."

Daniels tried to mask the emerging smile on his lips. "I just asked nicely."

Before Jack could reply the doors opened again and Amanda's trolley came into view, heading back to one of the cubicles.

"This young lady needs some rest, gentlemen." The senior A&E nurse standing by the cubicle curtain pursed her lips as Jack, Cooper and Daniels approached. "There really isn't the room for all three of you to be here . . ."

Jack felt his hackles rising and was about to jump in with a suitably terse response when a softening in the nurse's features stopped him in his tracks.

"*But* — if you promise to be quiet and not get in the way, I feel I can turn a blind eye." The nurse smiled, her tired eyes crinkling at the corners. "It'll be a while before we take her up to the ward. We need to find a bed first. Someone will be along to close the wound shortly, and then we'll perform some neuro obs."

Jack nodded his thanks as the nurse departed, closing the curtains behind her.

"Amanda?" Jack headed for her bedside. "How are you feeling?"

Cassidy looked out from beneath heavy-lidded eyes. "Like I've head-butted the windscreen of a car."

Jack grinned. "Well, funnily enough . . ."

"Did you get him?"

If Jack was concerned about Cassidy's power of recollection before, he wasn't now. He simply nodded. "We got him."

The taut look on Cassidy's face finally relaxed and she closed her eyes. "Good," she whispered. "Good."

After one of the doctors returned with a suture tray and proceeded to stitch the five-centimetre wound on Cassidy's forehead, and a nurse administered a further dose of pain relief, they were once again alone in the cubicle.

Jack perched on the side of the trolley. "We'll need you to give a statement of course, but not right away. Sullivan isn't going anywhere for the time being and he won't be interviewed until the morning. Depending when they let you out of here tomorrow, someone will come and pick you up."

"I'm not staying." Cassidy's eyes flew open, a sharpness returning to her gaze. She pulled herself up a little, leaning back against the thin pillows. "I'm fine. I don't need to be here."

Jack frowned. "Amanda, I . . ."

"Don't give me that '*I think you should do what you're told*' rubbish, guv . . ." Cassidy smirked. "You don't exactly set a good example, you know."

"That may be so . . ." Jack felt a smile twitch. "But I still think . . ."

323

"I'm not staying," she repeated, a firm defiance in her voice. "And they can't make me. It's just a headache. I'm *fine*."

Jack sighed and pushed himself up from the trolley. "I wouldn't dare make you do anything, Amanda. I'll go and find a doctor and see if we can get you discharged. In the meantime, Cooper . . ." Jack flashed a look at the detective sergeant. "See if you can find us some more of that disgusting coffee. I've a feeling we might be here a while yet."

* * *

For once, Jack was happy to wait for a doctor to come and deal with Cassidy's discharge paperwork. Although he knew she would be chomping at the bit to escape, Jack welcomed the opportunity to sit — and to think.

Adam Sullivan.

Sully.

It had come to him as soon as he'd seen the Welfare Truck in the middle of the screen of his laptop. He hadn't played the video recording right to the end before, always stopping once he'd seen himself disappear back into the night. He'd just assumed Spearing had cut the recording there and then, having got what he wanted — Jack seen in a compromising position, caught on film, that would be awkward to explain away.

But the crime correspondent had kept the recording going for a few more minutes. And when Jack saw the final frames, everything slotted sickeningly into place.

They'd been barking up completely the wrong tree with Barry Pierce and Julian Fisher. The real killer had been staring them in the face all this time — and staring at Jack in particular. He'd been inside a Welfare Truck before, on several occasions, and as soon as he'd seen the vehicle pulling up at the kerbside on The Causeway the penny had finally dropped.

The chocolate wrappers.

That was where he'd seen them before — inside the Welfare Truck.

The street pastors had a selection of snacks available to hand out where needed, and the chocolates were distinctive with their red and gold foil wrappers.

How had he missed it for all this time?

Glancing at his phone, Jack noted he'd missed four calls from the chief superintendent in the time it had taken for them to get from the station to where Sullivan had crashed the truck. The middle of the night and Dougie King was calling him — and not just the once. *Four* times. Even Jack knew that had to be a bad sign.

He also knew that not answering the calls would no doubt make an already bad situation a hundred times worse, but he did it anyway. Jack MacIntosh wasn't one to disappoint when it came to career suicide.

He'd managed to make a quick call to the custody suite, confirming that Julian Fisher was in the cells, and Barry Pierce was expected shortly, but the urgency to deal with them had waned over the last few hours. Whatever had led them both to become interwoven into the current investigation would be unpicked in due course — but tonight wasn't the night.

Jack sighed as a doctor approached to hand him Cassidy's discharge paperwork. He gave the man a tired smile and switched off his phone — not only to silence Dougie King, but also Ritchie Greenwood. The twenty-four-hour deadline for Jack to respond was already slipping away.

CHAPTER THIRTY-SEVEN

Time: 8.45 a.m.
Date: Saturday 17 January 2015
Location: Metropolitan Police HQ, London

"Adam Sullivan is in custody and as far as I'm concerned that's where he can stay for the time being. He'll be interviewed when we're good and ready. Pierce and Fisher are also in the cells, but again I'm in no hurry for them to be dealt with." Jack cast a hesitant glance towards the back of the incident room. "Amanda. Are you sure you're OK? You don't have to be here."

Cassidy shivered beneath an oversized anorak somebody had given her, her face a ghostly white. A bruise was beginning to form on her left temple where her head had connected with the side window when the car had crashed through the hedge and collided with the wall just inside the park on Grantham Corner. The laceration to her forehead had been neatly stitched.

"I'm OK. I'm fine." Cassidy's voice shook almost as much as she did. She pulled the anorak around her shoulders more securely. "I'm good."

Jack knew she was nothing of the sort but wasn't about to argue. Although the hospital hadn't been too happy to

326

discharge her, they knew there was little point in arguing the toss. Jack had promised that she wouldn't be left alone for the next twenty-four hours, and if there was any sign of a deterioration in her condition they would come straight back. Reluctantly, the discharge papers had been prepared and Cassidy was free to go.

But Amanda had insisted on coming back to the station instead of going home — as had the rest of the team. They all looked rather tired and dishevelled, even the usually dapper DS Cooper was sporting a decidedly crumpled look, but no one wanted to leave things how they were. They might have their man, but they still had some way to go yet before they secured enough evidence to charge him with any of the murders. And there was still Tanya Maund unaccounted for. The clock was ticking.

"You had a narrow escape, Amanda. You're allowed to be shocked." Jack leaned up against one of the desks, fixing his eyes on the detective sergeant. "I would still feel more comfortable if you took yourself home — we can handle everything here."

"No." The word came out more forcefully than Cassidy intended, judging by the sheepish look that followed. "Sorry. But I can't just go home. I won't rest. I won't sleep. I want to help nail the bastard."

"Well, the van has been retrieved from the scene and will be processed today. Elliott has already confirmed that they've sent away several water bottles and boxes of chocolates to the lab for analysis."

"So, he drugged me?" Cassidy's voice hitched. "I ate some chocolates in the truck and had some water, I think."

Jack shrugged. "We know he overpowers his victims in some way — so drugging would fit. The chocolates and water are being tested for any traces of sedatives or other drugs. We know nothing showed up in the post- mortem bloods of any of the other victims, but if he used something like GHB then that doesn't last very long in the system. We may have more joy with your bloods, Amanda. The hospital will let us know."

"Women out there trusted him." Cassidy's tone was taut. "He was meant to be *helping* them. Not killing them."

"He would have been a familiar face on the street," added Cooper. "They were more than likely to be comfortable getting into his van."

"Hopefully we'll know a bit more later on today." Jack checked his watch. "But we still need to locate Tanya Maund. Her disappearance unnerves me. We might not have found anything untoward in her flat but that doesn't explain why she's dropped off the face of the earth. Cooper — recheck the CCTV around where she was last seen. Anything to give us a lead."

"On it, boss."

"Daniels. You can come with me to see Sullivan's flat. Elliott and his team should be there by now. Apologies, but even the hero of the hour doesn't get a day off just yet."

Daniels' cheeks coloured. "I wouldn't call myself a hero. Amanda did all the hard work."

"That may be, Daniels, but credit where credit's due." Jack knew that Cassidy was thinking exactly the same as he was right now. If Daniels hadn't been out with his running club last night, then things could have ended very differently. He shrugged back into his creased jacket and scooped up the keys to the Mondeo. So far the chief superintendent had yet to catch up with him — and he wanted to keep it that way for a little longer. "Let's go, Daniels. Cooper – take Amanda home and make sure she gets some rest. The same goes for you. I don't want to see either of you until much later. "

* * *

Time: 9.15 a.m.
Date: Saturday 17 January 2015
Location: Metropolitan Police HQ, London — custody suite

He missed the discipline.

Agitation was beginning to set in, so he started pacing up and down by the side of the bed; if you could call it that. It was really a metal shelf jutting out from the wall with the thinnest of mattresses known to humankind. He hadn't slept since they'd picked him up and he had no desire to do so now.

Desire.

What he desired was the discipline.

As the minutes turned into hours, and night turned into day, he wondered what it had been that had finally tripped him up. He knew it was probably something he said. Did he feel sorry for himself now that it was all over? For he knew that it was all over now. No smart lawyer in a pin-striped suit could get him out of this one. And if he was being honest, he wouldn't want them to.

There was a part of him that felt disappointed that his killing spree was over, but there was an equal part of him that welcomed it. The euphoria that ending a life usually brought him wasn't the same anymore, and hadn't been for some time. It was no longer pleasure; it was hatred that drove him to do it. Hatred for the women, for what they stood for, but also hatred for himself.

And what he had become.

But he had only become this way because of one person. *Johnny.*

Even thinking of the man's name fuelled a fresh wave of revulsion.

As he paced, he felt a jolt of pain shoot through his leg every time he placed his foot on the ground. On arrival at the custody suite, he'd been seen by the doctor and offered painkillers — but he'd refused. Painkillers would mask his pain — and he needed to *feel* his pain. He wanted to revel in it, welcome it. It wasn't anything like the discipline, but it would have to do.

The discipline.

He wondered whether they would let him take it to prison with him. The thought made him chuckle — of course they wouldn't. But he *needed* the discipline; he needed it to snuff out the pain that almost consumed him every single day. If he couldn't have the discipline, he would have to find another form of punishment to control his anger.

The discipline.

Had they found it? He wanted it so badly he was almost prepared to tell them about the house — but if he told them about the house, then they would find the other two.

* * *

Time: 9.50 a.m.
Date: Saturday 17 January 2015
Location: Riverview Dental Practice, London

The flat had that unmistakable clean smell that was unique to dentists. Walking through the reception area only moments before, Jack had noticed the look of trepidation on some of the waiting patients' faces, as well as the reception staff, as a series of white-suited forensic investigators filed past.

Not their usual Saturday clientele.

He could see it now — the headlines when the press got hold of the killer's identity.

'Doctor Death' was sure to be one of them — Jack would stake his life on it.

Sullivan's flat above the dental practice was surprisingly spacious. Free from clutter, it wouldn't take the search team too long to complete their work.

Jack hovered by the front door as Elliott and his team started setting up. The familiar metal stepping plates appeared on the floor, and Jack was dressed head to toe in his protective suit. Daniels appeared by his side.

"You see what I see, Daniels?" Jack gestured towards a small table standing a few feet in front of them just inside the hall.

Daniels nodded. Two china bowls filled with the same brand of chocolates found in the crashed Welfare Truck, and, also at Acorn House.

Elliott Walker backtracked along the hall and gestured for Jack to step inside. "Morning, Jack. You might want to look at this."

Jack and Daniels trooped further inside the flat, keeping to the stepping plates. They had no idea at this stage if any of the victims had been brought here, either dead or alive, so the whole area needed to be treated as a potential crime scene. Jack suspected Sullivan was too clever to have brought any of the women here, or at least not stupid, but stranger things had happened. Sometimes killers slipped up.

Elliott waved a gloved hand towards a sleek sideboard that ran along the far wall of the flat's living area. With just a single candle in an ornate holder at each end, the sideboard was empty — except for a row of five hypodermic syringes and several glass vials all lined up next to each other.

"We'll bag them up and get them tested." Elliott waved an investigator forward. "Looks like GHB to me, looking at the label. Could be the link you're looking for."

Jack nodded. Amanda's blood and urine samples had yet to be processed, but if they contained what Jack thought they might, then this could indeed be the link. It would go some way to explain the periods of unresponsiveness and brain fog Amanda had experienced while in Sullivan's van last night. GHB, also know colloquially as the 'date rape drug' was colourless as a liquid, and with a slightly salty taste and almost no smell, it made it a perfect choice to spike drinks or foodstuffs.

"Cheers, Elliott." Jack and Daniels spent a few minutes looking around the rest of the flat, but soon left the investigators to it. Jogging down the stairs to the dental practice below, Jack continued to wrestle with the thoughts that had been tangling themselves into knots inside his head ever since last night's events.

Sully.

How had he missed it? He knew the man relatively well — or at least he thought he did. They weren't best mates or anything, but they'd shared the odd pint and pie in the pub on occasion — even as recently as last week. Had the man gone straight out afterwards to continue to prowl the streets?

Jack shivered as they headed outside. The killer had been right under his nose all this time, even sat next to him in the pub, and he still hadn't seen it coming. He felt like he was rapidly losing his touch.

CHAPTER THIRTY-EIGHT

Time: 11.00 a.m.
Date: Saturday 17 January 2015
Location: Metropolitan Police HQ, London

Jack looked up from his half-eaten bacon sandwich, the mug of strong black coffee that had accompanied it still untouched by the side. The enormity of what had happened last night was only just starting to sink in.

He had placed Amanda in extreme danger — there was no other way of putting it. Although she had gone willingly, had even come up with the crazy idea herself, it was Jack who had put her there. He could have put a stop to it — but he hadn't.

And look what had happened — or *nearly* happened.

The fact that they had managed to snare Adam Sullivan almost red-handed was unimportant right now. All he could think about was Amanda — and the huge bollocking he was about to get from Dougie King when the chief superintendent finally caught up with him.

Sullivan was being interviewed this very moment — Jack more than happy to sit this one out. His friendship with the man was a major red flag to him conducting the interview himself, and if he was being truly honest he would struggle to keep his anger under control if he were in the same room as the man right now.

"Jack? You're going to want to see this." Elliott Walker strode into Jack's office just as he began to wrap up the remains of the sandwich, appetite lost. "Here." The crime scene manager thrust a plastic evidence bag across the desk as he grabbed a chair and sat down. "Satnav lifted from the van."

Satnav.

Jack immediately straightened up and slapped a hand to his forehead. Of course. *Wake up, Jack — the satnav!* Jack took hold of the bag. "You've already had a look I take it?"

Elliott nodded. "I've had a quick squint, yes. It's still to go through a more thorough evaluation but I figured you'd want to know what was on there, sooner rather than later."

Jack smoothed out the plastic surface of the bag to reveal the satnav's digital display. He pressed the 'history' button to pull up the van's navigation log. Despite the lack of sleep, his brain immediately sharpened.

And there it was.

Eyes widening, he scrolled through the various addresses logged on the device's navigation history.

Acorn House.

Tanners Road Industrial Estate.

Cold Acre Road.

Riverview Dental Practice.

Those were the ones he instantly recognised, but then there were those that he *didn't*.

Grabbing a pen, Jack dragged a spare notepad across the desk and noted down the three addresses that had failed to register. "Thanks, Elliott. You're a diamond. This could be crucial."

"The van is being processed as we speak. But it'll be a while before you get any results."

Jack nodded. He knew how slowly the wheels could grind at times, but there was nothing he could do about that. At least the satnav information gave them something to go on in the meantime. Adam Sullivan could fester in the interview for a while longer for all Jack cared. The man had given a sample for DNA purposes, and the search was on for a match with any samples they had from the crime scenes so far. With any luck they would get a hit which would make even the smartest defence barrister squirm. They still had another twelve hours or so before they needed to decide what to do with him. If any of the addresses he'd noted down threw up where they might find Tanya Maund, then Sullivan wouldn't be going anywhere.

Tanya.

Jack's stomach tightened and he regretted wolfing down the bacon sandwich quite so quickly. If any of these addresses *did* lead them to Tanya, then there was no telling what they might find when they got there.

He handed the evidence bag back to Elliott as he rose from his desk. "Cheers, Elliott. I'll let you know what we find."

* * *

Time: 11.05 a.m.
Date: Saturday 17 January 2015
Location: Old Mill Road, Christchurch

Ritchie Greenwood had clambered over much of the Old Mill Road site over the last twenty-four hours and remained as unimpressed as when he'd arrived. Back in the seventies it might have been the height of sophistication, but now the building was nothing but a crumbling shack. Once or twice he'd lost his footing and nearly taken a tumble down the concrete stairs — the place was a death trap. The thought made him smile.

Gathering up the takeaway cartons that heralded last night's dinner, Ritchie surveyed the scene. 'You'd never know we'd been here,' he mused, satisfied with his work. He slugged back the remains of a bottle of water, then crushed the bottle and rammed it in the rubbish bag. Checking his watch, he mentally calculated how long he had before MacIntosh might put in an appearance. It was only a guess, but he felt it wouldn't be long. Despite the detective inspector insisting that he wasn't interested in Quinn, Ritchie knew a lie when he heard one.

James Quinn had murdered MacIntosh's mother — he wouldn't be able to resist.

Quinn himself was fluttering in and out of consciousness, but even when he was awake the man barely made sense so Ritchie had stopped listening to him. Quinn was merely a pawn in this game of chess — expendable.

The real checkmate would come with Jack MacIntosh.

* * *

Time: 12.45 p.m.
Date: Saturday 17 January 2015
Location: Greystone Rise, London

The first two addresses had shown nothing untoward. One was an unoccupied mid-terraced house, the other a flat occupied by an elderly woman in her nineties. The woman was shown a photograph of both Adam Sullivan and Tanya, but denied having ever seen either.

That just left Greystone Rise.

The house was an end-of-terrace in a quiet street. The windows looked grubby, with stained net curtains hanging in each one. Paint peeled from every surface giving it a distinctly unloved feel. Each house along the stretch of road had the same abandoned feel. Jack suspected the vast majority were uninhabited, judging by the number of graffiti-clad boards up at the windows.

In the tiny walled front garden area, three bins stood side by side plus a collection of rusting paint tins amid the knee-high grass. A cracked path, infested with weeds, led to the wooden front door.

"I've got a bad feeling about this, boss," muttered Cooper as they exited the Mondeo. Cooper had gone home for a few hours' rest as instructed, but Jack had found the detective sergeant back in the incident room devouring a bacon sandwich soon after Elliott had delivered the news about the sat nav. Despite still being sleep-deprived, Cooper had jumped at the chance to try and find Tanya.

"You and me both, Cooper." Jack led the way up to the front door. At least the overnight rain had stopped, which was a blessing, but the chill remained. While Jack had been at the flat above the Riverview Dental Practice, Cooper had been trawling through the CCTV once more. The Welfare Truck had been seen out regularly, patrolling the streets around where each of the victims had last been seen — it had just never registered as suspicious before now. Hiding in plain sight — the easiest form of camouflage.

"How do you want to play this, boss" Cooper stepped across the garden to the side of the house where a narrow path led around to the rear of the property. The way was blocked by a dense, overgrown bush encroaching all the way across. And it was a bush with thorns. "I don't much fancy pushing through that."

Jack took in the front door's appearance and then without hesitation gave it a swift kick. The wood splintered easily.

The smell hit them square in the face as they entered. Something rotten lived within. The entrance hall was dark — a lonely light bulb thick with cobwebs hung from the ceiling above but emitted no light — and it was narrow. As Jack and Cooper stepped further inside, the walls seemed to close in around them.

Grubby flock wallpaper graced the walls, faded and peeling in places. Jack had no idea what colour it had been originally but it was now dark brown with flecks of green mould. Ahead was a single closed door. As they neared, the smell that had greeted them on the doorstep intensified.

"Brace yourself, Cooper." Jack grabbed the door handle and pushed — feeling it resist only slightly before swinging open. As he stepped inside his insides curled. "Good God."

* * *

Jack had never thrown up at a crime scene before, and he had a job to keep his stomach contents where they should be as he stood inside the tiny kitchen. Swarms of flies buzzed around his head. Cooper pulled a handkerchief from his pocket and coughed. "Something strong in here, boss."

Jack could only manage a nod, not wanting to risk opening his mouth. He felt his eyes start to water as he batted away another swarm of blue- bottles. The kitchen was teeming with rubbish and decaying food. At least, Jack assumed it had been food at some point in its existence — there really was no obvious way to tell. The sink was overflowing with unwashed dishes, the water in the bottom a congealed murky brown. Every worktop was covered in takeaway boxes, more plates and more decaying rubbish. Mould clung to the walls and the window didn't look as though it had been opened in decades. Jack wasn't about to put his hand through the dirty net curtain to change that.

With his stomach settling, Jack stepped across the litter strewn floor towards the only other door in the kitchen. Wrapping the end of his jacket over his hand, he tentatively took hold of the handle and pushed it open.

If the smell had been bad in the kitchen, it was cranked up and multiplied in the next room. Cooper instantly lost the battle to keep his bacon sandwich in his stomach, heaving the contents on to the floor behind him. "Sorry, boss," he muttered, wiping the handkerchief across his mouth.

Jack merely shook his head, clamping his own mouth shut. The smell was indescribable, but he would take the distinctly unpleasant aromas emanating from the Westminster Mortuary over this any day of the week. This went beyond anything he'd ever witnessed before; it was beyond grime; beyond filth. The smell wasn't even of death.

It was worse than that.

Jack inched further into what he supposed was a living room. It was hard to say, but he suspected that nothing living resided inside — which didn't bode well for Tanya Maund.

If she was here.

The curtains at the window cast the room into a dimness that also squeezed the very oxygen from the air. Jack coughed and cleared his throat, as he continued to inch himself deeper into the room. More bags of rubbish lined the walls, plus stacks of old newspapers and magazines. Decaying plates of food were balanced on decrepit furniture, thick coverings of mould on everything. The air was heavy with decay and judging by the flurry of bluebottles still buzzing around, they were finding plenty to feast upon.

Jack shuddered. He sensed Cooper approach behind him and turned to see that the detective had fished out his torch. A concentrated beam of light swept around the confines of the room.

And then they saw her.

Tanya.

Jack immediately turned and vomited on the floor.

CHAPTER THIRTY-NINE

Time: 5.45 p.m.
Date: Saturday 17 January 2015
Location: Metropolitan Police HQ, London

"Tanya and Zara are both recovering in hospital." Jack collapsed into a vacant chair in the incident room. He knew that they were lucky to be alive — with the ropes tied the way they were, if either had panicked and started to move, the effect could have been catastrophic.

He'd sent Daniels home for some rest — the detective constable had been on the go all day, as well as the previous night, and looked fit to drop. Cooper and Cassidy had managed a couple of hours each at best, tiredness still encircling their eyes. Jack, on the other hand, was living off his nerves — and more caffeine.

"They were found at an address in Greystone Rise — drugged and with a tight ligature around their necks. The ligatures were tied together in such a way that if one of them moved, it tightened the one around the other's neck. Both had just enough room to breathe — but only just. Apart from that, their physical injuries are thought to be minor."

"What an animal," breathed Cassidy, shuddering. "It must have been torture for them."

Jack nodded. "The lab came back with some DNA results — profiles found in Acorn House and on the holdalls at the Tanners Road Industrial Estate have thrown up a match for Adam Sullivan. Interestingly, much of the drug paraphernalia found in Flat 7b was a match for Julian Fisher — both for DNA and fingerprints. A large quantity of GHB was found in the back of the crashed Welfare Truck, plus another quantity at Sullivan's flat above the dental practice. Traces have also been found in the water bottles and chocolates inside the truck."

"So that's what he gave me." Cassidy's shoulders shuddered again, her face still pale after the previous night's events. "GHB."

"It would appear so," agreed Jack. "Your blood and urine results from the hospital show quite high GHB levels."

"What about Barry Pierce and Julian Fisher?" asked Cooper. "What was their involvement?"

Despite his exhaustion, Jack managed a smile. "Well, here's the interesting thing. Pierce's lock-up was raided earlier today and it seems he deals in all manner of stolen items. My assumption is he then sells the stuff on to the residents of the three tower blocks. The lock-up had three chest freezers stuffed to the brim, full of various cuts of meat — beef, lamb, chicken, you name it. Plus, the mysterious silver suitcase was located inside, too, full of blood and offal. My guess is he used that to transport some of his wares around the estate. The lab confirms the blood inside is not human." Jack watched Cooper continue to munch his way through a packet of crisps, unsure if he felt hungry himself or not. What he really wanted was sleep, or maybe a stiff drink; neither of which he was likely to get for some time yet. "It would fit with the bloodied bedsheet we found inside his flat, and the knife. Again, both were covered in animal blood, not human. Not particularly pleasant, but at least it's not murder. He's currently being questioned about handling stolen goods but I'm not sure we can get him for much more than that."

"What about Fisher?" Cooper emptied the remains of the crisp packet into his mouth.

"He's being questioned about the illegal sale of prescription and non-prescription drugs. We have the evidence of Annie Palmer that he sold her painkillers, and we expect more residents to come forward once we do another door-to-door. A house belonging to his father, Bernard Fisher, has been found and searched — it's reported to be in a poor state of repair, but lo and behold quite a substantial stash of drugs was found inside. Looks like that's where he's been keeping his supplies. There's no evidence that he supplied Sullivan with the GHB, but it's a line of questioning we'll explore. Sullivan could equally have got his supply from his dental practice — I'm sure he's more than adept at doctoring the odd prescription or two, but it's more likely he got it off the street. Fisher's prints on the drug paraphernalia at Acorn House fits with the supply of drugs to the local gangs — enough of it went on inside Flat 7b, so I'm pretty sure he was involved somewhere along the line. He's been declared fit to be interviewed after being checked over by a doctor — he has some pretty nasty open wounds on his back caused by severe eczema."

Jack rooted around inside his jacket pocket, hoping to find a packet of paracetamol. There was nothing. Sighing, he continued. "Although Fisher seems to be quite wary at answering questions, I'm told that Pierce can't wait to sing like a canary. He's already confirmed that he and Fisher were better acquainted than we gave them credit for, and that he turned a blind eye to Fisher's drug dealing on the estate — I suspect it might have been in return for a backhander or two. Pierce has chronic low back pain from an old injury and takes an unhealthy amount of painkillers, judging by what was found in his lock-up. Could well be an addict, no doubt kept well-supplied by our friend Julian Fisher — I imagine in exchange for his silence. By all accounts, Fisher's financial services business hadn't been doing all that well of late and he's up to his eyeballs in debt, so I'm guessing the drug dealing was a way to make some fast easy cash."

"Which almost got him caught up in a quadruple murder," added Cooper, ripping open a second packet of crisps.

"Indeed. On the question of the house in Greystone Rise, Elliott reports that several dismembered body parts have been recovered."

Cassidy's face paled. "Shell Harris?"

Jack nodded, solemnly. "That's my guess, yes, unless . . ." He shuddered as the words caught in his throat. *Unless they belong to another victim.* The thought wasn't a pretty one, but they would find out soon enough. He decided to change the subject.

"Do you recall the neighbour me and Daniels visited over at Acorn House? The one who saw Pierce with the suitcase?"

"Watkins," confirmed Cooper. "The bin man."

A tired smile flickered across Jack's lips. "The bin man, yes. Well, it seems his kleptomaniac tendencies appear to have thrown another result our way. Some of the bags he pilfered from the communal refuse bins contained more than he bargained for — but give him his due, he rang it in more or less straight away. There was some bloodied clothing that has already been linked to Sullivan, and also some human-looking bones — namely ribs. These are being fast tracked at the lab to establish who they belong to."

"Lisa Wood?" Cooper's eyebrows peaked. "Dr Matthews mentioned only ribs number one to seven were found at Acorn House."

Jack nodded. "That would be where my money went if I was a betting man."

"There's something else, too, boss" Cooper crumpled the now empty crisp packet and tossed it into the bin. He waved a note in the air. "Before he went home, Trevor left a note about the unsolved cases he was looking into. In particular, the one from 1988 where two people OD'd and there was an attempt to dismember them?"

Jack nodded. "Go on."

"The deceased woman's name was Rita Sullivan. And the records say she had a son called Adam. Digging further into it, Trevor found out that the son was thirteen at the time of his mother's death, and he was the one to discover the bodies. Both victims had lethal doses of heroin in their systems, but also had ropes tied around their necks. There had been several attempts to hack their arms and legs from their bodies."

"A trial run?" The words escaped Cassidy's lips before she had a chance to stop them. "He was practising?"

Cooper continued. "The son Adam was then taken in by a foster family whose last known address was, you guessed it, Greystone Rise — where Zara and Tanya were found."

"Do we think these deaths in 1988 are a coincidence, Cooper?" A tired smile crossed Jack's lined face.

Cooper returned the grin. "You know what I always say about coincidences, boss . . ."

"Good, you're learning. I'll pass that on to the team interviewing him. I'm sure they'd like to ask him a question or two."

"What happens now, guv?" Cassidy stifled a yawn.

"*Now*, you and Cooper are going to get yourselves back off home." Jack knew by the look on Cassidy's face that his next suggestion of someone being at home with her while she recovered from her knock to the head would be met with fierce resistance, so he didn't pursue it. "Sullivan is in good hands with the interview team — they don't need us sticking our oars in."

"There's something about Sullivan that still puzzles me." Cooper reached for an energy drink to wash down the crisps. "How did he manage to get both Tara and Lisa into the flat in Acorn House without anyone seeing him?"

Jack had asked himself the same question more than once. "All I can think of is that in places like the Hillside Estate, sometimes it's safer not to see things. To keep your head down and not stand out from the crowd. There are some shady people hanging around that estate, some even live on it, so it's not surprising that many choose not to get involved."

Cooper downed the rest of the can of drink. "I guess that makes sense."

Jack got to his feet. "Barry Pierce and Julian Fisher are being interviewed, and we're taking a back seat on that one, too. As far as Dixon is concerned, we've got an extension to question him further. I reckon once he learns we have Sullivan in custody then he might decide to talk. But that can wait until tomorrow."

"Sullivan must have had some hold over Dixon to make him get onto a bus carrying two bags stuffed with body parts." Cooper crushed the can and dropped it into the bin. "I know he's not the brightest but . . . it's not a normal thing to do, is it?"

Jack gave another tired smile. "It's not normal at all, Cooper. But there are some strange folks out there. Don't forget, Sullivan is an expert manipulator. People like him feed on weaknesses — all he would need to do is find someone's weak spot and hone in on it. Dixon isn't bright, that's true — maybe he's another addict or has a mountain of debt. It wouldn't take much for someone like Sullivan to get to him." Jack made his way towards the incident room door. "But now, you two really do need to get off home."

"And what about you?" Cassidy's face was slack with exhaustion. "If we're going home then you should be, too. I don't think you've slept since Thursday night."

And the rest, thought Jack, but didn't say it. Instead he fixed a smile to his face which he hoped looked genuine. "Your concern is duly noted, sergeant. And once I've followed up on a few things here I'll be heading home, too. Scout's honour."

Jack had never been a scout and he suspected the team were well aware of that, but they seemed to swallow the lie with good grace and sloped out of the incident room. It was true — he did have a few things to follow up on, but most weren't urgent and could wait until after the weekend.

There was really only one place he needed to go right now.

* * *

Time: 6.15 p.m.
Date: Saturday 17 January 2015
Location: Metropolitan Police HQ, London

"We got a result. We got our man."

"The ends don't always justify the means, Jack. You know that. And *this* is one such example." Dougie King exhaled deeply. "You put DS Cassidy in extreme danger. It could have ended very differently. Very differently indeed."

Jack hung his head. "I know. I'm sorry."

"I don't want your apology, Jack. It's far too late for that." The chief superintendent drummed his fingers on the desk. "You do realise I have to take this higher, don't you? I can't bury everything."

Jack nodded. "I know. I did try and stop her, if that's any consolation."

"It's not." Dougie King's expression softened. "But it was a good result. I'll do what I can to soften the blow from upstairs, but they can be sticklers for procedure at the best of times. Especially if it's something that's going to land the reputation of the force into hot water. Have you interviewed Sullivan yet?"

"He was interviewed earlier today — initially he said nothing, but after taking legal advice he now apparently wants to talk. The interview team have got it covered, I'm keeping my distance for obvious reasons."

Dougie King's eyebrows hitched. "A confession?"

Jack could only shrug. The occasional update had filtered through to the team and although Sullivan may not have made a confession, he was at least talking — which was always a good start. "Even if we don't get a confession, the lab results and other evidence means I expect the CPS to authorise charges sometime later tonight or first thing in the morning.

Mobile phones and other items belonging to the final two victims — Cherry Eyres and Shell Harris — have been found in the property at Greystone Rise."

"Well, that's good news. And what about DS Cassidy? How is she bearing up?"

"She's doing well, by all accounts. She's been resting at home all day." The lie felt at home on Jack's tongue.

"Well, that's something at least. As soon as Sullivan is charged, I want to know. It might just sugarcoat the bitter pill I'll have to deliver upstairs. In the meantime, I suggest you keep your head down — maybe even take a leave of absence for a while."

Jack nodded. "Sir."

"I suppose the good news about this most recent lapse of judgement on your part is that the video recording is now yesterday's news. A full explanation has been released to the press, and none of the news agencies seem all that interested in pursuing it."

"Thank you." And this time Jack meant it.

"But I mean what I said about keeping your head down — I don't want to see or hear you in this building for the next few days. Maybe longer. This isn't over, not by a long chalk. Understand?"

"Perfectly."

Dismissed from the chief superintendent's office, Jack knew he shouldn't even be contemplating going to see Quinn. He should have deleted the messages from his phone and laptop the minute he saw them. But Jack wasn't renowned for doing what he should, as the heated conversation in Dougie King's office — otherwise known as a bollocking — had just demonstrated. He could feel a suspension in the offing — the man hadn't quite come out and said it, but he didn't really have to. Jack knew the score by now. He'd crossed far too many lines not to know what might be coming his way.

Pulling the images up on to his phone once more, he headed for the exit. If he was already facing a suspension — or even worse — what did it matter now anyway?

CHAPTER FORTY

Time: 11.05 p.m.
Date: Saturday 17 January 2015
Location: Old Mill Road, Christchurch

Jack left the engine of the Mondeo running. Not for the first time, he wondered whether maybe he should turn back. He really *should* turn back. The voices clamouring inside his head were screaming at him to turn back — *go home, Jack. Don't be such an idiot.*

Again.

He gave a faint chuckle instead — the sound instantly swallowed by the silence inside the car. Since when had being an idiot ever stopped him before? He eyed his mobile phone on the passenger seat. He knew he should call it in. James Quinn was a wanted man — and a man on the run. His face had been splashed across every newspaper the length and breadth of the country over the last three days. You couldn't move for seeing the man's piggy eyes staring back out at you.

After another minute or two, Jack switched off the engine and pocketed the keys. He knew he would do this, so there was little point in procrastinating any further. He had tried to

348

convince himself that he wasn't interested in meeting Quinn face to face — why on earth would he want to? But it had all been a lie. And Ritchie Greenwood was well aware of that. He knew just how to push Jack's buttons, a fact that infuriated him.

Stepping out of the Mondeo, he glanced around. Even in the dark, the place looked different to how he remembered. So different in fact that he began to question that he'd come to the right place. But, despite the intervening years, he knew this was it. Even though the building was crumbling now, and clearly in a state of mid-demolition if the piles of rubble were anything to go by, he knew he was home.

Home.

The Old Mill Road flats sat behind a wire fence which stretched for a good distance in front of him. At regular intervals, rusting metal signs warned of the perils of trespassing and the dangers that lay within. '*DEMOLITION IN PROGRESS*'. Judging by the litter on the other side of the fence — haphazard piles of beer cans, old spent barbecues, takeaway wrappers and cigarette packets — the warnings went largely unheeded.

Before slamming the driver's door, Jack caught his brother's eye. "Stay here, Stu. If I'm not out in ten minutes, you know what to do."

They'd argued for most of the three-hour drive down to Christchurch. Stu wanted to face Quinn, but Jack had firmly put his foot down. It was non-negotiable. He'd only brought Stu along because of the small voice in the back of his head warning him about going off on his own again. History told him to listen to these voices. Also, Jack was dead on his feet — and getting behind the wheel of the Mondeo wouldn't be the smartest move. But he'd made it clear to his brother; Stu wasn't to come near — Quinn and Ritchie Greenwood were Jack's alone to deal with.

Eventually, his brother had agreed — albeit reluctantly.

Jack now began to walk along the length of the fence and it was then that the memories started to come flooding back, falling over themselves in their haste to play out inside his head.

The derelict wasteland in front of him housed a variety of cumbersome machinery and several rusty skips; the ground littered with piles of splintered and rotting timber, swathes of bricks left to crumble to dust. An abandoned portacabin sat at the side.

But Jack ignored the building materials — for all he could see was the playground that used to be there. The slide that seemed to reach the clouds; the roundabout where he would yell *'faster faster'* at the top of his voice, while feeling the wind whip through his hair. Memories continued to tumble. A pair of swings. A tangled climbing frame.

A punctured football lay in the gutter. From its faded discoloration it must have been there a while. Jack remembered kicking a football against the side wall of the flats and a small grin found its way to his lips. He couldn't remember how many times old Mr Griffin from the ground floor had shouted through the window for him to stop making such a racket. Four-year-old Jack had merely kicked the ball harder.

Jack gave the deflated football a nudge with the toe of his shoe and sent it rolling lopsided along the gutter.

The main entrance to the flats was to Jack's left. The wire fence continued to weave its way along the perimeter, but there was now another metal cage encircling the entrance. More rusting metal signs warned the public to *KEEP OUT*. On this section of the fence there were additional warnings of *Danger of Death* and *At risk of imminent collapse*. Jack moved closer, spying yet more signs advising that CCTV coverage was in force, and that guard dogs were on regular patrols. Judging by the rust, Jack considered neither looked likely.

A gap in the fence — just wide enough for someone to push their way through — afforded a way inside. But were Ritchie Greenwood and James Quinn really here?

Giving the fence a shove with his good shoulder, Jack pushed his way through and supposed that he was about to find out.

* * *

Inside, everything looked and felt smaller than he remembered. Or was it just that he was bigger? Back in the day, the lobby had been an area full of bicycles, trikes and outdoor play equipment. Now, it was just an empty space, the walls closing in as he edged forwards.

The concrete floor below was damp, and Jack had to negotiate puddles of water at regular intervals as he made his way towards the stairs. A fetid, rotten aroma followed in his wake. Even though it was dark, he thought the stairs looked to still be intact, although a mound of fallen bricks and other rubble lay in a heap at the bottom. It was still passable on one side and Jack decided to head up.

Bringing out a pocket torch to illuminate the way, he cautiously made his way up, each step littered with broken tiles, bricks and pieces of metal piping. Jack glanced warily above his head as a fresh shower of brick dust fluttered down from above. Shielding his eyes with his hand, he plodded on.

This is a bad decision, Jack, he remonstrated with himself. *A very bad decision. Maybe one of your worst yet.*

But still he carried on.

Ritchie hadn't told him where Quinn would be found, but he didn't have to. It couldn't be anywhere else.

Jack made his way up the first flight of stairs. Brick dust continued to flutter down from overhead as he climbed, and there were other sounds now, too; water dripped from somewhere up above, the rhythmic drip-drip-dripping sound much louder in the confined space of the stairwell.

More disconcerting, however, were other noises he could hear. Every few minutes a deep, groaning sound echoed through the building — as if the very brickwork itself was in pain. At times, Jack could even feel the vibrations through his shoes. He wasn't quite sure what unnerved him the most — that or the thought of coming face to face with James Quinn.

But he was nearly there now; one more flight of stairs and Quinn would be his.

* * *

Time: 11.11 p.m.
Date: Saturday 17 January 2015
Location: Old Mill Road, Christchurch

Jack had been gone six minutes now and Stuart MacIntosh already had his hand hovering over the last 9 of 999.

Ten minutes was a long time when you were counting each second. What if Jack was already in trouble? The extra four minutes could make a difference.

Mac didn't trust James Quinn as far as he could throw him and he'd wanted to look the man in the eye — the man that had killed their mother — and ask him why.

Why?

That was it — that was the only question he wanted an answer to. It wouldn't change anything; or bring her back — it wouldn't alter the path his own life had taken. But he still wanted to know. He *needed* to know.

He knew Quinn was not to blame for the spectacular mess he'd subsequently made of his own life — Mac was pretty sure his downward spiral into teenage delinquency would have happened with or without the man's involvement. He couldn't lay that particular chestnut at Quinn's door; Mac was more than capable of pushing the self-destruct button without any assistance from anyone.

Seven minutes now.

Mac's finger twitched.

Seven minutes.

CHAPTER FORTY-ONE

Time: 11.20 p.m.
Date: Saturday 17 January 2015
Location: Old Mill Road, Christchurch

Jack found memory after memory somersaulting inside his head as he climbed. Playing on the stairs with an old tennis ball; making a parachute for his Action Man out of an old plastic bag, and throwing it over the bannisters to the stairwell below; waiting for George the milkman in the mornings, knowing the old man would give him a handful of sweets along with their daily two pints.

A small smile formed on Jack's face as he pushed on through the rubble. All these memories and many more besides were about to be ripped down along with the flats themselves, reduced to nothing but a pile of rubbish.

Quinn had to be here somewhere.

Although the radiator he'd seen in the photographs Ritchie had sent through could have been from any 1970s' building, Jack knew the picture had been taken here. There was something about the wallpaper behind it — exactly the same – that had been on the walls of their living room in the flat. Typical 1970s' brown and orange swirls, it probably hung in many a lounge or bedroom back in the day — but Ritchie hadn't shown it to Jack for any other reason than to let him know where they were.

It's your last chance, Jack.

He's here for the taking.

Just you and him — no one else.

Come on, Jack — you know you want to. You know you need *to.*

Ritchie Greenwood's words floated around inside Jack's head as he pushed on towards the flat. "Hello?" He wasn't quite sure whether he expected a reply. "Anyone here?"

The words bounced emptily off the damp walls.

The landing seemed far smaller than Jack remembered and the door to the flat itself had long since disappeared, wrenched off its hinges to leave nothing but a gaping hole behind. Jack stepped closer, wary now.

Inside, the hallway appeared narrower than he remembered too, but still had the same exposed floorboards, although sections of the wood had now decayed and Jack had to be careful where he put his feet. Water continued to drip from somewhere up above, sliding down the walls and pooling at the bottom before sinking into the rotten woodwork below. Huge, cavernous holes were ripped into the walls where the electrical wiring had been stripped from the plaster.

People would steal anything these days.

The first inkling that all was not as it should be came as Jack made his way into the living room. He could sense that the flat was unoccupied even before he swept the torchlight around inside. The radiator was indeed where he had remembered, the wallpaper behind the familiar brown with orange swirls.

But there was no James Quinn.

And there was no Ritchie Greenwood.

Taking another long look around the room that held so many memories, Jack tensed when his mobile chirped. Pulling it out, he saw who was calling and an intense irritation began to fester, which redoubled when the voice on the other end spoke.

"Boo!"

"Where are you?" Jack's tone was short, his jaw tense.

"Having a good look around are you, Jack?" Ritchie Greenwood's voice crackled in Jack's ear. "Good to be home?"

"This isn't funny. Where are you?" Jack waited for a suitably obtuse reply, but the phone remained silent.

Jack looked around the abandoned living room, realisation slowly dawning. Had he been lured here as some kind of joke? He wouldn't put it past Ritchie — it would be just the type of thing he would do to waste Jack's time. But why? And why here?

Jack's thoughts then returned to Kettle's Yard Mews. Was Ritchie's intention with this elaborate plan just to get Jack away from home? Jack didn't think he had much in the flat that would interest the gangland leader, but his thoughts then turned to Marmaduke. The cat would be alone in the flat now, curled up on the sofa or even on Jack's bed. Surely not even Ritchie would stoop that low?

Disquiet joined the irritation as Jack pocketed the now silent phone, Ritchie having hung up. He made his way out of the living room and headed for the landing. He had been wrong to come — to dance to Ritchie Greenwood's tune the way he had — *again*. Well, this was it. The last time. There would be no more.

* * *

Time: 11.25 p.m.
Date: Saturday 17 January 2015
Location: A31, Ringwood

Ritchie looked towards the dashboard clock and wondered whether it had happened yet. Part of him had wanted to hang around, to be there at the final moment — but he knew he couldn't. He'd set the trap well enough — all he needed was Jack MacIntosh to walk into it.

He pulled the van back onto the road and continued to put as much distance between himself and the Old Mill Road flats. Quinn was propped up in the passenger seat, his head bouncing against the side window every time they went a corner. The thudding sound didn't bother Ritchie — instead it made him smile.

He could have left Quinn back at the flats — let Jack have his final five minutes with the man that had murdered his mother. That might have been the decent thing to do. But where was the fun in that? Ritchie knew that Joseph Geraghty had wanted him to protect MacIntosh — to *help* him. It was the man's dying wish, and Ritchie had sworn to uphold it. But the very idea grated on Ritchie's nerves as much now as it had done back then. Even as he'd uttered the words at the top of the Skyline Apartments — *I promise* — he hadn't meant it. How could he? The idea was insane. And now MacIntosh had outlived his usefulness, it was time to end it.

He grinned and turned up the radio.

REM's 'It's the End of the World as We Know It (And I feel Fine)' filled the van.

* * *

Time: 11.35 p.m.
Date: Saturday 17 January 2015
Location: Old Mill Road, Christchurch

Jack had been shot at, stabbed, run over by a car and even shoved through a plate glass window in his time — but he'd never been blown up before.

Until now.

The force of the explosion ripped through the Old Mill Road flats, the vibrations still rumbling through its foundations long after the fireball had erupted. Jack felt the floor beneath his feet collapse and disintegrate into nothing, sending him plunging down to the floor below, brick dust following in his wake.

Although he couldn't see any flames, he could feel the heat coming from somewhere — and then the acrid smell of toasted almonds reached his nostrils. The noise was intense, as was the thick smoke that quickly filled the air.

As he fell, Jack's throat filled with coarse dust, forcing his airway to close down. Eyes clamped tightly shut, he saw little of the descent — which lasted all of six or seven seconds before his body hit the ground below. Lumps of concrete and twisted metal flew through the smoke — choked air, and then the continued rumblings as the flats themselves began to collapse.

And then there was the second explosion.

CHAPTER FORTY-TWO

Time: 11.35 p.m.
Date: Saturday 17 January 2015
Location: Old Mill Road, Christchurch

Sandy plumes of brick dust and other debris shot skywards as the explosion ripped through the already crumbling building.

"Jack!" Stuart 'Mac' MacIntosh attempted to wrench himself free from the forceful hands restraining him. "Jack!"

"You need to keep back, mate." Alan Barnes, Southern Fire Brigade's station manager, tightened his grip and pulled Mac away from the wire mesh fence that encased the dilapidated block of flats on Old Mill Road. "This place isn't safe."

Mac's heart hammered painfully inside his chest as yet another explosion tore through the building and rocked the ground beneath his feet. This time he allowed himself to be dragged backwards behind the bank of fire engines, his legs beginning to shudder.

"But, my brother . . ." Mac's face was caked in brick dust. "He's in there — I know he is!"

Alan Barnes nodded, eyes grave. "If that's the case then we'll do our damnedest to get him out."

358

"Alive?" Mac's eyes widened while he watched several fire-fighters kitted out in full protective gear and breathing apparatus heading for the wire fence. "You'll get him out alive?"

The station manager turned to look back at the devastation facing them, a steadying hand still resting on Mac's shoulder. After a second or two he gave it a brief squeeze. "Like I said — we'll do our damnedest to get him out."

* * *

Time: 12.35 a.m.
Date: Sunday 18 January 2015
Location: Knowles Farm, Dorset

Ritchie hated the countryside. He hated the look of it, he hated the smell of it — and he hated the people who lived in it. Luckily, the farm had long since been abandoned, so he was unlikely to come across the latter.

But he couldn't do much about the smell.

Although no longer in use, some of the farm buildings were being occupied on the quiet — something that Ritchie was quietly thankful for. For a small sum, a local farmer who was using one of the barns to house his pigs, was prepared to turn a blind eye to Ritchie and the gang's coming and goings over the past few weeks. The farmer had little choice really — he wasn't meant to be there himself.

The somewhat strained relationship, born out of a sense of mutual distrust, worked well for both parties concerned.

Before getting himself shot in the abdomen, Rhys had had his uses — securing the abandoned farm being one of them. Ritchie liked the lad, even saw a bit of himself in him on occasion. If he could rein in his enthusiasm a bit and do as he was told, then he might just live a bit longer.

Ritchie strode across the muddied front yard with relative ease, getting used to hauling Quinn up on to his shoulders by now. Maybe it was the thought of finally getting rid of the man, and MacIntosh to boot, that was putting a spring in his step.

The barn was the furthest one away from the farmhouse and, just as the farmer had told him, the corrugated iron sheet that acted as a door had been left unlocked. Ritchie didn't need to be asked twice.

Pulling the sheeting to the side he disappeared into the dark, emerging some minutes later. Without Quinn on his shoulders he felt lighter — both physically and mentally.

Now he just needed to wait for the catastrophic news from Old Mill Road to reach him and the deed was done.

* * *

Time: 9.15 a.m.
Date: Sunday 18 January 2015
Location: The Forest District Hospital, Nr Christchurch

"Jesus, Jack — how many lives is that now?" Chief Superintendent Dougie King pulled the cubicle curtain aside as he strode in. "Cats have nine — I'm not sure the same can be said for humans."

Jack managed a sheepish smile from his hospital trolley, instantly regretting even that small movement as a searing bolt of pain stabbed him between the eyes. "You know me, sir," he mumbled through gritted teeth. "I'm indestructible."

"*That* I very much doubt."

Jack knew better than to force the issue.

"Just what in God's name were you doing there?" Dougie King pulled the curtain closed behind him, the hum of the busy A&E department temporarily masked. "And I mean *really*. You could have got yourself killed. You very nearly did."

Jack was about to shrug, but thought better of it. The painkillers the nurse had rigged up for him were just about doing their job — but he didn't fancy pushing his luck. "I had intel that Quinn was there."

The look on Dougie King's face told Jack that the senior officer didn't buy it. "Even if that were true, Jack, why did you go in alone? You should have called for backup at the very least. Or let the local force deal with it. It wasn't your call to make."

"I did, sir. Call for backup, I mean." Jack knew he was being flippant, but technically he had. Or at least Stu had. His brother had been true to his word and as soon as ten minutes were up and there had been no sign of Jack re-emerging, he'd put the call in to the local police.

The chief superintendent's mouth twitched with a smile. "OK — well you should have waited until they actually got there before charging in with your size nines."

Jack knew Dougie King was right. He should have waited. Hell, he should have steered clear altogether. Neither Ritchie or Quinn had been anywhere to be seen and once it had finally dawned on him that he'd been lured into a trap, the explosion had ripped through the fabric of the building and sent him plunging to the ground.

Beneath the thin hospital gown Jack silently chastised himself.

Just then the cubicle curtain was swished aside and Sister Evelyn bustled in, eyeing Dougie King with a suspicious gaze. "I need to do Mr MacIntosh's observations — if you wouldn't mind?"

The look on her taut face told the chief superintendent that his presence wasn't wanted. He took a step towards the curtain. "I'll leave you in peace. You're signed off indefinitely, Jack, while you recover." He held up a hand to ward off the anticipated reaction. "And no arguments this time. You still need to keep a low profile — being blown up hasn't changed anything."

Once Dougie King had departed, Jack allowed the nurse to take his blood pressure and other observations, letting his head rest back against the pillow. He did feel quite rough to be honest — more than a little battered and bruised, and a little shaky, too. Not that he was prepared to admit that to Sister Evelyn. She had a look of Nurse Ratched about her.

He knew he'd been lucky — escaping from the devastation of the Old Mill Road flats with relatively minor injuries. Dust inhalation, a variety of cuts and scrapes, a fractured metatarsal in his left foot, and a deep laceration to the back of his head. After falling through the collapsed ceiling, he'd landed on his bad shoulder but thankfully another dislocation hadn't followed suit.

The chief superintendent wasn't wrong when he questioned how many times Jack had cheated death; it was fast becoming a regular occurrence. He was now living on pure luck.

With Sister Evelyn having completed the latest round of observations, she quickly departed to leave Jack alone with his thoughts once more. Her parting words were to issue strict instructions to stay where he was and not go wandering around while she found a bed for him on the ward. He was about to reply '*what do you take me for?*' but thought better of it. Going walkabout was exactly what Jack MacIntosh would ordinarily do.

When he'd been wheeled into the Forest District Hospital A&E department early that morning, he could recall with crystal-clear clarity Stu being rushed through the same doors only two years or so before. All he could think about as he was taken through to resus was seeing Stu hooked up to numerous lines, heavily sedated, bandages and other dressings swathing his burnt body. The aroma of smoke and burnt flesh still lingered in Jack's nostrils after all this time.

Jack was about to close his eyes and let the painkillers lull him to sleep when the curtain swished open once again to reveal a face he recognised.

"This is getting to be a bit of a habit." Station manager Alan Barnes stepped towards Jack's trolley, hand outstretched. "Good to see you. How's that brother of yours?"

Jack took hold of the firefighter's grip and smiled as much as the pain would allow. Alan Barnes had been the one to bring Stu's lifeless body out of the burning wreck that was St Bartholomew's Home for Boys nearly two years before. "Stu's doing well, thanks. He still has physio, but essentially he's back to normal. As much as he can be, anyway."

"That's good to hear." Barnes rested against the end of Jack's trolley, a sombre look on his face. "But you gave me a bit of a fright in there, I will admit." The firefighter paused. "How you managed to survive falling through that ceiling with barely more than a few cuts and bruises is beyond me."

"What can I say? I live a charmed life."

Barnes grinned and took a step back towards the closed curtain. "That you do. And that brother of yours. Must be in your genes."

"Something like that I guess."

The firefighter stepped outside the cubicle, calling back over his shoulder. "Don't take this the wrong way but I hope we don't meet again."

Just as Jack was about to close his eyes once more, Sister Evelyn reappeared, bustling Alan Barnes out of the way. "You're in luck, Mr MacIntosh. A bed has been found for you up on our orthopaedic ward. It'll be ready in just a few minutes, so we'll set about moving you."

Jack opened his mouth to respond, but saw Alan Barnes make a face and draw his fingers across his lips in a 'zipping' action.

"And no arguments," finished the nurse, affording the fire-fighter a hot look. "You're going to do as you're told for once."

CHAPTER FORTY-THREE

Time: 2.15 p.m.
Date: Sunday 22 February 2015
Location: Knowles Farm, Dorset

The message had come through late last night, just as Jack was heading to bed.

Bring your wellies.

Followed by a location on a map.

Jack didn't own a pair of wellies, hadn't done since he was a kid, and in any event he was still meant to be wearing the walking boot while the fracture knitted itself together. The rest of his injuries had healed well — the wound to his scalp stitched, the cuts and scrapes healing on their own. His ears had stopped ringing now, with just an occasional faint buzz when he tipped his head to the side.

He had been surprisingly obedient in keeping away from the station over the last four weeks or so. Adam Sullivan had been charged with four counts of murder, and the deaths of his mother Rita and her live-in-lover Johnny Makin were being investigated further. He answered a limited number of questions during interview, but had admitted to both Julian

Fisher and Michael Dixon being patients of his at the dental practice. That was how he had got wind of Flat 7b being empty and unlocked, and also given him Michael Dixon as a suitable pawn to be taken advantage of. Dixon had confessed in interview to an amphetamine addiction and spiralling debt. Sullivan had offered him a short-lived way out.

As Jack made his way across the farmyard, Adam Sullivan's voice echoed inside his head.

You'd be surprised what secrets some patients will divulge when they're sat in the chair. They treat it like a confessional.

Jack shuddered as he squelched through the mud.

Barry Pierce had been charged with handling stolen goods and had lost his job as caretaker of Acorn House. Julian Fisher was currently on remand having been charged with possession and intent to supply controlled drugs. In interview he admitted having been present at Flat 7b on the morning Lisa Wood and Tara Coe's remains were discovered, but that he'd gone to the flat to carry out a deal with a local gang. He saw the remains and chose not to get involved, instead lifting the women's mobile phones, thinking he might be able to sell them.

All in all, the result had been a good one — even if Jack, and his career, had flown a little too close to the sun at times.

The farm looked like a regular farm but had clearly been long abandoned. There were several tractors standing idly by — none of which looked to have been moved in a very long time. A row of barns was devoid of either hay or animals, and the farmhouse itself was crumbling, the window frames rotten and splintered in places.

Jack sniffed the air. It might not look much like a working farm, but it still smelled like one.

Without dogs or chickens running around, an eerie silence descended as Jack continued his way across the yard. As he limped through the mud in his walking boot, he wrestled with his thoughts as to why he was even here. Despite his better judgement he was dancing to Ritchie Greenwood's tune once again. He knew who the message had been from — it may have been a different number, it had Ritchie Greenwood written all over it — the farm was just another Hanged Man, but in the countryside.

With mud.

Jack was also convinced that Ritchie wouldn't be so daft as to show his face, but he kept a cautious eye out as he slipped and slid his way across the yard. The recent rain had done nothing to make the journey any easier. He didn't fancy adding another fracture to go with the one he already had.

Instinctively, Jack knew exactly where to go.

You know a pig will eat just about anything . . .

Jack made his way towards an outbuilding at the far end of the yard. A single piece of corrugated iron acted as a door, but it had been left unlocked and ajar. He took another look over his shoulder. Still nothing. Still no one. Once again he hadn't told the rest of the team where he was heading — it was clearly a habit Jack had no intention of breaking any time soon. Rob had been kind enough to drive him up in the Mondeo, a quizzical look on his face for the entire journey.

The pig shed was dark, but as soon as Jack pulled open the corrugated iron door and let his eyes adjust to the gloom, he immediately saw movement. And then he heard the snuffling. And the grunting.

Pulling a torch from his pocket, he swept an arc of bright light around three-hundred-and-sixty degrees. The pigs were huge; in Jack's eyes they were easily the size of a small horse. He quickly counted four pigs, all snuffling quite contentedly in their filthy-looking straw oblivious to their human intruder. None raised an eyebrow — if, indeed, pigs had eyebrows. It wasn't a question Jack had had to consider before.

You know a pig will eat just about anything . . .

Ritchie Greenwood's words echoed inside Jack's head once more, and the inference was clear. Quite what Jack intended to do if and when he found the remains of James Quinn, he was unsure. He knew what he *should* do — but that wasn't always the same thing.

A broom rested against the side of the pen. Jack took hold of it and leaned in as far as he dared and began to prod the dirty straw that lay thick on the ground. It looked to be more than a foot deep in places.

Each of the four pigs — what breed they were Jack hadn't a clue — were big, hulking creatures, noses constantly buried in the straw. Munching. Crunching.

Torch in his opposite hand, Jack prodded more fervently with the broom handle, now searching a muddier section of the pen. One of the pigs was enjoying a root around in the mud, ignoring the broom handle when it came too close. Jack's stomach began to churn in time with the pig's snuffles.

As he prodded deeper, the torchlight illuminated something in among the mud. Jack focused the beam on the glinting object, waving the broom handle in the pig's direction. Unable to avoid it, he hauled himself over the side of the pen, knowing there was no real alternative, almost landing headfirst into the mixture of mud and straw. The smell intensified and made him gag.

Mud now up to his ankles and covering his NHS supplied walking boot, Jack bent down. He could see what it was even before he picked it up.

A watch.

Using the broom handle again, he prodded more of the surrounding mud. It didn't take long for his stomach to lurch again. This time it was a tooth.

A human tooth?

You know a pig will eat just about anything . . .

Jack shuddered and took a step back. If James Quinn was indeed currently being digested by any one of the four hungry pigs in front of him, then he believed it couldn't have happened to a nicer guy. Visions of Cooper tucking into his customary bacon sandwich made Jack's stomach clench even more. Maybe Amanda and her health kicks had a point.

Instinct told him to turn and run.

Quinn wouldn't be missed.

On his way back across the yard, returning to where Rob was waiting with the Mondeo, Jack momentarily considered tossing the Fitbit in with the pigs. They might not eat it all, but it could be worth a shot. But instead, he smiled. He'd become quite attached to it in a strange kind of way.

Approaching the passenger side of the Mondeo, Jack bent down and peered in through the open window. "Rob?" He cast a look back over his shoulder towards the pig shed. "You fancy a pint? There's something I need to tell you . . ."

THE END

MESSAGE FROM THE AUTHOR

There are many people I need to thank for helping get *The Twelfth Floor* on to the bookshelves.

First, I must thank Detective Inspector Steve Duncan and Police Sergeant Rebecca McCarthy once again for their help throughout this book. As always, it is very much appreciated. If there are any remaining procedural inaccuracies, then I can assure you that they are mine and mine alone, and they are there for entertainment purposes only!

I must also thank Tracey Proctor for her expert advice on the use of luminol.

Thanks also go out to several of my colleagues at the West Suffolk Hospital in Bury St Edmunds who have loaned me their names for use in this book — Lisa Wood, Tara Coe, Cherry Eyres, Shell Harris, Sally O'Brian and Mike Dixon — thank you!

And special thanks also to Tanya Maund for agreeing to be a character in the book, it's very much appreciated.

My good friend Sarah Bezant once again deserves a very special mention — your brilliant attention to detail when reading my early drafts is invaluable. I honestly couldn't do any of this without you.

And, of course, I must thank everyone involved at my publishers, Joffe Books — and especially Kate Lyall Grant for continuing to believe in me and making my writing the best it can possibly be.

And, finally, it is you — the readers! Without you, none of these books would ever see the light of day. I thank each and every one of you.

To keep up to date, there are various ways to get in touch:

www.michellekiddauthor.com — join my author newsletter for information on future releases and special offers. I also give away free downloads, content not available anywhere else!

www.facebook.com/michellekiddauthor

Twitter @AuthorKidd

Instagram @michellekiddauthor

THE JOFFE BOOKS STORY

We began in 2014 when Jasper agreed to publish his mum's much-rejected romance novel and it became a bestseller.

Since then we've grown into the largest independent publisher in the UK. We're extremely proud to publish some of the very best writers in the world, including Joy Ellis, Faith Martin, Caro Ramsay, Helen Forrester, Simon Brett and Robert Goddard. Everyone at Joffe Books loves reading and we never forget that it all begins with the magic of an author telling a story.

We are proud to publish talented first-time authors, as well as established writers whose books we love introducing to a new generation of readers.

We won Trade Publisher of the Year at the Independent Publishing Awards in 2023 and Best Publisher Award in 2024 at the People's Book Prize. We have been shortlisted for Independent Publisher of the Year at the British Book Awards for the last five years, and were shortlisted for the Diversity and Inclusivity Award at the 2022 Independent Publishing Awards. In 2023 we were shortlisted for Publisher of the Year at the RNA Industry Awards, and in 2024 we were shortlisted at the CWA Daggers for the Best Crime and Mystery Publisher.

We built this company with your help, and we love to hear from you, so please email us about absolutely anything bookish at feedback@joffebooks.com.

If you want to receive free books every Friday and hear about all our new releases, join our mailing list here: www.joffebooks.com/freebooks.

And when you tell your friends about us, just remember: it's pronounced Joffe as in coffee or toffee!